In Search of
BRIGID COLTRANE

In Search of Brigid Coltrane by Seamus Beirne

Cover design: Christine Horner
Interior design: Jacqueline Cook

ISBN: 978-1-61179-390-1 (Paperback)
ISBN: 978-1-61179-391-8 (e-book)

10 9 8 7 6 5 4 3 2 1

BISAC Subject Headings:
FIC002000 FICTION / Action & Adventure
FIC014050 FICTION / Historical / World War II
FIC031020 FICTION / Thrillers / Historical

Address all correspondence to:
Fireship Press, LLC
P.O. Box 68412
Tucson, AZ 85737
fireshipinfo@gmail.com

Visit our website at:
www.fireshippress.com

To all my family,
both Irish and American

Also by
Seamus Beirne

Breakout From Sugar Island

Acknowledgments

First I must thank my wife Ann for her yeoman's work in editing this novel. She has crisscrossed the terrain of this book so many times that we've lost count. Thanks also to our three children, who have weighed in on numerous occasions with suggestions and insights. A special thanks to my professional editor Robert Yelling, author of *Voices*, *When We Were the Boys*, and *Beyond ADHD*. Along with providing excellent advice and direction, he helped me wrestle the book into manageable size. Last but not least, a big thank-you to my volunteer readers who grappled with rough drafts and provided me with valuable insight: Lynda Gibbs, Steve Veenstra, Ken Crilly, Gene O'Toole, Donal McCarthy, Stephanie Crilly, Jacky Young, and Joyce Cunningham.

In Search of
BRIGID COLTRANE

SEAMUS BEIRNE

To Stella!
Enjoy the adventure
5/4/19

FIRESHIP
PRESS

Seamus Beirne

Prologue

The Dungeon

Fourteen-year-old Brigid Coltrane never spent a night away from home until she was abducted. And it was nothing like the sleepovers her friends talked about. She was cold and scared, and she shuffled around in darkness. When they finally removed the blindfold, what appeared to be a large tic-tac-toe grid filled her vision. Strange, there were no X's or O's. Stranger still, the sound of a Gregorian chant seemed to be coming through the grid that shimmered while her eyes adjusted to the anemic light. In time the chanting faded, but the grid hardened into iron bars set high on a wall near the ceiling ...

Chapter 1

The Island

Ireland, Summer, 1941

Peter Coltrane eased off the bow seat onto the floor of the boat and took another swig from the flat bottle of Jameson's cradled in the palm of his hand. Head resting against the seat, he tried to focus his bleary eyes on the oar sneaking from the oarlock into the dark water and drifting away. Looking back it was the first sign of danger, but it didn't register.

It was the end of a long, disappointing day, especially for Brigid, his fourteen-year-old daughter, asleep in the stern of the boat. She wasn't as passionate about fishing as he was. The current gently pushed them toward a row of weeping willow trees that hugged the shoreline of an island known as Red Cow. It was one of many tiny islands dotting Loch Gorm.

The day had been quite warm. The boat nosed through a curtain of trailing willow branches that drooped into the water. Behind the curtain a concealed channel snaked along the shore, canopied by interlocking branches. He welcomed the cool shade of this secluded place. As the wind separated the willow streamers it allowed shafts of sunlight to flit across the water of the channel. He repositioned his head on the bow and closed his eyes. Brigid's gentle snoring and the gurgling of water against the boat lulled him to sleep.

***

Something jolted him awake. A current of unease crept through him. *Better get Brigid back to her mother at a decent hour*, he thought, pulling the collar of his coat up around his neck against the rising wind, *or I'll never hear the end of it*. Not to worry. He had many long summer days stretching ahead of him, one of the perks of being a schoolteacher. Ample time for his fishing luck to change. The words of an old rebel song rose from within: "*In Mountjoy Jail one Monday morning...*" he sang softly as he picked his way toward the stern to start the old Evinrude. He patted the scuffed cowl of the sturdy outboard motor, now paintless from age, as one might pet a dog. *No Pasarán*, he called her. She had ferried him safely on endless fishing trips across the length and breadth of the lake. "*... Kevin Barry gave his young life ...*" He laid his hand on the sleeping girl's head before leaning across her to pull the starting cord. "*... for the cause of...*" Out of nowhere came the sound that had awakened him.

A gust of wind parted the willow streamers. The hairs on the nape of his neck bristled against his shirt collar. A gunmetal-grey boat carrying several armed figures wearing hoods over their heads and faces, along with two others bound at the wrists, churned its way toward an inlet where the willow canopy had thinned out. Once ashore, the gunmen herded the two captives into a grove of twisted alder trees.

Brigid moved. "What's going on, Da—?"

"Shh." He pressed his hand so tightly over the girl's mouth that her teeth cut into his fingers. He pulled her into the belly of the boat and squeezed down beside her, atop lunch boxes and fishing rods. An eerie quiet descended. Even the birds stopped their chatter. When the tension became unbearable, he removed his hand from his daughter's mouth as one might release a grip on a captured songbird, unsure of its reactions. She trembled. He raised his head and parted the willow screen.

The bound men knelt among the trees. Clumps of bog grass spilled from their mouths. Their chests heaved like bellows. The hooded figures towered over them.

Several shotgun blasts and the sharp crack of a rifle reverberated across the water, flinging the kneeling pair into the underbrush. They bounced and twisted like rag dolls. "Jesus Christ!" Coltrane mouthed. A flock of ringed plover erupted skyward in a raucous, flailing mass. A familiar smell assailed his nostrils. Cordite. He knew it from his time in Spain fighting Franco.

One of the executioners pulled off his hood, propped his shotgun against an alder tree, and turned in Coltrane's direction. He removed his wire-rim glasses and rubbed his bloodshot eye with the heel of his hand. He looked in his fifties and had the face of a man in no great hurry. His close-cropped grey hair gave him a washed-out appearance. Scanning the lake, he slowly folded the hood and placed it carefully in a pocket of his trench coat.

The old bullet wound in Coltrane's jaw throbbed and for a moment he was back gasping for breath under a pile of bodies at the Ebro River in Spain, awaiting the *coup de grâce* from one of General Franco's *Regulares*.

He continued to peek through the willow screen, imagining the killer's eyes locked on his. His heart raced. His only weapon was a knife for scaling fish. Not much use against double-barreled shotguns and a rifle. But a few factors favored him: the sun was in the killer's eyes and the thick willow screen cast the area behind it in deep shadow. It provided adequate concealment for Coltrane and Brigid for now.

Abruptly the man turned his gaze back to the lake and shaded his eyes as if expecting someone. He cupped his hands and lit a cigarette, flicking the spent match into the water. The acrid smell of sulfur carried on the wind. The killer retrieved his shotgun, tucked it into the crook of his arm, and headed back to his comrades. Then he stopped abruptly and looked up and down the shore. His gaze wandered toward his two henchmen digging shallow graves near the tree line. He took a long drag from the cigarette and slowly expelled a steady stream of smoke through his nostrils.

Coltrane's temples pounded. He reached for the knob of the bow-hatch door and pulled gently. It creaked open, sounding like the squeal of a startled dog whose tail got stepped on. "Damn!" The assailant swiveled his head toward the willow trees, breeched the shotgun, and inserted two shells into the barrels. Coltrane pawed inside the hatch. Where was that knife? At last his fingers curled around the bone handle. The assailant snapped the shotgun shut and clicked back both hammers. Coltrane rose to a crouch, the knife in his right hand.

The gunman stepped into the water. As he moved closer, small waves sloshed against his waders. Coltrane must strike first. The gunman staggered, but righted himself. He kept coming, his shotgun raised chest-high. Coltrane braced himself in the boat and got ready to spring. Sweat dripped down his face. The gunman staggered again and tried to back up. This time he lost his balance and fell face-first into the water, discharging the shotgun.

His henchmen came running, and with considerable effort they dragged him to safety. They stretched him on the shore face-down, sputtering and gasping for breath. It took two of them to pull his waders off and empty them into the lake.

Hoisting their boss to his feet, they supported him as he stumbled back to the boat, coughing and swearing. The craft fitted with two outboard motors strained against its anchor in the lapping waves.

"Daddy," Brigid whispered.

"Shh." A new danger. Their boat was drifting toward the thinning willow trees. He rose on his hands and knees and crawled backward to grab the oars. An empty oarlock. "Christ!" In less than a minute they would be in full view of the assailants. He thought of grasping the trailing branches, but feared such a maneuver might breach the willow screen and reveal their presence.

He stood up and thrust the remaining oar into the water, hoping to ram it into the bottom. The water proved too deep, and his efforts only propelled the boat faster toward the hole in the canopy.

Brigid tugged on his shirtsleeve. "Daddy, Daddy, the engine?"

He was hoping not to reveal their presence by using it. But now it was the only course left. He grabbed the starting handle in the web of his fingers and held his breath. Bracing himself, he yanked and prayed. *No Pasarán* sputtered. He yanked again. Another stutter. The smell of petrol drifted on the breeze. Shouts from the other boat. Coltrane wiped his sweaty palm on the knee of his trousers. *Come on. Don't let me down now.* A third attempt and she roared to life. Blue smoke poured from the exhaust. He swung her around, cutting a turbulent furrow in the amber-colored water, and raced along the shoreline under the canopy.

He glanced behind him. "Get down, Brigid."

More shouts and commotion. Bullets whistled over their heads like angry bees. So far no sign of pursuit. Tending to their half-drowned comrade probably slowed their response. When he outran the willow canopy, he shaded his eyes to look at the sun. About an hour of twilight remained. He pushed the little motor flat-out until the shoreline gave way to a small inlet choked with man-sized reeds and bulrushes. He recognized it as the concealed entrance to a turn-of-the-century boathouse long fallen into disrepair, hidden from view by stands of white ash and birch trees. Part of the structure extended over the water on stilts.

He knew this spot. As a young boy he came here often with his father, a fish and game warden.

He killed the Evinrude. Using the oar as a paddle, he maneuvered through the reeds until the boat scraped against the cement ramp under the boathouse. Sections of the walls had rotted away, but enough remained to offer a measure of concealment. The reeds and rushes offered good cover but also left him blind, which made him uneasy. He turned to Brigid. "Sweetheart, I need to get into the boathouse to get a better view of the lake. You stay put. I'll be right back."

Brigid whimpered. "Dad, don't leave me. I'm scared."

He put an arm around her shoulders. "Listen, I'm not leaving you." He pointed to the underside of the boathouse floor. "I'm going to be up there. Not five feet away." Feeling she'd been reassured, he shimmied up one of the stilts to the first storey for a better view. The whine of an engine. He flattened himself on the floor.

The grey boat, with three men, nosed into the mouth of the inlet. He whispered to Brigid to remain still. The man who had taken a

14

dunking in the lake scanned the island with binoculars. He wore a woolen cap and shivered under a blanket draped around his shoulders. His face had a determined look. Coltrane knew men like him in Spain. They enjoyed the kill.

The minutes ticked by. Since his face was pressed against the pine needle-matted floor, he had to pinch his nostrils to prevent a sneeze. At last the assailant lowered the binoculars and the boat moved on. When Coltrane's heart rate stabilized, his thoughts turned to his wife, Claire. She would blame him for putting their only child in danger. Her oft-repeated complaints assailed him like a biting wind. "You keep Brigid out too long." "You're careless, you drink too much." "One of these days they'll be fishing you out of the lake, Peter Coltrane." He lowered himself to the ground and took Brigid in his arms. He felt her spasm. "They're gone, love."

"Who were those terrible men, Dad?"

"I wish I knew, sweetheart. I wish I knew." He looked over her head, taking stock of their surroundings. The island behind them wasn't big enough to hide a rabbit, and escape from the inlet could easily be choked off. Unless he was careful, it might become a snare, all set to trip them. They needed to get out, fast.

Chapter 2

Flight

He paddled to the middle of the reed patch. He figured it was the safest place to await the coming of darkness, since the reeds were tall and dense enough to prevent detection from either the lake or the island. With a little luck, using the reeds as cover, he could slip by the assailants should they return to the inlet and escape to open water. He didn't see any other option in this cat-and-mouse game.

The sun dipped behind the mountains at the western shore. It would disappear within a half hour. The boat bobbed gently on the water and emitted little gurgling sounds as waves slapped against its belly. They settled in and waited for dark, sharing the remains of the ham and cheese sandwiches Claire had prepared that morning.

He gazed at his daughter. She looked the spitting image of her mother with her Celtic red hair and freckled cheeks. He massaged his stubbled face with his thumb and forefinger and thanked the Almighty she hadn't taken after his side of the family with their black Irish features and dour dispositions. Looking at her made him feel content. But he suspected that her interest in fishing, tepid though it might be, was a ruse to escape the turmoil at home caused by his drinking. He halted the boat's drift out of the reed patch toward open water with a backstroke and took another bite of sandwich. Brigid sat on the floor, her back pressed against his legs.

His return from the Spanish Civil War hadn't brought peace of mind. He resorted to the bottle to ease the pain of adapting to the monotony of domesticity. He missed the adrenalin rush of combat, the threat of death lurking in the next shell crater. When Claire threatened to take Brigid and move in with her parents, he attended a few meetings of the local Pioneer Abstinence Association, but it did little to tame his need for the narcotic of danger.

"It's a good first step," Claire said. "I'm proud of you."

An uneasy truce prevailed on the home front.

The splash of a water hen skittering through the reeds mingled with the

high-pitched staccato call of a snipe. He finished the last of the whiskey and ran his tongue along the bullet wound in his jaw. Brigid looked away.

He felt more vulnerable now than he did waiting for the bayonet thrust of the mustachioed *Regulares* at the Ebro River. Then, he had a pistol. When the enemy raised his arms to stab, he shot him between the eyes. Now he had no gun. His only child was in grave danger. Still, he couldn't suppress the energy and excitement surging through him. Guilt tore at him.

"What are we going to do, Dad?"

"We'll figure something out," he rasped, his throat raw with tension. He extracted the hunting knife from his pocket and set it on the stern seat. "It's going to be dark soon, and unless they're waiting in ambush, I think we can make it back to the mainland."

Brigid wiped tears from her cheeks with the heel of her hand. "I'm so afraid. What if their boat is faster? Won't they catch us?" She sobbed until her body convulsed. He enfolded her in his arms, wishing he had easy answers to her questions.

"Not if they don't see us. I know the lake and they don't." In his heart, he knew that was a pathetic and unconvincing answer.

"How do you know they don't?" Her breath came in great gasps.

"Because they're not from around these parts. Shh. Lie down."

He maneuvered the boat through the reeds into a backwater channel. The assassins' boat emerged from a swath of tall bulrushes near the mouth of the inlet. It carried two men. Where was the third?

A splash … from behind!

Coltrane whipped around and yanked the Evinrude toward him, raising the propeller shaft from the water. He caught the swimmer lunging for the stern square in the chest. The attacker cried out, dropping a knife from his teeth. He clawed for a grip on the propeller shaft. Coltrane flung himself on top of the outboard. The extra weight tipped the boat backward. He grabbed the knife from the stern seat and thrust it into the attacker's neck. Brigid screamed. The body sank among the reeds, a trail of blood and bubbles marking its descent to the bottom.

"Quick! Brigid, stay down and hold on!" He cranked the Evinrude and circled the other boat, coming at it from the side. Concealed by reeds and growing darkness, the assailants didn't see Coltrane until he was on them. The sturdy prow of the *No Pasarán*, reinforced by a steel strap, sliced off one of their outboard motors, catapulting an assailant into the water. The impact spun the *No Pasarán* around. After fighting to get it under control, Coltrane steered toward a narrow channel between two islands strewn with underwater volcanic rocks and sandbars. He zigzagged through the maze.

When he emerged at the other end of the narrow waterway, a rifle crack sent a flock of mallard ducks screeching in a ragged arc from a patch of rushes.

Brigid raised her head.

"Stay down!"

The assailants' boat roared from behind Red Cow Island, churning a powerful wake, its prow high in the water.

Another shot.

A tongue of water leaped from the surface of the lake about a hundred feet in front of *No Pasarán*. Coltrane looked over his shoulder. A man in the pursuing boat crouched with a rifle to his shoulder. More shots, but they all went wild. Then what he hoped would happen, did: the pursuers ran aground on a sandbar in the narrow channel. Coltrane expelled air from his lungs in a mighty gush.

"Dad, Dad, water's coming in."

"Crawl back here and hold the throttle."

A bullet had punctured the planking above the waterline, leaving a hole the size of a fist. Every time the bow sank into the wave troughs, water gushed in. After staunching the flow with an oil rag that he found in the storage cabinet, he and Brigid exchanged places again.

"Keep your hand pressed against the hole, sweetheart."

He checked to his rear. The pursuers were still struggling to release their boat. Good. The lights of Kildallogue Girls' School beckoned from the mainland, over a mile away. He toyed with the idea of making a run for it but reconsidered, fearing the assailants might get their boat operational in time to catch them mid-crossing. Although they had lost one motor, they were still faster than *No Pasarán*. Despite Brigid's efforts, several inches of water sloshed around the bottom of the boat. Better stick to the shelter of the islands, just in case. He sought out one in particular, the Priests' Island, a wilderness of algae-covered bog holes hidden in thickets of heather and hazel trees. The setting sun was in the water. Darkness spread across the lake like a shroud, making it more difficult for their pursuers, but also making it a greater challenge for Coltrane to find the elusive island.

As he threaded his way down the narrow channels that separated the tiny islands, his eyes adjusted to the growing darkness. The putt-putt of his engine reverberated off the limestone boulders strewn along the island shores like prehistoric monsters crouching in ambush. He cut the motor and listened.

"Daddy!"

"Hush up and listen."

"To what?"

"Shh! Be quiet."

Off to their right, a faint bleating echoed across the water—the wild goat of the Priests' Island. He paddled in the direction of the bleats. The dark outline of an island loomed ahead. "I could kiss that goat."

The boat scraped the bottom and they jumped onto a rocky beach.

He unloaded the small cabinet underneath the bow, relieved to find one of his old jackets and a six-foot piece of rope. In the back of the cabinet, a length of fishing line anchored a life buoy to an eyehook. He handed Brigid the old jacket.

"Put this on. It's warmer than that windbreaker you're wearing."

"Yeah, but I'll look like the old woman of the roads in it."

A look of exasperation flitted across his face. "Do it. Right now style is not high on my list."

She obeyed with an irritated shrug. Then he undressed down to his shorts. Brigid whimpered at seeing her dad wade half-naked into the water and place a large rock in the bottom of the boat. "Daddy, have you gone loony?"

"Don't tell your mother about this."

"I couldn't explain this to Mammie."

"Help me get the boat back in the water."

When they pushed it clear of the rocks, he jumped in and paddled out onto the lake. Water sloshed around his feet. He was afraid the boat might sink in the shallows and be visible come daylight. About fifty yards from shore he removed one of the floorboards to uncover the ribbed hull. Lifting the rock, he stood and pitched it with all his might against the exposed ribs. Within seconds he sunk to his neck in cold water. With a powerful lunge, he pushed free of the sinking vessel and swam ashore.

Brigid pointed over his shoulder. "Dad, look!" Out on the water the life buoy had broken the surface and bobbed lazily over the capsized boat.

"Damn." He weighed the risk of leaving it there against going back out to cut it free. It was a much smaller target than the boat, so he gambled and left it.

He pulled his clothes on over his wet body, stuffed his feet into his rubber boots, and washed blood from the knife. "Give us your hand, love." Then they jogged into the tangle of hazel trees and mountain ash.

The sound of an outboard motor echoed across the water, weak at first, but gradually gaining strength. Brigid leaned into him. "Daddy, they're here."

"They still have to find us, and it won't be easy once we vanish into the bog." He sought to reassure her, but he knew that if there were locals among the assassins, their hiding place might be vulnerable. A half-hour jog brought them to a jumble of limestone boulders crazily juxtaposed one atop the other—by some ancient glacier, he figured. "Okay. We'll rest here awhile."

Brigid slumped to the ground at the base of the rocks. He pried the oilskin from her grip and wrapped it around her. Sleep came quickly. Then he climbed the boulders to survey the lake. A light moved out on the water. The hunters had arrived. This confirmed his worst fears. They must have local help; otherwise they could not have found him so quickly. Decision time. The rhythmic sound of Brigid's snoring reverberated off the boulders. She was exhausted. Should he allow her to sleep a little longer or wake her and press on? It was so dark he could barely see his hands. Chances were his pursuers would not make much headway until daylight. He gambled again. They would rest a little longer.

He lay down beside Brigid and wrapped his arms around her. Who were these thugs following them? What brought them to this quiet backwater? And the brutal murders. Something odd. The assassins were not trying to flee like most killers. On the contrary. The world was at war, but it had not touched Ireland yet. Or had it? Tension existed between the IRA and the local fascist group known as the Blueshirts, but it had not escalated to the point of execution-type killings. The gentle rise and fall of his daughter's breathing expanded and relaxed his arms, lulling him to sleep.

**

He awoke in confusion. Moonlight flashed off the leaves of the silver birch trees. This changed everything. He clambered up the boulder. No sign of a light. Not necessarily good news. Their pursuers might already have landed on the island. Time to go. He shook Brigid by the shoulder. "Honey, I'm sorry. Got to move."

"Wha-what? No, Dad … just a little longer."

"Can't risk it." She stumbled to her feet, rubbed her eyes, and staggered off behind him.

After jogging for a spell they reached the edge of the cutaway bog. A hundred years before, the bog had been connected to the mainland by a narrow neck of land, but the rising water had cut it off, leaving an island about a half mile from the mainland. Because of its inaccessibility it became a hideout for priests on the run during Penal Times. A century of turf cutting left a bog of water-filled rectangular trenches linked together by a web of turf bridges. Deep in the labyrinth, islands of solid ground had been spared the turf cutter's slane. These islands were inaccessible to all but a knowledgeable few. Having spent hundreds of hours trekking along the sinewy trails hunting for pheasant and grouse, Coltrane felt at home among the hazel trees and heather that blanketed the bog like a coat of chain-link armor.

From time to time they left the track and plunged into thick stands of ferns and heather to emerge again on the banks of large bog holes carpeted with green algae. At the edge of one of these he stopped and wrapped the rope around Brigid's midsection, securing it with a knot.

"Why are you tying me up?"

"From here on the path is treacherous and narrow. Don't want to spend time fishing you out of the water."

They walked in single file, looking like a master with a captured slave. When they stepped too close to the edge, chunks of bog broke off and gurgled into the green algae. Once Brigid stooped to soothe the burning pain of a nettle sting on her bare legs, nearly toppling both of them into the mire. "For God's sake, watch what you're doing. This is no time to start dancing around."

"But Daddy, these nettles are stinging the life outa me."

"I know, sweetheart, but there are greater dangers lurking than nettles."

Farther on, the path widened into a little peninsula, in the middle of which stood a sod hut. "Daddy, if the locals are in on this, won't the hut be an obvious place to look?"

"Right. That's why we're not going to linger here. There's no other obvious place to hide on this neck of land, and I hope they won't think of looking in the water."

"In the water?"

"We're going in. The biggest bog hole on the whole island surrounds this hut. It would be very difficult to spot anyone under the algae in this expanse of water."

"Aren't you forgetting something? We're not fish."

"Pray God we won't have to be. Wait here while I check out the hut."

A little later he returned with a short-handled slane, a tool used for turf cutting. He ran his finger along the steel blade, surprised to discover that it was still quite sharp. It might come in handy. After further exploration he found the carcass of an old pine tree beached on the little peninsula. Half of it lay concealed beneath the algae. It measured about ten feet long and two feet in diameter and had several knotholes in its bark. He threaded the rope into a knothole on the section that rested on the bank and waded into the water. Brigid followed. After taking a few steps they were up to their hips.

With Brigid's help he pushed and pulled until the tree trunk broke free of the bank and slowly nosed toward them like a tired old crocodile. Using the slane, he carved holes large enough to accommodate a person's head and shoulders into the soft underside of the trunk, beneath the upper knotholes. That done, he slid the slane into the hollow end of the trunk, and together they swam the log to the middle of the bog hole. Brigid sighed with relief as the cool water enveloped her, soothing the nettle stings. The algae closed behind them. Soon there was no trace that its fifty-year sleep had been disrupted in any way.

"When the time comes, we simply duck our heads beneath the water and insert them up through the holes into the cavity of the log," Coltrane explained. "There's enough air coming through the knotholes. Don't worry." But to make sure, he did a test and submerged, resurfacing again inside the cavity of the log. Touch and go. The water lapped underneath his chin. They would have to risk it. He slipped his head out of the cavity and rejoined Brigid.

***

He glanced at the luminous dial on his watch: 2:00 a.m. They'd been clinging to the log for almost an hour. Had they given their pursuers the slip? The moon played hide and seek with the clouds, its light flashing off Brigid's silver hair clasp. "Daddy, I'm awful hungry."

"So am I, child." But he was lying. What he really wanted was a shot of whiskey. The sounds of turf bank splashing into the water jolted him from his trance.

Chapter 3

A Red Glare in the Sky

Tom Ryan, the lone Irish guard standing outside the German Embassy at 58 Northumberland Road, Dublin, tightened the collar of his navy-blue trench coat against the wind barreling off Dublin Bay. He was looking forward to the 1:00 a.m. shift change, about an hour from now. Then home to the wife and kids, and a feed of rashers and sausage. The kids would be long in bed, which is why he couldn't wait till his turn came to rotate out of this assignment. To keep the circulation moving in his legs he walked up and down in front of the Georgian mansion that housed the Krauts, but whenever it rained he had to retreat into the little kiosk that provided shelter. He hated that damn box with the pointy roof. It reminded him of the compartment in a cuckoo clock out of which popped an ugly puppet signaling the hour or half hour.

He looked at his pocket watch and then up at the light in the embassy window. The Krauts usually stayed up half the night. Because of them he was out flat-footing it up and down the footpath with only a wooden baton for protection. Until two nights ago it had been a most boring assignment. And wouldn't you know it, an hour after that shift ended, someone torched a synagogue. Rumors were rampant that the Krauts were behind it, although German ambassador Herr Mueller denied it vehemently. Few believed him, given that German storm troopers had burned nine hundred synagogues in their homeland two years earlier. The orgy of destruction known as Kristallnacht was a dark portent of things to come.

A heavy shower replaced the wind. Tom scurried to his cuckoo-clock shelter. Although he wasn't supposed to smoke on the job, he lit up. Unlikely, he figured, that anyone from the infractions department would be trawling for unprofessional behavior after hours.

Suddenly the night screamed with fire sirens, some at a distance, others close, becoming shriller and louder with every passing moment. And wouldn't you know it, here came his replacement. He was expecting Guard Daly, but the man who approached didn't have Daly's gait. It wasn't Daly at all, but a fellow about ten years his junior. "Hello, my name is Gurn, Sergeant Gurn," the replacement said. *By God, he is indeed,* Ryan thought, eying the chevrons on his sleeve. Worse, he didn't recognize him.

Ryan extended his hand slowly, as if weighing the wisdom of petting a hostile dog. "Well, I suppose you're welcome, but what happened to Daly?" A searing pain reminded him of the cigarette between the fingers of his left hand. He dropped it to the floor of the kiosk and ground it out with the heel of his boot. *Son of a bitch; my lucky night.* The edges of Gurn's mouth twitched with the slightest of smiles. "They pulled Daly for a more exciting assignment. He made quite a nuisance of himself with the higher-ups griping about the monotony of this duty."

Ryan scrutinized the stranger. "I don't know you." A red glare in the sky distracted him.

"That's because they brought a bunch of us up from the country yesterday to reinforce you chaps, and by the looks of it, not a moment too soon." Gurn turned his head to stare at the glow expanding like a red balloon on the horizon.

The rain tapered off. Ryan stepped out of the kiosk to allow his replacement to enter. He glanced again at the fire. "At this point I normally tell Daly to stay awake. You won't have that problem tonight."

With that, Ryan retrieved his bike from the embassy driveway and tightened his trouser cuffs with bicycle clips.

"Looks like we're in for a real show," Gurn said.

"Stay dry." Ryan pedaled away.

"Safe home."

A couple of hundred yards down the street, Ryan jumped off his bike and fired up another cigarette. He sucked his burnt finger. He had barely taken a dozen puffs from the previous one before that damn sergeant arrived. *Of all the fucking luck. Those bastards from the country are as rigid as paling posts. Sure as hell, he'll report me to the brass. I know it, the fucker will, no doubt about it.*

A sound nearby caught his attention. At first he thought it was an animal, but as he listened, he realized it was a moan. He had stopped on a stretch of road without any streetlights. He took out his torch and shone it in the direction of the groan. A derelict house stood about twenty feet back from the road's edge.

His gut told him what he'd find before he pushed open the reluctant door and played his flashlight into a dilapidated room. Guard Daly lay in a corner, tied and gagged. Blood trickled into his eyes from a gash on his head.

Ryan pulled a spring knife from his pocket, cut through the ropes, and removed the gag. "Holy mother of Jesus, John. What happened?"

Daly put his hand to his head. "Got jumped from behind. Then the lights went out."

But apart from the nasty head wound, Daly seemed okay. Ryan helped his colleague to his feet and conducted him to the nearest house with a light in the window. He instructed the residents to send for a doctor. Then he jumped on his bike and pedaled furiously toward the guards' kiosk.

Outside the embassy, a car with dimmed lights and its engine running was dropping off several shadowy figures. The so-called Garda Sergeant Gurn glanced up and down the street as he hustled the visitors up the embassy driveway. Before Ryan could reach the car, it sped away. He slid to a halt, dropping his bike with a clatter in the middle of the road. The sergeant scrambled through the door of the residence after the others and slammed it shut.

Thanks to diplomatic immunity, the newcomers were untouchable behind the walls of the embassy. Unless the Irish authorities could link them to a crime, they were free to come and go as they pleased. He looked up at the lighted window in frustration. There wasn't much more he could do. He cycled to the nearest phone kiosk and called in a full report to headquarters.

Chapter 4

The German Embassy

Dressed in a double-breasted grey serge suit, Franz Mueller looked more like a bank manager than Hitler's ambassador to Ireland. He was a man in his mid-fifties, with thinning black hair that highlighted a hangdog appearance. A life-sized picture of Adolf Hitler draped the wall behind him. A German flag bearing a swastika hung from floor to ceiling on the opposing wall.

Mueller seethed inside when "Sergeant Gurn" gave his report on the burning of the synagogue. Gurn's real name was Obersturmführer Stiglitz, a lieutenant in the SS and a committed Nazi. If Mueller resembled a bank manager, Stiglitz looked every inch the model Aryan, tall, athletic, blue-eyed, his blond hair slicked back in a high tight cut. Prominent cheekbones added to his aggressive demeanor. Mueller stood at odds with his superiors about the burnings, not only on principle, but for practical reasons as well. They drew unnecessary attention to German activity in Ireland and threatened to undermine the much more important objective, the planned invasion of Ireland, code-named Operation Green.

Stiglitz stood at attention in the chart room. "Mr. Ambassador, we have achieved our goal of putting the Jews on notice. Ireland will not be a safe haven for them either." Mueller turned his attention from the map of Ireland spread across a large oak table that he was studying with a magnifying glass.

He pointed the magnifying glass at Stiglitz. "You've left a trail of breadcrumbs right back to this embassy. Attacked one Irish policeman and showed your face to another, Herr Stiglitz."

The lieutenant clinched his teeth. "We are carrying out the Führer's will, Herr Ambassador."

Mueller dropped the magnifying glass on the map. "The Führer has priorities, young man, and attacking Jews in neutral Ireland is hardly something he wants to have get out at this time."

"But Herr Ambassador—"

The ambassador gestured toward the door. "That's enough, sir. You are dismissed."

Stiglitz tightened his lips, raised his right hand, and shouted, "*Heil Hitler!*" then spun around and marched out of the room.

After he left, the ambassador turned the key in the lock. He had enough of that young whelp for one night. *He* and not the lieutenant would be standing next morning before De Valera, the Irish *Taoiseach*, fending off accusations of meddling in the affairs of a neutral nation. He hoped De Valera might try to keep a lid on things, given some of the pro-German and anti-Semitic feelings in the country—not to mention his desire to continue on the path of neutrality in the war. Ambassador Mueller felt this neutrality was a joke. German air crews who crash-landed in Ireland were interned as prisoners of war. Brits, Canadians, or Yanks in similar circumstances were allowed free passage to the British-controlled six counties of Northern Ireland.

A polite knock broke Mueller's ruminations. He opened the door and admitted his secretary, an elderly gentleman wearing a black suit and a starched white shirt. He had a worried look on his face.

"What is it, Klaus?"

"Major Adler just called, sir."

"Go on." Mueller's impatience showed.

"The Major ran into a problem, but he wouldn't discuss it on the phone."

"Then how does he expect us to deal with it?"

"He's on his way here, sir."

"Show him in when he arrives."

"Yes, sir."

Mueller felt a stirring in the pit of his stomach. This could not be good. When the secretary left the room, he went to a cabinet, poured himself a shot of Jameson's, and threw some logs on the fire before settling into a leather armchair. It was fifteen minutes past one and he was growing weary of Sturmbannführer Franz Adler's scheming. Adler was his second in command, but unlike Mueller, he was a member of the SS, with a rank equivalent to major. A rabid Nazi, he supported Hitler's final solution enthusiastically.

After finishing his whiskey he placed the shot glass on the side table and closed his eyes, letting the liquor work its effects. He didn't like Sturmbannführer Adler. He felt he had been planted to spy on him.

Next thing he knew, Klaus was shaking his shoulder to announce the arrival of Adler. The Sturmbannführer was standing over him giving the Nazi salute. "*Heil* Hitler!" Adler said it with more enthusiasm, Mueller thought, than a late-night greeting warranted.

He returned the salute, more a dismissive wave of his hand, and gestured Adler to an armchair on the other side of the fireplace. "Like a drink?"

Adler removed his wire-rim glasses and rubbed his eyes. "Thanks, Herr Ambassador, but I think I'll forego it for now." He took off his black leather coat and draped it over a chair.

Stunning. Adler never passed up a drink.

Adler cleared his throat. "A few days ago we captured two British MI6 intelligence agents in the West of Ireland. After some friendly persuasion they confirmed my suspicions that England *has* a plan to invade Ireland." A self-satisfied grin flashed across Adler's face. He reached into his breast pocket and pulled out a pack of Player cigarettes, offering one to Mueller before lighting his own.

Mueller waved a hand. "I find it hard to believe that Britain would risk entangling itself in the internal affairs of a neutral country."

Adler threw back his head and laughed. "Don't be naive. The

31

British still see Ireland as theirs. Thousands of Irishmen are in the British army." He flicked cigarette ash onto the stone hearth. "If I had my way, we'd have moved on this sooner."

Mueller's face colored. "Lack of hard evidence called for caution, Sturmbannführer. We can't go stomping around a foreign country as if we owned it."

"In time we will." He crossed his legs and flicked the half-smoked cigarette into the fire.

Mueller leaned back in his chair and steepled his fingers. "What of the two agents?"

"We had to dispose of them to protect our cover."

Mueller's stomach tightened. "This could undermine Operation Green. The British will know it was us."

"No, they'll blame IRA rage at discovering British meddling in their country again."

"I hope you're right, otherwise you'll have a lot of explaining to do to the Führer."

Adler rose from his chair, not looking so cocksure of himself anymore, and paced. "Unfortunately there's another problem."

"Oh, one of your henchmen blabbed?"

"Worse, a fisherman and a kid saw the whole thing." He walked back and forth punching his palm with his fist.

Beads of sweat rose on the ambassador's face. *"Mein Gott in Himmel.* I think we need to change our Irish invasion plan from Operation Green to Operation Disaster."

Adler's face darkened. "Through a stroke of ill-timing, they saw my face." He paused to light another cigarette. A thin column of smoke escaped his lips. "Despite our best efforts to apprehend them, they escaped. Sooner or later they'll discover who I am. Once the story gets out, it's only a matter of time before the Irish government comes calling."

"And I dare say the British are not likely to sit on their hands in the meantime." The ambassador's tone bordered on mockery, as if he was pleased Adler's scheme was coming to grief.

Adler continued his pacing. "Not to worry. The Brits may not feel as cocky as they did, now that their scheme has been uncovered."

Mueller turned in his chair to look at Adler, who was staring vacantly at the maps on the table. "The solution for you at any rate is simple enough."

"I don't follow. It's anything but simple. It's a total fucking mess. If we don't get rid of that fisherman and his daughter, months of careful planning will go right down the drain."

"What I mean, Herr Adler, is we can get you out of the country, you and Stiglitz. That way they can never identify you. Case closed."

Adler waved his cigarette. "Absolutely out of the question. Without me this whole operation will fall apart. I've carefully built a network of Irish collaborators. If I disappear, that support will dissolve like a sand castle in a strong tide. No, we need to find those two--and fast." He returned to his chair. "But what's this about Stiglitz?"

The ambassador reviewed the fracas that followed the burning of the Jewish synagogue. For a split second Adler's bloodshot eye seemed to glow. He smiled. "On second thought, I think that drink would hit the spot right now, if you would be so kind, Mr. Ambassador." Mueller welcomed the break in the conversation. After filling a shot glass for Adler, he politely excused himself to retire for the night, leaving the SS major nursing his drink before the fire.

As Mueller climbed the stairs to his bedroom, he mulled over Adler's options. The wisest choice of course would be for Adler to leave the country at once. Ordinarily he could order him to do so, but Sturmbannführer Adler had Hitler's ear, thus compromising the chain of command. Adler had deliberately kept Mueller in the dark about the details of Germany's clandestine plans for Ireland, due no doubt to Hitler's suspicions that he was not a committed Nazi. For now, Mueller served to portray the benign face of Nazism, sufficient reason to tolerate his lack of fervor. As far as Mueller was concerned, Germany had quite enough on its plate already without getting involved in an operation of questionable strategic importance. Once Britain was defeated, Ireland could be overcome in a matter of days. Why risk opening another front? He sat in a bedside chair, kicked his shoes off, and closed his eyes. This would not end well.

Chapter 5

The Bog

Coltrane and Brigid held their breaths and ducked under the algae, popping up into the cavity of the tree trunk. They stayed afloat by holding on to the lips of the knotholes from inside, thus stabilizing the trunk and preventing it from rolling. Spying the moon through the knothole, Coltrane felt as if he were floating in space. Everything had turned as quiet as a predator about to pounce on its prey.

Another loud splash. A muffled cry. "Good!" he whispered. "Someone's gone for an early-morning swim."

The tree trunk's inner wall amplified every sound. The snap of a twig and the swish of heather against a rubber boot announced the approach of the trackers. The rise and fall of Brigid's breathing filled the log cavity. Coltrane reached out and patted her on the head. "We'll get through this, love," he whispered.

A shotgun blast sent woodland creatures scurrying through the underbrush. "You damned idiot!" a gruff voice shouted.

"There's something out there in the shadows."

"Here's your shadow, you fool. Looks like an old pair of overalls snagged in the bushes."

"Maybe they've gone for a swim," someone snickered.

A chorus of laughter reverberated across the water. The searchers spoke with English accents. Coltrane wondered if he was wrong about the presence of a local. Then another voice announced, "Maybe yer man here is not such an eejit after all; maybe that's exactly what they've done."

"Done what?"

"Gone for a dip."

"Dip? What the hell's a dip?"

"Jaysus, yer an awful thick bunch! Dip? Swim! They could be hiding in the water, for Christ's sake."

"I suppose they brought their bloody diving gear with them."

"Don't need no bloody divin' gear. Over here, will ye; give us the shotgun. Ya know they could be hidin' underneath the algae and comin' up for air under the cover of the bulrushes near the banks. Did ye ever think of that?"

The night exploded in a cacophony of shotgun blasts that raked the bog hole with buckshot. Coltrane peeked through a knothole. Patches of algae, like swatches of wrinkled skin, leapt from the pond. The water roiled and bubbled like a prehistoric animal angry at being roused from eons of undisturbed sleep. Inside the tree cavity, the acrid odor of spent shells burned their nostrils. Several rounds of shot had peppered the trunk but expended their force in the sodden timber.

"Look out there in the middle of the water. What's that?"

"Can't rightly tell."

"Get a light on it." A flashlight beam played up and down the trunk, and then extended farther out. "Looks like a rotten tree trunk. Been there forever, I bet."

"Well, let's find out. Bergin, get out there and take a closer look," an English voice commanded. A loud splash and a round of swearing followed as Bergin waded into the water. The tree trunk rocked from the disturbance.

Coltrane grabbed Brigid by the arm. "Take deep breaths." A wave sluiced up the cavity and splashed over their mouths. As the heavy breathing drew closer, he alerted Brigid and ducked out of the tree trunk. Shadowy figures moved along the bank. He swam to the end of the log that was farthest from the approaching swimmer. He pulled his knife and waited. Better to confront the assailant out in the open than remain entombed inside the log. In the moonlight he saw Bergin's head bobbing up and down through the algae like a cork at the end of a fishing line. He weighed the practicality of drowning him rather than using his knife. His pulse quickened.

A series of shouts for help and the sound of arm thrashing. Bergin was in trouble. The thick skein of algae clinging to his arms and shoulders weighed him down. He was about to go under when his mates threw him a rope and hauled him back to dry land.

"There's fuck all out there," the exhausted Bergin said, propping himself up on his hands and knees. He coughed up bog water as his companions stood laughing.

"How would you know; you nearly drowned!" the English accent mocked. "It seems Mr. McShane here, who took our money in advance, has come up a little short on his promises."

McShane coughed. "Please, sir, Mr. Kincaid, I'm as good as me word. You'll see. I'll track them down. They're around here somewhere. I'm sure of it, and I know just how to find them, as God's me witness."

"God will be your witness, all right; he'll witness your execution if you can't find this pair by tomorrow."

"Don't worry, Mr. Kincaid, there's no way in hell they can get off the island with their boat at the bottom of the lake. I'll be here with the dogs in the mornin'. They'll make short work of them, I tell ya."

A chill went through Coltrane. *Dogs!*

After stomping around a little longer and firing random shots into the algae, the hunters noisily departed. Coltrane and Brigid swam the tree trunk back to the water's edge. When he was satisfied that they were alone, Coltrane hoisted himself up onto the turf bank and pulled a shivering Brigid up after him. "Daddy, have they gone?"

"I think so, but I'm not sure. It could be a ruse," he whispered, looking around.

"Oh." She fell silent for a moment. Then, "Who is Kincaid? How are we going to get off the island before he comes back?"

Coltrane didn't have an answer to either question, but felt he should take a stab at the first. "My guess is Kincaid's a mercenary, a hired gun who follows the money. Sounds like a disaffected Brit, otherwise he'd be in the army."

"What does 'disaffected' mean, Daddy?"

"Someone who's mad at the world."

Coltrane knew that with dogs in the picture they'd have to get off the island faster than he planned. He was certain he could swim the half mile to the mainland, but he feared that Brigid was not up to it after such prolonged exposure to the cold water.

They stood in the fading moonlight, sopping wet, their bodies covered in algae and mud. He coiled the rope around his neck and took the slane in his right hand. "Let's go, love. We'll feel better once we're moving."

The rising sun gradually blanketed the landscape in a weak light that made travel less treacherous.

They followed a path to a different spot on the shoreline. As they approached the edge of the cutaway bog, a dark form emerged from the underbrush and stood directly in their path.

Chapter 6

Ambush

The apparition tipped the brim of its hat. "Well, well, if it isn't Mr. Coltrane and the kid. Good morning to ye both. Oliver McShane here."

They froze in their stride and struggled to regain their footing. Instinctively Coltrane grabbed Brigid by the shoulder and moved her behind him.

McShane wore a jacket that once was grey but had acquired a glossy brownish sheen from wear and dirt. A frayed black scarf hung loosely around his neck. "Doing a bit of turf cutting, I see. Sure, I knew ye were here all along, but those morons wouldn't listen to me. You know how those furriners are: know-it-alls, cocky as hell. Well, I'd love to stay and chat, but I must be off to collect me money." He raised the shotgun.

"Let my daughter go, McShane. It's me they're looking for."

"Afraid I can't do that. You understand me predicament. Didn't know your girleen was along at the start, but she'll talk. Can't risk that."

"You'll risk an awful lot more if you kill us. Besides, why do Kincaid's dirty work for him?"

"Nothing personal, Coltrane; it's the money, nothing against you or the kid, although there is the other thing."

"But you can still get your money if you just turn us over to them. You don't have to do any killing, unless, Lord save us, you have a taste for that kind of thing."

McShane took a few steps back. "Little girl. Take the rope from your old lad's neck."

Coltrane couldn't tell if McShane was having second thoughts or setting up a more exotic form of execution. It wasn't just the money. McShane might be settling a personal grudge as well--that other thing. As Brigid moved in front of her father to remove the rope, he bent his head to accommodate her reach while tightening his grip on the slane. He could see McShane under Brigid's armpit. He had lowered the barrel of the gun.

"Now tie the girleen's hands, but first throw that slane to me. You're not likely to be cutting turf anytime soon."

Coltrane moved to take the rope from Brigid, but instead shoved her hard to one side and lofted the slane. Its sharp point caught McShane under the chin.

The gun went off. The blast tore the weapon from the would-be killer's grip, spiraling it over the hazel bushes into a clump of sedge. Blood gushed from McShane's neck, spreading a red stain onto the black scarf. With a choking gurgle, the man who a short few hours before called on God to be his witness collapsed in a heap by the side of a bog hole.

Coltrane tramped around in the long grass and located the shotgun by a wisp of smoke leaching from its barrels. After retrieving several cartridges from McShane's pockets, he rolled the body off the bank into the brown water and threw the slane in after it. Only then did he realize that Brigid was missing. In the adrenalin surge he didn't remember pushing her.

"Brigid!" An otter slid from its den into the water, causing hardly a ripple on the glassy surface.

"Brigid! Brigid!" He tramped around frantically in the underbrush, his heartbeat reverberating through his throat.

"Brigid."

He almost stepped on the red stockinged foot protruding from a fern patch on the lip of a bog hole. Brigid had passed out.

With cupped hands he scooped water from the bog hole and dribbled it onto her face until she stirred. For a time they clung to each other without talking. Then she sobbed, her body quivering in his arms. "It's over," he whispered. "He can't harm us now."

"Who was that, Daddy?"

"I don't know," he lied.

"But he knew who we were—how come?"

"All I know is, he's a gillie. I may have run into him a time or two during some fishing tournament or other." He picked up two more cartridges from the trampled grass and handed them to her. "Put these in your pocket. We may need them."

Brigid put them in the pockets of her windbreaker and buttoned the flaps. Coltrane wondered if he should tell Brigid about "the other thing." McShane had once been his rival in pursuit of her mother. But then a barrage of questions was sure to follow. He decided against it. It was of no consequence anymore. After glancing at the red stains bubbling to the surface of the bog hole, he slung the shotgun over his shoulder, grabbed Brigid by the hand, and they ran toward the shoreline. He suspected that McShane had known their identities all along and shared that information with his overseers. A nervous spasm gripped his stomach. This put Claire in jeopardy too. They loped along for a time without speaking, while keeping a lookout for another ambush. Their survival depended as much on luck as it did on vigilance. The swishing of the bog grass against their boots and their labored breathing competed with rising bird calls. The sun peeked over the horizon. He felt a drag on his arm as Brigid struggled to keep pace. Time to stop.

The taste of salt on his lips. Blood. He washed his face in bog water, but the smell remained in his nostrils. Birdsong grew louder. Daylight would bring the rest of the pursuers back to the island, if they weren't here already. He had to figure out how to get Brigid across a half mile-wide channel famous for its warring currents. In their exhausted condition that would be impossible; they needed some sleep.

He put an arm around the shivering girl and led her to a thick clump of ferns in a clearing under a bog oak. "We'll rest here awhile." They stretched out among the ferns and bantered a bit to take the edge off their predicament. "God, you look a sight, child," he joked. Swatches of green algae clung to Brigid's hair and clothing, and bog grasses adorned her neck and shoulders.

"Look who's talking; you should see yerself. You look like somethin' the cat dragged in."

"And you look like a nymph from an ancient forest."

"What's a nymph, Daddy? Is she ugly?"

"No, no, in this particular case she's quite beautiful." It amazed him that Brigid continued to hold up. Fear wrapped them tightly, but also steeled their resolve to do what had to be done to survive.

She hugged him. Tears welled up in her eyes. "I'm afraid we'll never see Mammie again." Anger and guilt tore at him as he tried to reassure her that if they kept their wits about them, they would be home by evening. He wasn't sure of that anymore.

"Listen, Brigid. We'll have to risk getting some sleep and hope our luck holds."

"What if we don't hear them coming?" she whispered hoarsely as she lay down.

"The dogs will rouse us."

He reached across her and tucked the jacket around her neck before stretching out among the ferns. A light breeze moved across them, bending the long bog grass beneath the birch trees. He loaded McShane's shotgun and laid it beside himself after cocking both hammers.

Chapter 7

Sturmbannführer Adler SS

With the ambassador out of the chart room, Adler picked up the phone and called the recreation hall located in the basement. "Adler here. Get me Stiglitz."

"Yes, sir."

"Tell him to come up to the chart room immediately."

"At once, sir."

When Stiglitz entered the chart room Adler stood with his back to him staring at the floor-to-ceiling swastika. In one hand he held a bottle of Irish whiskey, in the other a cigarette.

He turned and faced the young lieutenant, then walked to the wall cabinet and picked up a shot glass. "I heard about your escapades tonight. Can use a man of your ingenuity and imagination." He filled the glass and handed it to Stiglitz.

Stiglitz's face lit up like a sunrise. *"Jawohl, Sturmbannführer."*

"Come, take a seat." Adler refilled his own glass and sat opposite Stiglitz. "So the ambassador plans to send you back to the Fatherland." There was no concealing the look of shock and disappointment on Stiglitz's face. "I have other plans for you. A good SS man doesn't turn tail and run like a scared rabbit, right?" He raised his glass. "To the

Fatherland." He threw back the shot of whiskey.

Stiglitz beamed as he raised his glass."To the Fatherland," and downed the whiskey.

Adler studied him. "Good. Now go get your things and meet me at the back door in fifteen minutes." Stiglitz's face registered surprise.

Adler pointed to the door. "Go on. Go!"

Soon Stiglitz was back with a bulging duffle bag to await Adler's instructions. He looked as wound up as a hound before the hunt. Adler appeared a few minutes later. "I'm sending you to the west of Ireland on an important mission for the Reich. There you will join in a search operation that is underway as we speak. You will talk to a man called Kincaid, who will fill you in on all the details."

Stiglitz looked a little bewildered until Adler told him that a car and a driver awaited him beyond the wall at the end of the embassy garden. Adler then looked at his watch. "It is now two o'clock. You should be there by seven." He was about to dismiss his subordinate when another thought crossed his mind. "Incidentally, I should caution you that our friend Kincaid is a rather boorish Englishman lacking our sense of loyalty and discipline. That makes him unreliable."

Stiglitz narrowed his eyes. "An Englishman?"

"He's a mercenary working with a team of locals who put money before patriotism. Loyal to us as long as the money keeps flowing. So I am counting on you to keep an eye on Kincaid and this rabble." The two exchanged the Nazi salute. "Good luck Herr Stiglitz."

The young lieutenant stepped into the garden.

***

When Adler returned to the chart room, he picked up the phone. He checked his watch. It had been seven hours since he abandoned the search and returned to Dublin. "Operator, please put me through to the Western Road Hotel in Cloonfin."

The connection was made. Adler asked the clerk at the night desk to summon the occupant in room 212 to the phone. After a few minutes a voice weathered by cigarettes and whiskey came on the line. "Kincaid here."

Adler coughed. "Are you sure there's no one else listening in?"

"Not to worry, Boss. I'm in a phone kiosk in the lobby with a direct bead on the clerk at the night desk. He's thumbing through a magazine."

"Well, anything to report?"

"If there was I'd have called you, mate, wouldn't I?"

Adler bristled at the man's disrespect, but he held his temper in check because he needed his services. For now. "I take it the fugitives are still at large?"

A brief silence. "'Fraid they got away, Boss. After you left we tracked Coltrane and the kid to a small bog island, but we had to give up after it got dark."

"Give up? What the hell kind of talk is that? That's not what I'm paying you for!"

"Let me finish, Boss, let me finish. My trackers are pretty certain that Coltrane and his young one are trapped on that little island. Their boat is sunk and come morning we're returning with the dogs."

Adler felt relieved. But they wouldn't be safe until that pair joined the MI6 snoops under the sod of Red Cow Island. He poured another shot of whiskey. "If that fails, is there an alternate way to flush 'em out?"

Kincaid cleared his throat. "Yes, but it's risky."

Adler turned up his nose at the vulgar sounds of Kincaid slurping his pint over the line. "I'll be the judge of that."

"If it goes wrong it could attract a lot of unwanted attention. I'm mulling over the idea of snatching Coltrane's wife. If successful, we'd hold all the bargaining chips. One of my chaps says there isn't a lock he couldn't pick." Kincaid made a loud sucking sound as he took another long draft of the pint.

Adler drummed his fingertips on the table. "What are you waiting for? Do it."

"Frankly, Boss, part of my hesitation is the condition of my men. After spending half the night in that damn bog, they're wet and tired to the bone. Not what you might call up to snuff, mate. Plus, the last two hours they've spent in the hotel bar have degraded their concentration, I'll wager."

"I don't give a damn what condition they're in. Rouse their drunken arses out of there and go after that bitch!"

The grandfather clock in the lobby sounded the hour. "Jawohl, Boss, I'm on my way."

"Wait. Since I'm forced to lie low here at the embassy for a while, I'm sending reinforcements—a young officer named Stiglitz. He should be at your hotel by six o'clock."

***

Kincaid mouthed a profanity into the phone, but didn't utter it. "Appreciate the help, Boss, appreciate the help."

He slammed the phone into its cradle. "Nazi prick! I don't need no more fucking Krauts to assist me." He reeled toward the bar. After being drummed out of the SAS, a Special Forces regiment of the British army, Kincaid fled the country and landed in Ireland eager to sell his considerable skills to the highest bidder. As if that weren't enough, his wife drummed him out of her life at the same time and absconded with their fourteen-year-old daughter. Hadn't seen the girl in two years. Didn't care about the wife, but the kid. That was another matter. When he heard the kind of money Adler was offering for muscle, he jumped at the chance. It mattered little that he was signing up to sabotage England, the country of his birth. Much as he disliked it, he could tolerate the Nazi bullshit as long as the money spigot continued to flow—for now.

Problem was, the flow of German money had been sluggish of late. A nagging unease rippled through his stomach. Was Adler withholding it until he had captured Coltrane? He should have asked for the total lump sum up front. Instead he agreed to take half until the job was done, figuring that capturing or killing a rural schoolteacher would be a relatively easy task. Wasn't working out that way. Only later did he discover that the schoolteacher in question had turned in his jacket with the leather patches on its elbows for a trench coat. This guy had fought with the international brigades in Spain against Franco.

And Kincaid's new command? A sneer creased his face. A crowd of blokes like himself with no moral compass. Fair enough. A bunch of

Irish touts who were willing to betray their country for thirty pieces of silver. These birds of a feather were crowded around the bar in various states of inebriation. He pushed his way through to the counter and turned to address them. "Listen up, ladies. Finish your pints and follow me. We've got a new assignment." A crescendo of grumbling. He shot them a menacing stare. They staggered out the door after him still griping and cursing their ill luck.

Chapter 8

Home Invasion

Claire Coltrane removed her clothes and collapsed into bed around 3:00 a.m. She had spent the previous four hours at Loch Gorm with her next-door neighbor Lost John Toole, anxiously pacing the shore trying to keep the lid on her panic. One after another, search boats returned to the staging area without any word of her missing husband and child. At her insistence, the boats continued to scour the lake by moonlight until reason prevailed and the operation was called off until daylight.

Earlier that night, when she arrived home from her parents' place in the country, she learned from Lost John Toole that Peter and Brigid had not returned from their fishing trip to Loch Gorm. Their car was still parked at Doyle's Cove, where they left it. She refused to move it, fearing that such an action was a subconscious admission that they were not returning. That she could not deal with right now. Having lost her grandfather in a boating accident, she was leery of the water. It gave her a nervous feeling every time she saw her husband and daughter off on one of these lake excursions.

The knot of terror in her stomach woke her several times during the night and each time she confronted the awful possibility that her loved ones were gone for good. When she finally dozed off again, something jarred her awake. She sat bolt upright in bed. Instinctively she reached across the bed to shake her husband, but found only the cold pillow. The small clock on the bedside table glowed 4:45 a.m. Rain sprayed the windowpanes, sounding like tiny steel balls dropping on metal. She slid out of bed and pulled on her robe. Someone was coming up the stairs. Her heart soared. They were home! She hurried across the polished floorboards and groped for the light switch near the door.

Then she froze. The squeaking of the stairs caused her throat to constrict. Drafty windows and squeaky floors were a given in the hundred-year-old house she inherited from her grandparents, but age alone could not account for the unfamiliar sound coming from beyond her bedroom door. Every night for the last two years she and her family squeaked up the stairs to bed, beating out a rhythm on the loose stair steps.

Tonight the rhythm was off. The person climbing the stairs was neither her husband nor her daughter.

Her brain went into overdrive. Like an exhausted fox fleeing from the hunt, she darted around, looking for a place to hide. The armoire, her grandmother's sturdy piece of Victorian furniture, stood against the wall opposite her bed. Its open top, adorned with crown molding, butted up against the ceiling, concealing a trap door to the attic. As children she and her sister used it as the entrance to a make-believe world, when the attic was a place of wonder and mystery.

Now Claire hoped it would be a place of survival. She stepped into the armoire, shut the doors behind her, and readied herself to climb the shelves. The bedroom door creaked open. The light switch clicked. The intruder's breathing filled the room. The smell of alcohol. Through chinks in the wood of the armoire she saw the outline of a man but couldn't make out his features. He appeared unsteady on his feet. The sound of the bed being upended. Time to move. She climbed the shelves, pushed the trapdoor up and crawled into the attic. The armoire doors flew open.

Clothes hangers rattled. The intruder pawed through her coats and dresses. She crouched in the attic about two feet above his head, but since he wore a hat she got little sense of his identity. In apparent frustration he pulled most of her clothes from the armoire and threw them onto the bedroom floor. His heavy breathing sounded like it was coming through a water filter. Mercifully, he did not look up. The smell of alcohol remained in the armoire after he left. Heavy footsteps descended the stairs, followed by the metallic clack of the knocker as the front door slammed. She eased the trapdoor shut and stretched out on the attic floor until her heart rate returned to normal. Though she hadn't explored the attic for years, she still remembered the layout in detail from countless games of hide-and-seek with her sister. The attic extended over the living space of the entire house. It was littered with the bric-a-brac of fifty years: rocking chairs, toys, old lamps, and several boxes of books deposited over the decades. Its sturdy floor and extensive insulation lessened the chances of being heard from below. However, in certain areas she had to crawl on hands and knees to avoid the low-slung rafters supporting the hipped roof.

The rain had ceased. Light from a full moon filtered through the small window in the south gable. Her stomach churned when she realized that she might not be able to squeeze through the window as she had when she was a wiry thirteen-year-old. She thought again of her loved ones. The intruders' appearance rent the fragile tissue of calm she had wrapped around her panic. It shattered the hope that her husband and child were safe and would be found in the morning. Was the break-in a coincidence? Or was it somehow connected to their disappearance?

A voice shouted from below: "Search this damn place from top to bottom!"

Her movements camouflaged by the noise erupting beneath her, Claire managed to scoot a heavy box of books over the trapdoor. It wouldn't stop them for long, but it would slow them down. She ducked under the ceiling rafters and dodged around the darkened obstacles until she reached the window in the gable end.

The window overlooked the roof of a thatched cottage owned by Lost John and his sister Nora. It also shared a common gable wall with the first storey of her own house. Down below the intruders moved from room to room. Claire raised the lower half of the window and surveyed the dun-colored thatch in the moonlight. The ten-foot drop looked like twenty. There was another problem, too: the thatch was slick from the rain.

A shotgun blast scattered fragments of the trapdoor and sent chunks of books flying through the attic.

Time to go. She squeezed out onto the window sill feet-first, shut the window behind her and jumped into the moonlight. She hit the neighboring roof hard and slid down the slick thatch toward a vegetable garden. To slow her descent she grabbed at the thatch, which pulled away in explosive handfuls, leaving a trail of small craters in her wake. Her slide arrested, she clawed her way back up to the ridgeline and took cover behind the whitewashed chimney.

She peeked around it. A light appeared in the attic window as the moon ducked behind a rain cloud. An explosion of glass rained down from above. A flashlight beam played back and forth across the glistening shards embedded in the thatch.

"Not a soul up here!" a voice yelled.

"Better make damn sure."

"Well, unless she flew out the fucking window, there's no other way out of here."

"You're a genius, no doubt about it."

Lights came on in neighboring houses. As the noise continued, neighbors spilled into the street to investigate. Abruptly a flashlight beam danced along the gable wall, illuminating the face in the attic window. A voice from the street called out.

"You up there. This is Guard O'Connell. Stop this racket, or—"

A sharp pop like a firecracker rang out. The flashlight slipped from the guard's hand and he collapsed in the middle of the street. The face in the attic window disappeared. Stifling a scream, Claire slithered down the roof on her belly toward the vegetable garden. The wind and rain picked up again. As she made her descent, her thin nightgown bunched up around her hips like a wet rope, exposing her body to the broken glass and coarse wicker bindings that secured the straw to the roof.

Lost John's inattention to his roof appeared as large soft spots spread like sores over the expanse of the thatch. Claire swore at her neighbor for his negligence as she maneuvered across these islands of decay, now overgrown with a layer of moss turned to goo by the rain. Wisps of thatch snagged in her hair and clumps of moss, reeking with the odor of bird droppings, stuck to her arms and legs. At the edge of the roof she tied her nightgown in a knot around her waist and leaped into the vegetable garden.

***

Nora Toole thought that the tapping on her small bedroom window was the stuff of a recurring dream, until she realized that the noise was coming from outside. The luminous hands of her alarm clock pointed at 5:00 a.m., but it was still too dark to see anything clearly. Nora, a spinster, lived with her brother Lost John in their ancestral home next to Peter and Claire Coltrane. Its sturdy two-foot-thick walls had withstood the test of time, but they wouldn't be worth a farthin', Nora reckoned, up against the banshee crying her name outside the window. Scared to distraction, she threw on a brown cardigan over her nightgown and wrapped her thin yellow hair in a black head square. Then she launched into a sing-song volley of prayers, beseeching the Almighty to intercede as she hustled to rouse Lost John, who was sleeping in the lower room beyond the kitchen.

Nora cowered behind her brother on their way back to the kitchen. Not happy about being awakened from a sound sleep, he vented his frustration with a string of profanities. Even in his long johns, Lost John cut a powerful figure. Big-boned with a strong jaw and a face that reflected a life of ups and downs, he was not someone you would elect to cross without considerable reflection. When he raised a muscled arm to release the bolt on the back door, Nora croaked in her morning voice, "Hould on John 'til I get a weep drop of Knock holy water."

"You daft loon. If it's a ghost, holy water will just piss him off, and if it's a normal person, he probably needs a shot of whiskey more than a tinkle of holy water."

"Never you mind, you old heathen. It's yerself that needs the whiskey, isn't it?"

She scurried off to the dresser to fetch the holy water.

***

When Lost John yanked the door open, he went weak at the knees. The apparition in front of him was barefooted, half-naked, and streaked in dirt from head to toe. Straw and moss stuck out of its hair and clothing. A stream of blood trickled down one of its arms.

He reached behind the door and his left hand closed around the knob of his blackthorn stick. He was about to swing into action when Nora shot by him with the holy water, screaming, "Mother a Jaysus Claire, what happened to you at all at all? You look shockin'."

"One thing's for sure," wheezed Lost John, who had collapsed in a heap against the whitewashed kitchen wall. "She scared the livin' shite outa me."

"Would you shut your filthy mouth and go and boil some water so we can clean this girleen up, and while you're at it, throw on some clothes and go down to the sideboard in the sittin' room."

John staggered to his feet. "And?"

"And bring up the bottle of brandy and a glass. Not two glasses now, mind you." She threw him a look that could bubble wallpaper.

He straightened up and flung her a wobbly salute. "Bitch," he muttered into the fireplace as he hung the big black kettle on a hook that hung from the crane. The fire was still raked, so he freed the coals of their canopy of ashes and added fresh turf to get a blaze going. That done, he went to the bedroom and pulled on his clothes. Over the years his fondness for booze led to several lost weekends, so many that people started calling him Lost John Toole. Before he could tie his boots, she was on him again.

"What's keepin' you with that brandy?"

He grabbed the bottle and a glass from the musty sideboard in the sitting room and headed back. He stopped short of the kitchen door to take a hearty swig.

Entering the kitchen he saw Claire sitting by the fire, wrapped in a blanket.

Nora's face looked like parchment in the light of the struggling fire

52

and the brown age spots looked like moth holes. "Put some more turf on and then go milk the cow while I clean this poor—"

"Not before I find out what in the hell's going on, Nora."

"Murder and pillage is what's going on," Nora said. "Remember earlier on when I called down to you that I heard a gun go off and Mr. Know-It-All here told me I was daft in the head? Well, wait 'til you hear Claire's tale."

Lost John shuffled nervously from one foot to the other as Claire's story tumbled out, punctuated by sobs. "You mean to say Guard O'Connell is lying out there in the street this very minute?" he asked.

"He was out there while I was on the roof, but as I was trying to get down without breaking my neck I heard the neighbors gathering in the street."

"Jaysus Christ." Lost John ran to the front door. "I can't believe I slept through all that."

"Wait, wait," Claire implored. "Don't tell anyone you saw me."

Lost John's face gathered into a mask of confusion. "For Christ's sake, why not?" She pulled the plaid Foxford blanket tighter around her shivering body. "Because whoever came after me might come looking for me again."

"She's right, John," Nora said. "As soon as these bloody gossips get hold of this, you might as well put it in the newspaper." A look of concern flitted across Lost John's face and he returned to the fire.

"What's the matter, John?" Claire asked.

"I'm afraid if they killed once, they'll kill again. We could all be in danger."

"That's for sure," Nora chimed in.

Claire's mouth dropped open and she touched her cheeks with the tips of her fingers. As if reading her mind, Lost John cast his eyes at the floor and stroked the stubble on his chin several times. He remained rooted to the spot for a spell before rousing himself with a grunt. Then he strode across the floor and grabbed his shotgun and a box of cartridges from the three-cornered press. "By God, if it's a fight they want, they're bloody well going to get it."

Claire exhaled loudly. Lost John loaded the gun and snapped the barrel back in place before setting it back in the corner. Next, stick in hand, he marched to the front door, lifted the latch, and joined the hushed knot of people gathered in the middle of the street.

"Did you ever hear such old blowing in all yer born life?" Nora groaned. "Pay no attention to him a grá, shure now he thinks he's bloody Napoleon. The Lord save us and bless us, he's an awful case."

***

But Claire didn't think he was an awful case. On the contrary, Lost John's fighting words reassured her. *Yes*, she thought, *I am safe here. Better to have Napoleon on your side than a frightened rabbit.*

***

Guard O'Connell was not dead, but it appeared to Lost John that he was not far from it. His face was dishwater grey and his breathing shallow. Lost John knew that two things stood in O'Connell's favor—his youth, and the presence of Dr. Desmond Ford. As a young man, Ford had served on the frontlines of the Great War as a surgeon with thousands of other Irishmen who had volunteered for the British army. Having survived the slaughter of Verdun he became an expert in bullet wounds, among other things. A short, stocky man with a moustache, Ford used to joke that he extracted enough bullets out of the wounded to build a lead wall around his dispensary.

"I'll require help getting this man to my clinic. One of you go and roust Charlie Tobin." Wearing a grey tweed suit with a pair of brown leather boots, Dr. Ford looked every bit the country doctor as he bent to examine Guard O'Connell. "Tell him we need his van down here on the double. Then I'll need a few volunteers to get this poor bugger into it. The rest of you can leave."

Lost John returned indoors. After grabbing his hat and raincoat from a peg on the back door, he crouched down beside Claire at the fire. He struggled to get his words out. "I'm sorry to leave, but I must be off to the lake again to search for your kin."

Tears streamed down Claire's face and her whole frame shook. She laid her hand on John's arm. "God go with you."

54

Chapter 9

The Man in Black

Men with guns and dogs milled around two boats with outboard motors on the shoreline across from Red Cow Island. Feathered light brushed the horizon as the "coooleeee" of the curlew from a distant bog mingled with the excited yelping of the nervous bloodhounds.

Kincaid squinted at the pocket watch in his beefy hand. "Where the hell's McShane?" Clad in a long black overcoat and a grey felt hat, his six-foot-two frame was an intimidating presence. He pursed his lips while dragging on his pipe. When he exhaled, two rows of yellow teeth flashed through the blue smoke. The crunch of his large feet on the rock-strewn shore added another dimension of menace to his already threatening demeanor. His subordinates drifted out of his path, not daring to answer the big man's query. If he had a first name, nobody knew it. If they did, they were afraid to use it. Most took the safer tack and simply called him "Boss."

"Where the hell is he, you conniving weasels?" he bellowed again. "I told everyone to be here by six o'clock. Without McShane we haven't a hope in hell of finding Coltrane on that cursed island."

"He didn't come home last night, Boss; the wife thinks he went on a booze-up," someone said.

"That sniveling little coward; probably didn't have a clue where Coltrane was hiding and was afraid to show up today. Took our money, though. Well, by God, he'll pay dearly for this sooner than he thinks. After we get Coltrane, we'll scour every pub and shebeen in the townland and give him what he deserves … the filthy little get!"

During Kincaid's tirade, dogs barked and men shuffled nervously. Storm clouds mustered on the horizon like regiments before a battle.

"Boss," a quiet voice ventured, "I think I can find Coltrane's hiding place."

"Who's that? Stop mumbling and speak up, for Christ's sake."

"It's O'Reilly, Boss. Jack O'Reilly."

"You better be damn sure of what you're saying, O'Reilly, because if you fail, you'll become a permanent resident of that accursed island. I'll drown you myself in a bog hole; I'm sick of being led on these wild-goose chases by you clowns."

O'Reilly pushed back his cap, revealing a mop of black curls, and scratched his head. He had a ruddy face and lively blue eyes that danced back and forth. Like the other gillies he wore an oilskin coat and Wellingtons turned down at the top.

Kincaid felt edgier than usual, but it wasn't from the ineptness of his search party. What really disturbed him was Adler's likely reaction when he discovered they had bollocksed the break-in and allowed the Coltrane woman to slip through their fingers. He needed a win, and soon, if he hoped to collect the £200 balance of his fee from the Krauts, which he needed to repair the motor launch he had purchased from a nervous English tourist. The thought of it bobbing at anchor in a secluded cove on the Shannon River made him wish he were on it instead of sucking up to some Nazi clown.

Giving up on McShane, they loaded the guns and dogs into the boats. They were about to head off for the Priests' Island when a horn blared. Everyone looked up. A black sedan roared down the gravel road and enveloped them in a cloud of dust, stopping short of the lakeshore. A young man, looking prim in a short black leather jacket, jumped out. "The name's Obersturmführer Stiglitz. I am to speak with Herr Kincaid."

All eyes focused on the newcomer. Kincaid did not immediately identify himself. He stood with a rifle in the crook of his arm and glowered at the newcomer. He extended his hand slowly while looking him up and down. "Overfury what?"

"Obersturmführer Stiglitz, sir."

"So you're Adler's young pup."

Stiglitz's face turned ten shades of crimson. He gave the Nazi salute and clicked his heels, sluicing sand onto the tops of his polished boots. "Yes, mein Commandant, I am Obersturmführer Stiglitz." The Irish gillies snickered.

Kincaid lifted his hat and rubbed a bald spot. "First off, we don't do a whole lot of saluting in this outfit. Second off, I don't give a fuck about your rank. It carries no weight here. *Kapeesh?*"

"Y-Y-Yes, sir."

He threw his rifle to Stiglitz. "All I care about is how well you can use that."

"I'm a marksman."

Kincaid pointed to a tall blond-haired man in a camouflage outfit with a rifle slung over his shoulder. "Big deal. So is Hans." Hans arched his eyebrows at the newcomer. Kincaid spat into the lake. "Okay, let's load up."

They opted for oars instead of engines in hopes of maintaining the element of surprise. O'Reilly, riding in the lead boat, looked pale as whitewash. It appeared as if he already regretted his decision. Halfway across the channel they spotted another boat. It changed direction and headed toward them. "Damn!" Kincaid shouted. "There are coppers in that boat! Quick, somebody give Hans an overcoat to cover that camouflage outfit." He swiveled toward Hans and Stiglitz. "You Krauts keep your mouths shut."

They put the guns under a tarp and hauled out the fishing gear. As the boats got close Kincaid recognized Sergeant Cullen, a large man dressed in a rumpled blue uniform with a peaked cap framing a round pleasant-looking face. Accompanying him were Guard Ward and two local gillies.

The Sergeant signaled them to stop. "Good morning, lads. What are ye up to this fine mornin'?"

"Over from England for a spot of fishing, Guvnor," Kincaid said in his clipped British accent.

Sergeant Cullen raised his eyebrows. "Faith you'll catch no fish round here, as Jack O'Reilly well knows or should know." He turned to O'Reilly. "What are ye doin', Jack, trying to con the visitors?"

"Ara Jaysus, Sergeant. Shure we're headed to the Priests' Island, where I've been told the trout are as plentiful as flies in a cow shed."

Nervous laughter erupted on all three boats, which had drifted so close they were almost touching.

Cullen leaned forward, causing the boat to list.

Guard Ward shifted his weight to counteract the sergeant's. "Mother o' God, Sergeant, be careful."

"What's with the dogs?" the sergeant continued. "You realize it's not hunting season."

"You can blame me for that," O'Reilly volunteered. "When the Guvnor here explained that his wife was going to be away visiting her friend and that there wouldn't be anybody home with the dogs, I kinda encouraged him to bring them along. Shure what harm is it, anyways?"

"Not a bit of harm in the world, and that's the God's truth," Guard Ward chimed in, "and shure if yez aren't lucky yourselves, yez can always throw the Doberman in the water, and who knows? Maybe he can land a trout or two, if he hasn't torn someone's windpipe out in the meantime." More guffaws from all the boats.

Cullen glanced into Kincaid's boat. "You lads seem to have a hell of a lot of gear under that tarp."

Kincaid hooked his thumb towards his gillies. "That's grub for these hungry Irishmen, Guvnor, and I damn near cleaned out Reagan's traveling shop to do it."

"Well, I think you wasted yer money on that lot," one of the gillies on the guards' boat piped up. "All O'Reilly needs is a few spuds, a hunk of butter, and a bottle of stout."

O'Reilly gave the other gillie the bird. This brought on another round of laughter and derisive comments.

"Okay, okay," Sergeant Cullen interrupted, "I hate to break this up, but we've got some serious business to take care of. There'll be no fishing today."

Kincaid's crew exchanged anxious glances. Kincaid feigned an air of aggrievement. "Listen, Guvnor, I've spent a lot of money on this."

"We're pressing every boat on the lake into a search and rescue effort for Pete Coltrane and his daughter. They went missing yesterday on a fishing trip. Their car's in Doyle's Cove, but no sign of them or their boat."

O'Reilly shook his head. "My God, that's terrible."

Kincaid spread his arms. "We'd be honored to help; just tell us what to do."

"Great. If you and your boys could search the islands in this area, then we can go back and join the main search in Doyle's Cove."

"Why are you looking this far north of Doyle's Cove if that's where they were last seen?" O'Reilly asked.

"We got a report that two boats were in the area near the Priests' Island last evening around dusk, both traveling rather fast, much too fast for fishing, which is odd. There's probably nothing to it, but all the same I'd appreciate it if you boys would search that section of the lake. Good luck to yez."

A thin smile bared Kincaid's yellow teeth. "Let's do it, boys."

Chapter 10

Dangerous Crossing

Coltrane raised himself on his arm as the Doberman entered the clearing emitting a soft growl. It settled on its haunches, head tucked between its front paws. Its small pointy ears twitched nervously.

Coltrane eased his hand toward the shotgun as the Doberman rose from the long grass. It took a few hesitant steps toward him and paused, its black and pink-mottled tongue drooping over its front teeth. A low growl, ears slanted. A spring. Seventy pounds of flesh and muscle came at him with a roar. Blindly groping for the gun, he aimed it at the lunging beast and fired both barrels, barely rolling out of the way before the bloodied animal landed with a crash on his imprint in the crushed ferns. Brigid shrieked and retreated into the brush.

"It's okay!" he shouted after her, "he's dead."

She took a few tentative steps back into the clearing. "What's happened?" Her eyes were the size of duck eggs.

"This brute was here when I woke, one of their advance guard, apparently." He gestured to the mangled body in the underbrush.

She turned her face away in disgust. "I think I'm going to be sick."

"Not now, not now. We must be away. Unfortunately those shots will help them zero in on us."

He gathered their few items, grabbed Brigid's hand, and led her into the hazel bushes at a run. They waded through a field of bracken and came out on a little rise. There it was: the half-mile stretch of water that had to be crossed. The big question—how?

The answer sauntered out from behind a clump of hazel bushes, munching on sweet grasses that grew near the shoreline. The young pony raised his head in their direction. With a swish of his tail he continued grazing, apparently unruffled by their sudden appearance. Peter couldn't believe his luck. On occasion local farmers swam their horses and ponies over to the islands for brief periods to take advantage of the grazing. No point in letting the grass go to waste when they had animals to feed. He could have kissed them for their shrewd husbandry.

Barking in the distance.

He carefully placed the shotgun against a boulder and undid the soggy length of rope from around his neck. After several failed attempts he managed to corral the animal between two outcroppings of rock near the water's edge. He looped the rope around its head like a crude bridle and secured it with a knot. Grabbing the shotgun by the barrel, he launched it out in a wide arc over the lake. It landed with a splash about thirty feet from shore. Pity to get rid of a weapon, he thought, but keeping it dry crossing the channel would be impossible. Before getting into the water he double-checked the rope around the pony's neck—and noticed the cuffs of Brigid's jacket dangling six inches below her fingertips.

"Better give me the jacket, Brigid, until we get across the channel. If you got into difficulty out there, those long sleeves could be trouble." She passed it to him with a look of relief on her face. "No matter what happens to me, stick with the pony. He'll get you to the mainland."

"But Dad—!" The barking got closer.

"Do as I say. Let's go!"

They held on to the loop encircling the pony's neck and led him to the shore. Soon they were waist-deep. At this hour of the morning, before being stirred by the sun, the lake carried the frosty bite of a mountain stream that cut right to the bone. The pony proved to be a strong swimmer. It looked as if he'd been waiting around for someone to tell him it was time to head home. "You hang on, love, and I'll guide him!" Peter shouted.

With the aid of the pony they had a sporting chance of reaching the mainland. The cold water took their breath away, but the high-pitched yelping of the approaching dogs motivated them to keep moving. Halfway across the channel, where the currents were most powerful, the pony's breathing became labored. As it struggled to navigate the turbulent waters, its nose dropped intermittently into the waves. Jets of spray mixed with air wheezed through its nostrils, making a sound like a badly played wind instrument.

Peter realized the animal was not going to make it with both of them in tow. He had overlooked the strength of the cross currents. "Brigid!" he shouted across the struggling animal's neck. "The pony is weakening. I'm letting go of the rope, but I'll stay close."

"Daddy," she wailed, "I'm afraid."

"Stick with the pony!"

He released his grip. Almost immediately the weight of the waterlogged jacket, which clung to him like chain-link armor, pulled him under. He was back in the Ebro River, into which he had once crawled to escape the horror along its banks, battling the strong current. Past and present fused as he grasped at the floating corpses and struggled with the jacket before stripping it off to watch it drift away like a dark shroud. The suck of air into his lungs nearly knocked him out when he finally broke the surface of Loch Gorm.

Brigid and the pony had vanished.

Chapter 11

Hunting Coltrane

The man on the limestone boulder adjusted the sight on his Gewehr rifle and lined up the figure staggering from the water toward the tree line on the Morah Headland. He fired two rounds in quick succession. "*Scheisse*, I think I got him." For good measure, apparently, he cranked off a few more rounds.

Kincaid turned toward the German. "Then stop firing, Hans, for Christ's sake! Apparently you're not the marksman you fancy yourself if you need all those extra attempts. We don't want the whole countryside down on top of us. The coppers will have heard those shots and figured out they came from our section of the lake. We better have some kind of explanation."

Kincaid caught Stiglitz's sneer and was about to turn on him when someone suggested, "We could always blame the Blueshirts. After all they're constantly drilling, giving that stupid salute like that Italian guy Mussolini and walking around as if they own the damn place."

"Is it that bunch of eejits?" another said to general laughter. "I don't believe they even own a gun, God help us, so that excuse wouldn't hold much water."

Kincaid gave the speaker a cold stare. "Enough. The smartest thing for us might be to feign ignorance. We heard the shots too, but we don't know where they came from, okay?" After burying his favorite dog, he wasn't in the mood for levity; the Doberman would be hard to replace.

"Okay, Boss."

Kincaid turned to the rifleman, who looked agitated. "Hans! Are you sure, mate?"

Hans massaged his thin moustache. "Not von hundred percent, but ven I fired he fell."

Kincaid trained his binoculars on the headland. "Well, I can't see anything."

"No! More to der left ... up close to der tree line."

Kincaid grimaced as he adjusted his binoculars. "Still don't see a bloody thing."

The German stuck out his hand. "Hier, give zim to me." He took a quick look.

"There! There! In der grass near der large tree. I knew it." He handed the binoculars back to Kincaid.

"I see something, all right, but I can't be sure it's a man; could be a log or a dead animal. We need to make sure our Mr. Coltrane has departed this life." Kincaid lowered the binoculars. "Sure as hell can't allow his body to be found with a bullet in the back. He deserves 'a burial at sea,' so to speak."

"So what to do, Herr Kincaid?"

"Isn't it obvious? Someone needs to get over there and take care of business as quickly and inconspicuously as possible." He gazed at the gillies, who shuffled their feet.

Stiglitz stepped forward. "I'll go, Herr Commandant."

"I warned you about those fucking titles. No, you won't go, young fella. This is a job for a man, someone with experience. Coltrane's no pushover." As Kincaid talked, Stiglitz tightened his fingers into fists. "Can't risk the whole group going, either. We might run into Cullen and his men."

"But it's more than a half-mile swim to the headland," Bergen said.

The remark drew a roar of laughter. Even Kincaid joined in.

"Bergen, you moron, you've already established your reputation in the water. We're not sending a swimmer across, so you don't have to worry."

He cleared his throat loudly and spat into the wind. He took Hans aside and the two conferred for a few minutes out of earshot. Then Kincaid rejoined the group. He paused for a moment before announcing, "O'Reilly, you're it. You'll accompany Hans to the Morah Headland to confirm that Coltrane's dead. If not, *you'll* deliver the *coup de grâce*." A malicious smile played around his lips. Other than the beads of sweat that glistened on his forehead, O'Reilly didn't react. He looked at the lake, expressionless. "Now, let's get back to the boats!" Kincaid shouted, "and keep in mind we still haven't accounted for Coltrane's kid."

Led by O'Reilly, they retraced their steps in single file through the treacherous terrain of the cutaway bog.

A disturbance at the head of the line.

"Hey, Boss, take a look at this!"

Kincaid went to where Stiglitz stood pointing into the brackish water of a bog hole. "Down there, Boss, among the rushes."

Kincaid plopped onto his knees and squinted into the murky water. Two glassy eyes set in a ghostly white face stared back at him. "By God! It's that son of a bitch McShane."

"Seems like he had one too many for the road," guffawed another of Kincaid's henchmen.

Kincaid whipped around and bared his teeth at the speaker. "Sure, and he closed Duffy's Pub and came out here for a 'dip' in the moonlight, you fucking imbecile. Get the bastard outa there till we see what happened."

He rose from his crouch. The gillies hauled McShane up on the bank, crossing themselves several times out of respect for the dead.

"It looks as if Coltrane turned the tables on McShane and gave *him* a 'dip' instead," Kincaid said. "That scar on his throat didn't come from falling on a sharp stick during a drunken stupor."

"But McShane had a shotgun," Bergen said. "You'd think he had the advantage."

"Apparently not enough of one, otherwise Coltrane and the kid would be lying here instead of him."

Kincaid stuck his boot in McShane's midsection and pushed him back into the bog hole. As the body sank into the rust-colored water and settled back among the rushes, little bubbles spiraled upward and tarried briefly on the surface, ephemeral markers of McShane's resting place.

A series of gasps arose from the huddled gillies. "Jaysus, Mary, and Joseph," one of them said. "He was a conniving prick, sure enough, but we can't leave him to rot in a dirty bog hole; he's got a daycent Christian burial coming. We won't have a hapert worth of luck for the rest of our lives if we do this."

Kincaid grabbed the speaker by the waistcoat and slammed him against the trunk of a tree, pressing the tip of his Luger against the terrified man's forehead. "Well, count your blessings; *your* luck is still holding, but another word of this superstitious crap outa ya and you'll join him."

The frightened man slumped to the base of the tree. Kincaid glowered at the silent group to be sure they all got the message, then he lit his pipe, puffing slowly as he ran the match flame back and forth across the bowl until the tobacco glowed red. As he expelled smoke through his nostrils, he spoke from the side of his mouth to accommodate the pipe shank held firmly between his yellow teeth. "Whatever Coltrane used on McShane, he damn near took his head off. We need to get him soon or someone else's head will be lopped off."

When they reached the boats, Kincaid decided to stay put on the island with the main group until O'Reilly and Hans returned from the Morah Headland.

O'Reilly fired up the engine and took his place on the stern seat. The German sat facing him in the bow, his rifle clinched between his knees. Before O'Reilly got on the boat, he attempted to take his shotgun along, but Kincaid relieved him of it, claiming that Hans had enough firepower for both of them. "For now, O'Reilly, you're the chauffeur. If Coltrane's not dead, Hans will lend you his rifle."

***

As O'Reilly navigated the boat through the surging waves, a nervous spasm shot through his stomach. His mind raced. Maybe the German's orders were to take care of him too after making sure Coltrane was dead, since he hadn't delivered Coltrane as promised. Maybe his was the head to be lopped off. He had proof enough of Kincaid's ruthlessness. Look at the way he kicked McShane's body into the bog hole. He worked himself into a frenzy. He was in it for the fifty pounds, more money than he could make in a year taking fishermen from one God-forsaken spot to another. But a man's life was worth more than fifty pounds. He hadn't signed up to kill anyone. If it came to a *coup de grâce,* he'd turn the gun on Hans, not on Coltrane. He searched for ways to neutralize the German.

The clouds turned black and the wind picked up. A summer storm was brewing. The pewter-colored waves, crowned with whitecaps, thrust the bow upward and dropped it back into the troughs with a thump. Seeing that the German was nervous, O'Reilly plowed full throttle into the turbulent currents, where the waves rose even higher. The German's face turned white. He held on to the sides of the boat with both hands as the prow continued to land in the troughs with bone-jarring thuds, slopping sheets of spray against his back. The German attempted to move to the center of the heaving boat. He lost his footing and pitched forward, banging his head on the middle seat. The rifle slipped from between his legs and landed barrel-first against the seat alongside his head.

O'Reilly eased back on the throttle. He leaned forward, pulled the rifle toward himself, and rested it against the seat. The German appeared dazed. Fighting his way through the whitecaps, O'Reilly reached the spot on the headland where Coltrane was believed to have fallen. As the boat slid through the shallow water, he raised the outboard and pointed the gun at the German.

Hans cradled his head in his hands and groaned. When he saw the gun leveled at him his eyes became slits. *"Mein Gott in Himmel, was ist der problem?"*

O'Reilly raised the gun. "I like these odds better."

He motioned with it for Hans to get out of the boat. They sloshed through the shallows, entering the long grass near the tree line. After a half hour of picking their way over limestone slabs and exploring thickets of hazel trees, they came up empty.

"Are you sure this is the place?" O'Reilly asked, keeping well behind the German.

Hans answered with a contemptuous stare. He walked to the base of a pine tree and picked up several chunks of bark. "Look at these, and look hier." He pointed to fresh scars on the trunk. "Voodpeckers didn't do that. Bullets did. Bullets from my gun." He flung the bark into the brush and stomped around, inspecting the ground. Then he dropped to his haunches and ran his fingers across a moss-covered rock. "Das Blut." He touched his red-stained fingertips to his tongue while swiveling his head in all directions. "He's hit. He can't have gotten very far. Now, *bitte,* I'll have my gun beck."

He rose and stretched out his arm.

O'Reilly retreated a few steps, pointing the rifle at the German's midsection. "'Fraid not. Don't believe you have my best interests at heart, Hans."

The German pulled a knife from his waistband, and it looked as if he might rush O'Reilly, but he backed off when O'Reilly raised the gun to his shoulder. "This ist not der end of this. When I bury Coltrane and der kid, then I come beck for you," he hissed, drawing the knife through the air in a throat-slashing gesture.

"How impressed is Kincaid going to be if he finds out that his top trigger man was disarmed? You might want to think about that."

"He's never going to find out. *You* might want to think about that." Then the German turned and stormed off into the hazel thickets.

O'Reilly chuckled. *Good luck finding them in that direction.* If Coltrane and his kid had survived, they were probably heading north in the opposite direction—toward Coltrane's friend Brendan Law, a moonshiner operating in Hayden's Wilderness. That's what he would do if he were in Coltrane's shoes. But Coltrane was alone when he emerged from the lake. Where was the kid? Maybe she drowned. Keeping an eye on the hazel wood, he bent down to examine the rock. It was blood, all right. It amounted to little more than a stain, however, suggesting that Coltrane's injuries were minor. *The Kraut's on a wild-goose chase.* He cradled the rifle, waded into the water and got back into the boat. *There'll be no burial today.*

Halfway across the lake, O'Reilly decided not to tell Kincaid about disarming Hans, figuring he could play that card later. He tossed the rifle into the whitecaps. In the meantime, O'Reilly's threat to expose him might restrain the German from blabbing to Kincaid. Hans had as much to lose as O'Reilly.

***

Kincaid rushed to the water's edge when he saw the boat approach. "Where's Hans?"

"Gone after Coltrane."

Kincaid stared at O'Reilly. "What?"

"Couldn't find the body."

Kincaid tore his hat off and slapped it against his thigh."Stupid Kraut!"O'Reilly described the blood and told him that Hans, figuring Coltrane had fled across the Morah Headland, had taken off in hot pursuit.

"Then what the hell are you doing here?"

"Hans ordered me to come tell you to return to the mainland and cut Coltrane off before he reaches the main road."

Kincaid stared at him for a long while as if he were trying to divine from O'Reilly's face the real meaning of the words. Abruptly he turned away. "I get it. The old pincer routine," he muttered. He smiled as though visualizing the chase.

"And since we can travel faster by water than he can on foot, we'll be there to greet him with a real Irish welcome," O'Reilly said, his confidence returning.

A real Irish welcome, indeed. Kincaid chuckled to himself at the irony. That little bit of reversal appealed to his sinister instincts; after all, weren't the Irish all about throwing parties for the deceased? A wake, they called it. He got off on that macabre contradiction: a wake for the dead. Nice! He removed his greatcoat and started screaming orders to get underway.

Chapter 12

A Watery Grave

For the better part of an hour Coltrane slogged across the Morah Headland through a tangle of hazel trees and white ash. The terrain alternated between upheavals of moss-colored limestone and hollows filled with leaf mold. The powerful odor of decaying vegetation added to the eerie feel of the place. Several times he got disoriented because the woodland was so dense. If Brigid survived, he figured, she and the pony had come ashore on the southern side of the headland that he was attempting to reach. He could only hope that he was on course.

Fatigue eventually got the better of him. He slumped at the base of a tree to rest.

About three hours earlier he had staggered out of the lake onto the northern shore after battling the currents and losing Brigid. The last thing he remembered, before diving for cover, was the whine of bullets slamming into the tree above him. He awoke to a splitting headache from a bump on his forehead. The wind bent the pine trees and whipped the water into huge white caps that pounded the shore. He wobbled to his feet, took a few steps, and collapsed again.

The sound of voices had sent him crawling into a hazel thicket. He recognized the man with the gun as Jack O'Reilly, but who was the one speaking with a German accent? He considered showing himself, but the German looked like a wild animal stalking its prey, so he retreated deeper into the hazels. From snatches of conversation he gleaned that they were after *him,* but they seemed at loggerheads with each other. When the German pulled a knife and advanced on his hiding place, he rolled into a culvert overgrown with ferns and wild ivy and drew his own knife.

Coltrane's German was a little rusty, but when he heard the words *das Blut,* he figured they had discovered a rock with blood on it. That would account for the bump on his head. The German jumped across the culvert, his brown leather boots coming within a hair of Coltrane's face. He knew that in his weakened condition he would eventually lose this game of hide and seek. He decided to put some distance between himself and the trackers. During the standoff between O'Reilly and the German, he slipped out of the culvert and struck out for the southern side of the headland.

Now, hours later and deep in the headland woods, another question loomed: *Where am I?* Exhausted and still leaning against the base of the tree, he started to nod. He had to fight sleep for fear of waking up in the dark. So he forced himself to his feet and ploughed on. On one occasion he stopped to listen, spooked by someone or something crashing through the trees behind him. When a wild deer leaped across his path, he slogged forward again and chided himself for being so jumpy.

At last, slivers of light filtered through the branches. The sound of waves lapping against boulders.

By the time he exited the wood, the blood thrummed in his ears. His waterlogged clothes clung to him like wet paper. Growing concern for Brigid increased his misery and guilt. He replayed the circumstances of her disappearance. As a seasoned angler, he knew about the turbulent currents, but in his panic to get off the island he discounted the danger. If Brigid had managed to hang on to the pony, she had a fighting chance.

He scoured the sandy shore for footprints or any other clue of her survival. A light rain fell as squawking seagulls swooped in noisy forays, searching for food. He followed the shore southward, figuring that would be the logical direction for Brigid to take since it led to the main road.

He came to a rocky clearing with islands of tall grass and birch saplings sprouting stoically among the boulders. In one of these islands the pony stood munching peacefully close to a fresh-water pool, the rope still around its neck. His heart soared. He cupped his hands to call Brigid, but stopped. The crunch of footsteps behind him. He scurried into the tall grass. The German entered the clearing. With his back to Coltrane, he bent over and placed his hands on his knees, struggling for breath. Sweat glistened on his bare arms. He knelt down and slurped water from the pool.

Coltrane sized him up. He was tall, muscular, and about ten years younger than he. In a hand-to-hand struggle, he might not fare so well with this man. But a surprise attack? He watched the German for a while longer through the long grass, steeling his nerves. It was now or never.

With a roar, Coltrane launched himself at the stooped figure. He jumped on his back and knocked him face-first into the water. He tried to keep the German's head beneath the surface, but he shook him off as a dog might a rat, upending Coltrane into the middle of the pool. The water was surprisingly deep at its center, and Coltrane had to struggle to keep from sinking. The German, apparently unaware of the change in depth, lunged at him with knife drawn but quickly submerged. He resurfaced without the knife, arms thrashing, shouting, "Hilfe! Hilfe!" Coltrane's opponent couldn't swim. After taking a deep breath, Coltrane maneuvered behind the struggling man, grabbed him around the neck with both hands, and squeezed, pushing him deeper into the water. The German's feet flailed against him. Coltrane brought his knees up and rammed them into the small of the struggling man's back. Using his knees as leverage he pulled the German's neck back. He felt it snap in his arms.

When the air bubbles died away, he released his grip on the limp body. He knew that sneaking up on him from behind wasn't honorable, but he felt no shame. This man was his enemy, a soldier in a war against his family who took the risk all soldiers take. He looked down at the dead man, his blond hair floating beneath the surface like straw. *The vagaries of fate.* The mighty Ebro River was Coltrane's savior. For Hans this pool became his executioner.

He walked away without a backward glance and renewed his search along the water's edge, scared to death of what he might find. He cupped his hands. "Brigid! Brigid!" The squawk of sea gulls and the hiss of rain were the only responses. A little farther on he found a cattle track leading to the water. After tightening the laces of his fishing boots, he followed the track inland at a run until it entered a young pine forest. Here the trail widened, looping around boulders and shallow pools until the forest closed in again, shutting out the sun. When he got winded he slowed to a jog and stopped behind a boulder, bending over to catch his breath. Out of nowhere, a scream … angry voices … the sound of an engine. He peeked around the rock. Two men were trying to subdue a young girl with red hair who kicked and punched them. They struggled to get her into the back seat of a large black car. Coltrane seized a fallen branch and charged with a guttural roar. Brigid!

One of the men grabbed a rifle and, stepping calmly into the pathway, took aim. Coltrane didn't slow down. O'Reilly dashed from behind the car and body-checked the rifleman into the underbrush. The shot went into the trees. O'Reilly ran toward Coltrane, shouting, "Get back! Get outa here! They'll kill her!" But Coltrane kept advancing. His child was in that car and he aimed to get her. O'Reilly moved between Coltrane and the gunman. Another shot, this time from a large man wearing a black trench coat. The bullet spun O'Reilly around. He dropped to his knees. Blood spurted from his shoulder. The large man swung the rifle in Coltrane's direction. Coltrane retreated toward the trees. No winning this one.

He pulled up short. O'Reilly had just saved his life. He couldn't abandon him now. He dashed back and pulled O'Reilly to the ground. A volley of shots slammed into the pines. Coltrane dragged the wounded gillie through the grass toward the shelter of the forest. Once out of the line of fire, he pulled O'Reilly to his feet. They shuffled along for a time through the pines until Coltrane felt they had put enough distance between themselves and the gunmen. O'Reilly panted, "Jaysus Christ, what are you doing here? I thought by now you and the girl were safe and sound at Law's place in Hayden's Wilderness."

Coltrane grabbed O'Reilly by the neck and pushed him against a tree. "Give me one good reason why I shouldn't choke the life outa ya here and now. You came to kill me on the Morah Headland. You better have convincing answers."

O'Reilly looked as if he would pass out. "Had no intention of killing you."

Coltrane shook him. "Likely story. Who is the guy in the trench coat?"

"A chap called Kincaid, out to kill you for whatever it is you saw on the island. As far as I can tell, he's a hired hand like the rest of us. He's hooked up with the Germans somehow."

"Why are *they* involved in this?"

O'Reilly's answer came in a whisper. "Honest to God, I don't know. Kincaid offered me money and I took it."

"You bastard, you and the other Irish scum were willing to hunt us down for money?"

"Didn't know what Kincaid's intentions were in the beginning." O'Reilly began to fade. "When I did, I got out."

Coltrane bared his teeth.

Chapter 13

Dead Man Walking

Seamus Reagan ran the local post office in Cloonfin, an establishment that shared a space with his grocery and bar. He also ran a traveling shop from an old Bedford van that had seen better days. Because of wartime demand, petrol was rationed and expensive, so he could only make a grocery runs to country houses on Mondays and Fridays.

He went the extra mile to be of service to his customers. Every Friday he collected the old-age pensions from the post office for the over-seventies crowd along his grocery route. Strictly speaking it wasn't on the up-and-up, but everyone trusted Reagan. He saved the old folks trips to town, so they reckoned he'd earned their patronage.

On this particular Friday afternoon he had completed half his run and was driving up the lake road alongside Lough Gorm. He fancied a tasty dinner of cabbage, bacon, and potatoes, followed by the usual pint of Guinness at the Lake Hotel across from the Morah Headland, about two miles farther on. Since he made frequent stops, he left the sliding doors on both the driver and the passenger sides open for convenience. The trees were in full foliage and in some places locked their branches in a leafy canopy above the road, creating shady green tunnels that ran for a few hundred yards.

As he emerged from one of these tunnels the sun struck him square in the face, almost causing him to run down a ragged figure waving frantically on the road in front of him. He jammed on the brakes and skidded to a halt on the soft shoulder, spraying a shower of dirt and gravel into the dust-covered blackberry bushes on the side of the road. Loaves of Boland's bread, tins of condensed milk, and jars of Bovril flew off the racks like mortar shells and slammed into the screen behind his head.

Not bothering to turn off the engine, he vaulted out the open door, ready to give a piece of his mind to the moron who almost killed them both.

He stopped dead in his tracks when he recognized the haggard face of Peter Coltrane. "What the hell? Is that you, Pete? Damn near killed a dead man, then. Aren't you supposed to be drowned?"

"I'm sorry, Seamus; no time for explanations now. I need help."

"Is Brigid with you?"

Coltrane shook his head and choked up. "Only Jack O'Reilly, and he's in a bad way."

"Jaysus, I don't believe it; half the country is looking for you. What the hell happened?"

"Seamus, right now I need help with O'Reilly. I'm no doctor, but he's lost a lot of blood." Between them they lifted O'Reilly from behind the ditch and placed him on the floor of the van. Blood oozed from the crude bandage that Coltrane had wrapped around his shoulder. His right eye was swollen shut.

Coltrane motioned toward O'Reilly. "Until an hour ago he was in cahoots with a bunch of thugs who tried to kill me and Brigid."

Reagan's jaw dropped. "You better explain." Coltrane gave a brief rundown on what had transpired over the previous two days.

"You're a better man than me. I'd leave the bastard to die."

Coltrane hung his head. "His black eye came from me. I'm not proud to have beaten up a wounded man."

"Your decision, but as I said …" His voice trailed off.

Coltrane lay on the floor beside O'Reilly and Reagan jumped

behind the wheel. "There's a phone kiosk up the road a bit. I'll call Doc Ford and have him meet us at the Lake Hotel."

The phone call took less than two minutes, then they were underway again. Around the next bend Sergeant Cullen and two of his men flagged them down. Reagan had enough time to yell a warning to Coltrane before Cullen jumped up on the running board on the passenger side.

Reagan gunned the engine before applying the brakes. The sergeant's girth didn't help and he lost his grip, pitching head over heels into a ditch. In the rearview mirror Reagan watched Coltrane squeeze into one of the cabinets under the counter, a flimsy refuge at best, sure to be discovered with even the most cursory of inspections. O'Reilly lay in plain view.

"That was a damn stupid caper to pull, Sergeant," Reagan shouted, expecting the worst as the sergeant dusted himself off and ran panting to the van.

"All in the line of duty," the Sergeant huffed, looking more embarrassed than angry.

"I thought the line of duty called for protecting the general public, not putting it in danger. I've a good mind to report you to your superintendent."

The sergeant stood wheezing at the door. He made no further effort to enter the vehicle. Reagan stepped out of the van and stood in front of the door. "Now what has you so fired up?"

"We're searching for Peter Coltrane, who unfortunately is known to you from your IRA activities."

"Then you're searching for a dead man, or haven't you heard? Pete Coltrane and his daughter drowned yesterday in Lough Gorm. Lord have mercy on them both." He crossed himself with a flourish.

"That's the story that's out there, but new information suggests that he, at any rate, is very much alive and that he might have been involved in the killing of Oliver McShane."

"Well, alive or dead I haven't seen Pete Coltrane in over a week. If I do happen to run into him, you'll be the first to know." Reagan stepped into the van and started the engine. "And now if you'll excuse me, unless you have some other reason to detain me, I've got a date with a bacon and cabbage dinner and a pint of Guinness at the Lake Hotel. I'd be happy to continue the conversation there if you want."

Reagan took off, leaving the sergeant standing in the middle of the road, dust swirling around his legs.

Coltrane crawled from underneath the counter. "That was close. I can't believe he didn't insist on searching the van."

"He knew he'd done a reckless thing and didn't want to push it, but he may be back. About McShane. Are the rumors true?"

"Depends on what the rumors are."

"For Christ's sake, stop stalling. Did you kill him?"

"I'm afraid I did, but it was in self-defense."

"Any witnesses?"

"None except Brigid."

A heavy silence hung between them until they reached the hotel. Reagan parked in a secluded spot along one side of the ivy-covered building under a beech tree. "Listen. You must be starving, so I'll arrange to get you some food. Stay put till I return. I'm going to find Paddy Cassidy, the proprietor."

Coltrane looked at O'Reilly. "Get the doctor out here as soon as he arrives."

***

Reagan crunched his way along the gravel path to the hotel entrance. Once inside, he spoke to the barman. "Ronan, is Paddy in today?"

"He's in the back, in the office, I think." Ronan craned his neck down the hallway. "Well, he's back there somewhere, anyway."

"Don't worry, I'll find him."

Reagan sidled through the restaurant to a little office in back of the kitchen. He rapped on the door and stuck his head in. "Anyone home? Apparently not."

Loud voices boomed from the yard. Reagan went to investigate and found Cassidy in a heated argument with P.J. Harrington, head of the local Blueshirt organization, a right-wing fascist group modeled loosely on the Nazi Brownshirts and the Italian Blackshirts. Cassidy had been a boxer in his younger days and his flat nose and bulging biceps stood as testimony to that. "We have every right to march anywhere we like!" Harrington yelled.

"It's not just the marching you're about; you and that Blueshirt crowd are a bunch of hooligans, with your uniforms, your fascist salutes, and your arse-kissing attitude toward that dictator beyond in Rome. What the hell does that guy Mussolini have to do with Ireland?"

Harrington balled his fists against his hips. "The world is changing, whether you like it or not, Paddy Cassidy, so take heed of what you're saying."

Paddy stabbed his finger about two inches from Harrington's face. "You're a right bollocks, is what you are, trying to intimidate decent people. That's what's really going on."

"Ireland better be on the right side of the divide when the British get their arses kicked into the North Sea; neutrality isn't going to save us then. Put that in your pipe and smoke it!" Harrington roared, turning and marching out the yard gate.

Cassidy clicked his heels and raised an arm in a mock Roman salute. "Yeah, and give my regards to El fucking Duce when you see him."

"Working on customer service, I see."

Paddy whipped around ready for battle, but relaxed into a broad smile when he saw Reagan. "Don't let him get to you, Paddy; he's not the chap we should be worried about anyway; he's Sloan's lackey."

"What he is, is a proper pain in the arse, like the rest of the Blueshirt drones," Paddy replied, extending his hand. "Seamus! Good to see you."

"Likewise. Paddy, Doc Ford is on his way here to treat a wounded man, so I need a room right away." Cassidy's face became a question mark.

"Paddy, do it. I'll explain later."

Cassidy grabbed a room key from the office wall and said, "Right, Boss. Follow me."

***

The room had one bed, a chest of drawers, armchairs on both sides of an empty brass fireplace, and a large window draped in shabby green velvet. The drapes were pulled and a single ceiling light provided the only illumination. A worn carpet covered the floor. The smell of antiseptic lurked like fog.

When Dr. Ford finished working on O'Reilly's shoulder he looked at Coltrane, who was wolfing down a ham and cheese sandwich. He pointed to a lump of metal lying at the bottom of an enamel dish. "I know you recognize this as a bullet. O'Reilly was lucky that it missed an artery. What makes it special, however, is that it looks almost identical to the one I extracted from Guard O'Connell two days ago. I'm not a forensic expert or anything, but I've taken enough bullets from broken bodies to wager that this came from the same weapon that took down the guard."

Coltrane slurped large mouthfuls of hot tea from a mug stamped with the flying-trout insignia of the Lake Hotel. He stared at the doctor with glassy eyes as he took another bite of the sandwich. The doctor turned to Reagan. He pointed at O'Reilly lying motionless on the bed, his chest and shoulder swaddled in bandages. "Yer man here should stay at least tonight."

"What if he insists on leaving? I can't hold him against his will."

"Humph! I would've thought a man of your authority would have little trouble in doing exactly that."

"My authority doesn't extend that far."

"In any event," Dr. Ford continued, "given his drugged state, you won't have to use extraordinary measures to restrain him."

"We'll do our best, and by the way, Doc, keep all this under your hat."

"I don't have a hat big enough to contain all this. First Guard O'Connell, now this chap. What are you IRA lads trying to do? Start another civil war?"

Reagan reddened. "We were not involved in either of those situations, Doctor."

"All right, all right, I'll take your word for it."

"Appreciate it."

"Well, gentlemen, I have to visit the very pregnant Mary Healy, who incidentally doesn't need to see me since I saw her yesterday.

However, having told the guards at the checkpoint that I was on my way to visit her instead of you lot, it might be wise for me to shore up my alibi, don't you think?" He raised his eyebrows, picked up his black bag, and crossed to the door. He paused with his hand on the doorknob and nodded in O'Reilly's direction. "I'll be back tomorrow, so I expect him to be here. Should you need me sooner, don't hesitate to call." He smiled, bowed his head, and let himself out.

Coltrane wiped his mouth with the back of his hand and set the empty mug on the small table near the fireplace. "Jesus, they're setting up checkpoints. What's all that about?"

"What do you think, man? This has been all over the radio. With that and the shooting of Guard O'Connell, the whole countryside is nervous and locking their doors at night."

"Not half as nervous as I am right now," Coltrane said.

"I've a gut feeling there's something larger afoot. This is only the tip of the iceberg," Reagan said.

Cassidy looked from Reagan to Coltrane. "I'd like to know what the bloody hell is going on around here."

Reagan turned to Coltrane. "Why don't you fill him in?"

Coltrane did, and as he talked Cassidy got more agitated by the moment.

"Germans! What in hell are they doing here?"

"I'd like to know that more than you, Paddy," Coltrane said. "At the moment I don't have a clue. One thing I do know, their presence takes this out of the realm of the ordinary, if murder and kidnapping could ever be said to be ordinary."

Reagan nodded. "Which is why I said, "'Tip of the iceberg.'"

"Listen! I don't care if the whole fucking country is sitting right on top of the iceberg. That's not my priority."

Cassidy jumped in. "It's not?"

"Hell no, Paddy. I'm concerned about Brigid."

Cassidy looked a little sheepish. "Sorry, Peter. Didn't mean to come across as indifferent. Count on me to help you any way I can."

Coltrane nodded his thanks.

Reagan noticed Dr. Ford's hat on the chair. "Get some rest while I run after the doc, and keep the door locked."

***

Cassidy left with Reagan. Coltrane shot the bolt home into the metal loop. His eyes drooped. He sank into the overstuffed armchair. One thing was certain: it would be up to him to keep the focus on Brigid, especially if, as Reagan thought, there might be a greater threat on the horizon. Let Reagan deal with that. Brigid was alive and that was all that mattered. Coltrane's chest heaved as if he were drawing his last breath. His mouth dropped open. Sobs came in sharp staccato bursts. He had saved O'Reilly, who had tried to kill them and chickened out when it came to rescuing his daughter. But a gun is a hard thing to reason with. The ex-soldier wasn't that tough after all.

He glanced over at O'Reilly, watching the rise and fall of his chest. He nodded off. *Must get word to Claire that I am alive.... In no hurry to face her. Coming home without Brigid would devastate her.... She would blame me.... Weary beyond belief....* He and Brigid were in the bog, running for their lives.

An odd sound in the hallway jolted him awake. He grabbed the poker from the fireplace and stood by the side of the door, his back to the wall. Someone was tiptoeing up the hallway. The pounding of the carotid artery in his neck drowned out the sound of the doorknob turning.

Chapter 14

Coltrane's Dilemma

Reagan caught up with Dr. Ford as he backed his old Fiat from the parking area, which had more horses and carts than automobiles. On his way back to the room a young man running from the rear of the hotel bumped into him and knocked him to the ground.

"Hey, watch where you're going!" Reagan shouted, then jumped up and gave chase. The blond-haired runner, who appeared to be in his mid-twenties, ran flat out toward the outdoor eating area at the front of the hotel. He hesitated briefly at the wooden fence that separated the area from the rest of the parking lot. Laying his hand on a post, he vaulted over the fence, upending several tables and sending dishes and cutlery crashing to the ground. The angry shouts of the guests did not deter him. He sprinted across the road and jumped into a large black car idling in a small parking lot that fronted the lake. As the car sped away, its tires sprayed the outside diners with sand and gravel.

"By God, that chap's in quite a hurry!" Mick Murphy shouted ruefully, watching his spilled pint disappearing down a crack in the pavement.

Reagan ran up, his face flushed, gasping for breath. "Do you know who that hooligan is, Mick?"

"Faith, I don't, Seamus; all I know is that he and his mates aren't from this neck 'o the woods."

"You're sure?"

"Well, I couldn't swear to it, but I believe they're part of that fishing crowd over from England. There's two of them, a big bulky fella, must be about six feet. Always seems to be in a black trench coat anytime I've seen him. And the other bloke who caused all this mayhem. I've seen him around Cloonfin. Has kind of a military appearance about him."

"Thanks, Murph. Good to know that the locals are keeping tabs."

"Oh, by the way, I've seen that black Bentley that tore outa here a number of times, too."

"Eye like a hawk, Murph."

Since Murphy had the reputation of being a spinner of tall tales, Reagan didn't pursue it further. "Take it easy, Murph, see you around."

He walked back inside. Passing through the bar it occurred to him that Coltrane could use a drink. Stopping at the counter, he bought a half pint of Powers whiskey, then started for the back stairs. On his way he bumped into Cassidy, who gestured for him to follow him into the kitchen.

Cassidy turned up the old Bush radio on the kitchen counter. "Wait, come in here and listen to this."

"A search party looking for Peter Coltrane and his daughter made the gruesome discovery of a body in a bog hole on one of the lake islands. The dead man's name is Oliver McShane, a local gillie. Preliminary investigations suggest that McShane was the victim of foul play. In a bizarre twist to the story, rumors are circulating, so far uncorroborated, that Mr. Coltrane may have had something to do with McShane's death. Meanwhile the search goes on for Coltrane and his daughter. So far these efforts have yielded nothing, but the guards have expressed an interest in questioning Mr. Coltrane should he be found alive."

Cassidy turned off the radio."Has he told you about this?"

"Yes. Said it was in self-defense."

"Good enough for me." They tramped up the back stairs and banged on the door to Coltrane's room.

"Who's there?"

84

"It's me and Paddy; who do you think it is?"

They entered the room. "Jaysus, why doesn't someone turn on a light?" Cassidy asked. "I'm paying the bloody bill, so it's okay."

Reagan and Paddy turned to see Coltrane standing behind them in a defensive crouch, the poker raised above his shoulder.

"Boy, you're still on edge." Reagan handed him the half pint. "It seems that you need this more than I thought."

Coltrane looked as if he'd seen the Holy Grail. He grabbed the bottle and dropped the poker on the floor with a clatter. In less than a heartbeat he pressed the bottle to his lips, drank, then closed his eyes and exhaled slowly. He held the bottle into the light, admiring it as if it were a precious gem. "There were times in the last two days when I thought I'd never taste this sweet brew again. Out there in the bog, this was all I could think of. I'm ashamed to admit it, but it's true." He took another long swig.

Cassidy fidgeted with the chain of his pocket watch. "I think you're being a little hard on yourself, Coltrane. In similar circumstances it's difficult to say how any man would have felt."

"Aye, maybe so, but it's not difficult to say how this man felt, and that's the point." Coltrane jabbed his thumb into his own chest, as if he didn't want to let himself off the hook. "What do you say to a man like me who in the hour of greatest danger for him and his young kid, couldn't stop thinking about this?"

He waved the bottle and slumped into the chair. "What's the answer to that?" he whispered, unscrewing the cap for another long swig. "No wonder the canon dumped me from the school in Cloonfin." He brushed strands of black curls matted with dirt and algae from his eyes.

"We all know why the canon removed you, and it had nothing to do with drink. He's no stranger to the stuff himself. He got rid of you when he discovered you'd fought against Franco and the Catholic Church in Spain. But it didn't stop you from getting your current job, did it?" Reagan said.

"My current job is part-time. Big difference."

Coltrane traced the track of the old bullet wound in his jaw with the tips of two fingers. He crossed the room and carefully placed the bottle on the top of the chest of drawers. He pushed the bottle away slowly, with one finger, as if uncertain about the separation. "Goodbye old friend; you and me are through."

He slumped back into the chair and covered his face with his hands. Reagan and Cassidy exchanged glances. Outside the branches of the trees clawed against the side wall of the hotel.

Cassidy pulled back the drapes. "That wind is coming from the lake. Not a good sign."

Reagan looked at his watch; it was getting late. Soon it would be dark. What to do with the fugitives?

Reagan pointed to the poker. "So what's with that? You looked like you were about to brain someone when we came through the door."

Coltrane flashed a sheepish grin. "Oh, I got distracted by the bottle. About twenty minutes before you fellows showed, there were intruders out there in the hallway."

"You're sure of that?" Cassidy asked.

"Pretty damn sure; either that or nosy employees. Whoever was out there tried to open the door without knocking. Then something must have spooked them, because they left in a hurry down the back stairs."

"You think there was more than one?" Reagan asked.

"Unless he was talking to himself, I heard multiple whispers."

Reagan told Coltrane about the blond-haired man who knocked him down in the parking lot, and about his conversation with Murph.

Coltrane stood up and edged the curtain back from the window. "They're on to us, then. Might be a good idea to see if our friends in the Bentley are registered in the hotel."

"Wait a minute," Reagan said. "Aren't we getting a little ahead of ourselves? How do we know they're the guys who tried to get into your room? Like you said yourself, it could have been nosy hotel staff."

"Driving a Bentley? Not bloody likely," came a scratchy voice from the bed. O'Reilly struggled to open his eyes. "The car I rode in with Kincaid and crew was a black Bentley, and that's the car they drove off in with the Coltrane kid. Murph was spot on."

Reagan's eyes flared in anger. "Why should we believe you, you tout? If I had my way I'd have you shot for what you did."

Coltrane's face stiffened. "Ease off a bit, Seamus. He saved my life and probably Brigid's as well. Once they had killed me there would have been no reason to keep her alive."

The look on Reagan's face indicated that he wasn't mollified.

Armed with descriptions of Kincaid and the Germans, Cassidy went to check the registry at the front desk. Reagan stuck his head out the door and called after him. "While you're down there, cast your eyes around and see if there's anyone who doesn't normally frequent the place."

Paddy nodded. "Righto."

Coltrane then revealed that he had drowned Hans in the pool. "So unless the Resurrection is upon us and we don't know it, Hans was not in the hotel today."

Reagan looked startled. "Is there anything else that we should know about? And should we be concerned about getting on your bad side?"

A weak smile creased Coltrane's face. "Very funny."

***

A light tap on the door signaled Cassidy's return with roast-beef sandwiches wrapped in white butcher paper and a bottle of Guinness for everyone except Coltrane. He would have to make do with a Bullmer's Cidona. "God knows when you fellas might get a chance to eat again, for who knows what the night may bring."

Coltrane looked so pitiful that it prompted Reagan to ask if his declaration of sobriety might have been a little premature.

"No, no, I'm gallant. I know it's going to be difficult for a while."

Cassidy took a slug from his bottle of Guinness and pointed it at Reagan. "Right, according to the front desk, there are no people answering to Kincaide's or the German's descriptions registered at the hotel."

"Anyone else in the bar from outside the area?" Reagan asked.

"No, but there's a local here that I've never seen on the premises before. Not sure it means an awful lot, but then again, you never can tell."

Coltrane paced, beating out a squeaky rhythm on the ancient

floorboards. "Who is it?"

"Abbot Jonathan's caretaker, Arthur Cusack."

Reagan's head snapped up. "Doesn't he live on the abbey grounds?"

"Yeah, he rents the caretaker's house, or maybe he has it for free. I'm not sure," Cassidy said.

"Hunh, that's a fair bit out to cycle for a pint, isn't it, Cassidy? How far do you think it is?" Reagan asked.

"It's about three Irish miles."

"And you've never seen him out here before?"

"Not as far as I know."

"Here's something else you lads don't know," O'Reilly said. "Cusack on occasion comes out to the pitch-and-toss at Drinane crossroads on Sunday evenings, which is a stone's throw from the hotel ... so wouldn't it be the most natural thing in the world to come down here for a pint or two after the game is over?"

Cassidy scowled at O'Reilly. "Except I know the pitch-and-tossers who come in here on Sunday evenings and I've never seen him among 'em."

"I'm not sure we can glean a helluva lot from that." Reagan picked up the phone. "To be on the safe side, we need to get you chaps away from here as soon as possible."

***

After a few clipped exchanges during which Coltrane brooded, Reagan replaced the phone on the hook and announced that one of his men would collect them at a designated spot and spirit them out of the hotel later that night.

Coltrane's face stiffened. "Seamus, I'm not doing this."

Reagan grimaced "Not doing what?"

"I'm not running from these bastards. I can't afford the luxury of going into hiding while my child remains in their clutches."

"It's only for a while until you get your strength back and we can devise a plan to rescue her."

Coltrane fumbled to light a cigarette cadged from Cassidy. "How soon are you coming up with this plan?"

"Can't do it if we continue to waste time arguing about it, can I? Me and the boys are meeting in my place tomorrow night."

"Not going until I see Claire. She must be insane with worry by now."

"That seems the most reasonable thing in the world, but it's not a good idea," Reagan said.

Coltrane puckered his face. "Are you out of your mind? Why not?"

"For two reasons. One, the guards may be waiting there to pick you up, and two, Kincaid may be there to pick you off."

"I can see why Kincaid might be lying in wait. But the guards?"

Reagan recapped the radio broadcast and reminded him of Sergeant Cullen's intercept on the lake road.

"Sorry, I forgot. I've a lot on my mind. Someone must be feeding the guards false information and I've a feeling it's this guy Kincaid."

"It's not totally false. You did kill McShane."

"Christ, Seamus. Whose side are you on? I killed McShane before he killed me and Brigid. That's a helluva lot different than murder."

"Right, but if you're right about Kincaid, then he's winning the propaganda battle, which brings me back to my original thought. You've got to make yourself scare for now."

Coltrane wasn't happy. Given the events of the past two days, he felt better equipped than anyone to track this Kincaid. Not wanting to look a gift horse in the mouth, he reluctantly relented on the promise that Reagan would get word to Claire about Brigid and him. He felt bad that he couldn't do this in person, but he didn't want to make a bad situation worse and endanger Claire as well.

When it came time to leave, Reagan drove his van up front as a decoy and joined Cassidy for a drink on the hotel patio to make it easy for anyone trying to keep tabs on them.

Under cover of darkness, Coltrane and O'Reilly left the hotel by the back stairway and went to a bridge that spanned a small river. A car with its engine running took them into hiding.

Chapter 15

On the Run

The car sped along a country road bordered by giant trees whose dark silhouettes encroached on both sides. Coltrane cadged a box of matches from the driver to light a cigarette, and apart from the terse phrase necessary to complete the transaction no further words were exchanged. He felt like he was in a prison van being hauled to jail. He didn't have much luck either with O'Reilly, who seemed lost in thought. I suppose you couldn't blame him given what he'd been through in the past week, but in light of the fact that they were headed for a little rest and recreation, it didn't bode well. The whole situation bespoke the end of something ominous rather than the beginning of something hopeful.

The driver tipped his head back. "We've arrived."

"Is this Stapleton's?"

"Kinda."

"Do they know we're coming?"

"Yes and no."

"Look! Either they do or they don't. Which is it?"

"They're not expecting visitors at the farmhouse, and they don't know you'll be sleeping in their stable out in the pasture."

O'Reilly tipped his cap up and scratched his head. "Well, that's just fucking wonderful."

The driver flicked the butt of a cigarette into a drain at the side of the road. "Well, that's the best Reagan could do in the circumstances. He figured you could bed down here for the night and head off across the bog to Law's place in the morning. Stapleton will be none the wiser."

O'Reilly flared. "Well, I'll give Reagan a piece—"

Coltrane put his hand on O'Reilly's shoulder. "Not worth getting upset about it." They grabbed their duffle bags from the back of the car and headed up the field toward a squat stone building set in a corner of the pasture. Coltrane pushed the door open and flashed his bicycle lamp around the interior. A pile of straw against the back wall, a horse cart on one side, and miscellaneous farm implements in a corner. *Not bad. It'll do fine for one night.* They settled down in the straw and used their duffle bags for pillows. On the point of dropping off, he felt O'Reilly jostle him.

"Coltrane. Going to cut my losses and get out of here come morning."

"I'm planning on doing the same myself—wasn't thinking of making this my permanent residence."

"No, I mean I'm going farther afield than Law's place."

"What, going to your summer house?"

"Don't rub it in. Don't want to be a gillie all my life. I have some options, I'll have you know."

"Like what?"

"Have a brother in England. Thinking of paying him a visit."

"You've heard that there's a lot of bombing and shooting over there. It's called the war."

"I'll take my chances. There's not much of a future here."

He's bluffing. He's scared that Kincaid will track him down. Reagan's hostile attitude didn't help either. Doesn't want the IRA after him for collaborating with the enemy. Might feel the same way myself if I was up against all that.

"It's a long trek across the bog to Law's place. You'll feel different after a good night's sleep."

O'Reilly settled back in the straw. "Good night Peter."

"Good night. Jack"

The strident *caw, caw* of jackdaws pecking on the galvanized roof woke him next morning.

He sat up, rubbed his eyes, and looked around. O'Reilly was gone.

Chapter 16

Tony Geraty Makes a Delivery

Young Tony Geraty came flying up the street on his old Humber bike as if the devil in hell were after him: head down, freckled cheeks puffed out. The tail of his brown shop coat flapped like a sheet on a line on a windy day. He wanted to attract attention and he knew it didn't take much to do that in the little town of Cloonfin. The back wheel of his bike, absent a mudguard, had sprayed a skunk-like stripe of muck all the way up his back. He had attached two pieces of cardboard, fashioned from a Sweet Afton cigarette box, to the frame on either side of the back wheel. They caught the spokes and gave off the rat-tat-tat sound of a machine gun as he gunned his way around donkey carts or anything else that happened to cross his path.

After school, three evenings a week, he worked in Reagan's shop measuring meal, flour, and sugar by the pound or the stone into gray paper bags. In short he did whatever needed doing on a particular day, like delivering groceries as he was doing now. That was his favorite job. It got him out of the shop and out from under Mrs. Reagan's thumb. Unlike her husband she could be difficult to deal with, at least when he wasn't around. On the other evenings he did whatever odd jobs he could find, like running down to the shop for messages, hauling in a few bucketsful of turf on a winter's evening for the fire of a shut-in. Other times he took a bag of hay on the back of his bike to an animal in a far-off field. His industry earned him a few bob a month. He gave most of it to his mother. With the few pence left over he bought the odd stick of Sailor's Chew, or a Beano comic book. Now and then he sneaked a pack of Sweet Afton smokes.

After cresting the hill he freewheeled down the other side to a two-storey house with a well-kept lawn. It was enclosed by a white pebble-dashed wall topped by a thick privet hedge. Dropping his bike with a clatter, he retrieved the bag of groceries from the handlebars. Then he pushed open the little green gate with his knee and ambled to the front door which he vigorously pounded with the brass knocker. The click of a lock turning. The door opened a crack, revealing the tear-stained face of Claire Coltrane. "Hello Tony," she whispered hoarsely.

"Hello, Ma'am, I've come with the groceries from Mr. Reagan."

"Groceries? There must be a mix-up, Tony. I didn't order any groceries."

"All's I know, Ma'am, is that Mr. Reagan said take this bag up to you and on no account was I to leave it if you weren't in."

She took the bag. As Tony was turning to leave, she asked him to wait while she took a coin from a mug on the dresser. Tony folded the three penny bit in his hand. "Thanks, Ma'am, and I'm very sorry for your troubles."

***

Nodding, she closed the door and placed the bag on the kitchen table. From the open window she heard the rat-tat-tat fading in the distance. Absentmindedly she scanned the contents of the bag: a pound of rashers, cheese, bread, sugar, and tea. She filled the kettle with water and set it to boil. A good cup of tea might distract her from her troubles.

The knocker sounded again. She rushed to the door. Maybe there was news. Fear tightened her throat. What if—? She pulled the door open. Seamus Reagan stood on the threshold.

"Seamus?"

Reagan removed his hat. "May I come in?" He passed through and stood awkwardly in the middle of the kitchen, running the rim of his hat through his fingers.

Her breath congealed in her throat.

"Great news. Peter and Brigid are alive, but …"

She ran her fingers through her long hair." Oh my God, O my God." She collapsed in Reagan's arms, sobbing. He guided her toward a chair and set her down. Crouching on his hunkers he held both her hands in his. "On my advice Peter is gone into hiding for the time being. Unfortunately there's a hitch. Brigid is not with him right now."

She stopped breathing. "What? My child is gone?"

He explained to her the essentials of the kidnapping and his plan to rescue Brigid. A half hour later she ushered him to the door.

He paused on the threshold. "Best not to inform the guards right now, for the reasons I mentioned. You must trust me on this."

She stared at him in silence. Her mind was a thousand miles away.

"I'll arrange for some of our lads to keep an eye on your house." With that he tipped his hat and went down the path to the front gate.

She closed the door behind him and collapsed onto a chair. Caught between the conflicting emotions of joy and terror, she couldn't keep a coherent thought in her head. She should tell the Tooles, but she couldn't concentrate. She jumped up and walked in circles, running her fingers through her hair and biting her lip in an effort to keep from screaming. How could a simple fishing trip have turned into such a nightmare? Despite what Reagan said, she was tempted to run screaming up the street to the guards' barracks and ask for help. In an effort to calm her nerves, she turned on the radio just as the news was starting.

The first news item was about the war. Mind-numbing reports of the numbers of dead and wounded. The larger world had truly gone insane and now her world was being sucked into the same hellish vortex. Unable to cope, she turned the radio off. And Reagan's report that some gossips in the community were spreading rumors that Peter was involved in McShane's death? Outrageous.

She paced the kitchen for a few minutes until she got her emotions under control. It would not serve her well to fall apart. In this dreadful situation she needed all her faculties, and if she collapsed in a blubbering mess she would be no good to anyone. But despite her best efforts she was becoming increasingly disoriented. She felt dizzy. Everything appeared strange and threatening. In an effort to stop this emotional drift, she glanced around her kitchen and tried to anchor herself in the familiar. She attempted to regain control by verifying that the everyday things of life were still there. They had not changed: her wedding photo on the dresser; the photo of Brigid so pretty and innocent in her white communion dress; the old bookcase stacked with her husband's school books; the picture of the Sacred Heart on the wall with the little red lamp burning in front of it. Ordinarily she received consolation from these tokens, but now it all seemed distorted and hostile. The familiar was morphing into the alien. The kitchen with its everyday objects began to spin like a merry-go-round. Each item in turn mocked and taunted her. Her dizziness grew worse and she collapsed.

Chapter 17

Hooded Terror

When Claire picked herself up from the floor it was near dusk. She didn't know how long she had lain there, but the numbness in her left arm suggested that it must have been at least an hour. The music of the wind chimes hanging from the ash tree in the garden, ordinarily so melodic and soothing, now seemed threatening and foreboding. The spinning in her head had stopped, but the growling of her stomach reminded her that she hadn't eaten since breakfast. She added some coal to the range and set a kettle on top of it to boil water for tea. The bag of groceries beckoned from the counter. Rifling through it, she decided that a couple of fried rashers and a salad would hit the spot. The wind chimes grew louder. As she stood at the sink washing lettuce and slicing tomatoes, Lost John Toole's dogs, Buttercup and Finn, charged through a hole in the boundary hedge and darted barking past her kitchen window to the corner of her garden. They set up an unholy racket under the ash tree. Must be after one of the neighbor's cats that frequently preened and slept in its branches.

As she watched from her window she kept telling herself that she should go out and call the dogs off, but in her lethargic state she remained rooted to the floor. Not to worry, she thought, Lost John will be out any second now to take the situation in hand. She would give him the news about Peter and Brigid. Then something struck her as odd. The chimes continued to ring, but not a leaf was stirring. The cat must be disturbing the branch from which the chimes were suspended. She decided to go out and investigate. The air would do her good. As she stepped into the garden Lost John's booming voice came over the hedge, calling off his dogs. She continued to the tree to see if the cat was in any kind of difficulty. The chimes sounded again. In the semi-darkness she couldn't see the animal, let alone rescue it.

She moved closer to the tree. Two legs wearing Wellingtons emerged from the lower branches. A hooded figure dressed in black jumped to the ground. Claire stopped dead in her tracks, transfixed with fright. The dark apparition remained motionless. It wore a hood with a red cross on its face. She opened her mouth to scream. Her breathy croak was muffled by the sound of the wind chimes, which the dark figure held above his head.

The chimes broke the spell. Claire let out a scream and ran for her back door. She heard the heavy footfall behind her, but she managed to get through the door and bang it shut. As she staggered through the kitchen toward the front of the house, she turned and looked. The black hood with the red cross filled her kitchen window. As she exited her front door, Lost John came running toward her, shotgun in hand. "In the back garden!" she screamed.

Chapter 18

Blood on the Gate

Without breaking stride, Lost John charged through the front door. He reached the back of the house as the hooded figure was climbing the crossbars of the iron gate that led to the lower garden. Here Peter Coltrane had planted a dozen ridges of potatoes now in full blossom. As the intruder leaped into the potato field, Lost John took aim and fired. The shotgun pellets pinged off the gate. The intruder took off running down the furrows.

Lost John reloaded and followed. The potato ridges ran down a gentle slope. In the gathering darkness he had to be extra cautious running with a loaded gun. Reaching the end of the slope, he walked along the boundary hedge that separated Coltrane's property from a marsh that extended about a quarter of a mile before turning into a small lake. At this time of evening it would be impossible, he thought, to track someone over that kind of terrain. He contented himself with having driven the intruder off and walked back up the hill alongside the ridges. He looked at the luxuriant green stalks. With Peter missing would it fall to him to harvest the crop when potato-digging season arrived? A sixth sense prompted him to turn. A dark figure rose from the green stalks and limped through a break in the hedge into the marsh. He raised the shotgun to his shoulder, but lowered it again. No point. The masked man was too far away.

When he reached Coltrane's house, Claire was gone. Must be at our place, he thought. He had to bang on the door before Nora would let him in. "It's me, I tell ye!"

"Okay, okay, I'm coming. Take your time. How do I know who it is?" she said, opening the door.

"You don't know the sound of my voice after fifty years?" he asked, ducking his head under the lintel and entering the kitchen.

"All I know is, I'm scared out of my wits and poor Claire here is a basket case. Half the neighbors came banging on the door inquiring about the shotgun blast."

Lost John walked over and placed the gun in the corner. "What did you tell them?"

"That you were scaring rabbits away from the potato patch."

Claire sat in an easy chair by the fire wrapped in a blanket.

"Sorry, he got away. I couldn't track him in the half-light. He made it into the swamp. But I got a shot at the beggar, which should put the wind up in him if nothing else."

"Did you tangle with the blackguard at all?" Nora asked, inserting a pinch of snuff from a little tin box into her nostrils.

"Haven't you been listening? No, never got close enough to him. He had too much of a lead."

Claire squinted her eyes. "What's that on your hand, Lost John?"

He examined the bloody fingers of his right hand. "Well, I'll be damned if I know where that came from. Maybe I scraped them on a briar or something." Nora poured water into a little tin basin, and when she got through washing his hand there was no sign of a scrape or cut.

"Hould on a minute," Lost John said. "Where's me flashlight?"

Nora pointed at the dresser. "It's over there behind the tea canister where you always put it." He retrieved the flashlight and went out the back door. Seconds later he was back. "Just as I suspected." He displayed the bloody fingertips of his right hand. "There's blood on the top bar of the gate. I hit the bastard, but it must only have been a flesh wound, otherwise he wouldn't have been able to run the way he did. I must have picked up the blood when I climbed across the gate."

"Well, that's a relief," Nora said. "At least it's not you."

"It's not much of a relief. The creep got away, which means you can no longer sleep in your house, Claire. You'll stay here with us for the time being."

Claire fixed her gaze on Lost John. "Do you think he wanted to kill me?"

"From what you told me he had plenty of time to do that if he wished. My hunch is he wanted to scare the living hell out of you."

Claire began to cry. "Well, he certainly succeeded in doing that."

Nora put an arm around her. "There now, you're safe with us."

After Claire and Nora went to bed, Lost John raked the fire and turned down the double wicks of the oil lamp, plunging the kitchen into darkness. Pulling a small coal from the ashes with his calloused fingers, he popped it into his pipe. He puffed vigorously until a red glow appeared in the bowl. He stood for a while, looking out the window and wondering about the menace lurking in the night.

Chapter 19

The Canon's Mass

Tony Geraty turned over in bed to quiet the sharp pinging in his right ear, but it started up again in his left ear—more loudly. He realized the irritating noise was coming from outside, only now it sounded like a jackdaw pecking brazenly on the glass of his bedroom window. He shuffled to the window and looked out. Standing on the footpath, one storey below, was a blur of black and red that gradually materialized into the somber figure of Canon Roach.

Tony couldn't believe his eyes. The canon? At this hour? One or two blackbirds were just tuning up for their daybreak performance in the lilac bushes. Straining, Tony pulled the bottom half of the window up and stuck his head out, letting the frame rest on his shoulder blades. The pulley cords for keeping the window raised had unraveled.

"Rouse yourself, young man. I need you to serve Mass."

"At five in the mornin'?"

"No back chat, I'll be in the church. Don't keep me waiting!"

Canon Roach turned on the ball of his foot and walked briskly up the street, the red tassels of his cincture whipping his legs, until he disappeared in the morning mist. Tony dressed quickly, splashed some water on his face, combed his unruly black hair, ran downstairs and jumped on his bike for the short journey to the sacristy. The cardboard pieces attached to his back wheel would wake the whole neighborhood. He didn't care. *If I have to be up, so do they.*

When he arrived, Canon Roach paced the sacristy, fully vested in alb and chasuble. His prominent nose appeared the more so because of his thin face. His eyes nestled inert in their sockets. Since Tony hadn't served Mass in two years, he had difficulty finding a soutane and a surplice that fit. Under the impatient scrutiny of Roach, he blindly selected a soutane that barely covered his knees and a surplice a size too small. He felt like a stuffed goose as he walked from behind the altar. The church was empty, thank God. The long absence also degraded his memory. The Latin responses no longer fell automatically off his tongue. The canon started with a flourish, crossing himself dramatically as if thousands watched. *"Introibo ad altare Dei."*

"Ad deum qui laetificat jutum, tutum mmmm," Tony muttered.

He mumbled his way as best he could through the rest of the introductory prayers. Canon Roach zipped along in high gear, seeming not to notice. The words bounced off the cavernous walls like a handball. The unintelligible Latin duet played on, interrupted occasionally by the clinking of water and wine cruets. After twenty minutes, which seemed like two hours to Tony, the canon capped the early morning ritual with *"Ita missa est!"*

"Deo gratias," Tony responded.

The Mass was ended. Thanks be to God for that. They exited the altar smartly. Canon Roach removed his vestments while Tony returned to the altar to extinguish the candles. When he returned to the sacristy, the canon stood at the outer door. "Help yourself to the change in my suit coat pocket and hurry up. I must be off."

Tony retrieved several shillings from the canon's coat, which hung on a rack in the corner. He shed the surplice and soutane and stuffed the coins into his pocket. The door banged shut, leaving him alone. As he exited the sacristy the taillights of Canon Roach's Volkswagen disappeared around the corner of the driveway. Tony cycled home, checked his alarm, and crawled back into bed. It was 5:45 a.m.

***

Later in the day he sat in school bleary-eyed, waiting for Brother Edmund to take roll. He pulled out the coins and spread them on the two-seater desk, scarred by a generation of penknife cuts and ink spills. His desk mate, Eddy Flannery, spotted a weird object among the pennies and sixpenny bits. He elbowed Tony in the ribs. "Hey, what's that?" He pointed to an oblong piece of metal with crossed red diagonals on a field of blue and a red hand in its center. It had a hinged pin and catch on the back.

Tony turned over the object in his hand. "I haven't a clue. It looks like a broach or something you pin on your jacket. What do you think it is?"

He handed it to Eddy. After a brief examination, he declared himself stumped as well. "Where'd you get it?"

It dawned on Tony that it must have been among the change he took from the canon's pocket. He wondered if it was valuable and if he should return it. He asked Eddie what he should do.

"I think you'll have to give it back; stealing from a priest is a mortal sin and you'll go to Hell for all eternity."

"Don't be a bloody eejit; I didn't steal it and he's not just a priest, he's a canon."

"Well, that's even worse."

"How worse could it be, if I'm already going to Hell? Where else worser is there to go?"

Eddy had no comeback. As he put the object back in his pocket, Tony thought Seamus Reagan might know what the strange pin was. He would ask him when he got to work.

The day dragged along. When the final bell sounded, Tony bounded out of the schoolhouse like a runaway pony and headed for Reagan's shop.

Chapter 20

Cattle Fair in Cloonfin

At the end of a fair day in Cloonfin the streets still held their share of unsold cattle, watched over by owners at their wits' end to make a deal. As Tony wove through the moving throng, he was forced to jump over or sidestep the cow dung that smeared the streets in green. While executing one of these maneuvers he staggered into Arthur Cusack and P. J. Harrington, two locals in a high dudgeon about something or other standing by the side of the street. Cusack tried to clip Tony with his blackthorn stick. "Mind where you're going, you young blackguard."

"Where's your wheelchair, Cusack?" Tony taunted and disappeared into the crowd. As he progressed farther down the street, he dodged shopkeepers heaving buckets of water onto the sidewalks outside their premises to wash the day-long mess deposited by dozens of cattle. To his dismay, no one was outside Reagan's hefting buckets of water or manhandling a broom; the dirty work would be his. He walked into the shop, only to be met by an agitated Mrs. Reagan. She told him to get cracking with the cleanup.

"Yes, Ma'am, as soon as I get a pair of Wellingtons." He stowed his book bag in a room behind the shop where the employees took their breaks and ate their lunches. A pot-bellied stove sat in the middle of the room, its only function on a summer's day to boil water for tea. Two shop assistants, thumbing absentmindedly through the day's newspaper, sat at a large wooden table, its surface bleached white as a lamb shank bone, from years of scrubbing. An open packet of Goldflake cigarettes and a box of Patterson's matches lay next to a cheap ashtray stuffed with butts.

Tony eyed the leavings of a plate of ham and cheese sandwiches next to one of the shop assistants, who recognized the hungry look. "Take it." He motioned to the teapot. "Help yourself. After a day with old Edmund, you need all the bucking up you can get."

Tony didn't need to be asked a second time. He dove in. While he ate, Reagan entered the room, a preoccupied look on his face. He seemed different from his usual happy-go-lucky self. He stared at Tony. "Fine kid you are, Geraty, stuffing yourself and the footpath out there full of cow shit."

Tony jumped up, brushing the crumbs from his lips with the back of his hand, and attempted to speak with his mouth full. "I'm sorry, Mr. Reag—"

"Come into the office when you're done." Tony slurped the last of his tea and brushed the bread crumbs from his jacket before heading to Reagan's office.

He tapped on the door before entering. The office was a cubbyhole behind the stock room with a small window overlooking the back garden. It included a desk, two chairs, a bookcase crammed with files, and loose stacks of receipts hanging over the lips of the shelves. In a corner behind the desk sat a little safe, where Reagan kept the day's take before lodging it in the bank each evening.

Reagan sat at his desk, impaling daily receipts on a vicious-looking spike. He didn't look up. "Your mother asked me to tell you that Arthur Cusack called to your house complaining that you assaulted him on the street today and called him names. She figures he went to the guards."

Tony's jaw dropped. He tried to tell his side of the story. Reagan stood up. "Son, you don't have to explain to me; it's none of my business. I'm only passing on your mother's message. Off with you now and start cleaning up the mess outside."

Tony turned to go. Then he remembered the strange pin in his pocket. He slid the oblong piece of metal across the desk. "Mr. Reagan, do you have any idea what this is?"

Reagan raised his eyebrows. "Where'd you get it?"

"It was mixed with the change I got from Canon Roach for serving Mass. Why, is it important?"

"It could be."

"Is it valuable?"

Reagan turned the pin over in his hand. "As a piece of metal it's not worth a threepenny bit, but ... well ..." Reagan's voice trailed off.

Tony shook his head. "You know, Mr. Reagan, I don't understand a word you're saying. Brother Edmund can be hard to understand at times, but not this hard."

"You're a persistent little bugger. All right, I suppose you have a right to know, since it is yours. This pin is called a *Saltire*. It represents the Blueshirt flag, although the red hand in the center is a new and more ominous addition."

"You mean those eejits in blue that march up and down the street after Mass on Sundays?"

"Yes, although their leader, General Sloan, wouldn't like to hear them referred to as a bunch of eejits. Ideas can be more dangerous than guns. Sloan thinks he's protecting Ireland and the Catholic Church from communists, trade unionists, and other extremists."

"But I thought the government was protecting us?"

Reagan leaned back in his chair and gazed out the window. "That's what it was elected to do, but Major Sloan is infatuated by the likes of Hitler and Mussolini, so he organizes these big parades as a show of force to frighten and confuse ordinary people and suck up to a pair of ruthless dictators. In fact he's planning a massive Blueshirt march on Dublin, which the government is very nervous about."

Tony followed his gaze. "Do the priests agree with him? I mean, does Canon Roach agree with him?"

"The majority doesn't, but some do. Whether the canon is a follower, who can say for certain? But if I were a betting man ..." Using his thumb and index finger he flipped the pin at Tony. "I would say he tends in that direction."

Tony caught it and acted like it was a hot coal. "What should I do with this?"

"If you prefer you can leave it here with me." Tony threw the pin back on Reagan's desk.

"Anytime you want it back, come and get it; after all, it's only a piece of metal."

"What if the canon wants it back?"

Reagan's face lit up with an impish grin. "He can ask me for it." He impaled another bunch of receipts on the ugly spike.

Tony hurried outside to find his Wellingtons.

Chapter 21

Discovery in the Back Country

Tony Geraty took a break from his part-time job at Reagan's to spend the weekend with his uncle and first cousins, who lived in the mountainous back country. This was a region famous for its moonshine, known locally as *poitin*.

On this particular weekend Tony and his cousin Sean, along with Sean's dogs Diver and Molly, went up into the mountains to fish and hunt rabbits. Each carried a lunch of sandwiches prepared by Sean's mother and a billycan to make tea. Tony lugged these in a shoulder bag along with tackle and bait. Tony didn't object to being the donkey since he was freeloading at his aunt's house. He looked at his cousin and wondered why they didn't resemble each other more. Sean had blond hair and a freckled face. *His* hair was dark after his mother's side of the family. When he rubbed his cheeks he felt stubble. The way things were going he'd be shaving soon. His cousin had a missing upper front tooth, which caused him to spit involuntarily as he spoke. It annoyed Tony to no end when at the conclusion of Sean's enthusiastic outbursts *he* often wound up with spittle on his face.

An hour's fishing in a mountain pool from atop an overhang yielded only a half dozen perch between them. They relied on the dogs to do the hunting. So far nothing doing. The overhang was shaded by the branches of a giant oak tree. The oppressive heat of the day filtered through its canopy. Tony retrieved his line from the water and threw his fishing rod on the ledge. "Right. I'm ready for a swim. Are you coming?" He stripped naked.

Sean's eyes grew to twice their usual size. "If anyone sees you, we'll be arrested."

"Don't be daft. We're in the middle of nowhere. So what if we're seen? Who cares?"

"But—"

"Come on. Don't be a dick." Tony put his hands together, arched out over the ledge, and let himself go. The water surged around him as he sank. The sound of escaping air bubbles echoed in his ears as he reversed his plunge and shot toward the surface. It was colder than he'd anticipated. He looked up. Sean was still standing on the ledge in his underwear. "Come on. What you waiting for?"

Sean jumped feet-first, creating a wave that sloshed over the edge of the pool. Tony dove under the water and pulled Sean's underwear down around his ankles. They horsed around for a while, wrestling and pushing each other under the water until they were exhausted. Hunger eventually got to them. They crawled out and collapsed in a patch of ferns. They lay there for a spell, surprised that enough sun filtered through the canopy to dry them off. Tony stood up. "Okay, I'll go fill the billycan. You light the fire."

"Sure, give me the hard job," Sean said over his shoulder, running up to the overhang to retrieve his clothing.

Tony came panting up behind him. "What's so hard about gathering a few dry brambles and setting a match to them?"

"And all you have to do is fill the billycan from the pool. It'll take about ten seconds."

Tony shook his head in exasperation. He finished dressing and sat on the overhang to lace up his sneakers. "If you think for a minute that I'm going to drink water from that pool polluted by your dirty underwear, you've got another thing coming." He jumped up, grabbed the billycan, and ran, but he wasn't fast enough.

Two big pine cones bounced off the back of Tony's head. "Shag off," Sean said, as he foraged for more ammunition under the pine trees.

Tony laughed and shouted, "Dress yourself, you naked savage!" Although Tony pretended he was kidding about Sean's dirty underwear and knew Sean would interpret his remark as such, he wasn't. He was squeamish about that kind of stuff. He followed the tumbling stream a little farther up the mountain until he got to a smaller pool with crystal-clear water. He bent to fill the billycan. Staring back at him from the pool was his own face and the face of a stranger—a man dressed in black, half concealed by the foliage. Tony spun around. The man had disappeared. Was it a ghostly apparition, a figment of his imagination? He checked the brush. No one there, and no evidence that anyone ever was. He started trembling. Was this what it was like to go loony? Like his grandfather who complained of seeing rats after a weekend of binge drinking in the local pub. But he was too young for such a thing to happen. He quickly filled the billycan and headed back to the overhang at a fast trot. He wouldn't tell Sean.

His cousin was down on his knees blowing into a pyramid of dried twigs. At first a plume of smoke. A weak flame. Then a crackle and a blaze. He jumped up swearing when the smoke got in his eyes. Tony put the billycan on the fire and watched until the rising steam set the lid jangling. Then he emptied a little tin of loose tea into the bubbling water. When the tea was drawn, he retrieved two tin mugs from the shoulder bag and filled them to within an inch of the brim to leave room for milk. They ate in silence for the most part, Sean presumably happy that Tony's ribbing had stopped and Tony too frightened and preoccupied to engage in conversation.

Sean stopped chewing. "You look like you've seen a ghost. And what's all the looking over your shoulder? Are you expecting someone?"

Tony feigned a pained expression. "What? I'm fine. Just a little tired after horsing around in the pool."

Sean didn't pursue it for which Tony appeared grateful. They finished off the lunch and lay back on the ledge, gazing up at the sun coming through the canopy in flashes as the breeze stirred the leaves.

111

Tony raised himself and rested on an elbow. "Say, Sean, are any of the old copper mines being worked nowadays?"

Sean looked askance at him. "What are you talking about? Haven't those mines been abandoned since our grandfathers' time?"

"What about *poitin* makers?"

"That's a whole other story. I thought you were referring to copper miners."

A series of barks drew their attention to the woods. Diver, the black lab, darted excitedly out of the trees and ran around the pool, still barking.

Sean stood up. "He wants us to follow him. Let's see what's going on."

Tony got to his feet. "How can you tell?"

"From the way he runs at us and then backs up. That's a sign he wants us to go with him."

Tony looked around anxiously. "I don't see Molly." They trailed the dog up through the trees. Tony scanned to his left and right. The more he thought about it, the more convinced he became that the apparition at the pool was real. They emerged from the trees into a clearing to find Molly, a black and white border collie, sprawled on her side close to a shack at an abandoned mine shaft. They ran to her. Relief. Her chest heaved.

Sean sniffed. "What's that awful smell?"

Tony bent over the prone animal. "Not sure, but it reminds me of a doctor's office. It's making me dizzy." Off to one side in the undergrowth, Tony spotted a lump of white gauze. He went to pick it up, but the odor repelled him. "Whatever it is, I bet that's what knocked Molly out. She either took it into her mouth or got too close to it." By now Molly was coming to and attempting to stand up on wobbly legs. Diver circled her barking as if to encourage her.

Sean eyed his dog nervously. "She needs water. Let's get her back to the pool."

"Go ahead. I'll catch up in a little while. I'd like to check this place out." Sean took the half-drugged animal in his arms and disappeared into the trees, followed by Diver.

Tony grabbed a felled pine branch from the underbrush and with its tip nudged the door of the shack. It creaked open. A single metal cot covered with a ratty-looking quilt and a dirty tick pillow occupied one corner of the dilapidated interior. Panloaf wrappers littered a table. He continued to poke around and found a receipt from Dooher's grocery among the briquettes in the coal bucket. On the table with the wrappers lay a packet of the gauze material similar to what he found outside, absent the foul odor.

No evidence of a still or any ingredients for making *poitin*. He touched his fingers to the potbellied stove. Warm. The mystery man at the pool? Perhaps. But what was he doing here? Homeless or hiding out? He didn't look destitute. Far from it. Was he still lurking in the woods? Time to go.

Grabbing a pan-loaf wrapper, he stepped outside, retrieved the medicine-smelling gauze from the grass, and placed it inside the wrapper. After a quick look around, he left the place at a run to rejoin Sean and the dogs at the pool.

Chapter 22

IRA Meeting

A knock on the outer door a little after midnight. Reagan slid back the cover of the peephole. Barely visible in the dim light of the street lamp stood Paddy Cassidy, one of his old comrades-in-arms. Along with Reagan he had survived the Troubles, the Irish Civil War of 1921, and the bloody battles against Franco's Regulares in the thirties. He was a trusted lieutenant of Reagan's regional IRA council.

They were meeting tonight because of the Coltrane affair. They descended into the basement under Reagan's shop, a large space with whitewashed walls and a flagged floor. Along the gable wall in an alcove adjacent to a fireplace sat a single bed overlooked by a small window near the ceiling. After some small talk they settled in around a large table with two pints of Guinness. Concern etched their faces. Reagan stubbed out his cigarette and turned to Paddy. "We've had a small breakthrough on the Coltrane front."

"Thank the Lord for that. I wasn't looking forward to our next meeting with him without having some progress to report."

"It hasn't been that long. Not even two days."

"That's an eternity when your child is missing," Cassidy said. "So what's the breakthrough?"

"New information from the Geraty cousins suggests that young Coltrane spent some time at an abandoned mine in the back country."

"What's the proof of that?"

"Dr. Ford confirmed that a hunk of gauze with a medicinal smell, found by Tony Geraty at the mine, was laced with chloroform."

Reagan noticed the flash of skepticism in Cassidy's eyes. "Help me out here; what has that got to do with anything?"

"Question is, what was it doing there, especially in such an out-of-the-way place as an abandoned mine?" Reagan said.

Cassidy took a sip from his pint. "Good question, but since I'm not clairvoyant, I'd have to hazard a guess and say it was used to knock someone out for a spell."

"Or hold someone against their will whose presence you needed to conceal in an emergency."

Cassidy's eyes lit up. "Say from two young boys and their dogs."

"That's my take on it."

Reagan drummed his fingers on the table. "Is it possible that they're moving her around? If so, it's going to make it that much harder to find her."

Cassidy spoke. "I'm still skeptical. There's damn little to back this theory up."

Reagan coughed. "There's more. Tony claims that he saw the reflection of a large man in a pool he was drawing water from. Said he was dressed in black, but when he turned to verify it, the man had disappeared."

The clock on the wall chimed the quarter hour, causing a momentary halt to their discussion. After the pause, Reagan continued. "So where does that leave us?"

Cassidy emitted a loud grunt. "I'll tell you where it leaves us. It leaves us chasing the wrong person."

Reagan looked stunned. "What do you mean, Paddy?"

Cassidy leaned back in his chair, apparently needing a new sitting posture to infuse his insight with authority. "We may not know where Brigid Coltrane is, but we do know where that S.O.B. Kincaid is. And young Geraty's description, sketchy though it is, fits him. To put it bluntly, we need to grab him. Get him, and we find her."

Reagan stared off to one side. "Easier said than done."

"How challenging can it be? He's walking around in broad daylight."

"He's a slippery customer. Conned the guards into accepting his version of the McShane killing."

"Isn't it his word against Coltrane's?"

"One of his lackeys swore that he saw Coltrane pounce on McShane in the bog. And being afraid for his own life, he stayed hidden until Coltrane had left the scene."

Cassidy's face registered shock. "A boldfaced lie."

Reagan lit another cigarette and blew a puff of smoke from the side of his mouth toward the discolored ceiling. "It is, but Sergeant Cullen bought it."

"For Christ's sake, let's nab this guy and beat the truth out of him."

Reagan went over to the bottom of the stairs, and called up to his wife. "Marie, tell Paul to come on down!" A young man in his twenties with flaming red hair descended the stairs and stood there awkwardly for a moment. Reagan waved him to a chair and he took his place at the end of the table. "Despite my initial skepticism for your suggestion, Paddy, my mind was running down the same path as yours; that's why I've asked Paul Wyker to join us."

Wyker gave a sheepish grin, signaling his apparent discomfort in the presence of his older, more experienced comrades.

Cassidy looked at Reagan. "By the way, where is Law tonight?"

"Great second-in-command you're turning out to be. He's entertaining Coltrane and O'Reilly. Don't you remember? They went to his place to recuperate for a spell."

"Begod, you're right. Got to lay off the drink."

Reagan turned to Wyker. "Paul, take a few of the lads and see if you can't persuade Mr. Kincaid to accompany you to the sawmill. Then notify me."

Wyker had intense blue eyes set in a baby face, and when he spoke a slight smile played around his lips. On hearing his assignment, the smile disappeared and was replaced by a frown. He stared back at Reagan. "Just like that?"

"Kincaid thinks he's a tough guy and smarter than the rest of us, so he won't be expecting a tail."

Wyker released a hiss of breath through puckered lips. "What if he is?"

"Then you'll have to be smarter than he is. Bring enough backup to do the job." Wyker looked at the faces of the older men as if expecting further clarification. Getting none, he stood up. "Well then, I better get going." He raised the latch on the door and let himself out.

Cassidy had a worried look on his face. "You think he's up for the job?"

Chapter 23

German Spies in Ireland

"I'd feel a whole lot more confident if Coltrane was heading up that operation."

Reagan tapped his cigarette on the edge of the ash tray. "He's in no shape to do that in his present condition, Paddy."

The discussion then swung to the larger issue of the Blueshirts. Reagan suspected that they were tied to Brigid Coltrane's disappearance.

Cassidy frowned. "How did you arrive at that conclusion?"

"The Blueshirts are German sympathizers. There are Germans among the abductors. Therefore—"

Cassidy threw his hands up. "For Christ's sake, that's a false something or other. As much as I hate to say this, you can't conclude from that that the Blueshirts are into murder and kidnapping."

"Okay, okay, I've harder evidence in my possession." He paused before continuing. "The Brits suspect the Blueshirts *are* collaborating with the Germans."

"How the hell do you know that?"

Reagan shifted in his seat. "The British secret service unit MI6 has been working behind the scenes tracking German agents in Ireland for the past year, helped by our intelligence branch G-2."

"You're putting me on, right? British agents are currently in Ireland?"

"'Fraid so, and the government wants their presence kept secret, since certain factions in the country would go ballistic if it got out."

Cassidy jumped up from the table, knocking his chair over. "The government guessed right. After all the bloodshed, pain, and suffering we endured to get those bastards outa here, they're back in?"

Reagan raised his hands, palms forward. "Hold on, hold on, Paddy. Before you get a heart attack, let me explain."

Cassidy righted his chair, but remained standing. "Well, there better be a damn good explanation why our old enemy is back among us, that's all I can say."

"German agents have been infiltrated into Ireland, and they're not just passing through to England."

"So we now have both English and German agents in Ireland," Cassidy said. "Are there any fucking Irish agents in Ireland?"

"There are. You, me, and the rest of our lads."

"You and me? You must be joking?"

"We've been asked to assist our intelligence unit G-2 in tracking down these foreign spies and to keep an eye on the Blueshirts. All we have now are suspicions. Not enough concrete evidence yet for the government to reel them in."

"If these German agents aren't passing through to England, then what in hell are they doing here?" Cassidy asked.

Reagan slammed his hand on the table. "Damn it. Get off your high horse, Paddy, and listen, will you?"

"Okay, okay!" Paddy's cheeks remained flushed.

"We don't know yet."

"I'll hazard a guess. It's nothing good for this country."

"There's a more immediate problem facing us."

"Oh, and how could it trump what you've already told us?"

"The Brits are reporting, not publicly mind you, that two of their MI6 agents in Ireland have gone missing," Reagan said.

"By God, you don't think that ..."

"That's exactly what I'm thinking."

"The executions on Red Cow Island." Cassidy buried his face in his hands and shook his head.

"Why haven't the Brits enlisted the help of the guards to get to the bottom of this?"

"Reluctance to disclose they're meddling in Irish affairs even with the collusion of the Irish government."

"This gets uglier by the hour," Cassidy said.

"Uglier and more dangerous, especially for Peter Coltrane and the family, although I'm inclined to think that as long as Coltrane remains one step ahead of his pursuers, nothing will happen to the kid."

"Don't follow your reasoning."

"At this point I have to admit that it's only an educated guess. Both Coltrane and the kid can identify the killer from Red Cow Island."

"As far as we know."

"Coltrane isn't going to go running to the authorities for fear the kidnappers might retaliate and kill the kid. The killers know that, so it behooves them to keep her alive until they catch Coltrane, and then ..."

"And then they can dispatch both of them with less risk."

"Right," Reagan said.

Cassidy scrunched his face up. "Except..."

"Now what?"

"Neither Coltrane nor the kid knows the identity of the killer. They know what he looks like, they might even be able to pick him out of a lineup if he was captured, but that's a big if. So what great threat does she pose?"

Reagan put his face between his hands and exhaled loudly. "I thought of that, and here my logic might be a little weak. The killers don't want to run the risk that somewhere down the line Coltrane might discover the identity of the culprit. So they want to keep the kid alive as insurance to thwart Coltrane from blabbing if it should happen."

"That's plausible as a theory, but not bulletproof," Cassidy said.

"Never said it was. We may be grasping at straws, but I can't think of another reason why they'd want to keep her alive."

Cassidy sat down and looked around as if he were in pain. "Reagan, all this detective work has got me powerful thirsty. It's after midnight. He held up his empty glass. "Any chance we could nip upstairs to the bar for a refill?"

Reagan seemed relieved, as if he too was at his wit's end and needed a break. "I suppose I can't refuse you after all the free pints I got in your establishment."

Cassidy's eyes lit up. "Damn right."

They climbed the stairs to the bar and Cassidy eased himself onto a stool while Reagan drew two pints. Cassidy leaned his elbows on the bar in anticipation. After the drinks settled, Reagan slid one over to his friend and, taking his own in hand, sat on a stool facing him. Except for a light underneath the counter the place was kept dark to avoid attracting the attention of the guards on the lookout for pubs violating closing-time. The lights of a passing car projected a moving silhouette of the shop window along the ceiling before fading from sight.

"Something just occurred to me," Reagan said. "What if the kidnappers have a secret reason to keep the kid alive that we know nothing about?"

"Like maybe they're more vulnerable to discovery than we think."

"Could they be some high-profile operators, with a lot to lose if they were uncovered?" Reagan said.

"Like the Germans."

"And where are the highest ranking Germans in Ireland located?"

"The German Embassy."

"Worth keeping an eye on them, although I don't believe they'd run an operation like that out of their embassy."

"Yeah, better bring in thugs from outside that are untraceable for that kind of skullduggery."

Reagan yawned and looked at the clock over the bar—2:00 a.m. "Paddy, I'm going to call it a night. I'm all done in." After finishing their drinks he saw Cassidy out the door and secured the house. He felt guilty. Other than the plan to kidnap Kincaid, not much else had been decided. And that wasn't a sure thing. Glad he didn't have to face Coltrane right now.

Halfway up the stairs he heard a knock on the door. *Cassidy must have forgotten his wallet again.* He retraced his steps. Squinted through the peep hole.

"What in the name of Jaysus?" He pulled the door open. Coltrane stumbled across the threshold.

***

"I couldn't do it, Seamus; I couldn't go into hiding and leave Claire to fend for herself. It turns out my instinct was right."

"What are you going on about?"

"Something you promised you'd do but didn't."

"We're not going to get anywhere if you keep talking in riddles."

"I dropped by our house on the way here. The place was empty. Woke up Lost John ... said Claire had gone to her parents because of the attack."

"What attack?"

"What attack? That answers the question. A masked man chased her through the garden. Lost John drove him off. So much for your protection."

Reagan's face turned red. "I'm sorry. Our lads were supposed to be keeping an eye on your place. Can't believe Lost John didn't tell me about this."

"He told one of your so-called sentries. Probably scared or embarrassed to tell you that they had fallen down on the job."

Reagan tightened his fists.

Coltrane plopped on a chair, closed his eyes, and exhaled loudly. "I'm so hungry I could eat a horse."

Reagan shook his head and led him up the stairs toward the kitchen. "Did O'Reilly go on to Law's place?"

"Did O'Reilly go to England? That's the question. I don't know. Did he end up at Law's? Don't know that either."

Reagan paused on the stairs. "Are you okay?"

"Am I okay? Are you serious? My child has been kidnapped. My wife's been attacked and ran from the house and I'm in hiding. What's not to be okay about?"

Reagan took the remaining steps two at a time. "Jaysus, let's get

122

some food in you and a shot of Jameson's. Maybe that'll bring you back to your senses."

"Let's start with the Jameson's."

So much for swearing off the drink. He'd be more resolute next time.

Over a hastily pulled-together meal of bacon and sausages, complemented by several mugs of strong tea laced with additional shots of Jameson's, Reagan heard the story of O'Reilly's hasty departure. Reagan probably knew the question was coming, but when it did, when Coltrane asked him about the promised IRA plan for finding his daughter, he stumbled through what came across as a flimsy strategy when spoken out loud. When he mentioned Wyker's role in it, Coltrane plunked his mug down heavily, sloshing tea onto the table. "No, no, no! He's too young and inexperienced to tangle with Kincaid. This can't be botched. My child's life is on the line. I'll handle it." He raised his hand, signaling an end to the discussion.

Reagan acquiesced, in part, Coltrane suspected, because of the bungling of his wife's security. But he placed a condition on Coltrane's receiving IRA support: Wyker must be included in Coltrane's scheme. By the time Coltrane settled in for the night on the bed in the basement, the sky filling the little window had turned grey at the edges.

Chapter 24

The Bog Crevasse

Kincaid's favorite haunt was the Percy French Hotel bar on Bridge Street, which he and Stiglitz usually left around 2:00 a.m. Coltrane had two problems. One, he couldn't nab Kincaid outside the hotel since many patrons milled around on the sidewalk after closing, smoking and chatting. Two, once Kincaid left, Coltrane had been unable in previous attempts to keep up with the powerful, fast-moving Bentley in his little Ford Prefect.

Tonight he hoped for a different result. Wyker had procured a speedy motorcycle that he claimed had the guts to even the odds. Around 1:00 a.m. Wyker and he parked across the street from the Percy French under a large elm tree. Its long tendrils concealed the little black Prefect in which they were seated. The boozy hum from the hotel was the only sound disturbing the quiet summer night. Through the large plate-glass window, with signs advertising Guinness and Tullamore Dew, they observed Kincaid and the German downing drinks at a fairly fast clip.

"If they keep swilling at this rate, all we'll need to do is bump into them when they leave and they'll fall right over," Wyker said.

Coltrane rubbed the side of his face slowly. "Not going to be that easy. Kincaid looks like a chap who can hold his liquor."

"Maybe so, but I'll wager that right now his judgment is not up to snuff."

"Let's hope you're right about that, and about the caliber of the motorcycle you acquired."

"I tell you, it's a rocket. It's a Triumph Tiger 100. Got twin-cylinder carburetors and can do up to a 100 mph." Wyker's eyes danced with excitement. "I did eighty on the Longford Road yesterday and that wasn't even at full throttle. If you can handle it, you'll catch the Bentley, I guarantee it."

"I suppose there's no point in asking where you laid hands on such a machine."

"What do you care where I got it, as long as it does the job?"

Coltrane flipped the cover of his pocket watch. It was ten past two and still no sign of Kincaid or his drinking partner calling it a night.

"I thought the Percy French was fairly strict about after-hours drinking," Wyker said, rolling down the driver's window and flicking a cigarette butt onto the grass margin.

"Shows you don't get out much, son. Hotels are notorious for lax closing hours." The conversation returned to the motorcycle. They got so wrapped up in the features of the Triumph Tiger 100 that when they looked inside the bar again, Kincaid and the German had vanished. They scrambled from the car in time to see taillights disappearing around a bend on the Longford Road.

"Quick! The keys to the bike. Follow as best you can in the Prefect!" Coltrane yelled.

"Don't try challenging them on your own. I'll be at Scramogue Crossroads."

Coltrane mounted the motorcycle and roared off. The bike was as fast as Wyker claimed. It responded to the throttle like the animal whose name it bore, its deep roar vibrating up his arms. The wind, so balmy under the elm tree, now pierced his light jacket like a knife. The smell of petrol made him light-headed and his eyes watered. To lessen the buffeting he leaned forward, almost touching the handlebars. After rounding the turn at Farn, he saw taillights ahead on the straight road.

Kincaid's head start might be a stroke of good luck; he could keep the Bentley in sight while staying far enough back to avoid suspicion.

When the Bentley turned down a by-road, Coltrane killed his headlight and navigated by the taillights of his quarry. Tall pine trees loomed out of the darkness on either side like challenging sentries. The Bentley wove down the narrow road at a reduced speed before stopping in front of a large wrought-iron gate. It blocked the entrance to a residence that once served as a guardhouse for an old English estate. The house ran along the boundary line separating the lands of Glenfar Abbey from Hayden's Wilderness.

In his haste to keep pace with the Bentley, Coltrane lost contact with Wyker. As a precaution he parked his motorcycle a hundred yards up the road and walked the rest of the way to the entrance. Fearing that the creaking of the heavy gate might give him away, he scaled the ivy-covered wall that surrounded the estate. Without backup, the best he could do was confirm that Kincaid was inside. He pulled the whiskey bottle from his coat, hands shaking, and removed the cork with his teeth. He took a long swallow before returning it to his pocket. The adrenalin rush for the task ahead neutralized any twinges of guilt for this lapse.

He crept toward the building. Light came from a second-storey window and from the window on the ground floor. Through the muslin curtain of the downstairs window he spotted Kincaid and Stiglitz pouring shots from a bottle of Courvoisier before settling into easy chairs arranged around a coffee table. Two pistols rested on the table beside the half-empty bottle. He toyed with the idea of taking Kincaid, but he was outnumbered two to one. Maybe more, since there was that upstairs light. Again he regretted the absence of Wyker, since Kincaid and the German looked inebriated enough to be taken off guard. The voices coming through the window sounded garbled. Could *he* be a little tipsy? He banished the thought and took another swallow.

Pulling a pistol from his waistband, he reconnoitered the house. He stopped to look at the upstairs window. Was Brigid imprisoned up there? Rounding a corner, he discovered the Bentley parked next to a rear door. He lifted the latch and tried to ease it open. The door stuck.

126

Rather than push his luck, he retreated into the brush and returned to the motorcycle to round up Wyker. By the time he and Wyker returned, Kincaid and the German would certainly be plastered. He took another swig before throwing his leg over the saddle of the bike, but he misjudged and banged his foot against the back wheel. He succeeded on his second try, and was about to turn the key when a strange ringing erupted in his ears, followed by a blinding flash.

Then darkness.

***

"You know, I'm disappointed," Kincaid said, surveying Coltrane's inert form curled in a ball on the floor. "I thought he and I were destined for a grand finale, so to speak. Instead he goes out like a lamb. Pity."

Kincaid fished around in Coltrane's coat and found the empty bottle. "Ah, the curse of the Irish," he slurred, holding the bottle by the neck. "If it hadn't been for this, my friend, our situations might be reversed."

He dropped the bottle on top of the prone figure. Stiglitz pulled out his Luger and screwed on a silencer. Kincaid stayed his hand. He turned toward a man in a black hood standing silently in the background. "This gentleman has a more elegant method of disposal in mind for Mr. Coltrane."

Stiglitz's face sagged. He unscrewed the silencer.

The masked figure chuckled. "He'll never see the light of day again where he's going, Boss."

"Good, and see that you don't bungle it. Better he disappears off the face of the earth. Makes things simpler."

"Consider it done, Boss." The hooded figure hoisted Coltrane onto his shoulder.

"All that remains is to rid ourselves of the other family member who's been enjoying our hospitality for some time now. I think I'll handle that little chore myself first thing in the morning." Kincaid flashed his yellow teeth.

"What about the wife?"

"She's of no consequence now; she saw nothing. So be off and do what you have to do."

Kincaid gathered his belongings and ordered Stiglitz to bring the car around. "Let's get out of here. Coltrane may have backup." The hooded figure lingered outside the door shouldering his burden. "Why in hell are you still here? Something wrong?"

"What should we do with the motorcycle, Boss?"

"Burn it." Kincaid jumped into the waiting car.

***

The hooded figure moved cautiously through the heather. He didn't want Coltrane's grave to become his own. From time to time he used his small flashlight to find his footing. At this time of night he doubted anyone would be up and about, especially in a God-forsaken spot like Hayden's Wilderness. Even though the hood impeded his sight and progress, he didn't remove it. He wished Stiglitz had finished Coltrane off so he wouldn't be stuck carrying dead weight across rough terrain. By the time he reached the crevasse he was too exhausted to spend much time searching for its deepest part. After a cursory survey, he let the body slip from his shoulder headfirst into the yawning chasm.

He was confident the body would never be found. Irish bogs were known to hold their victims for a thousand years. He chuckled. That should meet Kincaid's requirement that Coltrane disappear off the face of the earth. Once he heard the thump of the body hitting bottom, he moved back into the heather and took off his hood.

Chapter 25

The Prisoner

During the long hours of confinement, Brigid watched the shaft of light sneak through the little barred window near the ceiling of her obscure chamber. Gradually it worked its way across the bare limestone walls, illuminating the room until it disappeared with the movement of the sun. She wasn't sure how long she'd been in this new place, or how she got here. They had moved her many times, originally to a mineshaft, then to a house in the woods, and now here. The last thing she remembered was the man with the foreign accent pressing a strange-smelling cloth over her nose and mouth. When she awoke, it was dark and her head pounded.

She slipped in and out of wakefulness. At one point she thought she heard singing, but she couldn't be sure. Maybe it was a dream like the one she often had of her mother opening her arms wide to embrace her. But the light streaming through the window wasn't a dream; neither was the metal cot on which she lay. And where was that strong smell coming from? She realized it was from her. Her hair and clothes stank.

The last time she touched water was in Lough Gorm, where she struggled to keep her head above the waves by clinging to the neck of the pony. That seemed a long time ago. She ached to see her mother and fall into her comforting arms. She thought about her dad. She last saw him struggling to stay afloat after letting go of the pony. Had he survived? She took consolation in the thought that he was a very strong swimmer. She lost sight of him when the current swept her and the pony around the headland. Was he looking for her? Was anyone looking for her? She missed her school friend Julia. She even missed school. She missed gossiping with Julia on the playground about the curly-haired boy who sat in front of them in history class. Would life ever return to normal? Many nights she cried herself to sleep, wondering when the nightmare would end. Or if it would end.

She sat up in bed and pulled the dirty bedspread back, swinging her feet onto the floor. The flagstones were cold. After taking a few steps, she trod on something moist and sticky. She jumped back in fright. Just a plate, holding the remainder of a meal. Grabbing the edge of one of the grimy sheets, she cleaned between her toes and almost gagged as she viewed her surroundings. A thin sliver of light trickled from underneath the door. The singing resumed, very faint, not anything she'd heard before. Almost as though it came from another world. So that wasn't a dream either.

As she tried to sort everything out she gazed up at the barred window, about ten feet from where she stood. She wished she could reach it to look out. Patches of mold ran along the sill and green tentacles crept two feet down the wall. The only other object in the room was the metal bed. Standing on it wouldn't give her enough elevation to see through the window. But if she propped the frame on its end against the wall, she might be able to climb up the cross-hatched springs.

Footsteps approaching. She jumped back in bed.

A square of light appeared at the bottom of the door. A hand pushed a tray holding a plate and a mug through a little hinged flap. Then the little flap snapped shut again. Brigid took the tray and sat on the edge of the bed, balancing it on her knees. The meal consisted of bread, cheese, a lukewarm bowl of porridge, and a mug of milk. She ate ravenously. Stowing the empty tray in a corner, she turned her attention again to the window. Yeah, she thought, the bed idea might work. She removed the mattress, dragged the frame over, and placed it on its end against the wall. Removing her shoes she dug her toes into the springs and began to climb.

When she reached the window she was surprised to see that the sill was on a level with the ground outside. Now she understood the source of the green spots. Surface water seeped through the mortar that bound the stones together, creating wet patches on the interior. Her prison was a basement. She grabbed the bars to heave herself higher and nearly toppled off her perch when the bars shifted, loosening several stones that clattered onto the floor.

Fearing the noise might have alerted her captors, she scrambled down the springs and placed her ear to the door. Silence. She looked up at the window again. A large hole had opened up on one side of it. She shifted the bed underneath the opening. Tying her shoes together by the laces, she draped them around her neck and climbed. When she reached the window, she levered the stones back and forth, opening up a larger hole. She managed to get her head and shoulders through the opening. Voices. Growing louder. She buried her head in the long meadow grass, sprinkled with daisies and buttercups. The sweet smell filled her nostrils. The crunch of gravel. She thought of easing back into the basement, but feared knocking the bed frame over. So she stayed put, pressing her face as close to the ground as was physically possible.

The footsteps crunched closer. Hems of black skirts and black shoes appeared in her field of vision. She closed her eyes in the childish hope that if she couldn't see whoever was passing, they couldn't see her. She lay still, listening to the echo of her heartbeat against the earth. The footsteps and voices gradually died away. She raised her head slowly. Two nuns engaged in an animated conversation moved down the path. Nuns! That explained the singing. They looked like her teacher Sister DeSales. Surely they would help her. For an instant she contemplated calling them. A sixth sense kicked in. Maybe not. She waited until the sisters were out of sight before hauling the rest of her body onto solid ground.

The path the nuns had taken meandered down an incline to a large cluster of buildings. She figured it to be a convent. The building in which she was imprisoned looked like a granary. Not a sound came from within. Of course she couldn't be sure that her jailer wasn't lurking inside. It occurred to her that, since the building was isolated from the rest of the structures, maybe she was being held in secret from the community of nuns. Or could the nuns be involved in this? Too ridiculous to entertain that idea. Near the convent a road snaked off into a pine forest in one direction and disappeared into a cluster of low hills in the other. She had no idea where the road led, but if she could reach it she might find help. She decided to follow it toward the forest. Easier to hide there if she ran into trouble. About a hundred yards from her present position a wheat field extended down a hill in an undulating wave all the way to the road. Excellent cover if she could reach it unobserved. She put on her shoes, sprinted across the open space and plunged into the tall stalks.

So far, so good. She set off running. She felt bad about trampling the farmer's crop, but fear of being caught quickly banished that guilt. Exiting the wheat field close to an iron gate, she stopped to survey her surroundings. The way forward seemed clear. In a final rush she sprinted toward the gate, climbed over it, and jumped onto the tar road.

She alternated walking and running for about ten minutes. The sound of a car prompted her to flee into the pine forest. Sooner or later she would have to change her tactics. If she hoped to put distance between herself and the convent, she would have to risk stopping a car and hope her luck held. She stepped into the road again and walked for another twenty minutes. Her feet hurt and sweat ran down her back. She pulled off her filthy cardigan and draped it across her shoulder. The sounds of summer filled the air. Bird calls, the soft bleat of sheep with blue and red markings on their backs, the music of the wind in the pine trees. A quiet, peaceful world in contrast to the world of terror she was fleeing.

From behind her the rumble of an engine. She steeled herself and turned to raise her hand. The face of the big man with the yellow teeth filled the windshield. She screamed. Her feet rooted to the ground. The man with the chloroform rag jumped from the car and pulled her inside.

Chapter 26

"Why Am I Still Alive?"

Coltrane regained consciousness through a pounding headache. He opened his eyes and tried to assess his situation. The smell of wet turf filled his nostrils. As far as he could tell, he was wedged between the narrowing flanks of a bog crevasse. The sides of the trench felt cool and slippery. Almost imperceptibly he was sliding headfirst toward a ledge that overlooked a twenty-foot plunge to an algae-covered bog hole. The salty taste of blood filled his mouth. He dug his hands into the soft turf on either side to gain traction. Gradually he righted himself and elevated his head toward the sun. He rammed his hobnailed boots into the flanks. Little by little, he clawed his way to the top and pulled himself over the lip of the crevasse. He rested for a spell before crawling a few feet into the heather and passing out.

When he awoke, the sun was high in the sky. His head felt like it was levitating off his shoulders. How long had he been in the crevasse? In the heather? How had he gotten there? Gradually the haziness dissipated and he began to stitch together the chain of events that led him to the house the night before. He cursed his stupidity at being taken so easily: *Why didn't I return for Wyker before casing the house? Why am I still alive?*

He stood up. The terrain looked familiar. Hayden's Wilderness. He focused on a two-storey house at the edge of the heather and staggered toward it. As he drew closer he recognized it as the house from last night. Deciding to play it safe, he ducked down in the heather and listened. He ran his fingers through his hair and discovered an egg-sized bump on the back of his head.

Detecting no signs of life around the dwelling, he let himself in through an unlocked rear door that opened onto a small kitchen. A fireplace occupied one wall. He touched his finger to the ash pile on the hearth. Cold. No fire there in quite some time. He tiptoed across the flagstone floor and entered an adjacent room through an open door. A half-empty bottle of Courvoisier sat on the glass coffee table in the middle of the floor. The sitting room. He was back in the lions' den. Sunlight streamed through a double window, casting the shadow of the yellow muslin curtain on the coffee table. He had stood outside that window the night before and spied on Kincaid and the German.

His first instinct was to run, but on reflection he decided a search of the house might yield clues to Brigid's whereabouts. The occupants appeared to have left in a hurry. Someone with a drinking habit like Kincaid's wouldn't willingly abandon an expensive bottle of cognac. The liquor reminded Coltrane of his great thirst. It tempted him. But a stab of regret reminded him that his foggy state of mind the previous night contributed to his capture. He passed on the Courvoisier and foraged around until he found a bucket of spring water in the kitchen with a ladle handle protruding from it. After satisfying his thirst, he took the bucket outside and poured a few ladlefuls of water over the wound on his head. He winced, but afterward felt revived and almost human again.

He took the bucket back to the kitchen and returned to the sitting room. A Sacred Heart picture with a glowing red lamp hung on one wall, and next to it a picture of the Holy Family. Whoever lived here was devout. Why would he entertain a guest like Kincaid?

He opened the door to a small study and found himself facing a desk in front of a large bay window set in the back wall. A tall brass pedestal stood to one side. From it hung a flag with a white X-shaped cross imposed on a field of blue. The image of a red hand occupied its center. *Hunh!* He scoured the place, looking for something—a picture, a name, anything—that would reveal the identity of the owner. In a desk drawer he found an envelope with two faded photos. One showed several men in uniform holding a flag with an X-shaped cross on it. A street sign in the background read "Plaza Major." And underneath, written in a neat hand: "Madrid 1936."

He immediately recognized one of the soldiers: Arthur Cusack, Abbot Jonathan's caretaker from Glenfar Abbey. That was it; he was part of the Blueshirt contingent that fought with the fascists in Spain. Cusack must have been the one who ambushed him last night and most likely the local informer helping Kincaid. His presence in the Lake Hotel wasn't random, then. He wondered if Abbot Jonathan was aware of his caretaker's extracurricular activities. The other photo was not inscribed. No need. It was Generalissimo Franco posing in full military regalia.

***

Heavy footsteps outside. He scurried into the sitting room and edged back the muslin curtain. A balding man with the physique of a prizefighter trudged up the driveway and headed to the rear of the house. It was Cusack, all right. Good, Coltrane thought. I can slip out the front door. He hurried to the front entry alcove, passing a coat tree with rain gear and umbrellas. The back door creaked open.

"Here, Kitty, Kitty." A timid meow.

Then Coltrane understood why Cusack was using the rear entrance. The lock was missing from the front door. In its place a length of two-by-four fastened to the jambs at either end by screws effectively rendered the front entrance impassable. The sound of food being poured into a dish. A series of meows. He was trapped. He looked around for a weapon. Cusack's heavy footsteps approached the sitting room. Coltrane grabbed a walking stick hanging from the coat tree and edged to the baffle wall that shielded the entry hall from the sitting room. He didn't know if Cusack was armed. Fair chance he was, given his connection to Kincaid. Even if he wasn't, Coltrane was in no shape to take him on after his ordeal in the crevasse.

From the sitting room, the sound of liquid being poured, followed by the creaking of couch springs. Coltrane grabbed the stick by the butt. The curved handle could deliver a hefty blow if landed in the right spot. This might be his best chance to rush Cusack. One problem. The couch faced the entry. Suddenly another problem. "Meow." The cat came into the alcove and massaged its body along Coltrane's legs, purring rhythmically.

"Here, Kitty Kitty." The squeak of springs again. Heavy footsteps drawing close.

Coltrane raised the stick and nudged the cat toward the sitting room with his foot. A whiff of Courvoisier wafted into the alcove. Coltrane waited. Another meow. Two beefy hands reached into the alcove at floor level and scooped up the cat.

"There now, Kitty. You know you can't go outside through here." Cusack plodded into the kitchen. Coltrane sped across the sitting room into the little study. He hoped to escape through the bay window. He barely made it into the study before Cusack was back in the sitting room. But he forgot to shut the door.

"I could've sworn that door was closed," Cusack muttered.

Coltrane scurried for cover in the well of the desk and pulled the swivel chair in behind to hide his presence. Cusack entered the study. The sound of a bolt-action rifle being reloaded. Beads of sweat dripped down Coltrane's face. Cusack pawed around the desktop. "Must be that damn Frenchie drink." He moved to the window and stood with his back to the well of the desk. With the tip of his rifle he edged aside the curtain and surveyed the garden. Cusack's labored breathing filled the room. If he turned around, Coltrane was a dead man.

"Jaysus Christ! Those damn rabbits are playing hell with me cabbage." He rushed out of the study. Coltrane extracted himself from the desk and peeked out the window. Cusack ran up and down the garden, shouting and throwing clods at a rabbit scurrying through the cabbage furrows. Coltrane waited until Cusack's frustration was spent and he returned to the house.

Sounds of Cusack puttering around in the kitchen. It was now or never. Coltrane undid the catch on the bay window and pushed. Nothing doing. Multiple coats of paint had sealed it tight. Heart pounding, he grabbed the flagpole and rammed its heavy pedestal through the window, spraying a shower of glass fragments into the cabbage patch. He leapt through the jagged aperture and tromped through the cabbage to the tree line, still holding the flag pole. A bullet ricocheted off the brass shaft. Coltrane turned and lofted it like a spear at the figure standing with the gun in the ruined window. "I'll be back, Cusack! I'll be back!"

The rifle spoke again, slicing chunks of bark from an ash tree behind Coltrane's head.

Time to go.

He turned and scrambled into the woods.

Chapter 27

The Magdalene Laundry

The walls of the Magdalene Laundry stood twenty feet high, capped by a row of broken glass mortared in for security. Its occupants, mostly young mothers, were sent here for having had children out of wedlock, either by their embarrassed parents seeking to hide the shame from neighbors or by aggressive state and church officials out to protect public morality. In almost all cases the women were imprisoned against their will without the benefit of due process or appeal. After a life spent washing laundry, many would die here and be buried in unmarked graves.

Escorted by Kincaid, Brigid Coltrane arrived here in the dead of night per an arrangement worked out between the abbot of Glenfar Abbey and the mother superior of the Magdalene Laundry, whose order of nuns ran the institution. The mother superior, whose name was Brónach, was a tall, spare woman with the emaciated appearance of a long-distance runner. She was virtuous in that she followed the rules of her order without question, and saw no contradiction in a path to holiness that tolerated the harsh treatment of sinners while simultaneously preaching the golden rule of "Do unto others ..." After all, suffering was the path that led to purification, which ultimately bought salvation. It all worked out in the end.

Mother Brónach released a thin smile. "Tell the abbot that we will take good care of this hussy, Mr. Kincaid."

Kincaid withdrew an envelope from his pocket and handed it to her. "The abbot assures me you're a competent woman, Mother. I have faith in you and your institution, unlike the last establishment we housed this little vixen in."

"We aim to do God's work." She ushered him out a side door to a courtyard where Stiglitz awaited him behind the wheel of the black Bentley.

***

A nun dressed in a black floor-length habit shook Brigid awake. A close-fitting linen coif framed the nun's face, making her already plump cheeks plumper, like those of a peasant woman in a Rubens painting. The small room had a single bed and a chest of drawers with Brigid's street clothes stacked on top. A Saint Bridget's cross hung on a whitewashed wall. The nun threw a large towel on the foot of the bed. "Get down to the bathroom at once, you filthy creature, and don't come back until you look presentable."

Brigid sat up, stunned by the sudden apparition. "Who are you, and where am I?"

"You're in a place where you don't ask questions. Now get." She grabbed the towel and flung it at her. "As to who I am, you will find out soon enough." She pulled a small silver pocket watch from the folds of her habit. "Be back here in ten minutes."

Brigid contemplated resisting, but the prospect of bathing took all the fight out of her. She scurried toward the bathroom at the end of a long hallway. Even the tub with its clawed feet looked menacing. Paint peeled off the walls and the place smelled of mold. Brigid trembled. Filling the tub took almost five minutes, leaving barely enough time to get wet, but she sensed that she should not dally. She flung off her nightgown and stepped into the soothing water. As she lay soaking up its warmth, she took stock of her situation. She had landed in a nightmare. To survive she would have to be tough. Tiredness overcame her and she lost track of time. Her head drooped.

The plump-cheeked nun stormed through the unlocked door, grabbed Brigid by the ear, and hauled her out of the bathtub. She had barely enough time to wrap herself in the towel before she was in the hallway racing to the little room. As she stood there, dripping on the floorboards, the nun continued to twist her ear until she screamed.

"Now let me introduce myself, missy. My name is Sister Ursula, and I am in charge of discipline. Rule number one: when I give an order, I expect it to be obeyed. Ten minutes means ten, not twenty."

"But I didn't—"

The nun twisted her ear again. "Rule number two: don't speak unless I ask you to." Brigid hung her head as tears welled up.

Sister Ursula opened the door as the sound of many footsteps echoed in the hallway. "Go to the bathroom and get your nightgown." Seeing Brigid hesitate, she pushed her across the threshold. "Off with you."

Brigid stood shivering in her towel as a column of young women marched past, their hobnail boots beating out a military rhythm on the tiled floor. They wore shapeless calico dresses that hung below the knee and grey woolen socks that came up to mid-calf. Brigid turned red as a rooster's comb as she tried to cover herself, but apart from the noise of the boots on the polished floor, no one made a sound or looked at her. A buxom older lady, also dressed in calico, walked alongside the procession, her eyes darting from one girl's face to another as if she was checking for silent defiance. She seemed ready, even eager, to use her short bamboo cane.

By the time Brigid reached the bathroom, the hallway fell silent. She threw on the nightgown, wrapped the towel around her shoulders, and ran back to the room. Sister Ursula was pacing. Folded neatly on the bed were cotton underwear, a grey calico dress, a pair of heavy woolen socks, and a strip of calico about nine inches wide and two and a half feet long. Three pairs of hobnail boots of different sizes sat on the floor at the foot of the bed.

The sister pointed to the folded pile. "From now on, this will be your attire. Get dressed."

Brigid paused as she looked at the calico strip. Sister Ursula grabbed it from the bed and told her to raise her arms over her head. Then she wrapped the strip around her breasts and tied it in a knot at her side.

"You must atone for your sins and strive to be chaste like Our Blessed Mother. This piece of calico is a reminder that we must fight the impulses of the unruly flesh. Now lower your arms."

Brigid didn't have the foggiest notion what the sister was talking about, but she knew better than to speak out. After dressing and selecting a pair of boots that nearly fit her, she followed Sister Ursula to the wash house, a large building that extended along a riverbank, forming part of the perimeter wall with broken glass on top.

When the sister opened the door a blast of hot air hit Brigid in the face, nearly knocking her over. Through the steam she saw row upon row of tubs. In front of each a young woman labored over a washing board. Against the gable walls of the wash house stood several tall shelving units where soap and washing supplies were stored. On both sidewalls near the high ceiling, a row of small windows opened outward like stunted glass wings. As the nun escorted her among the rows, Brigid noticed that the girls' hands were wrinkled and yellow; in some cases their knuckles bled. When Brigid reached the tub assigned to her along the back wall adjacent to the river, Sister Ursula took the large brass crucifix that hung from her waist by a chain, and tapped one of the heating pipes. The girls stopped working instantaneously, as if someone cut the power to their arm muscles.

"We have a new addition to our community," the sister announced, standing rigid among the rows. "Her new name is Alana, meaning peace. Like you, she is here to wash away her sins, and through hard work and penance obtain Almighty God's forgiveness for her past misdeeds."

The sister stopped and looked around, checking for any signs of disagreement or rebellion. Satisfied that everything appeared in order, she turned and faced the large wooden crucifix on the front wall over the door and made the sign of the cross. All the girls followed suit, except Brigid, who was quickly yanked into position by the girl standing at the tub next to her.

141

When Sister Ursula turned around, the girls assumed their accustomed places. "Now back to work, and remember this is for your own good." She walked over to Brigid, who looked bewildered. "Your neighbor, Lily, will show you what to do."

Without another word the nun swept toward the front door, her long black skirt brushing the moist floor tiles.

***

Lily, a girl of about sixteen with cropped black hair, took Brigid through the basics. "Be careful not to get on the wrong side of Ursula, she's a regular bitch," she whispered. "We all hate her."

"I've already had a taste of what she's like."

"Shh! Aunt Mona is coming. We're not supposed to talk."

An older lady with a pageboy haircut and a broad impassive face advanced along their row, carrying a short cane. After she'd passed behind them Brigid ventured to ask, "Who's she, anyway?"

"One of us. She's been here since the place opened. She's a minder, but really she's a spy for Mother Superior." Lily kept her whisper barely above the noise of the washboard.

"What do you mean a 'minder'?"

"She's like a supervisor of sorts, but not really. Several of the older women, the lifers, patrol the washrooms and the dormitories at night to see that the rules are being kept. They're the eyes and ears of the nuns. If they catch any of us breaking the silence or being away from our proper place, they report us to Mother Superior or Sister Ursula."

"Sounds like a jailer to me," Brigid replied.

Lily blew a strand of hair away from her face. "This place is a jail, except it's worse. In a jail you're there for a specific amount of time. You could be here for life, that's the difference."

"Why are you here?"

"For being an orphan. How about you?"

"For being in the wrong place at the wrong time."

Brigid whispered her story to her workmate. Lily looked stunned. "You shouldn't be here at all." She vigorously pummeled a bloodied butcher's apron over the corrugated glass surface of the washing board.

"Does anyone ever try to run away?"

Lily was about to answer, but fell silent when the five o'clock bell sounded for supper. Led by Aunt Mona, the girls marched to the dining hall, a large austere room containing four wooden tables with bleached white surfaces standing end to end in two rows. Mother Superior and her nuns sat at a fifth table placed strategically to provide optimum surveillance of the girls. The whitewashed walls were devoid of decoration except for a large picture of the Virgin Mary wearing a halo and a sweet smile. Brigid gazed at the picture and wondered what the Mother of Jesus Christ was doing in a place like this. They ate their meal of fish, vegetables, buttered bread, and tea in silence. At five thirty the Mother Superior rang a bell signaling the end of the meal. Brigid was thankful that the day was over. Then she discovered that it was back to the wash house until seven before retiring for the night.

For the next week Brigid endured the monotonous, back-breaking work of washing, scrubbing, and bleaching an avalanche of sheets, tablecloths, shirts, aprons, and other sundries disgorged from a van that visited the laundry daily. On its return journey the van carried away large wicker baskets stacked with clean clothes taken from the sorting room.

At the end of each ten-hour day Brigid fell asleep as soon as her head hit the pillow. By the end of the third week she had adapted to the routine and forged a solid friendship with Lily. She also discovered that not all the nuns were like Ursula. One in particular, Sister Dorothy, was more relaxed about the rule of silence when it was her week to supervise the wash house. She allowed several five-minute work breaks during the day. Also, Lily had grown close to Sister Dorothy. More than once Brigid observed them deep in conversation.

After one such session Lily returned to her workplace. "Remember you asked me if anyone ever tried to escape?"

Brigid had hesitated to bring the topic up again.

Lily fixed her with a sharp gaze. "You can swim, right?"

Brigid brushed back a wisp of hair with a sudsy hand. "I'll say. I've spent more time in the water than a duck in the last month."

"Good, because if you couldn't there'd be no point in telling you

143

this." Visions of her trip across the channel hanging on to the pony flashed before her eyes.

Lily looked around, apparently to check Mona's whereabouts. "When I told Sister Dorothy your story, she was horrified. She agreed with me that your life is in greater danger the longer you stay here, so she wants to help us both escape."

"How're we going to do that?"

"Haven't figured that out yet, but our options are limited. Either we scale the wall or we sneak out through the main gate."

Out of the corner of her eye Brigid saw Mona moving toward them. "Shh."

Mona stopped behind them and with the tip of her cane lifted the shirt Brigid was scrubbing. "Put more elbow grease into it or go without supper," Mona smacked the cane against the folds of her calico dress.

"Bitch," Lily whispered when Mona moved on.

Brigid suppressed a giggle. "But the wall must be twenty feet high, and the gate's got an alarm on it."

"I know. That's the reason I don't have much of a plan, yet."

"Then why'd you ask if I could swim?"

Lily vigorously rubbed a bar of soap over an apron on the washboard. "Because the crazy notion I have in my head involves swimming."

Brigid frowned. "Is crazy another word for real dangerous?"

"It's not quite as bad as that, but it's risky. It involves jumping from our dormitory window into the river."

"Jesus! How far to the river?"

"A long way, and the water may not be deep enough to accommodate the plunge," Lily said.

"I feel better already."

"Knew you would."

Brigid straightened and pressed her hand against the small of her back. "What about Sister Dorothy? Couldn't she help us with this?"

"She'll provide us with traveling clothes and money and assign a friendly minder to our dormitory who won't raise the alarm the night we make a break for it."

"Great good that will do if she can't figure a way to get us out of here," Brigid whispered, her voice shrinking with disappointment.

"I know, but that's as far as she's willing to go. She's scared. We've got to figure a way out on our own."

The wash house echoed with sounds of water sloshing, washboards croaking, and workers coughing. Clouds of steam drifted upward and escaped through the stunted windows. Perspiration glistened on the girls' faces. Outside the light faded.

***

That night as she lay tossing and turning, it occurred to Brigid that there might be an easier way into the river than from the dormitory window. The row of tubs against the back wall of the wash house lay over the water. At one end of that row, near the washing supply shelves, an iron grate was embedded in the floor through which, in bygone days, the girls had hauled buckets of water from the river to fill the washtubs. Modern plumbing had replaced buckets, so it was no longer used. What if she or Lily could squeeze through the opening?

At her workstation next morning, Brigid, on the pretext of getting additional bars of soap, made her way toward the supply shelves. She used the opportunity to inspect the size of the iron grate. Back at her workstation she eyed Lily surreptitiously to assess her bodily dimensions. Then she leaned over and whispered, "I'm not a hundred percent certain, but I think we could slip through the grate with a slather of soap around our butts."

Lily stood bolt upright and took a quick look around the room. Mona had stepped outside. "What the hell. Speak for yerself, Miss Fat Arse." Both dissolved into laugher, and when the spasm ended they were surrounded by disapproving looks. Lily fixed her coworkers with a wicked stare. "What's the problem? Mind yer own business."

The tramp of heavy boots outside sent everyone scurrying back to scrubbing. Mona entered the room and resumed her patrol.

Lily whispered. "Not a bad plan. Unfortunately it introduces an additional problem."

"Which is?"

"Getting in. We have to get in before we can get out."

A puzzled look crossed Brigid's face. "What?"

"The wash house is under lock and key at night." Lily glanced around anxiously, to see if their whispering had attracted Aunt Mona's attention. The old lady nodded on a chair near the front door, her vigilance sabotaged by the swirling clouds of steam. Seeing Brigid's crestfallen face, Lily leaned over. "Not to worry. Sister Dorothy should be able to help with that quandary."

Brigid's eyes brightened. "How soon do you think we can get out of here?"

"Believe me, I'm for blowing this joint right away, but we'll have to check with Sister Dorothy before doing anything."

"You said she was scared. I hope she doesn't have second thoughts."

"If you believe in prayer, say a few that she doesn't."

Next day Lily didn't show up at her workstation. *Had she fallen ill?* When she didn't appear on the following day or the day after that, Brigid considered the worst: Mother Superior had discovered their plan, and she was being punished. Or worse still, they had moved Lily to another institution. It was only a matter of time before they came for Brigid too.

Chapter 28

Washboards, Minders, and Calico

At the end of three days, Lily showed up at her accustomed station. Brigid couldn't hold back tears of joy.

"God I'm sorry, Brigid," Lily whispered. "I did a stupid thing. I've been on punishment detail for the past three days."

Brigid's voice trembled from anxiety and relief. "What happened?"

"I got into a fight with another girl in the dormitory after lights out, and I spent three glorious days on my knees scrubbing floors."

"Oh, I'm sorry," Brigid said, relieved that their plan hadn't been compromised, but sad that her friend had been punished.

"Don't be. I used my time well. We're all set to go tonight."

Brigid shook her head, "No." How could she be ready that soon?

"It's got to be tonight. Sister Dorothy is being replaced in the supervision rotation tomorrow by Sister Ursula. And you know what that means."

Lily described one of her punishment chores: scrubbing and waxing the hallway in the nuns' quarters that ran past Sister Dorothy's bedroom door. On the pretext of having her room waxed, the nun invited Lily inside. Once there, Lily shared her escape plan. Over the next few days Sister Dorothy pulled together traveling clothes for the girls and money to cover bus fare and food.

Most importantly, she handed Lily a key to the wash house door.

Lily straightened and looked around. Mona was nowhere in sight. "Here's the plan. Put on your bathrobe and go to the toilet at eleven o'clock tonight. Carry your boots in your hand. That will be the signal for the minder to unlock the dormitory door. Don't worry, she's on our side. If you run into anybody, tell her the toilet in the dormitory is blocked and you're going to the one on the first floor. I'll be waiting for you downstairs in front of the main door."

Brigid looked around as inconspicuously as she could. She reached into her calico pocket, took out an apple, poked Lily in the ribs, and passed it to her.

"My God, where did you get this?" She stole a bite and passed it back to Brigid.

"I whipped a few from the orchard the day after you disappeared, when we were hanging out the wash."

"You could spend a week scrubbing floors for this, but good on ye and give us another go."

They passed it back and forth until there was nothing left but the core, which Brigid broke up and flushed down the sink. Spirits lifted, they left the wash house at quitting time, more hopeful about the greater challenge ahead of them.

***

Brigid had to pinch herself to stay awake. Fear and excitement consumed her. At last the downstairs clock struck eleven. Slinging her shoes over her shoulder she tiptoed among the snores to the toilet. There she blocked the bowl with a roll of toilet paper to provide an excuse if challenged for going to the first floor. When she reached the dormitory door she found it unlocked. The minder was nowhere in sight.

She pushed open the door and stepped onto the landing. At the bottom of the stairs Lily emerged from the shadows carrying two bundles wrapped in oilskins, one of which she handed to Brigid. After putting on their boots, they slipped through the Gothic front door and

148

dashed across the gravel compound to the wash house. A full moon sailed from behind a cloud, bathing the compound in a silvery light. They hustled to get into the shadow of the building. Accessing the wash house wasn't a problem, since Sister Dorothy had provided them with a key. Lifting the heavy iron grate was another matter. It wouldn't budge. Through the grate they saw moonlight glistening on the fast-flowing river about three feet below.

"There's gotta be something here to pry this loose," Lily said. "Pity we can't turn on a light."

Then Brigid remembered old man Cummings, the maintenance man. He worked out of a utility closet at one end of the wash house when he came to fix the boiler that generated power for the steam presses. She mentioned this to Lily. "By God, you're the observant one. I've been here two years and I didn't know that."

Aided by the moonlight streaming through the stubbed-wing windows, they found a spanner hanging from a hook on the utility closet wall. They inserted its head between the bars of the grate and rocked it back and forth until it began to give. A few more heaves and it sprang free.

Easing the grate out of its casing, they slid it away from the opening. "What happens now?"

Lily narrowed her eyes. "'What happens now?' Are you joking? We drop into the bloody river and swim for our lives. That's what happens." Lily shook her head and continued. "We're aiming for a railway bridge that crosses the river about a half mile downstream. A hundred yards beyond that is a little cove with fishing boats. One is a cabin cruiser named *Ave Maria*. That's where we'll spend the night."

"Wouldn't it be easier and less dangerous to swim to the opposite bank and walk to the little cove?"

"Here's something you wouldn't know but I do. The riverbank directly across from the wash house rises about six feet and is covered with whin bushes that could tear you to shreds. You know, the ones with the beautiful yellow flowers that conceal prickly thorns underneath. Kinda like Mother Superior. Sweet smile on the outside, claws on the inside. It doesn't level off until beyond the railway bridge."

Brigid winced. "Thought I'd ask."

"That's okay," Lily replied. "Besides, it'll be less exhausting to drift with the current than to climb that bank."

They stripped to their underwear at the edge of the grate. Now came the test. Would they get through or get stuck in the opening and have to wait ignominiously to get rescued when Aunt Mona unlocked the wash house door a few hours from now? Brigid recoiled at the consequences. Lily made the sign of the cross on her forehead and lowered herself through the opening, pulling the oilskin bundles behind her. She made it, but barely. Brigid was not as lucky. Having more meat on her bones, her hips got stuck.

"Jaysus, hurry up; I'm freezing," Lily hissed from the river.

"Can't. I'm stuck."

"The soap, the soap."

"What?" Lily's voice was muffled by the sound of the rushing water.

"The fucking soap!"

"Oh right." Brigid extricated herself from the opening and retrieved a bar of Dirt Shifter soap from an adjacent washbasin. She turned the tap on it and lathered up. Next she soaped the iron rim of the opening. This time she almost got through . Lily grabbed her legs and pulled. Brigid hit the water as if shot from a cannon. They tied the bundles to each other's chests with the belts from their bathrobes. When they moved away from the bank, the strong current swept them into the middle of the river. Lily's head bobbed in front of Brigid on the moonlit surface. Lily was a strong swimmer. The gap between them grew. Frightened of losing her, Brigid quickened her pace and was surprised at the buoyancy of the oilskin bundle. But it was a two-edged sword. On the one hand it helped her stay afloat, but it was also a drag on her forward movement. When she lost sight of Lily, she readjusted the oilskin bundle, moving it to the small of her back. This allowed her arms more freedom of movement. In a burst of nervous energy she doubled down on her strokes. So intent was she on catching up to her friend that she hadn't noticed the current pulling her toward the shore with the tall embankment.

Something scratched her leg. It was her first clue that she'd drifted off course. Without warning she found herself amid a tangle of waterlogged tree branches and abandoned fishing nets. What lurked beneath the black water was of more concern. She lunged toward midstream. A sharp tug at her midsection pulled her back. She tried again but failed to break free of whatever anchored her. She slid her hands down her waist and discovered the belt of her bathrobe pulled taut toward the river bottom. Shifting the oilskin bundle must have loosened the belt, allowing it to trail freely until it got snagged on some underwater obstacle.

She took a deep breath, ducked beneath the water, and began pulling on the belt. It moved, but when she tried to surface only her head broke through. Whatever was holding her had shifted into deeper water pulling her down. With her mouth barely above water she found it difficult to take deep breaths. She began to tire. The underwater obstacle continued to move. It pulled her deeper until her head slipped below the surface.

Chapter 29

Caught in the Undertow

Desperately she clawed at the oilskin pack. Images of a grieving mother passed before her eyes. The sounds of escaping breath bubbled from her mouth. Down to her last reserves of oxygen. In a final heave she yanked the pack around to her stomach and pulled it free of the restraining belt. She kicked her feet in a frantic lunge and shot to the surface, sucking air in great gasps.

Lily had disappeared. She flipped on her back to rest, and she let the current carry her for a spell, all the while keeping a wary eye out for the embankment. The water had gotten colder, and the cold seeped into her bones. The abrasions on her hips from the grate opening stung. She would have to get out soon, doubled-arched bridge or not. She flipped back over and did the sidestroke. It was less demanding than freestyle. Her first break. The double-arched railway bridge loomed in the darkness. Under the bridge the river narrowed and the current strengthened. Beyond the bridge the river widened again and the going got easier. This had better be the right place, because she was done in. Even if Kincaid was there to meet her, she wouldn't put up a fight. She let the current sweep her under the bridge. When it slowed, she made her way over to the little cove.

"Over here, over here." A shadowy figure stood on a boat, shouting and waving its arms. Brigid swam toward it, clawed her way up the anchor rope, and collapsed alongside Lily on the dilapidated deck of the *Ave Maria*. She lay there panting and trying to control her anger. She felt Lily had abandoned her.

"Where's your pack?"

Brigid didn't answer.

Lily bent over her. "Are you okay?"

Brigid had a fit of coughing. "No thanks to you."

"I'm sorry. The current was stronger than I anticipated. I figured if the worse came to the worst, the oilskin bundle would keep you afloat."

Brigid staggered to her feet and faced Lily. "The oilskin bundle nearly did me in."

Lily's eyes narrowed. "What?"

In heaving sobs she related her ordeal in the river. Lily took her in her arms and began to cry. "My God. I am sorry. I am so sorry."

They clung to each other for a while in silence. Brigid felt as if the life were draining from her body, but she couldn't remain angry at Lily forever. They needed each other to survive.

Lily wrapped an arm around Brigid's shoulder. "Let's get you in out of the cold. It's freezing. You'll catch your death."

She opened the cabin door and led Brigid inside. The interior wasn't much to look at. A torn muslin curtain hung limply from a porthole window. A ratty frayed mat covered the floor. But it offered protection from the elements. Best of all, there were no washtubs or screaming nuns.

Lily dug into her oilskin bundle. "Lucky for you I brought some extra clothes. Since we're about the same size, these should fit." She handed her a woolen jumper and a plaid skirt. "Take off your underwear and put these on. We'll dry our underwear in the morning sun."

A little smile crept across Brigid's face. "With my luck it'll be pouring rain in the morning."

After putting on dry clothes and eating a few of the sandwiches, they felt revived and less antagonistic toward each other. They slept snuggled together on the floor under a thin blanket, not minding the discomfort. What discomfort? It was their first night of freedom!

Brigid awoke to the sun streaming through the little porthole. Lily was already outside scouting the road along the riverbank. Brigid didn't know how late it was, but sensed it was mid-morning. If so, news of their escape had been out for hours. Since they hadn't replaced the grate in the opening, it would be apparent they had fled by way of the river. This made her nervous, because she was sure that by now the mother superior had alerted the authorities. She didn't mention her fears when Lily returned. They discussed the next part of the plan.

"I hung our underwear out around seven this morning. They're practically dry already," Lily sputtered through mouthfuls of what remained of the ham and egg sandwiches.

Brigid leaned over and touched Lily's hand. "I'm sorry for getting mad last night."

"You had every right. I've had to fend for myself so long that I'm not great when it comes to thinking of others."

Brigid took a bite of sandwich followed by a gulp of water. "I hope when this ordeal is over we can remain good friends."

Lily had a faraway look in her eyes. "Yeah, maybe."

They continued eating in silence. This could be their last meal for some time. Lily wiped her mouth with the back of her hand and stood up. "Okay. Time to talk about what happens next. First things first." She pulled two pairs of new sneakers from a duffel bag. "Sister Dorothy figured we'd need footwear after the river."

"Oh, thank God. I was worried how it would look walking along the road barefoot."

"Speaking of roads. The main road is two fields up from here, but right now it appears deserted. According to Sister Dorothy, the bus to Cloonfin comes by here between ten and a quarter after."

Brigid knitted her eyebrows. "But we don't know the time."

Lily raised her right hand and extended two fingers. "Hold on." She pulled a small waterproof pouch out of her pocket and extracted a wristwatch from it.

"Sister Dorothy thought of everything. I'm beginning to think she must have worked in a prison," Brigid said.

154

Lily threw back her head and laughed. "She already *is* working in a prison." She checked the watch. "It's half past nine. That gives us sufficient time to gather our things together."

Brigid giggled. "Things, what things? We've nothing but the clothes on our backs. And even those aren't ours."

"Borrowed or stolen at that."

The smile faded from Brigid's face. "Do you think they'll follow us?"

"Unusual if they didn't. That's what makes me nervous about that bus."

"Then why are we taking it?"

Lily stepped from the boat to the river bank. "Because I believe in luck, and I think the Almighty owes us some. Don't you?"

"I believe in luck too, but if the last few weeks are any guide, I don't expect to get any."

"It's not likely to come calling if we don't get out of here. Let's get a move on."

Brigid put the tips of her fingers to her cheeks. "Wait, what about our underwear?"

"Oh, begod, aye. Gotta have underwear on in case we get killed. Wouldn't want to scandalize the good people of Cloonfin."

Brigid cracked a big smile. They dressed hurriedly. Lily led the way through the fields to the main road.

The whine of the Leyland engine echoed through the quiet countryside long before the bus lurched into view. Brigid caught the whiff of petrol fumes. The driver, in response to their raised hands, brought the vehicle to a halt with a mournful squealing of brakes.

The girls settled into a double seat. The conductor approached. "Where to?"

Lily looked up. "Cloonfin." The conductor cranked out two tickets from a dispenser hanging around his neck.

Lily produced the required fare for both of them. The bus moved forward.

As it picked up speed, Lily looked behind her. "There's a vacant seat near the rear door." She got up and beckoned Brigid to follow her.

"Better to be close to an exit in case we have to make a quick getaway."

Over the course of a half hour the bus made several stops to pick up passengers. Most of them, as far as Brigid could tell, were old-age pensioners traveling for free. The vehicle lumbered along, swaying and rocking into the turns of the country road. Brigid dropped off to sleep. An elbow in the ribs from Lily. She woke with a start. The bus had stopped to pick up two young men who sat in a seat near the middle. They both wore grey felt hats and double-breasted suits. The younger of the two had a thin moustache giving him a gambler's look. The older man's face puckered in a scowl.

These two were definitely not pensioners. Brigid noticed something odd: the conductor never asked them for a fare. "Be ready to move when I give the signal," Lily whispered.

The one with the moustache walked up front, leaned over the bus driver's shoulder, and whispered into his ear.

"Did you notice that, Lily?"

"Do you think I'm blind?"

At the next passenger pickup, Lily murmured, "Let's go!"

She ran to the back exit and jumped out the rear door like a young gazelle. Brigid prepared to leap. A bony hand shot out and clutched her arm. The two young men raced to the back of the bus.

The pensioner lady who had seized Brigid wagged her finger. "I knew there was something suspicious about those hussies, especially the one with the short black hair. Looked like Maggies to me from the start."

She released her grip. The man with the scowl grabbed Brigid by the forearm and yanked her toward him like a hunter pulling a frightened rabbit from its burrow. The pensioner inserted a pinch of snuff from a little tin box into her nose. "God above, the country's going to rack and ruin."

"Thank you ma'am, we'll take it from here," the scowler replied. He and his companion grabbed Brigid by the forearms and escorted her from the bus. Lily had long since disappeared into the young pine forest that bordered the road.

***

Brigid struggled to convince the two detectives who she was, but they were unreceptive. The scowler scowled. "These tarts get younger all the time."

"It's not as if we have nothing else to do," his colleague replied as they brusquely led her from the small rural Garda station and forced her into the back seat of a waiting car.

"My name is Brigid Coltrane," she protested. "I was reported drowned in Lough Gorm a couple of weeks ago, except I wasn't."

They rolled their eyes without responding. The scowler slid into the back seat beside her, while his colleague got into the front and started the engine.

Brigid addressed the driver. "Where are you taking me?"

"Now, where do you think? Back to your Maggie friends at the laundry."

"No! Not to that place. They'll kill me." Tears spilled down her cheeks.

"They'll whip some sense into you, which is what your kind bloody well needs, is all," the scowler said. He gave directions on the shortest route to the Magdalene house.

A half hour later they drove through the laundry gates and pulled up to the side entrance of the large stone structure. Mother Superior and Sister Ursula were waiting. The detectives dragged Brigid from the car and turned her over to the waiting nuns. She flailed her arms and kicked, trying to wrest herself from their grasp.

"This one is quite a handful. Do you need any help getting her inside, Sisters?" the scowler asked.

The superior stared, her face a blank slate. "Don't worry; we know how to deal with her kind."

"Call my mother in Cloonfin," Brigid wailed at the departing detectives. "She'll tell you the truth."

The mother superior made eye contact with the detectives. She shook her head from side to side. With Sister Ursula's help, she dragged Brigid across the threshold, through the kitchen, and out another door into a small courtyard. A large black Bentley waited, its engine running. Brigid recoiled at the sight of Kincaid and Stiglitz. Stiglitz pressed a gauze pad over her nose and mouth. She struggled to twist her head away.

***

Kincaid bared his yellow teeth at the mother superior. "If it was up to me, you'd be handing that envelope back," he snarled as he and Stiglitz pushed Brigid's limp form into the car. "It appears the vaunted reputation of your establishment as a place of confinement is overblown."

He jumped into the driver's seat and slammed the door without waiting for a reply. As the car roared through the main gate, the superior, her gaunt face a mask of anger, turned to Sister Ursula. "Have Sister Dorothy in my office within five minutes. I don't like being made a fool of by a pair of sniveling outcasts."

Ursula's linen coif expanded as a crooked smile rippled across her plump face.

"Right away, Mother."

Chapter 30

Planned Execution

Kincaid put the Bentley in gear and raced down the road, swearing at high volume. "The minute we turn this little bitch over to our so-called allies, she manages to escape. I can't fucking believe it!"

He pounded his hands on the steering wheel. Stiglitz sat in the back with Brigid, pressing the rag over her mouth. "She's out, Boss."

"See that she stays that way until we get to the lake." He slammed the brakes to maneuver around a herd of cows. He looked over his shoulder while weaving through the lowing animals. "Can't credit this damn country. Why you people are interested in it is beyond me."

"I follow orders, Herr Kincaid. Not for me to say."

"Well, good luck in trying to subdue this lot, that's all I can say. We were at it for eight hundred years and made a proper bollocks of it."

For over an hour they sped down a country road fringed by towering pine trees so dense that the route was in perpetual shadow. They turned down a lane that ended in a sandy cove on the shores of Lough Gorm. Large antediluvian boulders lay strewn along its length on the sand and in the water, as if the gods had abandoned them in a fit of pique after a game of jackstones. Behind one, a motorboat bobbed at anchor. Brigid stirred. Stiglitz took the chloroform rag from his pocket.

Kincaid wore a rueful look. "Leave it, makes no difference now. Get her into the boat." While they maneuvered the boat through the rocks to deeper water, the whine of an engine intruded. "Let's get a move on. Someone's coming."

"Sounds like a motorcycle," Stiglitz said, guiding the boat toward the center of the lake.

Kincaid looked to the shore. "Take cover behind Red Cow Island. Don't want to risk being seen."

Brigid was fully awake and looking around her. Her voice quivered. "Where are you taking me?"

Kincaid bared his yellow teeth. "To meet your Daddy, luv. Don't you think he'll be happy to see his little girl, hunh?" He turned his back on her while screwing a silencer onto his pistol. His hand shook. His daughter's face swam before his eyes. Beads of sweat bubbled on his forehead. She'd be fifteen by now.

Two shots shattered the silence.

Stiglitz pointed at a man standing on the shore with a gun in his hand. "Mein Gott, who is that?"

Kincaid bristled. "Cusack, by God. Swing the boat around!" Brigid cowered before him, her eyes big as saucers as she faced the pistol pointed at her head.

Cusack waded out up to his hips to meet the boat. Fear etched his face. Behind him the Triumph Tiger lay on its side, petrol seeping from the tank. He stuttered."C-C-Coltrane's alive."

Kincaid shifted the gun away from Brigid's head and pointed it at Cusack. "I should kill you right here on the spot, you incompetent imbecile." Then he turned and shouted at the German. "Get her back in the car!"

As they walked to the Bentley, Kincaid turned and aimed the gun at Cusack struggling to right the motorcycle. "I thought I told you to burn that bike, you greedy bastard."

Cusack opened his mouth to reply, but before the words came out, Kincaid raised the Luger and fired twice. The bike's petrol tank exploded, pitching Cusack into the bushes.

***

When Cusack came to he was on his own. Apart from a pounding in his ears and a splitting headache, he had escaped serious injury. The Triumph Tiger lay gutted all along the lakeshore.

Chapter 31

Blueshirt Parade

The marchers assembled for the Blueshirt parade after second Mass on Sunday. They strutted about in their crisp uniforms, their shiny brass buttons and leggings polished to a glassy sheen. Their captain, P.J. Harrington, astride a black horse of dubious pedigree, barked orders at his subordinates. His potbelly, sagging like a roll of dough over his Sam Brown belt, marred the trim of his freshly pressed blues. His ruddy face and handlebar moustache, its extremities waxed into spikes, only reinforced the impression that the Blueshirts were not an outfit about to engage in trench warfare.

This comedic façade, however, did little to camouflage the Blueshirt enthrallment with Hitler's right-wing paramilitary organization, the Brownshirts, and Mussoulini's Blackshirts, after which they were patterned. Although the Blueshirts had not engaged in the violent tactics of their Continental counterparts, they might yet, many feared, given time and opportunity. Ads in the weekly newspaper and church bulletins had drummed up considerable interest in the event, as had word of mouth. A sizeable crowd consisting of both young and old lined the footpaths on either side of the parade route. A brass band tuned up with snappy kettledrum riffs and short trumpet blasts.

A man wearing a light gabardine coat and a brown hat pulled over his eyes mingled with the onlookers. He did not engage in any chitchat or pleasantries. Coltrane was taking a risk coming to Cloonfin in broad daylight, but he gambled that in a crowd swollen with strangers from the surrounding countryside there was a good chance he could move around incognito.

After his brush with death in Hayden's Wilderness and his narrow escape from Cusack's house, he had taken refuge with Lost John Toole. Information had come to him that one of Kincaid's Irish collaborators, the gillie Sweeney, had jumped ship and gone into hiding. Since Sweeney had fled from Kincaid's employ soon after Brigid was abducted, there was a chance he had knowledge of her whereabouts. It was a fragile hope, sure enough, but what else did he have? He avoided the Cloonfin guards, their ranks augmented by reinforcements from neighboring towns. They expected trouble. Across the street, Lost John moved through the throng, backslapping and glad-handing people he barely knew while foraging for information on Sweeney. Reagan and Paddy Cassidy kept an eye on the Blueshirts. They too expected trouble.

When Harrington raised his arm in a Roman salute, the march got under way, the brass band first, followed by the Blueshirt contingent. Several Saltire flags fluttered from the ranks of the marchers, but none from the onlookers. The more vocal spectators fell in behind the Blueshirts, and some gave the Roman salute, but most drifted along the footpaths, caught up more by the spectacle than by the politics of the event. Coltrane allowed himself to drift with the crowd, figuring it made him less conspicuous than if he stood apart from it. A commotion erupted at the head of the parade. The throng surged forward, dragging Coltrane with it. An angry IRA supporter had apparently unhorsed P.J. Harrington as the parade turned into the market square, where a public address system had been set up on the back of a lorry. That's all it took for the IRA crowd to charge the Blueshirt line. They ripped up their flags and sent the Blueshirts reeling into the discombobulated band members, whose trumpets and drums were soon commandeered as weapons. It took the guards thirty minutes to separate the combatants before finally restoring order. Both sides began shouting insults: "We don't want your Nazi tactics here!" the IRA crowd yelled, drawing choruses of "*Sieg Heil!*" and "*Heil* Hitler!" from the other side.

A bedraggled Captain Harrington attempted to mount the lorry and address his followers, but the guards quickly hustled him away. As the crowds dispersed, Coltrane felt something brush against his coat pocket. When he checked to see if the few pounds he carried were still there, he was surprised to discover a pack of Sweet Afton cigarettes, a brand he didn't smoke. Inside the pack, nestled among the cigarettes, he found a folded scrap of paper with the message *Meet me in the church after the Angelus bell rings. Got important information.* He looked at the faces in the crowd. Who had passed the note? Impossible to tell. He checked his watch: ten to twelve.

By the time he reached the church, the bell was tolling. Several people stopped to recite the Angelus, the customary midday prayer, but he forged ahead, arriving in front of the large Gothic doors as the last peals sounded.

Inside it was cool and quiet. Rays of sunshine pierced the rose-colored windows on either side of the nave, dappling the floor in patches of rainbow-colored light. As he walked up the center aisle, glancing from side to side, he appeared to be the only one in the church. A sharp knock to his rear. He turned and saw Oliver Dow, the church sacristan, standing in the choir loft. Dow beckoned him forward and pointed upward toward the belfry.

When Coltrane reached the choir loft, Dow's heavy footsteps sounded on the stairs above him. One of the sacristan's duties was to ring the bell at twelve and six o'clock every day. If Dow wanted a clandestine rendezvous, it was understandable that he would use the belfry. But even for an ex-Guard Dow was going a bit overboard on the secrecy thing, Coltrane thought. He checked the gun in his waistband.

Climbing the more than thirty steps to the tower winded him. He worried that he would be at a disadvantage in a confrontation, so he paused to catch his breath. The door to the belfry stood ajar. Dow stood inside with his back to the wall, facing the door. Although Dow was at least ten years older than Coltrane, he seemed unfazed by the climb.

Dow beckoned him in. "Sorry for the elaborate precautions, but you know the way it is."

Coltrane put out his hand as if to push the door open, but instead slammed his boot against it, sending it crashing back against the interior wall.

A scream came from inside; something clattered to the floor. Coltrane pulled his gun and stepped into the room. Dow's face turned ashen. He raised his hands. "I swear I had to—"

"Move!" Coltrane barked, motioning with his gun in the direction of the door. "Now pull it back and let's see what we have here."

Coltrane backed toward the other side of the room. The stout rope that descended from the great bell brushed his shoulder before disappearing through a hole at his feet. As he backed up farther he tripped over a young boy lying bound and gagged in a fetal position on the floor. His throat tightened. He thought it was Brigid.

During that moment of inattention a figure with a bloodied face emerged from behind the door and came at him with a knife. Dow retreated into a corner, his face a mask of fear.

The assailant circled him, brandishing the knife. "You're a hard man to kill, Herr Coltrane."

"That bump on your forehead has scrambled your brains, Kraut. I'm the one with the gun. Tell me where my daughter is, and I'll let you live."

The German laughed. "Kill me and you'll never find her."

He bared his bloodied teeth. Then he lunged. A sharp pop from behind brought him to his knees. Oliver Dow lowered the Luger that he'd recovered from the floor. Coltrane trained his gun on Dow and commanded him to bend down and place the pistol on the ground. Dow quickly complied.

He raised his open palms before his chest. "They threatened to kill my son if I didn't go along, I swear. Please, let me untie the lad."

"Go ahead, but then you better start talking."

Coltrane rolled the dead German onto his back and went through his pockets. Empty.

Hanging from the man's neck was a chain with a lightning-bolt insignia attached. He showed it to Dow, who now held his son tightly

165

in his arms. "Is this what I think it is?"

"That depends on what you think it is." Dow tightened his grip on the boy.

"Apparently we don't have a meeting of the minds here, Mr. Dow." He touched the barrel of his gun to Dow's forehead.

"It's … it's a Nazi symbol called a Sig Rune. I'm frightened, that's all."

"You've a right to be. Unless I get straight answers, you'll not walk out of this belfry."

"I'll tell you what I know, which isn't much."

"Let me be the judge of that." Coltrane waved his gun barrel in dead man's direction. "Who is he, and why is he here?"

"He's part of the German contingent working with Kincaid."

Dow went on to explain that the Blueshirts, as well as being Nazi sympathizers, were also tied to the English fascist groups under Oswald Mosley, with whom Kincaid was associated. He dabbed sweat from his forehead with a grimy handkerchief. "All these right-wing characters think Hitler is the Messiah, and they're waiting for him to establish a new order and cleanse Europe of communists, Jews, trade unions, and other riffraff."

Dow maintained that he was a low-level Blueshirt operative who had gotten himself drummed out of the guards for his extremist activities. Recently, however, he claimed to have a change of heart, which angered his overlords. When Kincaid and company cast around for bait to spring their trap, Dow's young son provided the leverage they needed for his father's cooperation.

Coltrane eyed him closely. "They abducted your boy, is that what you're saying?"

He nodded in his son's direction. "Got nervous that they were up to something, but I never thought that *he* might be in danger."

"I'm waiting. What happened?"

"When he didn't return from the shop yesterday, I knew something was wrong. That's when they told me what to do or else."

"Why didn't you report this to the guards?"

"What good would that do? They didn't make much of a shift to find your kid after the first few days, did they?"

"But they think Brigid drowned."

Dow curled his lip and laughed. "No they don't, or at least the higher-ups don't, and that's what counts. They know both of you are alive and have for some time."

"They've got a pipeline to Kincaid, then. That's the only way they could have found out that Brigid was alive. The news bulletin speculated about me having survived, but it didn't include her."

Dow looked at the dead German and then out the belfry window. "I suspect so. However, the mischief here runs deeper than you think. Finding you and your kid may have been the last thing the guards wanted."

That statement had the ring of truth to it, Coltrane thought. Collusion between the guards and the Blueshirts (and by extension Kincaid) wasn't as farfetched as it seemed. After all, the first commissioner of the Guarda was also the founder of the Blueshirts.

Coltrane still didn't lower his gun, but he did raise his voice. "You *suspect*. Then how did you find out about it?"

"Oh, you know, I heard it being kicked around by some of Kincaid's lieutenants."

Coltrane narrowed his eyes. "Is that a fact?"

"If it's okay with you, I need to get away from here fast, and I suggest you do the same. They'll be waiting for word from the German."

"Or from you."

"Don't think so. My hunch is that after the German took care of you, me and my young fella were next."

Coltrane lowered his gun and they hurried down the stairs.

"Your note said you had important information for me—or was that a come-on to lure me into the trap?"

"You know, you can be too suspicious for your own good, Mr. Coltrane. The word is out that you're looking for the gillie Sweeney. As luck would have it, the other day I was on an errand for the abbot to Kiltrustan Parish and the sacristan there told me that Sweeney attended Mass at Kiltrustan the previous Sunday."

Coltrane returned the gun to his waistband. "Does Kincaid know this?"

"Not from me he doesn't. I knew that they were trying to get their hands on Sweeney, but I said nothing. Now I need to be away; it's not safe around here anymore. You don't know who to trust. Good luck."

Dow and the kid disappeared around McHale's corner.

***

Dow removed his arm from the boy's shoulder and grabbed him tightly by the forearm. "Give me what's comin' to me," the boy said, struggling to free himself.

Dow snarled and yanked him off the road toward a vacant lot choked with long weeds and enclosed by a dilapidated stone wall. "You'll get what's coming to you all right, don't worry, you little beggar." A rusty galvanized shed stood in one corner, almost concealed by the weeds. Things had gone terribly wrong. Coltrane was supposed to be dead by now, not the German. But there was nothing else he could have done. Knowing Coltrane's reputation, he was scared to take him on, but if the German started talking the game would have been up. He killed the Kraut to save his own skin. To sound convincing he was forced to reveal information that might cost him his life if he didn't make good on his promise to get rid of Coltrane.

His fingers closed around the ebony-handled knife in his pocket. There was one more loose end to take care of. He'd hide the boy's body. Who would waste much time looking for a missing gypsy? After this he'd lie low at home for the night. Although it was getting dark, he glanced around a few times to see if anyone was watching. As he struggled to push open the shed door with his left hand, the boy planted a kick on Dow's shin with his hobnailed boot. "Fucking little get!" Both hands shot to his wounded ankle, allowing the boy to pull free. The young gypsy dashed through the long weeds and scaled the wall like a rabbit. He disappeared into the woods.

Dow hobbled toward the wall, but he knew it was useless. Even if he could run, he would never find the boy in those woods. He limped home by a shortcut and entered his house through the back door. His wife would be asleep by now, so he decided not to risk waking her. He stretched out on the couch in the sitting room after setting the alarm for 5:00 a.m.

Chapter 32

Adair's Sawmill

Paddy Cassidy spent the night in jail for unseating P.J. Harrington from his mount at the parade. The authorities charged him with assault and battery, conspiring to incite a riot, and hooliganism, the last a catch-all in case the authorities missed anything. Harrington demanded a public apology.

"Hell no!" was Cassidy's quick reply. The incident might have landed him in the county jail had it not been for the intervention of Seamus Reagan, who convinced Sergeant Cullen that Cassidy's continued incarceration would only add fuel to an already inflammatory situation, not only in Cloonfin, but throughout the county. Added to that was Cullen's questionable decision to give Harrington a parade permit in the first place, given the bad blood between the Blueshirts and the IRA.

Consequently Cassidy was released on his own recognizance, on the promise of good behavior.

Such was the state of affairs next morning when Coltrane and Lost John approached Gerald Adair's sawmill along the Bella Coric River. Located two miles from the town, the mill had been down for a month owing to a drop in the Bella Coric's water level. The large undershot water wheel, which powered the mill and towered ten feet above the building, stood motionless. Pushing through the outer doors they followed footprints in the sawdust, past stacks of lumber and the silent belted wheels that drove the huge circular saws. They climbed a wooden stairway on the back wall to the second storey, which housed Adair's base of operations. At the top of the steps they entered a room with several windows allowing close-up views of the mill wheel, its buckets empty like the outstretched hands of mendicants. Adair's desk sat in one corner and tucked beside it, a swivel chair with a broken wheel. A bookcase containing thick binders ran along the back wall. Reagan and Cassidy sat at a round table in the center of the room, smoking.

Reagan had picked this spot for the hastily convened IRA meeting because of its isolation. Adair, his friend, lent him the mill. The acrid smell of cigarette smoke, combined with the odor of pine resin from milled planks, made Coltrane's sleepless head spin. As they began their deliberations a shaft of sunlight permeated with dust bathed the table in a yellow glow.

Reagan snuffed out his cigarette. "Coltrane! Where the hell did you disappear to yesterday?"

"From what I heard, you had your hands full without worrying about me."

"Just the same, it would've been nice to know you were still alive."

"That's the point, Seamus," Lost John said. "He came damn close to not being." Coltrane related his encounter with Oliver Dow and the German. That quickly shifted the focus of attention. It also let Cassidy temporarily off the hook with Reagan, furious at his hotheaded behavior during the parade.

As Coltrane and Lost John settled in around the table, Reagan spoke. "Our friend Coltrane apparently has as many lives as a cat. First there's his brush with death on Red Cow Island. Next he's nearly buried alive in a bog, and now this thing in the church belfry. One wonders if his run of luck is near played out." A wave of nervous laughter rippled through the group.

Coltrane's face took on a sad expression. "Luck, is that what you call what I've been going through? Well, whatever it is, I hope it lasts long enough for me to see my kid again. Still no closer to finding her, though."

"Not so sure about that," Reagan said, looking a little chastened. "Cusack and Dow's involvement with both Kincaid and the Blueshirts confirms our suspicions that these two groups are working hand in hand."

Coltrane held his arms out. "Old news. Kincaid and the Blueshirts are in cahoots. So what."

Lost John scraped the bowl of his pipe with a penknife. "To my mind, it also confirms something else,"

Reagan threw Lost John a hard look. "What?"

"Cusack and Dow both work for the Church." He pressed tobacco into the bowl from his pouch.

"Circumstantial evidence at best. We have no direct proof the Church is involved," Reagan said.

Lost John cracked a match and lit his pipe. "The welt on Coltrane's head is proof enough for me." He puffed vigorously, wreathing the table in a blue cloud of sweet-smelling smoke.

Coltrane shifted his weight. "Lost John may be on to something. The Church financed a Blueshirt contingent to fight alongside fascist forces in Spain. But if the guards are implicated in this unholy alliance, it makes it more lethal."

"That's Dow's story, but how trustworthy is Dow?" Cassidy asked. "After all, he's a 'blow in' to Cloonfin. No one knows that much about him except that he was bounced from the guards. Not great credentials for criticizing your former employer."

"Maybe, but at least one pillar of the community trusts him," Coltrane said."Who?" Reagan asked.

"The Church."

"Hunh!" Lost John leaned back in the chair, puffing his pipe. "That tells us more about the Church than about Dow, which is the point I was trying to make earlier."

Footsteps on the ground floor. Cassidy jumped up and cracked the door. "It's all right, it's only Law."

When Brendan Law, the moonshiner from Hayden's Wilderness,

trudged into the room, he looked exhausted and irritated. Before sitting, he shook Coltrane's hand.

Reagan cocked his arm to look at his wristwatch. "Glad you could make it. We missed you at the parade yesterday."

"So which complaint do you want me to address first: why I'm late, or why I missed yesterday's fiasco?" He sank into a chair and threw his cap on the floor, forging ahead without waiting for a reply. "All I can say is *mea* friggin' *culpa* to the first and not on your life to the second, although I confess I'm sorry I missed seeing Cassidy toss Harrington on his arse in the gutter."

That brought a round of guffaws, which Reagan skipped due to his irritation with Cassidy, who bit his lip to avoid joining in the merriment and undermining his sham contrition.

After a moment of awkward silence, Coltrane pulled a photo of Arthur Cusack from his pocket and threw it on the table. "Any further word of this joker?"

"He's disappeared," Reagan replied. "The abbot stonewalled when Wyker paid him a visit, and nearly ran him off the property. As far as he was concerned, Cusack was an ex-employee and no longer any of his concern."

Coltrane shook his head. "Not disappeared. Gone into hiding, more like it. I'm convinced he's the local snitch."

"We're not giving up on him, I hope—I mean on Cusack," Lost John said.

"We're not giving up on either Kincaid or Cusack. Wyker's assignment is to find them," Reagan said.

"Let's hope he has better luck than I had," Coltrane said, putting Cusack's photo back in his pocket. "Lost John and I have to be on our way. We're on the hunt for Sweeney. Any word on him, Brendan, from your neck of the woods?"

"Not so far. But I'm confident that when Sweeney surfaces my boys will hear about it."

Coltrane turned to Reagan, disappointment showing in his eyes. "Could we hurry this up a little? I'm anxious to get moving."

"We're almost done. One other national item that may have

significance for us locally ..." Reagan paused to cough.

"Get on with it," Coltrane said.

"I'm assuming you've all heard about the march on Dublin?" He scanned the faces arrayed around the table.

"Who's doing the marching?" Law inquired.

"Mainly Blueshirt units from across the country. The march here in Cloonfin was merely a preview of the big event by our local branch."

Coltrane rose to his feet. "Well, I hope the outcome is the same."

Law started laughing. "It will be if Cassidy attends. Jaysus, what's this country comin' to? On the one hand you have the guards playing hide-and-seek with the law, and on the other this bunch o' fools strutting about in their uniforms and shiny boots supporting Hitler."

"The word is, it's going to be quite a spectacular event—mounted riders, bagpipe and accordion bands, the whole fucking show," Reagan said.

Law held Cassidy's half-smoked cigarette between his nicotine-stained fingers to light his own. "A fucking show is what it is, nothing more. I wouldn't knock the hot coal off my foot to go see the bastards."

"Well, hot it's going to be for the likes of you gob shites when the Blueshirt General Sloan and his boys take over, I'll tell you that," Cassidy said, trying to get a rise out of Law. "He'll turn the kids in Fianna Eireann into the Hitler Jungen. And you better enjoy your gin and tonics now, your pints and your poitin, because there'll be damn little of either when Il Duce Sloan is running the show."

"Pray God it'll never come to that," Law said.

Reagan opened his eyes wide. "God will have little to do with it, as He has damn little to do with what's going on in Germany today. The march on Dublin may be the first step to see that it does come to that."

"When is this supposed to happen, anyway?" Law asked.

"Within a few weeks, I'm told, and it's making the Taoiseach and the boys a little nervous," Reagan said.

Cassidy made a quick inventory of Adair's office with his ferret eyes. "All this talk of conspiracy has gotten me a little thirsty. I don't suppose we have the makin's of a mug of tea in this joint, since there's nothing better to drink."

Law pulled a small flat bottle from his pocket. "Speak for yourself." He rummaged around until he found glasses in a cupboard, and poured a generous dollop of poitín into each.

"Good man yourself, Brendan." Cassidy grabbed a glass and threw back the contents with gusto. "Great stuff! Almost as good as me own." He wiped the back of his hand across his mouth.

"Apparently we're not going to be able to test that boast today, since you came empty-handed," Law shot back.

Taunts and laughs followed as the friends went for seconds. Coltrane forced himself to pass and settled on a mug of tea that he brewed from supplies in Adair's cupboard. The effort sprouted beads of sweat on his forehead.

By the time the meeting finished, the yellow shaft of sunlight, had eased off the table onto the floor. Lost John rose from his chair, walked over to one of the windows filled by the mill wheel, and gazed outside. He turned to Coltrane. "How old would you say Dow's son was?"

"Twelve, thirteen at the most."

"Well, now we got another problem."

"We do?"

"Yeah. All Dow's kids are in their twenties."

Chapter 33

The Undershot Waterwheel

Oliver Dow crossed the Bella Coric River at a shallow spot about five hundred yards upstream from Adair's sawmill, his presence shielded from the mill's occupants by the woods. Since the water level was low, he had little difficulty navigating from one stepping stone to another until he reached the opposite bank. In one arm he cradled a Gewehr rifle with a telescopic sight.

A twig snapped. He whipped around, bringing the gun waist-high, but the woods looked empty and quiet. He waded into the tall fern patches and checked the nearby stands of Scots pine dotting the riverbanks. *Must be an animal or my imagination.* Reversing direction, he followed the course of the river, sticking to tree cover until he was within two hundred feet of the big undershot water wheel.

The immobile wheel reminded him of Ireland's current predicament—bogged down and in desperate need of a new start. He felt he was on a mission to give it that start. What luck to have run into Brendan Law in O'Neill's shop while buying cigarettes earlier that morning! He didn't know Law well, but he knew he was a friend of Peter Coltrane's. Other than that, Law was known to be involved in the illegal whiskey trade. When Dow overheard Law telling the shopkeeper that he was late for a meeting with Seamus Reagan, he figured that where Reagan was, Coltrane might be too. So he followed Law to the sawmill.

Now he had to make a decision: go inside and see if Coltrane was there, or chance his luck and wait until Reagan and his IRA buddies came out. The latter was the smartest action because he could then pick off Coltrane from a distance and escape. But it involved biding his time and running the risk of coming up empty-handed if Coltrane was absent. Since he wasn't a patient man and couldn't tolerate uncertainty, he gave his rifle a final check and entered the sawmill.

Dow made his way to the bottom of the stairs, listening to the voices above. He mounted the first step. It squeaked. He would never make it to the landing undiscovered. Surprise was his main weapon; without that, the outcome was uncertain. Something else: judging by the voices upstairs, he guessed he was outnumbered by at least three to one. It was impossible to tell if one of those voices belonged to Coltrane.

He had to be certain that Coltrane was up there. So he hustled outside around the exterior of the mill, ending up at the base of the undershot water wheel. There he hit on the idea of climbing the buckets until he was parallel to the second-storey windows. Slinging the rifle over his shoulder, he began his ascent. Out of breath he reached a bucket across from a window. Huddled around a table were Reagan and his fellow subversives. Coltrane was walking toward them, mug in hand.

Dow's pulse raced. Unslinging his rifle, he lined up Coltrane's head in the crosshairs. He would have to be fast and get it done before the others reacted.

A high-pitched voice came from the ground. "Hey, Mister! Gimme what's comin' to me."

Panic roiled his gut. He swung the rifle around and pointed it downward. The young gypsy who kicked him in the shin stood at the base of the wheel, along with an older man. In a fury, Dow took aim.

The older man raised an arm over his right shoulder and in a blur of movement released a long thin knife. The blade caught Dow in the

Adam's apple, deflecting his shot into the river. He dropped the rifle and struggled to his feet before plunging headlong into a lower bucket. This caused the wheel to rotate downward until it deposited him at the gypsies' feet.

Coltrane and Lost John reached the bottom of the mill wheel in time to see the gypsies disappear into the woods. They turned the body over and wondered at the arabesque carvings on the knife handle in Dow's neck. Coltrane stared at the wood. "John, I think we better find Sweeney fast before the rest of my cat lives run out."

Chapter 34

Hunting Gillie Sweeney

A black van missing its front bumper turned off the tar road and sped down a narrow lane, kicking up loose stones and trailing clouds of dust. It skidded to a halt before a herd of cows meandering single-file into a farmyard. A young lad with a sally rod and a sheepdog brought up the rear and herded the last of the animals through a double iron gate, allowing the van to continue. As the vehicle pulled away, the young boy waved the sally rod in the air.

Lost John turned toward Coltrane. "Did you see the way that kid looked at you? I think he recognized you."

"And I think you're paranoid. The kid was being friendly. You've been saying that all day and it's getting on my nerves."

"Being cautious. That's all."

"Caution is a good thing, but it can be a pain in the arse. We have to take some risks if we ever hope to find Brigid." Coltrane shifted up to second gear.

They had been on the road for a week, checking with gillies and anglers across the lakefront for sightings of Sweeney. So far, no luck. They got some promising leads, hearing that he'd been seen in this pub or that, but at the end of the day Sweeney remained a phantom.

Then there was Dow's story, but given that Dow tried to kill him twice, Coltrane was skeptical about its value. He figured that fear had driven Sweeney underground. But he also figured that a gregarious fellow like Sweeney, known to be fond of a jar, would tire of life on the run and surface somewhere. The most likely spot for this resurrection would be in some pub off the beaten track. Coltrane had put together a list of all such pubs within a three-mile radius of Sweeney's last known residence.

Their greatest fear was that Kincaid had found Sweeney and eliminated him. However, Coltrane thought the odds were against that, since Sweeney's natural cunning and extensive knowledge of the area would enable him to stay hidden for a long time. When Brendan Law's sources reported that Sweeney was spotted eating at the Kiltrustan church presbytery, they took Dow's information more seriously. They arrived at the church early and chose the last pew under the choir loft, in case Sweeney came inside the church, figuring he would be less noticeable inside than outside with the stragglers, in full view of the world.

To be on the safe side, Coltrane left the pew and mingled with a dozen or so late arrivals who crowded into the space between the last pew and the back wall, next to the holy water font. Here he could keep watch not only on them, but on the late, late arrivals shuffling around outside the open doors. From time to time as the Mass progressed, Coltrane surreptitiously glanced outside, but no sign of Sweeney. This is nothing more than a wild-goose chase, he thought.

Then Sweeney appeared, all five feet eight of him, dragging his skinny frame up the steps. He glanced around furtively while slowly sliding his battered tweed cap off his head. As Coltrane turned around to get Lost John's attention, the booming voice of Father Moran, who had taken to the pulpit to deliver his sermon, filled the church.

"Half the eyes of the nation are gazing hypnotically into upturned porter glasses on any given Sunday after Mass." The crowd under the choir loft shuffled. "It's a disgrace. If Hitler decides to invade this country, he should strike after second Mass on Sunday." The volume of groans and nervous coughing elevated considerably as Moran stormed on.

Coltrane turned around again. Sweeney was gone. He alerted Lost John and, risking Father Moran's wrath, they dashed out of church in the middle of the sermon, but Sweeney had vanished. The few stragglers outside either saw nothing or were unwilling to say if they did.

Fresh from that disappointment, he and Lost John got back in the van and headed to the townland near Doyle's Cove to talk to Sweeney's parents.

***

Two miles from where they had encountered the herd of cows, they turned down a winding road and rolled to a stop alongside a gate near a large oak tree. Coltrane wiped the sweat from his forehead with the back of his hand. "This must be the place." The weather had been very close, and the heaviness of the day lingered long into the evening. Sweeney's parents lived four fields up from the road, a throwback to a time when living beside a road was regarded as dangerous.

A cart track ran through the fields to the house, and each field had a pass-through gate to the next. By the time Lost John had opened and closed all those gates, he was done in. After parking the van on a gravel patch in front of the little farmhouse, they walked toward the open kitchen door. A large black and white border collie came charging at them from a shed that stood at a right angle to the house.

An elderly woman with gray hair tied up in a bun came to the door, wiping her hands on a frayed apron and called the dog off. "Blackie, back inside." Sweeney's mother, Coltrane thought. The dog trotted meekly into the shed and lay at the door panting, tongue hanging sideways from its mouth, apparently content to watch the intruders rather than make believe he wanted to devour them.

After identifying themselves and asking to speak to Vinnie Sweeney, a gruff voice from inside shouted, "Stand in line with everybody else! You're not the first to come looking for our lad." A stocky, balding man is his sixties emerged from the kitchen wearing Wellingtons and a gray serge pants held up with red suspenders over a white shirt with blue stripes. Sweeney's father.

"How much you offering for information?"

180

"Nothing," Coltrane responded, a little taken aback by the man's attitude.

"Well, good, because we got nothing to give. We don't know where he is, and even if we did, why should we tell you?"

"A young girl's life may depend on what he knows."

"What's this little girl to you?" The man with the red suspenders asked in a milder tone.

"I'm her father, and—"

"Is our Vinnie in danger?" Sweeney's mother asked, fear showing in her eyes.

"He could be if the wrong people get to him before we do." Her face relaxed as she fidgeted with her hair. Visibly relieved, Sweeney's father went on, "We haven't seen him in weeks, and that's the God's truth. If he still likes his Guinness, and I've no doubt he does, you stand a chance of catching him in Duffy's Pub up on the Black Stick Road. That is, if he has any credit left with old man Duffy. I can't say for sure he'll be there, but it's as good a place as any to start, and a hell of a lot better than the places I sent those other chaps who came looking."

"So we aren't the first?" Coltrane said.

"Faith, you're Johnnie-come-latelies." He ran his thumbs under his suspenders. "Yesterday a big English fella in a black trench coat came sniffing around in a great black car. Sent him way to hell and gone on a wild-goose chase, I did." His belly heaved with laughter.

Sweeney's mother clasped her hands before her bosom. "And two days before that, two guards arrived, Sergeant Cullen and another fella." So we're in a three-way race here, Coltrane thought.

"Not to worry," the elder Sweeney said. "We didn't tell those damn guards nothing neither."

Coltrane's face brightened. He offered the Sweeneys his hand. "Thank you. You've been a great help." Then he and Lost John climbed into the van and retraced their steps to the road.

Duffy's Country Pub was a run-of-the-mill two-storey house with white pebble-dashed walls crowned by a slate roof. A Guinness toucan sign hung from a corroded metal frame bolted vertically to the wall over the front door. It creaked noisily in the wind, its rusty refrain only adding to the dreariness of the day. A wooden sign attached to the wall above the large plate-glass window simply said "Duffy's Pub." Cars and horse-drawn vehicles were parked haphazardly on a flat gravel area in front of the premises. The building itself was set back twenty feet from the road, against the backdrop of a large mountain with shoulders rounded down by a million years of ice. Sheep clung to its sides like little white dots grazing on the rough sedge in apparent defiance of the laws of gravity.

The pub was unique in one way: what you saw when pushing open the double doors was not a pub at all, but a room chock-full of hardware and grocery items randomly thrown together. Boxes of apples and tomatoes, along with blocks of country butter, shared the general space with hammers, pitchforks, and bags of nails. As far as anyone knew, no retail strategy dictated this arrangement, unless it reflected Steven Duffy's rough and ready attitude toward life in general.

As Coltrane and Lost John made their way through the outer shop, they passed a counter high enough that a child couldn't reach without standing on tip-toes. On the left stood a barrel filled with brooms, placed heads up. Beside that a half dozen blue-print aprons hung from a hook, and next to them stood a nested stack of galvanized buckets leaning to one side like the Tower of Pisa. The bar was back of this area, a small dingy place with a low-slung tongue-in-groove ceiling gone a sallow brown from half a century of cigarette and pipe smoke. Two strips of flypaper swung from it, looking like yellow tongues smeared with insects.

In a far corner, abutting the bar, was a women's snug—a small room with two entrances. One from the bar and one from the outside. A small pass-through window gave access to the bar. A woman could have a drink there in private. No one would be able to identify the disembodied hand that pulled back the shutter to retrieve the glass of sherry from the barman.

A few young fellows were throwing darts at a board on the back wall and several others sat on stools scattered throughout the pub, laughing and talking. Cigarette smoke spiraled toward the ceiling and hovered there, inert as winter fog. Coltrane and Lost John pulled stools up to

182

the counter and ordered two pints of Guinness. The clock over the bar mirror showed 10:15 p.m. Faced with the temptation to bury his face in a creamy pint, Coltrane caved again. Sweeney was nowhere in sight.

As they waited for their pints to settle, Lost John chatted up the barman, a young lad in his twenties with the beginnings of a moustache. He plied him about the goings-on in the neighborhood and the frequency of Garda raids after closing time. "I suppose you're kinda casual this far out about quitting time."

"Ah, begod, we stick to the regulations all right," he replied, looking over their heads to the bar beyond while wiping spillage off the counter top.

Lost John chuckled. "Oh! I know you stick to the rules, insofar as you close the doors on time, but since you're out here in the back of beyond, do you close the bar on time? That's the real question."

"Ara go way outa that, we may be off the beaten track, but we're not so far off that the guards don't drop in from time to time."

"You mean to tell me that if a few locals come calling after closing time, you wouldn't let them in?" The barman shrugged but didn't answer, running his fingers through his wavy red hair. Coltrane could tell by his body language that the answer was probably yes. "I'm right, amn't I, me boyo?" Lost John laughed before raising his glass and taking a long draught of his Guinness.

The barman lit up a cigarette. "I'm not saying we would or we wouldn't, but since you're not a local, the chances of you getting a pint in Duffy's after hours are next to nil."

"Way to go, young fella," Coltrane said. "Pay no heed to this amadán, him and his after-hours nonsense. Getting a rise outa ye is what he's doing, you can be sure of that." He took a long swallow from his pint.

"I can believe that; I see characters like him in here all the time." He dragged at his cigarette and looked askance at Lost John.

"After-hours nonsense, is it?" Lost John raised his voice and twisted around on his stool toward Coltrane. "You must think I have amnesia, and you spending most of your time in the boozers after hours before you went on the wagon, which by the looks of things didn't last till the water got hot. You and that fella Sweeney."

"You're daft, so you are. 'Most of the time'; will you listen to him? I'll tell you what, next time we see Sweeney, we'll get to the bottom of this," Coltrane said.

"I don't need Vinnie Sweeney to get to the bottom of it. I've been there with you on many occasions meself. Seriously! You need to take a run up to Doc Ford to get the old noggin checked."

The barman looked sharply at Lost John. "You mean Vinnie Sweeney from Curraghbawn?"

"The very same chap." Coltrane leaned in. "Why, do you know him?" "Kinda, he comes in here every now and then."

"There you go," Lost John shouted, slapping Coltrane on the back. "We'll settle this tonight when he walks through that door."

"I thought you said you didn't need Sweeney."

"I don't, but I'm not going to look a gift horse in the mouth all the same."

The barman laughed. "Well! Begod, you won't settle it tonight, gift horse or no. Sweeney only comes in here on Friday nights."

"Fair enough," Lost John replied. "Come Friday we'll be back here and settle this, once and for all."

"I can't, Claire doesn't get home from playing whist at the parish hall until after eleven, and I have to babysit until she does," Coltrane said.

Lost John smirked and adjusted his cap. "Which proves my point, you couldn't get to the pub before closing time even if you wanted to."

The barman took a pull from his cigarette and exhaled with a flourish. "You'll be time enough if you get here by twelve. Come to the back door and ask for Aidan," he whispered.

"Great," Coltrane said.

Lost John rubbed his hands together. "Five pounds that Sweeney proves me right."

"You're on."

"By the way," Lost John asked, turning to the barman, "Do you hold bets?"

"Can't; old man Duffy would have me head."

"Pity, because this cheapskate never pays when he loses."

So as not to arouse suspicion they each had another round before leaving. When they got outside, Coltrane turned to Lost John. "By God, you missed your calling; you should be in the Abbey Theatre, I swear to God."

"It worked, didn't it?" Lost John was hardly able to contain his excitement.

"Let's hope so."

They got into the car and headed back down the road to Shane Doyle's, where they had arranged to stay the night. They might nab Sweeney, if the barman was on the level and if their luck held. Two big ifs.

Chapter 35

The Canon's Radio

Canon Roach was a model of correctness, from the crown of his meticulously coiffured salt-and-pepper hair to the spit-polish shine of his expensive Oxfords. His outward appearance reflected his inner orientation. He observed the status quo unless it threatened his beliefs or lifestyle. He felt at home in the clerical world of ritual, deference to tradition, and adherence to religious orthodoxy.

On a warm August night he paced the floor of his second-storey study, waiting for the transmission from his Nazi overlord, Sturmbannführer Franz Adler. He glanced at his watch: sixteen minutes after midnight. Adler was ten minutes late. Not like him. The canon grew anxious, a bit irritated. As he awaited the coded message he adjusted and readjusted the dials on the ham radio to ensure that he was tuned in to the right frequency. He wasn't an expert in Morse code, which deepened his unease.

At last the radio came to life. He grabbed his fountain pen and quickly scribbled the essential parts of Adler's transmission. He acknowledged receipt of the message, but its contents startled him enough to ask for a re-transmission.

The second transmission confirmed that the commencement of

Operation Green had been moved up by a few days. This gave him considerably less time than planned to prepare to rendezvous with the submarine. The weather forecast for the night of the drop-off was rain with gale-force winds. Everything would become exponentially harder and more dangerous. He re-read the copied message again, put it face-down on the desk blotter, and rubbed his hand vigorously over it to dry the wet ink. He shut the radio down and set it inside the desk drawer. Then, fearing its discovery in his absence, he retrieved it and stowed it in the boot of his car.

Next morning after saying Mass, he packed his suitcase into the back seat of his Volkswagen, slid in behind the wheel, and drove off. His first stop was Glenfar Abbey, located about two miles outside Cloonfin. Abbot Jonathan, a tall hooded figure in a black habit, his hands tucked beneath his scapular, stood at the corner of a building to greet him. When the canon stepped from the car, the abbot removed his hood to reveal a sallow, gaunt face with a stubbly grey beard. He directed the canon to park inside a large double-doored barn in the cobblestone yard beyond an archway. "Your car will be safe here until you return." He helped the canon transfer his suitcase and ham radio into a larger vehicle. "The items you requested are already in the boot. I believe you will find them satisfactory, if the measurements you gave me are correct."

"Let's hope so, Abbot, because if not, we will be hard put to make on-the-spot adjustments in either the suits or the individuals they are intended for."

The abbot stiffened. "My remarks were not intended to question your competence, Canon, but more an expression of concern about the details of the operation, that must work together flawlessly for us to succeed."

"I think I can handle my responsibilities, Abbot."

The abbot's sunken eyes held the canon in an icy stare. "Well, then, I hope you know what you're doing with the radio. A slip-up in that department could land us all in a world of trouble."

The canon loosened his jacket, sat into the car, and started the engine. "As I said, I can handle my end of this; I suggest you worry about yours. I didn't request this assignment, Abbot. In fact, this change of plans could be a harbinger of disaster."

"My dear Canon, enough with the melodrama. Some of us are taking far greater risks than you. Keep in mind you are nothing more than a taxi driver. We all serve the same master." He traced the sign of the cross on his forehead before turning his back and disappearing beyond the arch.

The canon drove away, dismissing the abbot as a crank and a boor highly unfit for his position. Fortunately he was cloistered behind the walls of an abbey with limited exposure to the public. Yet he had the ear of the higher-ups. It rankled the canon.

***

After stopping at the coastal town of Westport for lunch, the canon crossed the Eriff River Bridge at three in the afternoon, about fifteen minutes from his destination. Around the next bend he ran into a checkpoint manned by two guards. *Damn! The ham radio!* He hoped he could bluff his way out of being searched or, failing that, explain why a priest would be transporting a ham radio. Maybe there was a chance these country guards wouldn't recognize it as a ham radio set.

One of the guards tipped his cap when the car stopped. "Good afternoon, Father."

"For your information young man, I should be addressed as Canon, or don't they teach you anything in the Academy? Now if you don't mind, I need to be on my way; I have little time for this silly nonsense."

Without waiting for a reply, he put his foot on the accelerator and moved forward. A Garda sergeant who had been leaning casually against a stone wall jumped in front of the car. "Stop the engine, Father, and get out."

"I'm on a sick call. Please clear the road at once."

"Strange, I'm not aware of anyone in these parts in need of the Last Rites. Now please get out of the car."

Realizing that he had put his foot in it, the canon stepped into the road. "Why in Heaven's name are you stopping me on a road to nowhere?"

"If it's going nowhere, then why are you on it? What's the name of the nobody that requires your services?"

"I apologize for the white lie, but I've been under a lot of stress lately and I was so anxious to get to my destination for a few days' holiday that I momentarily acted rashly. I have to confess, it's been happening too much recently, as my poor parishioners know only too well."

"What's your destination?"

"The Leenane Hotel on Killary Harbor."

"You don't have to tell me where the Leenane is." After a cursory search of the interior, the sergeant walked to the back of the car and pointed to the boot. "Open it."

Chapter 36

Duffy's Pub

Coltrane and Lost John left Shane Doyle's place and headed for Duffy's Pub on the Black Stick Road. The wind came in squalls with rain intermittent all day. "I hope we can conclude our business indoors," Coltrane said to Lost John, who sat puffing his pipe in the passenger seat. "I'd hate to be outside in this dirty weather." About a hundred yards shy of the pub, Coltrane eased the van off the road into a field entrance and killed the engine. "Sweeney might get spooked and take off if he saw a strange vehicle."

"Sound thinking. No point in taking chances."

Over the pub door the Guinness sign creaked back and forth. The place appeared closed for the night. They walked to the back entrance. Several bikes were parked under the trees. Lost John nodded toward them. "It's going to be one ugly ride home for these lads in this weather."

Coltrane knocked lightly on the door. When challenged, he answered, "Aidan." Inside the pub five or six locals sat on high stools chatting quietly before the bar. To avoid being dragged into a conversation they picked a spot in a corner where the lighting was bad.

Coltrane and Lost John ordered a round and waited. Coltrane checked his pocket watch. It was 12:15 a.m. Lost John whispered,

"Did you notice that there's a different barman?"

"Just as well. The fewer people in here who know us, the better."

At one o'clock, still no sign of Sweeney. Rain pounded the slate roof sounding like the roll of a kettledrum. As people came and went, they remarked how crazy it was to be out on a night like this. The minutes ticked by. Coltrane wondered if Sweeney hadn't thought the same thing and decided to give Duffy's a miss. Again, luck was against them. The barman announced the last round and Lost John went up to the counter to order. When he returned with the drinks, the look of disappointment on Coltrane's face must have been evident. In an apparent attempt to lighten the mood, Lost John inclined his head toward the end of the bar. "That's one tough woman in the snug."

"How so?" Coltrane asked indifferently.

"Well, in the course of an hour she's gone from glasses of sherry to pints of Guinness."

"Maybe she's had a rough day."

"Rough day or not, she's got to be one tough customer to be out alone on a night like this chasing her sherry with pints of Guinness."

Then it hit them. They jumped up, knocking Lost John's fresh pint to the floor in an explosion of glass and porter. As they burst into the snug, a door banged against a wall. Through the open rear entrance they saw Sweeney jump on one of the bicycles and take off down a by-road that skirted the side of the mountain.

Coltrane shouted above the noise of the wind. "Quick, John, you follow him and I'll go back and get the van!"

"Way ahead of you." John commandeered a bike and sped after Sweeney.

As Coltrane ran for the van, a late-night carouser yelled, "Me fuckin' bike's gone!" He stared bleary-eyed at the empty space under the tree.

Coltrane caught up to Lost John at a junction where a smaller road diverged and headed up the mountain. "That way, up the boreen." Lost John grabbed a flashlight from the bike and jumped into the van. "Less than a minute ago."

"That's headed straight for the mountain."

"Right, and it's madness on a night like this."

"He sure as hell's not going to get far on a bike."

As they sped up the road, Lost John shone the flashlight out the side window. "I don't know, in this weather we'll never find him. Stop! Stop!"

Caught in the glare of the flashlight beam something flashed red from behind a hedge. Coltrane doused the lights. They entered the field by way of a stile and discovered a bike hidden in the bushes. Its red safety reflector winked back at them. "That's his bike for sure," Coltrane said.

"It's the one he commandeered, at any rate."

"There's no point to this. We can't track him down in the pitch dark."

"Even if we try to follow him up through the fields with the flashlight, he'd see us coming a mile away," Lost John said.

"My hunch is he's hiding close by and will make his move early in the morning."

"Plus he's got a thousand-foot mountain in front of him, and since he's not a sheep or a mountain goat, most likely he'll go around it."

"Either that or head back toward Duffy's on the main road, which I don't think he's going to risk doing."

"Well, if he takes the mountain route, he'll probably veer to the left at the foothills close to the road to avoid the climb."

"That's what I'm counting on," Coltrane said.

"And we'll be waiting for him when he does."

"Not we—me."

Lost John eyed Coltrane. "And where will I be?"

Coltrane jabbed his hand into the darkness. "You'll continue up the field we're in now. Position yourself between the mountain and Duffy's Pub to our right. If my theory is correct, when he sees me he'll head back in the direction he came and run right into you. Between us we should be able to trap him. For now, however, I think our best bet might be to sleep in the van and be up before daylight and ready to move."

The rain intensified. They hurried back to the van, parked in a gap off the side of the road, and settled down for a fitful few hours' sleep.

***

Sunrise saw them on the move. Lost John took off up the fields with his shotgun and Coltrane drove the van to where the road made a sharp turn at the base of the mountain. He parked about twenty feet shy of the bend in the shelter of a hedge so the van couldn't be seen from the fields. Anyone coming along the foothills at this spot would have to pass within a hundred yards of the road. Large lichen-scabbed boulders, dumped eons ago by passing ice, littered the area between the road and mountain. Several majestic chestnut trees grew among the boulders, islands of shade in a desert of stone. The boulders provided perfect cover to observe the foothills all the way back to Duffy's Pub.

Coltrane grabbed his shotgun from the van. In order to get to the boulder field he had to jump across a little drain overgrown with sedge and briars that followed the contours of the boreen. A barbed-wire fence with tufts of sheep's wool on its prongs filled the gap where the hedge faltered. Ensuring that the hammers were down, he grabbed the gun by the barrel and lifted it over the fence, stock to the ground, before climbing across himself. As he advanced through the boulders, the terrain grew steeper. Leftover rain pooled in the hollows of flat rocks. He laid his weapon down and scooped water from one of these pools, suddenly realizing how hungry and thirsty he was, not having eaten since six o'clock the previous evening.

As he bent to drink, the watery sun of early morning reflected in the shallow pool, promising a day of more rain. The bleating of a startled sheep caused him to jerk his head around.

Sweeney stood ten feet away, pointing the shotgun at his midsection. "I could say something stupid, like 'Imagine bumping into you in a place like this,' or 'Never leave your shotgun unattended,' but I'm not. I'm tired of being followed by you and that gangster Kincaid." He leaned back against a boulder with an exhausted look on his face.

Sweeney was bleeding from a wound over his eye, most likely the result of a fall on a sharp rock in the dark. "I see you didn't get your beauty sleep last night."

Sweeney shifted his weight from one leg to the other while sharply jerking the gun upward in line with Coltrane's head. "Don't get smart with me, or I'll be giving you more sleep than you bargained for."

His wet clothes steamed from the heat of the sun. Coltrane figured he could take him before he got a shot off, but a more vigilant part of his brain cautioned him that the rush of adrenalin, even in an exhausted man, could make up for physical deficiencies. He decided on a lower-key approach. "I'm not out to harm you or turn you into the guards. I seek only information about my daughter."

Sweeney laughed. "I'll say you're not going to turn me into the guards. That's a bloody good one, turn me into the guards. They're out looking for you, not me. You're the one wanted for murder, or haven't you heard?"

Sweeney coughed so violently that he was unable to keep the gun steady or maintain his balance. Coltrane dove in under the weapon and hit him in the midsection, discharging the gun and hurling it behind one of the massive rocks. The shot echoed through the boulder field like artillery fire.

A flock of crows exploded upward from a nearby chestnut grove and flew in a raucous circle over the struggling men. From their vantage point it would have been difficult to determine who would gain the upper hand. More evident, though, was the big black car moving cautiously up the boreen toward the boulder field.

Apparently getting another rush of adrenalin, Sweeney burst free of Coltrane's grip and dashed through the boulders. Coltrane gave chase, but soon lost him in the forest of stone. Hoping to alert Lost John to Sweeney's position, he climbed up on one of the boulders.

He spotted Sweeney exiting the boulder field and Lost John advancing to cut him off. Believing they now had Sweeney trapped, Coltrane got ready to scramble from his perch when a black car eased in behind his van. He jumped to the ground and pulled a pistol from his waistband. "Damn," he hoped they hadn't spotted him. Now he faced a crucial decision: follow Sweeney and help Lost John? Or stay and engage his nemesis? He crept forward toward the barbed-wire fence, using the boulders as cover.

Kincaid and his henchmen emerged from the car. There were five in all: two rifled through the van, and three others toting guns advanced on the barbed-wire fence. Once beyond the fence, they spread out. Five to one. Not great odds. He risked being outflanked, so he retreated into the boulders and sprinted down the slope in search of Lost John.

Chapter 37

Sweeney's Confession

When Lost John heard the gunshot, he raced through a pasture with Shorthorn cattle to a fenced gap that led to a neighboring wheat field. He mounted the fence and spotted a lone figure running from the boulders toward the wheat. He couldn't tell who it was, but the appearance of a second runner in clear pursuit cleared up his uncertainty. Since the runners had to come through the wheat field, and the gap was the only way out, he decided to wait there. He checked the cartridges in his shotgun and crouched behind the hedge near the grazing Shorthorns. Three horizontal wooden poles anchored to uprights spanned the gap.

Only the sound of cattle lazily munching grass disturbed the quiet until the heavy breathing of an approaching runner intruded. When the runner climbed over the fence, Lost John stepped out and smacked him alongside the head with the barrel of his shotgun. Sweeney collapsed in a heap. He didn't want to hit him at all, but feared that Sweeney would bolt when he saw him. And since shooting him was not an option, he chose the least harmful course of action. Lost John pulled him off the exposed wet clay of the gap and onto the grass verge, surprised that he fell so easily. He hadn't hit him that hard. Now he could see why.

Sweeney was skin and bone, from living rough, he figured.

***

A shout from the wheat field. "My God! You didn't kill him, did you?" Coltrane stood transfixed on the other side of the fence.

"He's fine; he fell crossing the fence poles."

Coltrane threw Lost John a disbelieving look before negotiating the fence. Then he scooped water from the drain along the base of the blackthorn hedge and splashed it on Sweeney's face until his eyes flickered. "Let's get him out of here."

Lost John looked puzzled. "Aren't we going to question him before we take him back to the van?"

"No, we can't take him back to the van. Kincaid and his cronies are already there going through it. They may even be coming down the wheat field, although I don't think they saw either Sweeney or me."

"Shit, someone in the pub must have tipped them off."

"That or they're clairvoyant."

They got Sweeney to his feet, but it was clear that he was not up for a long walk. Since they couldn't take him back to the van, they needed to come up with an alternate plan to move him to temporary safety. Sweeney shook uncontrollably; when he tried to stand, he staggered toward the drain. Lost John stopped his fall. The man was in no condition to answer questions.

Coltrane removed Sweeney's wet jacket and shirt. Then he took off his own shirt and put it on him while Lost John helped Sweeney into his overcoat. Coltrane glanced at Lost John. "The only logical thing to do now is get back to Duffy's Pub and call Seamus Reagan to pick us up."

"But won't Kincaid's crowd be watching the place?"

"We're not going onto the premises. There's a public phone box off to the side of the shop; I think I can get into that unnoticed. Besides, I have this." He removed the Glock pistol from his jacket pocket.

"Just thought of something," Lost John said. "There're some sheds behind the pub. Noticed them on our last visit. We might be able to slip into one of them unnoticed, and I could sneak around to the phone in the front."

Coltrane gave a dismissive wave. "No, I'll make the phone call; you've already put yourself in enough danger on my account."

"I think you're putting yourself in jeopardy needlessly, but if that's the way you feel, okay with me."

"That's the way I feel, so it's a deal, then."

The warm shirt and overcoat brought Sweeney around. He stopped shivering and looked steadier on his feet. They grabbed him under the arms and set off for Duffy's, sticking to the hedgerows. They arrived at a field behind the pub without incident and took refuge in one of the sheds. It had a cement floor that was strewn with an assortment of large empty chests, the kind used to ship bulk tea. One corner held about a dozen sacks of meal, stacked one against another. Several worn shop coats hung from a hook inside the door. A small window set in the gable end provided a view of the back of the pub and the side entrance to the road.

Sweeney made a beeline for the meal sacks and was soon snoring heavily.

Coltrane removed Sweeney's wet boots and covered him with the discarded shop coats. "We better see that he gets well, fast. He's our only link to Brigid, so keep a close eye on him while I'm gone."

Coltrane slipped through a gap into a field dotted with haycocks, ducking along the hedge until he was parallel with the pub. A group of men stood in a huddle near the phone box. One of them was Kincaid.

Unfortunately another was the bartender from the previous night. That settled it. Time for plan B. A young lad of maybe sixteen carrying a bag of groceries sauntered from the shop. He jumped on his bike and set off down the road, whistling. Coltrane sprinted to a gate that opened onto the road on the other side of the field and intercepted him. "I need a favor, son. There's a shilling in it for you."

The young lad's eyes lit up. "A shilling, eh? Depends on what you want me to do."

"I need to make a phone call, but I can't let old man Duffy spot me. You see I owe him a few quid, if you know what I mean."

The kid laughed. "How long will it take? They're expecting me home with this stuff for the tea."

"No time at all." Coltrane took the butt of a pencil from his pocket and wrote the number of the Lake Hotel on the back of an empty matchbox. "Call this number and ask for Paddy Cassidy. Tell him to send Seamus Reagan out to Duffy's Pub on the Black Stick as soon as he can, and to come in round the back. Tell him that Pete Coltrane asked you to make the call. Think you can do that?"

"Sure," the kid replied, putting the money Coltrane handed him for the phone call in his pocket.

"When you come back, the shilling is yours."

The kid headed to the phone kiosk. Within five minutes he was back.

"Well?"

"Cassidy wanted to know what the hell you were doing in this godforsaken part of the county."

"And what did you tell him?"

"I told him to fuck off because I lived in this godforsaken part of the county."

Coltrane burst out laughing, gave the kid the shilling, and sent him on his way. "Oh, begod, hold on! Did he say anything else?"

"Not a damn thing," the kid yelled over his shoulder before disappearing around a bend. Coltrane stood in the middle of the road, stupefied. He ripped the cap from his head and threw it on the ground. "You conniving little bastard!"

Then the kid reappeared. "Getting a rise out of ya, mister, that's all. Cassidy said, 'Hang tight and that he'd be along.'"

The kid took off, whistling at the top of his lungs. *Now there's a kid after my own heart,* Coltrane thought. He experienced again the pain he often felt at not having a son. They tried for a second child, but it never happened.

When he got back to the shed, Sweeney was sitting up on the meal sacks, hunched inside the overcoat that appeared two sizes too big for him. He looked like an errant schoolboy caught without his homework. Lost John sat on a balled-up shop coat on the floor, his back against the opposite wall. Coltrane pulled the Glock from his belt and sat on a meal sack beside Sweeney. Fear leapt into Sweeney's eyes. "Unless you want to be on crutches for the rest of your days, you'll start talking. Where's my kid?"

"As God is my witness, Mr. Coltrane," he stammered, "all I know for sure is that Kincaid knows, and I suspect so does the ..." His voice trailed into incoherent babble.

"Go on." Coltrane leveled the pistol at him. Sweeney's eyes darted back and forth, as if expecting an escape route to open up by magic in one of the cement walls.

"Why are you stalling, man?" Coltrane asked, more exhausted than angry.

"I'm afraid you'll think I'm lying."

"Try me. Who else is involved?"

Sweeney dropped his head and examined his hands."Who, goddammit?"

He pressed the tip of the pistol against Sweeney's right kneecap. Beads of sweat broke out on Sweeney's forehead. He whispered as if he were in a confessional box. "The canon."

Lost John jumped to his feet. "Son of a bitch."

Coltrane turned cold. "You mean Canon Roach from Cloonfin?"

"What other canon is there?"

"I think you're asking to get your kneecaps adjusted, because that beggars belief."

Sweeney scooted farther up the meal sacks. "You better believe it. After capturing your kid, Kincaid took her to the sacristy behind the high altar in the church."

"In broad daylight?"

"No, in the middle of the night."

"And you saw this?"

"I was there, but I quickly figured I wasn't supposed to be from the look on the canon's face when he saw me."

"Go on."

"They moved outside the door and argued what to do with her, and my name was mentioned several times. I could tell the canon was none too happy that I'd seen him."

"Get on with it, man!"

Sweeney opened his arms wide. "I put two and two together, seeing what Kincaid did to O'Reilly, and got to hell outa there."

Coltrane rubbed his forehead and closed his eyes."So you have no idea where they are hiding my kid?"

"Amn't I tellin' ya that the canon must know where she is?"

Throughout Sweeney's rambling account, Coltrane's stomach churned, almost causing him to throw up. Cassidy was right. The canon had it in for him. He probably fired him from his teaching job not because of his drinking, but because he fought against Franco and his Blueshirt allies in Spain.

Lost John sidled up to the window and peered out. "I never liked that hypocritical prick, but not in my wildest dreams did I think he could be mixed up in something like this."Coltrane turned away from Sweeney. "But you had your suspicions."

"I did sure enough, but not to this extent."

"Me neither, but we all wear masks, John. Just depends on what we're trying to hide."

Lost John had a blank look on his face as if the news he had just heard was too difficult to process. "What now?"

Coltrane reached out and touched his shoulder. "We continue our hunt and hope the top half of the hourglass still has a little sand left." After admonishing Sweeney to go see his parents, Coltrane let him go with a warning that if he was lying about the canon, he would track him down and kill him.

Chapter 38

Answer in an Old Newspaper

Coltrane jimmied the catch on the kitchen window of the presbytery, Canon Roach's residence, while Lost John kept watch on the driveway. Earlier in the day they had called at the house, but nobody was home. Subsequent inquiries revealed that the canon was on holiday at an undisclosed location and would not be back for two weeks. Coltrane couldn't afford to wait; Brigid might not survive that long. So this was the only option left. Once inside he pulled the drapes to hide the flashlight beam. He unbolted the back door and let Lost John in. Looking for clues to the canon's whereabouts, they ransacked the house, rummaging through drawers and closets and emptying wastepaper baskets.

Nothing. "John, I'm heading upstairs."

John had a smile on his face. "Gallant, I'll continue with my plunder down here." In an upstairs study, near a washbasin, Coltrane rummaged through a bookcase crammed with philosophy texts as well as the works of Machiavelli. A mahogany desk faced a window overlooking the side wall of the church. The drawers were locked, but within seconds Coltrane cracked them open with the blade of his commando knife. In one he found a small brown book fastened by a leather strap with a clasp on its end. It contained a list of the canon's appointments—dates and times of masses, marriages to be performed, a meeting with Abbot Jonathan of Glenfar abbey, and other sundry items. Still, nothing about its owner's travel plans.

Disappointed, he was about to put the book back in the drawer when he noticed a bulge in the inside flap of the back cover. He reached in and pulled out a St. Anthony's scapular and a clipping of an *Irish Times* article about the Dublin Horse Show. Nothing unusual about any of this, even the clipping, since the canon was known to be part of the "horsey set." What grabbed his attention, however, was the accompanying photo and caption that read, *Ambassador Mueller and members of the German Legation enjoy a day out at the Dublin Horse Show.* Coltrane perused the article for a few seconds and was set to put it back in the flap when the hair on the back of his neck grew rigid. "Son of a bitch. It's him!" he shouted down to Lost John. "Come up here!"

When Lost John puffed up the stairs, Coltrane met him on the landing and shoved the clipping into his hand. "Take a look at the guy second from the left."

"Who is he?"

Coltrane grabbed the clipping back. "Strum ... Sturmbannfu ... Oh, hell, some guy called Adler from the German Embassy."

"Some Kraut at the horse show, so what? I thought you had found a lead to the canon."

"Maybe I have and don't know it. I tell you it's the bloody assassin from Red Cow Island."

"Holy Christ! The German ambassador?" He lifted his cap and scratched his head as if trying to stimulate his brain.

"No, no, but close enough. The deputy ambassador, seems like."

"So it's not a rogue operation, then."

"Apparently not. Looks like this goes all the way to the top. "

"But I thought Ireland declared neutrality."

"That's the point. It has."

"Bloody subversion."

"Reagan was right about *the tip of the iceberg.*"

This provided the imprimatur for Sweeney's story about the canon. They searched the house with renewed urgency. Lost John returned to the first floor and Coltrane continued his search of the canon's office. *My child is caught in an international conspiracy.* He turned his attention to the desk again; its top was clear except for a phone, a gold fountain pen, and, placed neatly on the white blotter, a stack of the canon's personal letterhead. He was surprised to see the fountain pen, since the canon was known to display it ostentatiously in his top jacket pocket when he traveled. *Looks like he left in a hurry.* As he turned the pen over in his fingers, he was drawn to the white blotter. Lurking there were the usual indecipherable hieroglyphic patterns of dried ink. But running vertically up the right side of the pad, a combination of letters and numbers stood out.

He held the blotter up to the mirror over the washbasin. Written in the canon's neat script were the lines, "(WGS84) L 53 37 00, L-9 52 00." Using the canon's gold fountain pen, he copied them onto a sheet of the canon's letterhead and hurried downstairs to join Lost John, who was picking his way through the mess left by their frenetic ransacking. Coltrane recognized the script as longitude and latitude coordinates. He knew this from time spent during his summer breaks from university working on fishing trawlers that plied the waters off Iceland in search of herring shoals.

He played the flashlight beam along the canon's bookshelves. "John, I think I found something else."

"And now you're looking for what, exactly?"

"An atlas would do the trick."

Lost John pointed his flashlight at the battered spine of a world atlas. "Up there in the corner."

"God bless your eyesight, man."

Coltrane took it down and laid it on the floor. He ran his finger up and down the map of Ireland, stopping at the location indicated by the coordinates on the blotter. Longitude -9 was not shown, so he had to guess. He jabbed his finger against the map. "Somewhere on the Galway coast line."

"Yes, but where? That covers a lot of territory."

"That's what the rest of the numbers narrow down. I believe they're called minutes and seconds, but unfortunately my expertise stops there."

"Which puts us back at square one."

"Not exactly. A Garda buddy of mine who worked alongside me on the fishing trawlers is a dab hand at this. I'll give him a call. We can kill two birds with one stone."

"Excuse me. You're calling a cop. Are you out of your bloody mind? I thought you said the guards might be involved."

"I know, but this guy is solid as a rock. We fought together in the Connolly brigade against Franco, so I trust him."

Lost John shook his head. "This revelation about the canon has pretty much depleted my faith in the clergy."

Chapter 39

Spitfires' Revenge

Guard Tom Ryan dozed in the day room of the Rathmines Garda Station, his feet on the desk. This week he was pulling the late shift. Except for the chirping of crickets, the night was still, which suited him fine.

The phone rang, sounding like the local church bell against the silence.

"Jaysus Pete, you scared the livin' shite out of me; do you realize its fuckin' three o'clock in the morning?"

"I thought you were one of the country's official night watchmen," Coltrane said. "Who else am I supposed to call with a problem, the local butcher?"

Ryan cleared his throat a few times. "Problem, for fuck sake, we're up to our arses in problems up here with all this Blueshirt crap." Then he apparently caught himself and coughed nervously. "Forgive me for being such an insensitive prick, but is there any word on your girleen?"

"That's part of the reason for my call. I may have a lead on one of her abductors, and you can assist me in tracking him down."

"Jaysus, anything I can do to help, legal or otherwise. Do you want me to bust some heads?"

206

Coltrane chuckled. "No, this involves using your brain." He read the coordinates over the phone.

"Oh, begod, let me get a jotter and a pencil and I'll call you back."

Within minutes the canon's phone jangled. "Little Killary Bay in County Galway."

Coltrane gasped. "You're sure of that Tom?"

"Listen, you were the better fisherman, but you couldn't navigate your way out of a paper bag, so yes, I'm sure."

"I knew I could count on you."

"I'm sorry I can't get down there to help you, but with all the shite that's going on up here I'm tied up for the—"

"Not to worry, I've got a trusted ally down here. Now brace yourself for this next morsel of news." He told Ryan about Adler's connection to the Red Cow Island executions.

Ryan jumped to a standing position, knocking back his chair with a clatter. "Holy mother of Jaysus. I knew those bastards at the embassy were mixed up in this somehow. Have you told any of the bigwigs about it yet?"

"No, I'm relying on you to do that. Can't trust your colleagues down here."

"Leave it to me, old friend. *No Pasarán!*" he shouted, using the famous Spanish Civil War Republican rallying cry, "They shall not pass."

"*No Pasarán,*" Coltrane replied. He hung up the phone.

Lost John leaned back in the canon's easy chair. "What's next on the agenda, Boss?"

"Killary Harbor."

***

In the early hours of a summer morning, Ambassador Mueller accompanied SS Major Franz Adler under police escort to Baldonnell Aerodrome. There Mueller put him on board a Junker's Ju 52 tri-motor German bomber for a secret flight to Norway. Mueller and the major exchanged few words as Adler boarded the plane through the freight-compartment door behind the wing. At the top of the ramp he turned with raised fist and shouted a defiant *Sieg Heil!* in farewell. The only response was a one-fingered salute from a lone Irish guard on the tarmac stamping his feet against the cold, a cigarette stuck in the bunched fingers of his raised hand. By then, Ambassador Mueller had turned his back and was walking away.

A combination of diplomatic immunity and the unavailability of the primary witness saved Adler from a jail cell. Nevertheless, Ambassador Mueller thought it best that Adler leave Ireland as soon as possible. The Irish government concurred, allowing him safe passage from the country—or so it was believed. As soon as Guard Ryan was tipped off by Coltrane, he went straight as a string to the British Embassy. A few days later, after getting wind of the secret flight to Norway, he'd alerted the Brits again.

Ryan watched the Ju 52 trundle down the runway and lift off, soon to disappear into the rain-laden skies. "*Go n-éirí an bóthar leat,* literally, you bastard," he said, using the old Gaelic farewell for *May the road rise up to meet you.* He took one last drag of his cigarette, dropped it to the ground, and crushed it out with his boot. No use pushing his luck with the brass. He'd done all he could. Now it was up to someone else to see that justice prevailed.

***

Next day Ryan got word from Irish Intelligence about Adler's fate. According to MI6, two British Spitfires out of Sullom Voe in the Shetlands blasted the wings off the Ju 52 and watched the fireball cartwheel toward the ocean. On its plunge the plane disappeared into a towering black cumulus cloud, no more than a thousand feet above the water. Satisfied, the Spitfire pilots called off the attack and headed back to base.

A broad smile creased Ryan's face when he heard the news.

Chapter 40

Too Close for Comfort

The canon's face went pale as he opened the boot of the car. When the sergeant saw the radio, he stepped back as if stung by a wasp. "What's this?"

"Oh, that's something I've had an interest in since I was a young lad. I used to spend hours listening to shortwave radio from places like Luxemburg, Moscow, and Vatican City, and one night I even picked up Ankara."

"So did I, Canon, but what's that to do with a ham radio, and why are you carrying it with you on holidays?"

"Well, there's kind of a natural progression from shortwave to ham radio. My studies prevented me from doing much with it for a long while, but lately I've taken it up again and I must say it's a lot of fun."

"How are you intending to use it on holidays?"

"Mainly to brush up on its operation. I'm not going to be doing any transmitting."

"So you're a ham radio operator, then. Is that correct?" The sergeant's tone suggested serious doubts about the canon's story.

"Yes, I am, but I must confess that I'm a little rusty."

"Do you have a license to use it?" The sergeant picked up the radio and scrutinized it. The canon panicked because he wasn't aware he needed a license, having received the radio only two weeks before.

"You know, Sergeant, I think that may have slipped my mind as I'm so busy with the church building program. Outside my clerical duties, the new addition to our church pretty much takes up my spare time. Part of the reason for coming on this holiday was to get away from the pressure and indulge my youthful interest."

"I'm afraid, Canon, we'll have to confiscate the radio until we can get to the bottom of this. Also, you'll have to accompany us to the Garda barracks to fill out a statement."

The canon started to protest, but pulled up. "By all means, Sergeant, but could I first go and check in at the hotel so I don't lose my reservation? Then if you give me directions, I will proceed right away to the Garda barracks."

"Tomorrow is fine, but we'll retain the radio. In case you're wondering, we're checking for foreign agents all along the west coast. We have intelligence that the Germans are trying to infiltrate spies into the country."

The canon's hand flew to his mouth. "How outrageous—and Ireland a neutral nation."

After giving his name and address, he received the sergeant's permission to continue to Leenane, minus the radio.

Alone again in his car, he shook violently. That was close, but it could have been worse. The guards, distracted by the ham radio, hadn't searched his suitcase or the large parcel with three black suits and three pairs of black shoes, all of different sizes. How would he have explained *that?*

The canon arrived at the hotel without further incident. After the porter delivered his bags to the room, he gave the man a handsome tip and locked the door. He always tipped hotel staff generously, because one never knew when their services might come in handy for items not on the menu. A satisfied porter is a cooperative one. Although the sergeant had told him to drop by the station at his leisure, the sergeant's attitude suggested that he should be on his guard.

Before going down to dinner he spread a map of Killary Harbor and its little brother Killary Bay on the bed. He traced over the route to the rendezvous point with a red pencil, planning to do a dry run the next morning to avoid last-minute foul-ups. Earlier he had purchased a small compass at a pawnshop in Westport to assist in finding the landing spot on the north shore of Little Killary Bay. Unfortunately the weather forecast called for rain and gale-force winds. The silver lining within that cloud of bad news was that the foul conditions would keep most people indoors, lessening the possibility of discovery.

After he finished dinner the canon took a snifter of brandy to the elegant sitting room with its magnificent view of Killary Harbor. To think that King Edward VII and Queen Alexandra had once graced this very room with their presence made him long for the time when such elegance would be restored to his country again. He could taste salt in the air as the muslin curtains of the large bay window ballooned into the room before charging wind gusts that announced the gathering storm. As he settled back in an armchair to enjoy the spectacle, he noticed the dour sergeant from the checkpoint sitting in a car across the road. The Garda were watching him.

Nothing for it now but to cancel his trip to the rendezvous point with the German U-boat. Better to let the Germans fend for themselves than betray their whereabouts to Irish authorities. If he didn't get a message to his backup, Alfred Hayes, a disaster could ensue. However, he dared not risk a call for fear of it being monitored, or leave the hotel and risk being followed. Through the open sitting-room door he caught sight of the young porter carrying suitcases into the lobby. He felt sure that for a decent tip the lad could be persuaded to carry such a message. He would attend to that first thing in the morning.

Before retiring for the evening he went to his room and penned a note on a clean sheet of paper: *Unable to collect package this evening due to unforeseen circumstances.* If the backup received the message in time, he would pick up the Germans at the rendezvous point.

Next morning he awoke to the howl of the wind roaring down the harbor and the sound of rain beating on the windowpanes. Before heading to breakfast he put the one-line message inside an envelope and inserted it in an oilskin pouch. When he finished eating he approached the porter and told him he needed a letter delivered to the church in Kilmore. He caught the look of hesitation on the young man's face, a look that vanished when he spotted the two ten pound notes between the canon's thumb and forefinger. That was probably more money than he could earn in two months. He eagerly agreed to deliver it.

The canon wagged his finger. "This is a donation for the church in Kilmore, but I like to keep my good works private. Is that understood?"

"Fair enough, Canon."

"How soon do you think you can get going?"

"Right after my shift ends."

The canon handed him a ten-pound note. "Once you make the delivery, I will pay you the balance."

"Sound, Father. It's as good as done."

The canon walked into the sitting room and looked out the window. The sergeant was gone. He wondered if his concern was all for naught. Maybe this notion of being watched was a figment of his imagination. However, as he passed through the lobby on the way to his room he saw the young guard from the roadblock, dressed in civvies casually lounging in an armchair reading the morning newspaper. His panic returned.

***

The canon's visit to the guards' barracks later that morning turned out to be routine, so far as he could tell. After he signed the statement, a written version of his verbal explanation, he was allowed to leave— without his radio.

He grew increasingly nervous as the day wore on. Several gin and tonics broken by spells of fitful reading did little to restore his calm. As house lights began popping on, the porter returned to the hotel. He was drenched to the skin and looked exhausted.

The canon approached from the sitting room. "Well?"

"I did as you told me and put the envelope into the collection box at the Shrine of Our Lady."

"Was the box secure?"

"It had a padlock."

The canon let out a sigh of relief. "Good." He handed the tired youth another ten-pound note and sent him on his way.

When Alfred Hayes, the church caretaker at Kilmore, made his daily rounds of the collection boxes, he would retrieve the message and know what to do. The canon spent a restless night tossing and turning as the storm outside his window gradually abated. He looked at his watch. 2:15 a.m. By now the Germans would be safe in Hayes's house.

If things went well.

***

The porter massaged the two crisp ten-pound notes. He felt a twinge of guilt because he hadn't been entirely truthful with the canon. When he arrived at Kilmore church it was filled with people attending a funeral service. He panicked. Crowds made him nervous. The shrine to Our Lady was near the altar, and he was far too self-conscious to make that long walk up the middle aisle in front of all those people. Since the weather was awful, he didn't want to get caught in the dark, so he couldn't chance waiting until the service was over. God only knew how long that would take.

However, his conscience, and his desire to collect the remaining ten pounds, forged a compromise that he could live with. Grabbing a pencil from a table at the church entrance, he removed the envelope from the oilskin pouch and addressed it to *The Parish Priest, Kilmore*. Then he walked next door to the parish house and slid the envelope under the front door.

***

After the funeral service the parish priest found the letter and read the puzzling message: *Unable to collect package this evening due to unforeseen circumstances.* Since he had no idea what the cryptic note meant, he cast it on his desk intending to ask the sacristan, Alfred Hayes, about it the next day. However, an early morning assignment took him away from the parish and he totally forgot about the enigmatic note.

213

Chapter 41

Chapter of Faults

Brother Michael, the young infirmarian of Glenfar Abbey, led Dr. Ford to see Abbot Jonathan, who was tending his bees in the orchard. The doctor had come to drop off some medication for Brother Edmond, one of the sick monks. He appeared surprised to learn that all medicines had to be delivered into the abbot's hands before being administered to the patient. Arriving at the orchard, Michael paused with his visitor at the perimeter fence.

Abbot Jonathan seemed to glide in slow motion among the hives, placed in rows amidst the apple trees in full bloom. He wore oversized gloves that ran halfway up his arms and a black hood with a gauze mask. From a distance his movements seemed predatory as he lifted the honeycomb frames from each hive and placed them in his collection cart.

The bees registered their displeasure with aggressive attacks. He retaliated with volleys from a brass smoker, which he waved around his head like a machine gun. After each confrontation, a pall of acrid smoke drifted over the apple trees blossomed in pink and white, like a noxious haze over a battlefield. On this summer day the buzzing waxed and waned almost hypnotically in response to the beekeeper's movements.

Michael ran his fingers through his cropped black hair while throwing furtive glances at the beekeeper. "The bees are in an ugly mood today. See how they fight him. *He's* going to be in a foul mood too."

Dr. Ford looked taken aback. That didn't deter the infirmarian. "He doesn't tolerate disobedience cheerfully, from either man or beast."

Dr. Ford puffed his cheeks out and exhaled loudly. "Brother, why don't I come back at a more opportune time?"

That snapped the young brother out of his trance. He lifted his narrow shoulders and took a deep breath. "No, I'm the infirmarian, and I should have the right to accept medicine from a doctor." He extended his hand. "So, if you please ..."

Dr. Ford passed him the bag of medications. "Hope this doesn't get you in trouble."

"I'll tell him later. Besides, Brother Edmond needs his medication today, and not two or three days hence—or whenever the abbot gets around to releasing it to the infirmary." He took the bag and headed back the way they had come. Dr. Ford followed. At the front door he bade farewell to the doctor and disappeared into the abbey.

***

The monks filed silently into the chapel and took their customary positions, awaiting the abbot's arrival for the Chapter of Faults. The abbot conducted this ritual once a month. Its purpose was to air infractions of the rules, on the premise that public disclosure would deepen the individual's humility by curbing pride and ensuring stricter adherence to the discipline of religious life, thereby drawing the individual closer to God. That was the theory, but whether it brought about the desired results was difficult to measure.

Outward observance of the rules was no guarantee of inner acceptance; the appearance of humility could be the cloak of hypocrisy or, worse still, "silent contempt." Nevertheless, the abbot shared the opinion of those who held that suffering and humiliation were good for the soul, especially when inflicted publicly. As one of the young monks, Brother Michael sat close to the front of the chapel. Most likely the abbot would call upon him to confess some infraction.

When the abbot arrived he crouched on a chair on the elevated steps of the altar facing the assembled community, his lanky six-foot frame bent over like a question mark. Red splotches covered his nose and cheeks where bees had won the battle. Dark circles circumscribed his deep-set rheumy eyes, giving the impression of keen concentration.

He regarded those before him with a fixed stare, made more haunting by his sallow looks. His opaque gaze hinted at menace, adding to the mystery and tension that surrounded him.

***

Brother Michael's stomach churned at the thought of having to reveal his disobedience pertaining to Brother Edmond's medication. He didn't fear what the others might think, but what the abbot might impose as a penance. He could opt to reveal nothing, but he suspected that eventually the abbot would discover his indiscretion. As the monks filed forward and knelt in front of the abbot, heads bowed, they confessed the usual infractions: breaking the grand silence, eating between meals, sleeping during prayer, sleeping in after the morning bell, and failure to complete assigned tasks. The abbot imposed routine penances ranging from foregoing a meal to spending extra time at prayer or work.

When Brother Michael's turn came, his courage failed him. Whether out of fear of the abbot or of jeopardizing his eternal salvation, he unburdened himself and awaited his sentence. The abbot's stone-faced demeanor did not change. This could mean that Michael had run the gauntlet successfully and might escape with a routine reprimand. Then the abbot's rheumy eyes flickered. Michael's heart sank.

Instead of automatically assigning one of the pro-forma penances doled out to the preceding twenty individuals, the abbot stirred himself in his chair. "Brother Michael not only questions the rules of our order; apparently he also sees fit to question my authority and take matters into his own hands." A long pause followed as the abbot slowly scanned the assembly before again fixing his gaze on Michael. "Maybe he feels that he should be abbot and that I should be infirmarian. After all, he has been with us for … how long, Brother?"

"A-a year, Abbot."

"A year, is it? I can see how you might feel it's time you should be moving up to bigger and better things." He raised his right hand high above his head. A current of nervous laughter rippled through the chapel. "Such ambition should be preceded by a rigorous trial period, Brother, don't you think, so you can demonstrate to all of us your aptitude and fitness for my position?"

The abbot's mocking behavior angered Michael.

"The first step in your training, Brother, will begin tonight in this chapel, where you will stay until one o'clock in meditation before the Blessed Sacrament, seeking guidance on how best to conduct yourself in your new responsibilities. Do you understand?"

Michael bowed his head."Yes, Abbot."

"Unfortunately you will miss supper, but such a sacrifice, I'm sure you will agree, is a small price to pay for such high ambition. The next step in your education will begin tomorrow in the fields, where you will spend your day with Brother Bernard. You were raised on a farm, I'm told."

"Y-y-yes, Abbot."

"Good. To unburden your conscience I'm relieving you of your job as infirmarian. That way your moral dilemmas will be confined to the treatment of livestock rather than humans."

The Chapter of Faults ended at seven o'clock. Led by the abbot, the brothers silently filed from the chapel to the refectory for the evening meal. Brother Michael began his long vigil. The odors of supper wafted through the open windows. His stomach growled. It would be a long night, but he had a plan to acquire sustenance before it was over.

It was a beautiful mid-summer's evening, so it was still light outside. The mellow song of blackbirds echoed from the lilacs beyond the chapel wall. It reminded him of the happy carefree days of childhood, when he used to help his father on their little farm. Now he wondered what his father would think.

The monks reassembled for night prayers at half past eight. After they dispersed, Brother Michael had the chapel to himself. The fading evening light added to the eerie feeling of the chapel with its high-vaulted ceiling, Gothic columns, and large circular rose-colored window over the altar. A candle burned in its red glass container before the tabernacle, signifying the presence of the Blessed Sacrament. For a while the yellow flame bent and wove like an exotic dancer behind the smoky glass. He turned off the lights, except for those over the altar, and settled in for a night of meditation and prayer.

Some of the time he passed on his knees, but even for a young man's joints that became stressful, so he alternated between sitting in the pews and walking up and down the aisle for the remainder of his allotted time. The church was cool and peaceful and he found a certain solace in the quiet of the semi-darkness.

As the one o'clock hour drew near, he mulled over his scheme to acquire food. He crept down the darkened hallway toward the kitchen, listening for anything out of the ordinary. But all he heard were the timbers of the old structure creaking and crickets chirping in the darkness. His heart skipped a beat—a light shone from the abbot's room across the compound. Although he had a flashlight in his pocket, he didn't dare turn it on in this part of the hallway with its many windows, for fear of being discovered. Brother Gabriel, the cook, locked the kitchen at night to deter midnight visitors like him, but he usually hid the key nearby. The challenge: find it or go hungry. Placing his handkerchief over the flashlight, he searched the area outside the kitchen door, crouching low to the ground. Eventually he found the key under a coal scoop and let himself in.

Although the kitchen was in a secluded spot with no windows opening onto the dormitories or other living areas of the abbey, he didn't turn the lights on, but relied on his flashlight. A large pantry occupied the space to the right of the door where Brother Gabriel stored foodstuffs and supplies to feed a community of over fifty people. In the middle of the kitchen floor sat a long wooden table surrounded by a half dozen chairs. Brother Michael made a beeline for the old refrigerator purring against the opposite wall, hoping to find leftovers. He was not disappointed: an ample supply of chicken, cheese, fruit, and eggs was on the racks.

He cobbled together a chicken-and-cheese sandwich, poured a glass of milk, and sat down at the large table. Off in the distance he heard the whistle of the 2:00 a.m. train to Dublin and wondered what it would be like to ride with no purpose other than to be aboard, not knowing what lay at the end of the line. As he ate, his mind meandered back and forth among unrelated topics.

From deep in the bowels of the house a telephone rang. At first he thought his mind was playing tricks on him. Then the distant sound of voices approaching. The casual violation of the grand silence suggested that there were outsiders in the house. Unusual in the dead of night. Whether the outsiders were headed toward the kitchen, he couldn't tell, but this was no time to gamble.

He quickly cleared the table and put his plate and utensils into the sink, hoping for a quick getaway. When he poked his head outside the door he realized that the voices were too close for him to escape to the library. He closed the door and ran to the pantry, hoping the visitors' destination wasn't the kitchen. Once inside, he edged the door shut and pulled a large sack of flour away from the wall to create a space in which he could hide. His next thought chilled him: *I left the key in the kitchen door!*

Panic gripped him. He rose to retrieve the key, then stopped. The doorknob turned. The abbot's gruff voice followed. "This is highly unusual. Brother Gabriel is so cautious about putting this key in a secure place."

"Looks like he forgot," another voice added.

"He won't forget a second time, I assure you." Michael heard several other voices and the scraping sound of chairs being pulled back from the table.

"Why would anyone be down here at two o'clock in the morning?" a familiar voice asked.

"No one should be anywhere near here this time of night. That's why I decided to have the meeting here in the first place. It's the most secluded spot in the abbey," the abbot replied. "I suppose it's possible Brother Gabriel simply forgot to hide the key, but to be sure we're on our own, Arthur, go ahead and search the place."

All the lights were turned on. Brother Michael steeled himself for what might follow. As he hunkered down he noticed that the neck of one of the flour sacks was open. He reached in, scooped up several handfuls of flour, and dumped them on his head, face, and shoulders. The pantry light, a solitary, grimy bulb hanging from the ten-foot ceiling, left shadows in the corners. With a little luck they might not spot him behind the flour sacks camouflaged in white.

The pantry door opened. A hand reached in and flipped the switch.

Chapter 42

Into the Celtic Sea

Sturmbannführer Adler stood on the heaving deck of the sailing ship *Orion* as it punched its way through the froth-capped waves and gale-force winds of the Celtic Sea pounding Ireland's southern coast. The ship was rigged as a fishing vessel to camouflage its real mission. Overhead, the sails puffed out like the breasts of white swans running for takeoff. The wind and spray whipped through the shrouds, creating a high-pitched wail like the cry of a frightened animal. As the wind intensified the wail changed pitch, becoming almost a scream. He held on to the lines with a death grip. The howl of the wind brought back the terrifying night he'd spent in the mountainous North Sea waves after bailing out of the stricken Ju 52 bomber. As far as he could tell, he'd been the only survivor.

In spite of the ribbing he took from the crew of the Ju 52, his sixth sense prompted him to don a parachute and life jacket. Despite his secret departure from Ireland, he suspected the British would get wind of it. It wouldn't surprise him if Ambassador Mueller fingered him. But the new order would take care of fence-sitters like Mueller. Whatever Aryan gods were up there that night must have been looking out for him. Against all odds he'd washed ashore on the Norwegian coast near

Bergen. A sympathizer of the Nazi puppet government rescued him and took him to the German occupying forces. Within days he was back on his feet, having suffered only superficial burns on his arms. Soon he made his way to Berlin. Given his connection to Hitler and his previous work in Ireland, it wasn't difficult to persuade those in command to put him in charge of the advance team about to embark for Ireland to prepare for Operation Green.

Now three days out from the French port of Brest, the *Orion* was bound for Killary Harbor on Ireland's northwest coast. Adler and his companions were to rendezvous with a German submarine off Inish Bofin, a small island off the Galway coast, to ferry them unseen to the landing zone.

He had his doubts about the *Orion*'s captain, Hans Von Schroeder. A day before leaving Brest, Van Schroeder discovered that the boat's large diesel engine was missing an external propeller. Since it was too late to get a replacement without missing the submarine rendezvous, Adler decided to head for Ireland under sail. Given the heavy weather, he was beginning to reassess that decision.

"Major Adler!" a voice from behind shouted, "I think it might be advisable to come inside. This is likely to get worse once we round Mizen Head."

The interruption of his reverie annoyed him. "Right away, Captain! As soon as I have one more smoke."

"As you wish."

Tucking his head into the collar of his raincoat, Adler succeeded in lighting his Player cigarette on the third try. Smoking was a moral failing he tolerated without too much guilt, even when smoking an English cigarette. As the captain predicted, once they cleared Mizen Head the boat was broadsided by the full force of the wind barreling down Ireland's west coast from the Atlantic. Moving to the relative shelter of the main mast at center deck, he retrieved a southwester from his pocket and fitted it on his head, securing it with a drawstring under his chin while clinging to a capstan attached to the mast. He was not ready to go inside yet.

He mulled over the plan for the Irish operation. How would all the pieces come together? How reliable were the Irish allies? His experience with Kincaid and the Blueshirts was not reassuring. Bumblers, all of them. Of even greater consequence, how committed was Hitler? Given his mercurial nature, Der Führer might call the whole thing off on a whim.

As Adler slowly blew cigarette smoke through his lips, the wind snatched it away with such speed that he almost questioned whether he was smoking or dreaming. Twenty-five feet above, the French tricolor stood straight out from the main mast as the wind pulled it almost to the ripping point like a ravenous animal tearing a piece of meat from a bone. The *Orion* sailed under French colors so as not to attract the scrutiny of the Royal Navy, which prowled in search of German subs. The subterfuge's success depended on a certain amount of luck, and on the *Orion*'s camouflage as a fishing vessel heading for the mackerel beds off Ireland's west coast. Once there, the plan was to mix with the other vessels during the day and head for the rendezvous point with the submarine under darkness.

By the time he took the last drag on his cigarette and flipped it overboard, the wind had lost some of its intensity. This might be a good time to catch some sleep. After a little small talk with the captain and crew, he turned in for the night.

He awoke several hours later to the news that two Royal Navy cruisers were spotted on the horizon about five miles west of Inish Bofin. Too close to the rendezvous point for comfort. The submarine would not surface under those circumstances. He'd grown cautious after his gaffe with the mask on Red Cow Island. He considered an alternate plan that called for the *Orion* to rendezvous with the sub at the mouth of Killary Harbor, Ireland's only fjord, between Galway and Mayo. A reliable agent would meet them and conduct them to a safe house. Come morning, if the British cruisers still lurked around Inish Bofin, he would implement this plan.

That part of the operation was crucial. Many sea-based clandestine operations failed in the initial hours after landing. He checked his watch and realized it was almost time for the meeting with his fellow agents. A dark scowl crossed his face. He was not a hundred percent sure of these fellows. In his mind they were a bunch of mongrels, young and inexperienced, two of them South African Germans, the third an Indian national. Worse, only one spoke passable English. But since he joined this phase of the operation at the eleventh hour and caused a ruckus by ousting the original commander, he had little input in picking the team.

As far as he could tell, all that bonded the team was a passionate hatred for the British. That in itself would not get them through. While he shared their attitude toward the Brits, he knew that rage without power and direction fizzles. He didn't want to be their nursemaid, but accepted it as the price he had to pay for his tardy arrival.

When he joined the team in the captain's cabin, he could smell their resentment. He was a Johnny-come-lately. They clustered around a table smoking nervously and talking loudly in German. He raised his hand. "*Heil* Hitler!" They didn't bother to return his salute. "Gentlemen," he said, his face flushing, "this might be a good time to practice your English. The Irish don't speak German and probably won't buy the tourist bit." Fear registered on their sullen faces. "Remember, your compatriots are dying of frostbite and dysentery on the Russian front, so whatever cover you were given better be convincing enough to explain why you're not with them."

"But Major Adler," one of the South Africans said, "if we are detained by Irish authorities, it will be very difficult to disguise who we are, despite what our South African passports say."

"The challenge, then, is not to get stopped. We—you, rather—are relying on the skill of native Irish collaborators to provide alibis that sound and look convincing. I hope it's not necessary to remind you that we address each other by our aliases. Mine is Aaron ten Boom, a Dutch Jewish merchant on the run from Germany."

"What are ours?" the Indian asked.

"You'll get them from our Irish contacts when we arrive."

The three looked at each other. The Indian joined his hands and raised them to his chin.

As they discussed operational details an ear-shattering roar rocked the boat and faded into the distance, only to return with the same deafening howl before fading once more.

When they picked themselves up from the floor, the captain rushed in. "British Sunderland seaplane. From a base in Northern Ireland, I suspect."

"Our cover is blown already?" one of the jittery South Africans asked.

Adler gave him a contemptuous stare. "Probably buzzing our boat to confirm that we are who we appear to be."

"That's right," the captain said.

This abrupt shattering of their fragile security convinced Adler to put plan B into action. He wrapped up the meeting and directed Captain Von Schroeder to abort the rendezvous at Inish Boffin and sail on for Killary Harbor. "Captain, inform the submarine about the change in plans, and get confirmation. Last minute changes have a way of getting fouled up."

"*Jawohl*, Major." The captain saluted and hurried from the cabin.

Chapter 43

Secrets of Glenfar Abbey

The searcher crossed the threshold of the pantry. In his mind's eye Michael saw the intruder's head swiveling from side to side. The smell of brandy mingled with those of the fruits and vegetables. "All clear in here," the voice said, pulling the door behind him.

Although Brother Michael couldn't see anything, he recognized the voice of Arthur Cusack. He shook his head free of flour. A shaft of light streamed into the pantry. Cusack had left the door ajar.

He listened for a while to the mumble of competing voices until curiosity got the better of him and he crept toward the partially open door. Half a dozen men, including the abbot and Cusack, sat around the large table. The rest were strangers. The abbot stood at the head of the table. A large man in a black trench coat occupied a seat at the other end. To the abbot's right sat a man in his mid-forties with salt-and-pepper hair and a neatly trimmed moustache. He was immaculately dressed in a blue suit, red tie, and a matching red handkerchief tucked into his top pocket. He had a military bearing. On the floor by his right foot sat a leather satchel. He reached inside it and retrieved a folder and a small flag with red bars crossed on a field of blue mounted on a pedestal

"This meeting of the Army Comrades Association will now come to order. Please stand." He raised his arm in a Roman salute. "*Sieg Heil!*" The others stood and followed suit.

Blueshirts. Why in Heaven's name was Abbot Jonathan mixed up in a group like this?

"Reverend Abbot! Would you please open the proceedings with a prayer?" the leader asked after motioning everyone to sit down.

"I'd be honored, General Sloan." The abbot bowed his head and placed a small wooden crucifix on the table next to the Saltire, while those with caps removed them. He crossed himself and intoned, "O Lord, bless these proceedings undertaken on your behalf here tonight. We renew our commitment to defend and perpetuate Holy Mother Church in Ireland and throughout the world. Confound our enemies, we beseech you; strengthen our courage; stiffen our resolve to do what must be done to establish a government and a society worthy of your church on these shores. Amen."

Sloan spoke to an individual dressed in a blue military uniform across the table from him. "Captain Harrington, as secretary, would you please stand and read the first item on the agenda and give us a report; that is, if you can stand after your ignominious performance at the parade."

Harrington coughed to clear his throat. "Y-y-es, sir," he stuttered, avoiding the general's gaze. "This first item has to do with money. As you all know, we rely on our German friends to supply a good portion of it. Without their generous contribution, we could not hope to carry out our objectives."

"We are well aware of that, Captain Harrington. Would you please get on with it and give the group the update on Operation Green?"

The man in the trench coat fixed Sloan with a menacing stare.

Harrington cleared his throat. "Of course, General Sloan. One of our most trusted agents is already at the contact point awaiting the arrival of the German ship. Things are proceeding according to plan."

Sloan turned to the abbot. "How reliable is our agent?"

"Have no fear, he's totally committed. His profession gives him unquestionable access to all levels of society, and especially to the local authorities."

"Good. Moving on."

Cusack interrupted. "If I may ask a question, General Sloan ..."

Sloan dabbed his nose with his handkerchief. "Go ahead, but make it short."

"What does the German support amount to in terms of money? I mean, there are a lot of people who have to be paid—"

"Who are getting damned irritated about the sluggish pace of remittance for services rendered," the man in the trench coat interrupted.

Sloan's face stiffened. He appeared to have been caught off guard. "Mr. Kincaid, don't worry. There will be enough to pay everyone, although as far as I can see, it seems like throwing good money after bad with the results we've gotten so far."

Cusack gave a hoarse cough into his cupped hands. "I don't follow, sir."

Sloan spread his arms. "You can't even track down a simple schoolteacher. Every time you go up against him, you get your heads handed to you. Give me a few men like Coltrane and we wouldn't have to rely on German help."

Cusack shuffled the papers before him. "Excuse me, sir, Mr. Kincaid has more on that situation," his tone indicating that he was only too eager to turn it over to the Englishman at the end of the table.

Brother Michael felt his insides turn. If he was discovered, he had far more to fear than the abbot's wrath. Like a witness transfixed by a horrible road crash, he continued to watch and listen. Kincaid prepared to say his piece. He had a booming voice and looked ready to jump across the table and choke the life out of General Sloan with his bare hands.

"I've never come across such gall in all my life!" he bellowed. "On top of the money screw-up there's the local assistance fuck-up. I ask for help on the premise that these blokes have enough skill and knowledge to find one man and one kid in an area they are supposed to know like the backs of their hands. But what do I get? The first gent goes and gets himself killed by Coltrane, as does Dow, our supposed ace in the hole, not to mention Hans, my so-called right-hand man, who's gone missing." He pointed at Cusack. "And this incompetent can't kill someone lying prostrate on the ground in front of him. So much for local talent."

Cusack jumped from his chair, knocking it back on the floor. "Now just a bloody minute! I resent that."

"Enough, enough! No wonder Coltrane has run rings around you. You are a bunch of fools, all of you." The abbot swept the table with his rheumy eyes. Here he wagged a boney finger. "You storm ahead like a herd of elephants, shouting and making noise when you should be like cats, silent and listening."

"With all due respect, Abbot Jonathan, aren't you forgetting something? We've captured Coltrane's daughter, haven't we?" Cusack said, his face flushing.

The abbot shifted uncomfortably in his chair. "Well, that's another issue. It appears the young one is a chip off the old block. Her father's impossible to find and she is impossible to hold."

"I'm afraid I don't follow."

Kincaid leaned forward with his elbows on the table. "What he means is she's escaped from his bloody custody, twice."

"I can't help it that I'm dealing with a bunch of incompetents," the abbot replied. He grasped the brass crucifix suspended from his neck and rubbed it vigorously up and down his chest, as if warding off evil spirits.

"Sure, blame your subordinates. The bottom line is she was your responsibility and you muffed it."

"This bickering will get us nowhere," Sloan cut in. "The question is, where is she now?"

"She's in a secure place, back under my protection," Kincaid said.

"I repeat. Where is she being held?" the general pressed, transfixing Kincaid with a look that suggested, *Don't cross me.*

Kincaid hesitated and looked over at the abbot.

"In the interest of security and to prevent another fiasco, I've decided that it is in the best interest of the cause to limit knowledge of her whereabouts to myself and Mr. Kincaid." The abbot fixed the general with his opaque stare.

The general didn't press the issue further. "I suppose that's prudent. As long as she remains in our custody, it gives us some leverage over her father." His tone suggested he was looking for reassurance rather than a guarantee.

A disgusted look crossed the abbot's sallow face. "I wouldn't bet my life on that, General Sloan. From what Mr. Kincaid has reported, Coltrane appears to be anything but intimidated. This whole Coltrane affair has been a major distraction from our main objective and to my mind threatens it, unless we conclude this business pretty soon. The window of opportunity is closing, and the Germans are getting impatient at the interminable delays."

Kincaid threw his hands up. "The Germans. I'm sick of hearing about their so-called problem. If that son-of-a bitch Adler had kept his mask on, we wouldn't be in this mess."

Sloan grimaced. "That's water under the bridge; we have to deal with things as we now find them. And by the way, your foul language doesn't add credence or weight to your opinion, so please refrain from using it in the presence of the abbot. Keep in mind we are in an abbey."

"Believe me, that irony has not escaped me."

"Mr. Harrington, what else is on the agenda?" the general asked. "It's almost half past three, and for obvious reasons we have to be out of here before the monks rise for morning prayers."

Harrington gestured toward Kincaid. "Well, sir, as I said, Mr. Kincaid has an update on the Coltrane situation."

"Needless to say, we haven't apprehended him," Kincaid began, shrinking back in his chair. He sat in silence for a while before continuing. Then he slapped the table. "But we had him, we had him." He jerked his thumb at Cusack. "Until this imbecile misjudged the thickness of his skull."

"Mr. Kincaid, we're aware of that. Now what are the prospects for remedying the situation?" Sloan asked.

"He's a tough nut and has IRA protection. He's after the gillie Sweeney, as are we. He came damn close to capturing him a few days ago out at Duffy's Pub, but we're confident Sweeney slipped through his clutches."

"Why is it important to catch Sweeney, since I assume he doesn't know where the girl is, anyway?"

Kincaid stretched his lips in a tight smile. "He doesn't have direct knowledge of her whereabouts, but he does have a piece of information that could be dangerous if Coltrane got his hands on it."

Sloan leaned back and folded his arms. "Then see to it that you get to Sweeney before he does."

After an awkward silence, Harrington said, "Since the hour is getting late, I suggest we move to General Sloan's report without further ado."

Brother Michael's back ached from standing on the cement floor. His life was in jeopardy. If he was discovered, his next Chapter of Faults would be with the Almighty.

Chapter 44

Eavesdropping

Sloan cleared his throat, rose from his chair, and paced the length of the table. "Very Reverend Abbot and gentlemen. I assume I don't have to tell anyone seated here that this country, like many, is facing a grave crisis. The Bolsheviks and their minions, the trade unionists and the socialists, are on the march across Western Europe." A murmur of agreement arose. All eyes turned toward Sloan. "General Franco had the wisdom to see the threat they posed to Spain under the so-called banner of democracy. With the help of allies like Germany, and yes, I am proud to say, a contingent of our Irish Blueshirt brethren financed by the Catholic Church, he stalled their forward march."

Many stamped their feet in support of the speaker.

"I use the word stalled deliberately," Sloan continued, "because he didn't crush them. Now, like a virus, the red tide of communism in its many guises is washing ashore on the beaches of Ireland. Unfortunately our Taoiseach De Valera either doesn't see the threat or, worse still, is a collaborator. He has declared the country neutral in this great struggle and covertly has made common cause with our ancient enemy, the British, against Germany and Italy. If the Bolsheviks succeed, goodbye democracy, goodbye capitalism, and goodbye Catholic Church." He waved his hand in a grand flourish after each goodbye.

"Hear, hear, hear!" they shouted, applauding.

Sloan forged ahead with renewed vigor. "We see how the Republicans, the lap dogs of the Soviets, treated our Catholic brethren in Spain. Murder and mayhem became the order of the day; priests and nuns were butchered. That must not happen here. That will not happen here."

"It is not by accident that we are meeting in this abbey. This good man," he gestured toward Abbot Jonathan, "and many of his Catholic brethren see the real threat to the Church in Ireland. We are grateful for the personal, financial, and moral support they have given our crusade of righteousness.

"If De Valera and our government stand in the way of this noble cause, then he and it will be removed by force of arms, if necessary."

A loud roar arose from the gathering. Michael put his fingers in his ears in disbelief.

"In conclusion, I agree wholeheartedly with Abbot Jonathan: the Coltrane affair must be wrapped up immediately." He moved his finger back and forth between Kincaid and Cusack. "It's distracting us from our main objective. So do what must be done to get rid of him. In the meantime, keep the daughter secure. Her fate will be decided once we have achieved our objectives. Bear in mind that sometimes even the innocent have to be sacrificed for the greater good."

He paused and scrutinized the faces of his listeners for a reaction. The majority nodded their heads in silent support.

The abbot raised his hand. "One final item, General. See to it that our friends the Germans bring their payments to our comrades current. As the Gospel says, 'The laborer is worthy of his hire.'"

The general took a deep breath. "Rest assured, Abbot." After a few concluding comments, Sloan led the others in the Roman salute and a chorus of *Sieg Heils*. The clock in the kitchen sounded 4:30 a.m.

Michael retreated to his hiding place. As he squeezed behind the flour sacks he heard chairs scraping as the lights were switched off. He waited for a short while to be sure he was in the clear. He rid his hair and habit of the flour as best he could in the darkness before returning to his cell. He closed the door as the first streaks of dawn daubed the horizon. Sweat beaded his forehead.

***

After breakfast, a tap on Brother Michael's door. The abbot wished to see him in his office. His head swam. They couldn't have discovered him so soon! Or could they? He climbed the circular staircase, his heart pounding. Before knocking he took a deep breath."Enter." The abbot sat behind a large mahogany desk. A Blueshirt flag decorated the wall to his rear. Off to one side sat Brother Anselm, a young lad in his teens with a country face topped by a shock of red hair. He looked pale and ill at ease. The abbot directed Michael to stand in front of the desk and wasted no time in getting to the point. "Brother Anselm will assume your duties as infirmarian. Walk him through his new responsibilities and then report to Brother Bernard on the farm. That is all. Both of you may go."

Relieved beyond measure, Brother Michael hurried from the room with Brother Anselm in tow. Once out of the abbot's earshot, Brother Anselm confessed his apprehension about his new assignments in light of the unjust treatment he felt Michael had received during the Chapter of Faults.

"I wish I could tell you that his bark is worse than his bite, but sadly I can't. His bite matches his bark. He's also arbitrary and capricious," Michael said. "My best advice, Anselm: stay out of his way unless you absolutely have to speak with him. Now, let's go up to the infirmary and I'll introduce you to the sick brothers." On the way Michael discussed the conditions of the patients. Most were suffering minor ailments, including flu and colds. "It's important that they take their medicine. Many of the older brothers simply forget or lose track, and so it's up to you to remind them."

Then he told Anselm the story of Brother Edmond's medication.

"You mean that caused all the furor?"

"Indeed it did, and if you know what's good for you, you won't repeat my mistake." Brother Michael laughed nervously as they entered the infirmary. The room was well ventilated by three windows cut into the whitewashed walls lined with single beds. Paint was chipping off the iron frames. Beside each bed sat a small locker. Five of the beds were occupied.

"Good morning, Brother Edmond, did you take your medication today?"

Edmond rubbed his eyes. "No, not yet." For a moment Michael wondered if the abbot had failed to return the medication after confiscating it, but he was relieved to see the bottle with Edmond's name on it in the medicine cabinet.

"Here, let me help you." Michael filled a glass with water and gave Edmond his pill.

Before putting the bottle back in the cabinet, he decided to count its contents to make sure Brother Edmond wasn't taking more than the prescribed dosage. The label on the bottle said 30 capsules. His count revealed 25.

"Brother, when did you receive these pills from the abbot?"

"Yesterday."

"And you took one yesterday?"

"Yes."

He recounted the pills. Twenty-five. Taking into account the two pills taken thus far according to the dosage, twenty-eight should remain. Three were missing. He checked the medications of the other patients and discovered the same disturbing pattern. When the abbot returned the medications after his so-called inspection, each bottle was missing three to four capsules or tablets.

So that was it! The abbot's opaque stare was due to medication, not meditation.

Chapter 45

Rendezvous with the Submarine

After a day of rough sailing up the west coast of Ireland, Adler and his team arrived at the rendezvous point and hove to over the horizon off the Galway-Mayo coastline. The sub was nowhere in sight. Adler's three companions vomited over the side. He wondered if the old Irish curse of bad luck shrouded the boat in its black folds. He checked his watch: 3:00 a.m. He was restless to get underway.

The sub was supposed to ferry them to Little Killary Bay at the mouth of Killary Harbor. Since it could run submerged, there was less chance of it being spotted and a greater chance of their being dropped as close as possible to the landing spot. He scanned the surging waves. Nothing. He paced the rolling deck, pulling the southwester tighter over his ears. The others had disappeared below: 3:30 a.m. Lights on the horizon. He swore. The sub or the two British cruisers? Hard to tell at this distance. His heart pounded.

At last. About a hundred yards from the *Orion,* the dark shape of a conning tower surged from the water. As the rest of the sub rose to the surface, Adler felt hopeful for the first time since he set out from Brest. The head and shoulders of a man emerged from the conning tower.

Once Adler and his mates boarded the sub, Captain Schroeder

hoisted the *Orion*'s sail and headed for the open sea. No point in tempting fate. Adler couldn't quite decide if he was better off staggering on the rolling deck of the *Orion* or cramped in the tight space of the sub fifty feet below the rolling Atlantic. After the fresh sea air, the pervasive smell of diesel and sweat in the cramped quarters of the sub nauseated him. He couldn't wait to get back on solid ground.

The sub surfaced about five hundred yards from a small headland in Little Killary Bay, within a quarter mile off the village of Rosroe. As they paddled ashore in a small dinghy, Adler saw a light in one of the village houses, that cut through the pitch-black night. He stepped onto the weather-beaten rocks on the shore, relieved that the first stage of the operation had been successful. They were here, and by all appearances in one piece. He undid his pack and donned his oilskin against the rising wind and drizzle. The others followed suit, and crouched down in the shelter of large boulders scattered at intervals along the shoreline.

Adler expected to hear the agreed-upon signal at any moment from his contact. He looked at his watch: 5:00 a.m. Still no sound. He put his fingers to his lips and gave several sharp whistles: 5:30 a.m. No response. Despite his best efforts to avoid a mess, it became apparent with every passing moment that something had gone wrong. By half past six, with the wind rising and the drizzle intensifying into a fairly steady downpour, he decided to find shelter off the beach. Without it they would be like sitting ducks in the largely barren landscape of exposed rock and scattered clumps of bushes jutting from a ragged carpet of sedge grass.

From his pack he drew a worn pair of Wellingtons, a tweed cap, an overcoat, and a pair of work pants. He changed hastily. He put his oilskin back on, directed his comrades to stay put, and moved cautiously up a small lane in the direction of the village, unlikely to attract attention, he hoped, in his present attire. The solitary light in the village had long been extinguished; he put his trust in the lane to lead him in the right direction.

A short distance ahead, the dark outlines of buildings emerged. They couldn't hide out in the village, that was obvious, so he looked for an outlying barn or cowshed that would harbor them for a few hours. He doubled back and followed another lane that branched off the one he was on. A hundred yards on he found a small squat shed in a sheltered corner of a field. It had stone walls and a rusty galvanized roof held down with large rocks to secure it against the wind.

When he pushed the door open, the faint smell of stale cow manure pricked his nostrils. The building was a shelter for animals in winter. Now it was warm and dry. Nothing else mattered. The drumming of rain on the galvanized metal sounded like a distress code urging him to get his men off the beach and under cover before daylight. By the time that was accomplished, it was half past six. Faint wisps of light pushed through the dark clouds.

Whether the crashing waves or the piercing cries of seagulls riding the air currents awoke Adler, he wasn't sure, but he panicked when he discovered that it was almost 10:00 a.m. The morning had dawned bright and clear over a bay reflecting the azure blue of the sky. Shafts of light coming through the door cracks had been too weak to stir them. The loud snoring of the others underscored the stress they'd endured.

They weren't likely to be bothered for the time being, since no cattle grazed in the field and the shed appeared unused for anything else. Now that he was rested and could think clearly, he reflected on how badly the operation's first phase was botched. After all the meticulous planning, they were in a perilous situation due to either the stupidity or the cravenness of his Irish contacts. Had the entire operation been compromised? He didn't want to entertain the idea, but why did the highly recommended contact fail to make the rendezvous? Despite his suspicions, Adler knew he had to act on the assumption that incompetence and stupidity, rather than treachery, led to this *faux pas*. Why should that surprise him in light of the numerous botched attempts to capture Coltrane!

Before leaving the shed, Adler roused the others. "I'm on my way to reestablish contact with the Irish agent. Stay hidden until I return." As he walked up the lane toward the village, he hoped that his cover as a Dutch Jew seeking asylum from Nazi terror would hold up if challenged. In dress he looked like the locals, so he wasn't expecting trouble.

The few people on the streets barely gave him a second look. To his great relief, he spotted the green and beige phone kiosk outside the small post office at the end of the street directly opposite the Catholic Church. Although Catholic, he hadn't attended church since he was a teenager. The new German order would require little need for churches or priests. He climbed the steps to the great front door set in a Gothic arch. Once inside he eased into the last pew to collect his wits. How would he explain what a Jew was doing in a Catholic church? He figured the odds of being confronted on that score were low. The grey morning slid through the narrow Gothic windows, lighting the interior. Apart from an old lady lighting a candle in front of the St. Anthony's statue, he had the building to himself.

He leaned his head against the wall, closed his eyes in the soothing darkness, and felt the comforting shape of the Luger in his pocket. Momentarily the excitement of the mission distracted him from his present predicament. He extracted a slim notebook from his pocket and ran his finger down a list of names until he found the coded number of his contact. Walking outside, he slipped into the phone kiosk and dialed. The voice on the other end was quite businesslike and expressed surprise that the package had not been picked up. "I'll get back to you at this number in one hour," the voice said. Trying to contain his anger, Adler hung up the phone, sauntered down the street to a café selling tea and sandwiches, and sat at a little table beside a window overlooking the street. It was eleven o'clock.

While waiting for his sandwich he nipped next door to the post office and returned with the *Irish Press*. "Blueshirt March on Dublin," the main headline announced. How ironic that as one of the major players in this event, he might not make it on time. When he finished his meal he ordered chicken sandwiches for his companions, which he intended to supplement with a few bottles of beer from a nearby pub. He glanced at his watch. It was almost time for the phone call, so while the sandwiches were being prepared he retraced his steps to the kiosk.

About twenty yards shy of his destination, the phone rang. Two guards came down the street in his direction. *Great, nothing like the look of a stranger rushing to a ringing telephone in an empty call box to attract attention.*

He tipped his hat to the guards, who glanced at the kiosk. They showed little interest and strolled on. Adler stepped inside the kiosk and pulled the door after him but it jammed due to a faulty hinge. He picked up the receiver. "*Jawohl.*"

"Himself says to get to the ruins of Cluan this evening after dark, and you'll be picked up," the voice said.

"How the hell does himself think we're going to get there without transportation or cover? Both of which he promised to provide and is now dumping in my lap?"

"There were some unfortunate complications, best not talked about here, but we've addressed those now and are finally ready to move."

"*Finally ready*—that's rich. Why not give me the damn train timetable? That way we can all queue up at the station this afternoon and buy tickets to Galway in Deutschmarks without bothering you lot at all."

A long silence on the other end. Then, "For one thing, sarcasm won't get you to your destination. For another, there's no train service from here. No one is suggesting that you get to Cluan on your own."

"Why should we believe you now, since—"

"Once it gets dark, we'll provide a guide to shepherd you over the hills. It's the safest route and almost guarantees your getting there in total secrecy."

Not reassuring. At all. "Can we count on the guide's arrival this time?"

"You have my personal guarantee," the voice said. "We contact you at your current address at zero one hundred hours."

Adler rolled his eyes and opened his mouth to respond when the phone went dead.

Zero one hundred hours my arse. You'd think he was the coordinator of a bombing squadron, the puffed-up prick. He shouldered open the jammed kiosk door and strode down the street to pick up the beer and sandwiches.

***

The guide, a young woman named Maura, arrived at the shed a few minutes after midnight. *A woman? They have to be kidding.* Things were going from bad to worse. Adler bit his tongue until the overall situation clarified itself.

Maura picked up on his attitude. "Major, you can cool your arse here in the Irish drizzle or follow me across the mountain. I don't give a damn, it's up to you." Her fiery red hair and freckles matched the intensity in her eyes. "Either way I'm heading out, so hayfoot strawfoot, if you're up to it, let's go."

They slogged up the steep incline for an hour against a biting wind that scoured their faces, finally cresting a hill. Adler's breathing came in sharp spurts and his heartbeat thrummed against his ribs. He wasn't used to this and neither were his comrades, judging by their struggles to keep up with the guide. The deserted village of Cluan lay before them, a collection of ruined cottages abandoned in the Great Hunger a century before. As they waited for their deliverer among the derelict houses, Adler got spooked and moved outside the ruins. He didn't like graveyards, and this was as close to one as you could get absent mounds and crosses. Not a good omen. He imagined he could hear the voices of the dead, but it was only the moan of wind through the loose stones of the ruined walls. The headlights of a distant car flashed up the mountain road, in their direction.

"Don't show yourselves until we're sure who this is," Maura said. "I expect it's our man, but we need to be sure it's not some stray driving home from a pub who's taken a wrong turn."

The car's headlights disappeared and reappeared in the hollows and hills of the road as it slowly climbed toward them. The alternating pattern of light and darkness seemed to taunt them with the promise of salvation—or destruction.

Chapter 46

Quick Exit

Michael found Brother Bernard by the hayshed, unloading hay from a tractor bed. The brother and his helpers, in a rush to finish before the rains came, paid little attention to the newcomer. Bernard, a man in his mid-forties, had an ascetic face, which at first glance seemed at odds with his fit, outdoor look. But those who knew him well saw no contradiction.

Bernard continued forking clumps of hay up to a man inside the shed who was tramping it into a great square reek. Not wanting to disturb the work, Michael sat down on the cobblestones and waited, his back against the barnyard wall. Great clouds of dust rose into the air and gusts of wind sent errant wisps of hay flying in all directions so that the ground around the base of the tractor looked like a golden carpet of seed and chaff. When Bernard finally spotted him, he jumped from the tractor and came over and shook his hand. "Welcome to the farm. I heard you were coming, and I was most pleased. Nice to get a country lad who knows something about the land."

Michael returned his greeting warmly. "I can't tell you how happy I am to be here, Bernard."

Although Michael knew Bernard as a community member, they

weren't close. But almost immediately they struck up an easy friendship. That evening Michael unburdened himself of his secret.

"Do you think I should tell the guards?"

"From what you've told me, I wouldn't," Bernard said. "No telling where the tentacles of this group extend. For all we know, some of the guards might be involved in this."

"A few weeks ago I would have thought such thinking was madness, but now—"

"Now we need to get you out of here and pass word to the Coltranes about their daughter. I'll work on a plan tonight."

***

Next morning a notice on the bulletin board announced a Chapter of Faults the following day. Unusual to hold two so closely together, Michael thought. When he got down to the farmyard, Brother Bernard stood in the shelter of the hayshed beckoning wildly at him. "Did you hear about the Chapter?"

"Read it on the bulletin board. I'm afraid they're on to me."

"You think? If my hunch is correct, you'll be the star of this session. You'll have to get out of here sooner than we planned."

"I figured as much," Michael replied. "But that aside, do you know what prompted this?"

"According to the rumors I heard this morning, the abbot gave Brother Gabriel a royal chewing out for leaving the key in the kitchen door. Ever since then Gabriel has been chafing at the bit to clear his name. He steadfastly maintains that someone else must have entered the kitchen after lights out. Apparently he found evidence to confirm that."

Michael slapped his forehead with the palm of his hand. "The bags of flour."

"You got it. Gabriel discovered white footprints leading from the pantry to the kitchen. He didn't report it until he was sure none of the lay help were involved. But when he was satisfied that they were above suspicion, he was only too eager to run to the abbot to get back in his good graces."

"But how do they know I was involved? It could have been anyone."

"They didn't originally, but you became the number-one suspect because of another piece of information that's floating around."

Michael arched his eyebrows. "Which is?"

"Apparently when you got back to your cell, someone was awake. When Gabriel launched his investigation, the eavesdropper came running to him and turned you in, probably with the expectation of being granted some after-hours kitchen privileges."

"So much for brotherly love."

"Human nature won out, son. So this is not going to be a Chapter, but a kangaroo court before the entire community, which will be completely in the dark as to its real purpose."

"If I admit that I was the culprit, I'm as good as dead."

"That's why you have to leave as soon as possible. In fact, if it were me, I'd do it tonight after lights out. Come down here to the hayshed where I'll be waiting."

"But the Chapter of Faults hasn't taken place yet."

"Use your head, man! There's a real possibility that someone in that kitchen cabal may jump the gun and not wait for the Chapter of Faults to take action. I'm amazed they've let it go this long."

Michael buried his face in his hands. "Oh my God."

"I know you're put out to think of this happening in an abbey, but you're young and obviously not up on the ways of the world."

"C'mon, I'm not a complete innocent. After all, my background isn't that different from yours."

Bernard laughed. "I hope it is, unless you worked on the Albert Docks in Liverpool." Michael had no comeback. "Look, I lived a little before becoming a monk. In rubbing shoulders with the world, I quickly learned that humankind isn't all that different whether on the docks or in an abbey."

"Then what possessed you to come into religious life?" Michael asked.

"Looking for redemption, I suppose."

"Do you think, knowing this, you can find it here?"

"I hope. Fortunately the road to salvation doesn't run through the

Abbot Jonathans of the world. So no, I'm not scandalized, if that's what you mean; I learned long ago that who we are and what we become depend on ourselves."

***

After lights out, Michael sat on his bed with his worldly possessions tucked into a small duffel bag on his lap. The walls of the dormitory seemed to pulsate with snoring. But chances were not all were asleep, so in deference to the few insomniacs he tiptoed along the corridor, down the stairway, and into the night.

Chapter 47

Dissension in the Ranks

When the car drew level with the ruins of Cluan, it flashed its lights twice and stopped, its engine still running. Maura returned the signal. A tall man uncoiled himself from the driver's seat and stepped onto the roadway. He wore a grey felt hat at an angle that concealed his eyes. Maura walked out to meet him. Adler followed.

Maura extended her hand. "Alfred, I'm right glad to see you."

"Likewise, Maura, but I'm afraid we've had to change our plans."

Adler's eyes narrowed to pin pricks. "You were the gent I talked with on the phone, right? Why wasn't I consulted about a change of plans?"

Alfred Hayes looked quizzically at his questioner, as if trying to conjure up who he was. "And you are?"

Adler stood ramrod straight. "Adler, Major Adler, commandant of this operation."

"Well, Commandant, you above all should know. We're at war; things change without warning."

"How much of the original plan has changed?"

"Quite a bit, because of increased Garda activity."

Anger gave way to anxiety. "What do you mean *quite a bit*? Are you

246

saying the whole operation is ... off?"

"Circumstances have forced us to improvise. We've made arrangements to get you across Killary Harbor by boat to the Louisburgh Road instead of traveling by car to Galway. Once there you'll be picked up and taken to Westport."

"Westport?" Adler almost choked in surprise.

"Yes."

"So Galway is out?"

"It's too risky. Guards are all over the place because of Blueshirt and IRA activity in and around the city."

Adler fumbled to light a cigarette and paced. Hayes opened the trunk and returned with a parcel containing several black suits. "These are the duds for your disguises, Commandant." He turned to the guide. "It might be better to have them change right here, Maura, than at the boat."

"Let's not forget these." She walked forward with four pairs of black shoes. "It wouldn't look the part to have clerical students walking around in black suits and brown boots."

"Between me, you, and the wall, I'm not sure they'd fool anyone, even if they dressed up as bishops," Hayes whispered to her.

"Jaysus, you got that right."

"Did you ever see this chap Adler before?"

"'Fraid not."

"Well, I have, but I can't place him."

"That's not our worry, is it?"

"Maybe not, but this guy gives me the creeps."

Maura tossed her hair back. "Maybe we need a creep for this job."

Alfred stifled a laugh. He shouted to Adler and his cohorts changing behind the hedge. "It will be morning in about two hours and we need to have you across the harbor before daylight, so get a move on."

***

They sailed from Derrynacleigh Quay across Killary Harbor in a boat borrowed from a sympathetic fisherman, who manned the helm. Since the waters were still choppy from the powerful gale coming off the Atlantic, the sail on its own was insufficient. Adler and the Germans had to row not only to complete the crossing before sun-up, but also to keep the boat on course toward Bundorragha Quay on the Mayo side. The wind roared in squalls and whipped salt spray into their faces, burning their eyes and lips.

With every wave that slammed against it, the bow plunged and bucked, causing the German agents to occasionally miss the water with their strokes and fall back into the bottom of the boat. Each time this led to a torrent of German obscenities. Here and there through ragged holes in the storm clouds, the light of a solitary star shivered briefly before the clouds congealed and the sky turned ink-black once more.

Because of the need for stealth, the helmsman used his bow light sparingly, adding to the hazards of the crossing. Hayes wondered if running the gauntlet of checkpoints might not have been a safer option than this nightmare. Maura's assignment, to return the car to the church, was the better end of the deal. On top of that, Adler swore profusely and berated Hayes for landing them in such a mess.

Hayes threw him a dark look. "Stop bitching and row. I've got to make the return trip, so don't bellyache to me; soon enough you'll all be warm in your beds in some fancy hotel in Westport."

Adler shouted over his shoulder. "No thanks to you or that damn canon, if we are."

***

What a typical Irish cock-up. He struggled with the oars not so much to save the mission, but to save his skin. Wouldn't it be ironic, after surviving the Ju 52 crash, to perish while rowing a boat? The unfolding screw-up convinced him to sever contact with the others at the first opportunity. This would free him to fulfill the mission and let them attend to their objectives on their own timetable.

As dawn broke, they reached the other side. Exhausted and chilled to the bone, they dragged themselves up the steps of the crumbling cement stairway that ascended from the water to Bundorragha Quay. In a final push, they staggered up the embankment to the Louisburgh Road. Ahead of them, the dark outline of a car with its engine running.

Canon Roach exited the car and greeted Alfred Hayes while slipping an envelope into his hand. After a brief conversation they shook hands, and Hayes tipped his hat and returned to the boat.

***

On seeing Adler, shock registered on the canon's face. He scrambled for words.

"Major Adler? I thought that you—what in Heaven's name are you doing here?"

Adler rubbed his unshaven face as he glared at the canon through his wire-rim glasses. "Because of your incompetence, this whole operation nearly died in its cradle."

Blood rushed to the canon's pale cheeks. "Now see here—"

"I am not interested in your lame excuses. Please get us out of this miserable hole before we freeze to death."

The canon seethed. The Germans shambled behind him toward the car. Against the grey light of early morning, they looked more like shipwrecked refugees than agents of the mighty Third Reich in their crumpled suits. He was appalled at their condition, and despite his shabby treatment from Adler he realized he had to get them under cover as soon as possible in order to make them presentable.

Adler sat up front in the passenger seat, silent and brooding. By the time they pulled up outside the hotel in Westport, the rain bore down in torrents, which was fortunate. It would explain the soggy condition of the so-called "clerical students." The canon spent more time than necessary unloading luggage from the trunk, taking a good soaking himself. By the time he rang the bell at the front desk of the Regent Hotel in market square, he didn't look much better than his passengers.

While the German agents slept, the canon spent the better part of the morning getting the clerical attire cleaned and pressed. Then he drove to the railway station, where he bought four tickets on the morning train to Dublin for the following day. He was eager to be shut of his charges, especially the cantankerous Adler.

Apparently Adler had the same idea. When the canon awoke the next morning, Adler was gone. What a relief—but then, fear. What if his unpredictable behavior endangered the mission? The canon called General Sloan. He wasn't in Sloan's inner circle and wasn't privy to all the details of the master plan, but Adler's defection, or whatever it was, warranted Sloan's attention.

The general didn't seem overly concerned about Adler's disappearance. "Your responsibility, Canon, is to get the others to the German Embassy in Dublin before the march."

"And speaking of Adler, how did he end up?"

"That's none of your concern," Sloan said." You fulfill your mission and let Adler get on with his." An abrupt buzz. The phone went dead.

For the rest of the day the canon carried a sense of foreboding mixed with anger. They'd used him. Sloan's attitude was inexcusable. And what about Adler popping up out of the blue? Wasn't he supposed to have been deported back to Germany? He would show them. Once he boarded the Germans on the train, he intended to wash his hands of the whole mess. They couldn't treat him like some flunky.

One more thing to do. It might arouse suspicion to see clerical students traveling with duffel bags, so he walked up and down Main Street until he found a shop selling suitcases. He purchased four just in case Adler showed up again. He instructed the Germans to empty the contents of the duffel bags into their new luggage. He was curious to see what they carried. When his charges headed to the hotel bar for pre-dinner drinks, he returned to their rooms to rifle through their stuff.

Apart from the usual underwear and toiletries, they carried maps with locations circled in red ink. Each man also had a pistol in a leather holster, along with copies of Irish newspapers (certain article headings underlined), and an array of items that surprised him: fishing reels, pliers, insulating tape, and Irish pound notes—a lot of them. The fishing reels seemed out of place, since it was obvious that they'd have little time for recreation.

Next morning when the German agents showed up in the hotel dining room for breakfast, they were decked out in clerical garb. The canon had to admit that unless something unforeseen happened, they would avoid detection. He felt a little chuffed at that.

After a hearty breakfast of rashers, eggs, black pudding, and fried tomatoes, the canon delivered his charges to the train station. He waited on the platform until the last carriage trundled around a bend.

There were no goodbyes. He was delighted to be rid of them. Pulling up the collar of his top coat against the wind, he left the station and hurried to his car. While the engine ran he sat for a while, staring and smoking. Absentmindedly he extended his hand with the cigarette through the open side window, examining it as one might inspect a newly shaved face for razor nicks. His hand shook so badly while inserting the cigarette back into his mouth that it knocked ash onto the knees of his good pants. He barely noticed. After taking a few more pulls, he flicked the half-smoked cigarette out the window. Then he put the car in gear and drove back to Leenane to collect his belongings and head for home.

Chapter 48

Coltrane Pounces

The canon trudged up the stairs to his hotel room without checking at the desk for messages. His exhaustion was so great that he could barely insert the key in the door. Once inside the room, he fell on the bed fully dressed and sank into a deep sleep.

The sound of running water awoke him. The bedside clock said 5:00 a.m. A strange smell irritated his nostrils. He staggered into the bathroom and switched on the light. The tap was running. He reached to turn it off. The smell, stronger now, made him lightheaded. A hand clamped around his mouth. Everything went dark.

***

He fell backward into Lost John's brawny grip. In one swift maneuver Lost John flipped him face-down on the bed. Coltrane dropped the chloroform-soaked rag into a paper bag. "That should keep him quiet for a while."

Lost John opened the bedroom door a crack and peered up and down the hallway. "Everything's quiet out there."

Coltrane nodded. "This may be as good a time as any to make our move."

"Let's hope the night porter hasn't gotten cold feet," Lost John said.

"The prospect of getting another twenty pounds should keep his feet warm enough, don't you think?"

Lines of concern wrinkled Lost John's face. "Just the same, I'm going to slip down the back stairway to see if he's is still there keeping watch and as committed as when we gave him the money."

"Good idea. No sense in putting too much reliance on the chap's greed."

"I don't think it was all greed. As you know, his failure to deliver the canon's letter got him in the shit when the canon complained to the hotel management, so he wants to get his own back on sleeping beauty here."

Lost John took off down the back stairs. Within ten minutes he returned with a large blanket and a canvas stretcher. "That young fella has his wits about him, all right. He insists we use these in case someone bumps into us. We can claim the canon has fallen ill and is being taken to hospital."

"Bloody fast thinking, I'd say, not to mention how much easier it's going to make our job getting him out of here."

Coltrane removed a twenty-pound note from the canon's wallet. After covering him with the blanket, they lifted him onto the canvas pallet and placed his overnight bag at his feet. Moving down the winding staircase proved tricky. Following some dicey maneuvering they reached the ground floor, where the porter met them.

Shuffling along the hallway, Coltrane inclined his head toward the twenty-pound note sticking from the canon's top pocket. The porter eased it out expertly. After verifying its denomination against the dim hallway light, he saw them out the back door, wishing them Godspeed. They slid the stretcher into the rear of the van and secured the stretcher's leather straps around the canon to ensure he made no precipitous moves once he came to.

Lost John took the wheel. "Now where to?"

"As far away from this place as possible before the reverend is missed and we get caught in a dragnet."

"Can't move fast enough for me." Lost John started the engine.

"I've a cousin living in Ballycastle in North Mayo," Coltrane said. "It's a few hours' drive and off the beaten track, but an ideal spot for an interrogation. Do you still have that hammer on you?"

"Why? Do you want me to wake him up?"

"No, leave him be for now. To tell the truth I'm a little nervous, because I don't trust myself once he starts trying to bluff his way out of this. Sooner or later, though, we may need that."

"Nervous? Coming from the man who almost decapitated McShane?"

"What if I go too far before getting anything out of him?"

Lost John attempted a sincere smile. "Don't worry. I'll keep an eye on ye."

It was still dark when they crossed the Eriff River Bridge and headed toward Westport. About the time they entered the town, the canon stirred and Lost John reached for the chloroform rag to prevent a scene as they passed through.

An hour from Ballycastle, the canon woke up. He was confused and complained of a headache. "If you're smart, that's as bad as this has to get for now, but if not, you'll pray for a headache before it's all over," Coltrane said.

The canon attempted to speak, but only a rasping croak emerged. After a few swigs of water from a canteen, he regained his voice. A frightened look crossed his face upon recognizing Coltrane. He masked it with outrage. "How dare you treat me with such disrespect. You shameful reprobate! You will pay dearly for this."

Coltrane looked at him coldly. "Wait until the good people of the parish hear about your role in the kidnapping of a fourteen-year-old girl. Something tells me you're about to learn the true meaning of disgrace and shame."

The canon clenched his jaw. "I'm sure I don't have the faintest idea what you are talking about."

"There's no point in bluffing. We know."

"Know what, you lunatic? I insist you free me at once. Speaking of kidnapping, you'll be the one charged with that."

"You can continue to play this game, but you know where my

daughter is being held," Coltrane said.

The canon wouldn't budge. He looked a little worse for wear. His hair was disheveled and one wing of his clerical collar had become undone, giving his neck a raw look.

"Okay, have it your way. Round two is coming up. I guarantee you, before it's over you'll be singing a different tune."

"Maybe we should tell him where he's going," Lost John said.

The canon twisted his head toward the voice. "So you have a partner in crime. I demand to know his identity."

"You're in no position to make demands. As for his identity, you'll know soon enough, but not to keep you totally in suspense, here's his calling card."

Coltrane pulled the ball peen hammer from Lost John's belt and dropped it on the canon's testicles.

The canon screamed. "You ignorant barbarians, your days are numbered, take my word for it."

"That's only a starter to the sumptuous meal we're preparing for you."

An hour and a half later they pulled into a farmyard and parked in one of the empty barns. Leaving the barn they ran into Kevin Foley, Coltrane's cousin, coming from the fields with a spade over his shoulder. A black and white sheepdog trotted by his side. Due to his Coast Guard duties Kevin had a phone in his house allowing Coltrane to notify him beforehand that they were en route. Coltrane figured it would be bad manners to drop in unannounced with a trussed-up cleric. Since the extended family knew of Brigid's disappearance, Kevin was eager to help.

Coltrane had another good reason for taking the canon to Kevin's farm. As a lookout, Kevin's chief responsibility was to watch for German submarines from an observation shack on Downpatrick Head, a raised promontory with a sweeping view of the Atlantic Ocean about a quarter mile from the farm. For interrogation purposes the shack was ideal. It perched on a cliff hundreds of feet above the crashing waves. A fall from such a height offered little hope of survival, a most powerful incentive to loosen the tongue of an obstinate prisoner.

The landscape offered another, more spectacular feature: a blowhole, the product of millions of years of algorithmic savagery by the sea against the fragile coastline. Situated near the top of Downpatrick, the Old Fire Hole—*Poll an Sean Teine* as it was known to the ancient Irish—possessed sheer funnel walls that dropped nearly a hundred feet to the churning waters below. In stormy weather, large geysers sluiced up through the funnel and were sucked down again into the watery abyss in an earsplitting roar.

With the reluctant canon in tow, they trudged up the hill toward the lookout shack. Above them the sky reverberated with the cries of seagulls and razorbills gracefully riding air currents or diving frenetically toward the turbulent sea in search of fish. This circling canopy of noise compressed the fierce wind coming off the ocean into an echo chamber until it sounded like an oncoming freight train. They dragged the canon to the edge of the blowhole. He recoiled in terror.

"I think he's got the picture!" Coltrane shouted to Lost John. "Let's get him into the shack."

The small shelter held a table and two chairs; its one window overlooked the rolling Atlantic. A life buoy and a pair of binoculars hung from a hook on one wall. Off in a corner sat a little primus stove with a kettle on top. A detailed map of the North Mayo coast was attached to the facing wall by thumbtacks. The trembling canon slumped into one of the chairs, his face a mask of fear.

"That was just a preview to clear your sinuses after the chloroform, and hopefully clear your head of any notion that you can bluff your way out of this," Coltrane said, his voice a flat monotone. "I'm going to ask you one more time: Where's my daughter?"

The canon straightened himself in the chair, his jaw set in defiance. "And for the last time, I'm telling you. I know nothing of which you speak. You were the one with your daughter when she disappeared, so why ask me, unless you're trying to assuage your guilt for having abandoned her, you drunken sot?"

"Kevin, get the ropes."

Coltrane wrapped the heavy rope around the canon's chest, shoulders, and armpits in the manner used to lower somebody from a burning building. The canon struggled as he was being harnessed, but his efforts were futile in a three-to-one contest. They dragged him outside to the rim of the blowhole. "A brief history lesson, Canon!" Coltrane shouted. "Legend has it that St. Patrick created this blowhole to save the subjects of a cruel chieftain who used to throw them into a fire on this very spot for failing to pay their rents."

"What a coincidence. Looks like the canon's rent is about to come due any minute now," Lost John chuckled.

"I hope he can pay up, John. The fire may be gone, but the blowhole will do as well."

A jet of water roared ten feet above the rim, drenching them and forcing them back from the edge.

"How ironic, Canon, that we have to use this same blowhole to save the life of an innocent young girl from one of St. Patrick's ignoble clerical descendants."

The canon's face stiffened. "You don't have the nerve for something like this."

Without another word they dragged him toward the edge and pushed him into the hellhole of wind and water, bracing themselves for the pull when the rope played out. A terrified scream echoed up the rock chamber before the rope caught hold and arrested the canon's fall. As they struggled to haul him out, the blowhole roared again, spitting him atop a great column of spume onto the boggy terrain close to the rim. The seagulls and razorbills continued to wheel lazily under the dark of the gathering rain.

The canon lay crumpled on his back on the spongy earth. They rushed toward him and for a heart-stopping moment Coltrane feared he had passed from this world, taking the secret of Brigid's hiding place with him to eternity. In the violent maelstrom one of the ropes had pulled free of the canon's armpit, leaving an ugly red gash where it settled around his neck. His shoes were gone and his coat hung from his body by one arm. They scrambled to turn him over and slapped his back to dislodge the water from his lungs.

The canon coughed. He coughed again, spitting up a stream of spume. Relief softened Coltrane's face. They carried him into the shack and laid him on the floor.

Lost John placed a rolled-up jacket under the canon's head and covered him with an overcoat while Kevin fired up the primus to make tea in case the canon confessed his secret. If he didn't, it wasn't tea he'd be drinking, but more salt water.

However, the fight was out of him. As Coltrane hunkered down to question him again, he lifted a shaking hand. "I don't know where she is, but I can name someone who does."

Coltrane's heart skipped a beat. "Then out with it."

The canon closed his eyes as if he didn't want to look at Coltrane. "Abbot Jonathan of Glenfar Abbey."

Lost John shook his head. "Told you so." Coltrane's face turned hard as stone. The Blueshirts. The Church. The Nazis. all actors in the Spanish Civil War, people he had fought against. His past had just come back to haunt him.

The canon wasn't done talking. He confessed his part in smuggling Adler and the German agents into Ireland in preparation for Operation Green and providing them with disguises and alibis.

Coltrane's jaw dropped. "Whoa, back up. What's this about Adler and Operation Green?"

"Hitler wants to add Ireland to his conquests. Not that he cares a whit about Ireland."

Coltrane sucked in his breath. "Hitler sees it as a jumping-off point for an attack on England. Right?"

"Right."

"Did I understand you to say Adler?"

"I did indeed, and a more nasty, dangerous, and disagreeable person I can't think of."

You mean the Adler from the German Embassy?"

"One and the same."

Coltrane felt the kind of chill one gets when frightened without warning. His mind harkened back to the island, peeking through the willow screen, staring at those grey malevolent eyes. He could feel Brigid's breathing against his chest.

He scrambled to make sense of what he'd heard. "I thought the

Irish government sent him packing from the country."

The canon's face gathered into a smirk. "It did, but it appears he came right back. He's a very determined fellow is our Adler."

Contrary to reports, the Spitfires hadn't done their work, it seemed. What if Adler was after Brigid—*Oh my God!* But on reflection that didn't make sense. Surely Adler had bigger fish to fry. His cover was already blown. On the other hand, Brigid might still figure in whatever dark purpose lay behind his sudden reappearance. To be on the safe side he had better get word to Guard Ryan and Seamus Reagan.

"But he's disappeared and you have no idea where, or what he's up to?" Coltrane said.

Lost John handed the canon a blanket, which he pulled around his shivering body. "I can say with certainty that I don't know where he is, that I did not put him on the train in Westport, and with equal certainty that wherever he is, he's up to no good." He put his hand over his mouth and fell into a coughing spasm.

"Why in the hell do we care where Adler is?" Lost John whispered. "Haven't we gotten what we want out of the canon?"

"Because I suspect they're all part of the same nest of vipers. Whatever Adler is up to could have unforeseen consequences for Brigid. I can't take that chance, so we need to get as much information on him as possible for Ryan and Reagan."

After his spasm ended, the canon started up again. "There is one person who *I* suspect knows where Adler is and what the true nature of his mission is."

Coltrane lit a cigarette. "Who?"

The canon gazed longingly as Coltrane took a deep drag. "Forget it. Get on with your story."

"General Sloan."

Coltrane shook his head. "You mean the Blueshirt bigwig?"

"The very one. Although in a recent conversation with me, he clammed up when I mentioned Adler."

"By God, haven't you been the busy beaver? Up to your clerical collar in all of this, it seems. Go on! How did you reach that conclusion?"

With the apparent attitude of "in for a penny, in for a pound," the canon suddenly seemed eager to divulge what he knew, even if part of it was sheer speculation. "My gut feeling is that Adler is on a special assignment that only the higher-ups are aware of, but Sloan was enigmatic on that point."

"But since Adler and the others are an advance team for Operation Green, isn't that special enough?"

The canon burrowed deeper into the blanket. "Can't say for sure, but I have a feeling something else is in the wind."

Coltrane pulled out his pocket watch. He turned to Kevin. "We must be away. If I don't get back to you within the week with good news," he nodded in the canon's direction, "down the blowhole with him."

Chapter 49

The Sky Falls In

To bide his time after walking out on his charges, Adler holed up in a rooming house in Westport within sight of the Regent Hotel. He wanted to see which way the wind was blowing before making his move. From his second-storey window he had seen the canon take the others to the train. When the coast was clear he walked down to a nearby confectionary shop and bought the *Irish Press* to scan over breakfast. He rushed to a restaurant, two doors down from the rooming house, hoping to get a spot before it filled up. He lucked out in finding a table under a stairway where he could read in relative peace.

He spread the paper out on the table. One headline dominated the front page: "Thousands Converge on Dublin by Rail and Bus." So the march had started. *Good, now let's see what happens.* Farther down the page, a photo caption: "Sloan Addresses the Blueshirt Faithful." Sloan was pictured on the back of a lorry speaking before a microphone. On the edges of the crowd a large contingent of guards was clearly visible. The article quoted inflammatory, almost seditious, passages from the speech. If Sloan was this courageous, the coup must be imminent, Adler thought.

Something about the presence of the guards in the picture caused him unease. The guards were presumed sympathetic to the cause, but what if Sloan got it wrong and they weren't?

Adler returned to his room. He went through the items in his duffel bag for the third time. How much of this equipment he put to use depended entirely on what happened in the coming days. As far as he was concerned, the one essential piece of equipment was the disassembled Gewehr rifle. He was tempted to ditch the rest.

After completing his check, he settled in the quietest corner of a very crowded pub with a scotch and soda. The place was abuzz with people, young and old, drinking and socializing. He eavesdropped on the banter about the Germans, the British, the Americans, and the war. One would think that the British Parliament were sitting in special session in Westport. There was no shortage of experts on everything. *Say your piece now, you self-styled gobshite know-it-alls. This bullshit is going to end, and not a moment too soon.*

***

Next morning over breakfast, the sky fell in. The newspaper headline screamed: "German Spies Arrested in Roscommon Railway Station." The article went on to say, "Local guards aided by the military intelligence unit, G-2, arrested three German spies masquerading as clerical students." A front-page photo showed them being led off the train in handcuffs. Displayed on a table outside the station were an assortment of guns, incendiary bombs, detonators, and Irish currency totaling over £800.

He put the newspaper down on the restaurant table and pushed away his hardboiled egg, his appetite gone. *That incompetent canon blew it.* By the looks and tone of the news article, it was obvious the authorities had been tipped off in advance. It wasn't blind luck. Someone squealed or made a stupid mistake that blew their cover. For the first time he realized what Kincaid was up against. He paid the bill, lit a cigarette, and walked to the pub, where he ordered a double scotch and soda. He needed time to think.

The news only got worse. Despite the static on the pub radio, the message came through loud and clear: Irish Taoiseach Eamon De Valera banned the march on Dublin and declared the Blueshirt organization illegal. To put muscle into his proclamation, he called on the army and the guards to disperse those who challenged the ban.

Apart from a few minor scuffles in some provincial towns, it was amazing how quickly the whole thing fell apart. Next day's paper described the efforts made to round up the ringleaders: Sloan was arrested dressed as a nun, trying to board a ferry for England. Several of his lieutenants were nabbed scrambling to cross the border into Northern Ireland. *When the going got tough*, Adler sneered, *Sloan did what he did in Spain: headed for the exit.*

There was no point wasting time and energy on a post mortem. He had work to do. After all the months of planning and hard work he wouldn't lie down or run off with his tail between his legs like the cowardly Sloan. To continue with phase one, the disruption of essential services, would be suicidal. That ship had sailed. It was time to implement phase two.

The following morning before breakfast he scanned the paper for any signs that his identity had been compromised. Sloan and his cohorts apparently kept their mouths shut, hoping against hope, he surmised, that he, Adler, might resuscitate a situation rapidly deteriorating into a lost cause. But in the back of his mind he clung to the idea that maybe there was a chance to turn this disaster around. Dicey to be sure, but while many of the top brass were now behind bars, most of the revolutionary cells and their leaders were still intact.

If he hoped to resurrect the mission he must strike soon, before these cells were disrupted or their members fled the country. He finished his coffee and returned to his room. After packing his belongings, he settled up at the front desk. Then he walked nonchalantly into the square and mingled with shoppers. His instincts told him that he should avoid public transportation, so he set off toward the edge of town and waited for a good Samaritan to give him a ride to Galway.

Chapter 50

Kincaid's Quandary

Kincaid paced the lakeshore in the gathering dusk, his briar pipe gripped firmly in his yellow teeth. Tobacco smoke wafted into the chilly air only to be whipped away in an instant by the surging wind gusts. The roof had fallen in. Operation Green had turned into a rout. The rats were fleeing the sinking ship. Sinking with it was his last chance to recoup the money owed him by the Germans.

Decision time. Should he flee now and try to make it to his boat on the Shannon? He could hide out there until things blew over. But there was the girl. Not much point in holding on to her anymore. Not much point in killing her either, since German involvement in the Red Cow Island killings had already been exposed. She couldn't give the authorities any information that they didn't already possess.

He toyed with the idea of holding her for ransom, but quickly dismissed it. Even if Coltrane had money, which he hadn't, Kincaid would never be able to pull it off given the current climate in the country. Plus it would only draw attention to him. Hidden out here in this remote spot lulled Kincaid into believing that he'd dropped below the radar. Better leave it like that.

He scanned the lake: whitecaps across its entire expanse breaking on the shore like ocean waves. Ink-black clouds hovered low on the horizon. Escape by water was his best chance. He looked at the motorboat tied to the jetty. Smart thing would be to get out right now before the storm got worse. He'd have to travel light, which meant leaving Stiglitz behind with the girl. He took the pipe from his mouth and mulled that over. Couldn't risk it. Stiglitz was a damn Nazi. He'd kill her for sure, which would be senseless at this point.

Now that everything had broken apart he thought about his own broken family, especially about his little girl. He saw her face now every time he looked at the Coltrane kid. Another thought crossed his mind. The abbot had probably spilled his guts about their hiding place. If so, he could expect a visit from the guards at any time. That did it. He didn't fancy spending the rest of his life in an Irish jail for kidnapping. Or a worse fate, if Coltrane got wind of his whereabouts.

He looked at the lake again. The whitecaps had gained momentum and were sloshing over the jetty. Too dangerous to leave right now. He tapped the bowl of his pipe on a rock to empty it and hurried toward the boathouse. He would leave as soon as the storm abated, hopefully first thing in the morning. As he entered the house another thought occurred to him. The Coltrane kid could identify him to the authorities. That could complicate matters.

Chapter 51

The Prostitute Fights Back

Adler passed through the Garda checkpoint outside Galway hidden under a filthy bunk bed in a rainbow-colored gypsy wagon. In return for the favor he paid the gypsy leader fifty pounds; for an additional twenty the gypsy sold him a knife with arabesque etchings on its bone handle. Told him that it would bring him luck. Adler didn't believe it, given his run of terrible reversals so far. But at this stage of the game he was willing to entertain any belief, no matter how flimsy or idiotic, that might turn his fortune around. Bidding farewell to his hosts, he shouldered his duffel bag and walked to Shop Street, dropping a shilling into a banjo player's collection cup outside a pub. He proceeded to the docks, where he found a cheap boarding house near Spanish Arch, figuring a foreigner could lie low there until the furor died down.

This area of the city possessed an interesting stew of colorful personalities with equally diverse cultural and economic backgrounds. Here musicians, shopkeepers, dancers, farmers, prostitutes, and bookies mingled with easy informality. The population abided by the precept "Live and let live." However, Adler considered himself destined for greatness; he wasn't some uneducated yahoo whose only ambition was a pint or a cheap night of illicit pleasure. He couldn't tolerate this mind-numbing anonymity for long.

***

A young prostitute with fiery red hair named Maraid earned money on the side by keeping her eyes and ears open for tidbits of information that her IRA handlers might deem important.

On this night she hit the jackpot. A middle-aged man with a foreign accent paid for her services. When their tryst was over, they talked.

"Ara go on, you're having me on; if you're that important what the bloody hell are you doing in a flophouse like this?" she inquired as they sat up in bed smoking in the light of a solitary ceiling bulb.

"Don't you worry; very soon I'll be moving to posher digs up in Eyre Square."

"Oh ye will, will ye?" She laughed. "I'll believe that when I see it."

His face reflected anger at being mocked by a whore. Apparently to reclaim his dignity and prove his point, he revealed more information about himself and his business than he should have. "Very soon, strumpet, everyone in the country will know the name of Major—" Then he caught himself.

She laughed even harder. "Major! In whose fucking army, the Salvation?"

He reached for the bottle of Powers on the floor and refilled both their glasses. "Here, let's dr-r-ink a toast to the day in the new order when places like this sh-sh-it hole will be burned to the ground and your kind will not be allowed to walk the streets."

"What the bloody hell are you talking about, you foreign prick? Shitholes like this wouldn't exist and people like me wouldn't be walking the streets but for arseholes like you."

She threw her whiskey in his face, jumped out of bed, and pulled on her dress.

He tried to grab her, but in his inebriated state he was no match for her. When she pushed him back onto the bed, his head hit the wall. He reached beneath his pillow and pulled out a pistol. "I'll kill you, you b-b-itch."

Again she got the better of him. As he struggled to level the gun, she hit him with the chipped-enamel chamber pot, slopping the contents all over his head and shoulders. Making another effort to grab her, he fell out of bed and landed atop the duffel bag, the whiskey bottle, and the empty pot. He lay there dazed and watched as she helped herself to the money in his wallet and fled.

***

She couldn't believe her luck when she examined the money under a streetlight and discovered two fifty-pound notes, and another note with foreign writing on it. Sure enough, this was not just another braggart blowing hot air. Her contacts would like to know about him.

At the next corner she found a kiosk and made a phone call.

Chapter 52

Graveyard Reckoning

As Brother Michael passed beneath the arch into the cobblestone yard, a slight breeze that hinted of rain rustled the leaves of elm trees bordering the little graveyard. Once inside, he paused and listened to make sure he wasn't being followed. Silence, save for the chirping of crickets and the croaking of frogs.

Satisfied, he moved along one side of the yard, sticking close to the buildings until he reached the hayshed. This large structure consisted of a steel skeleton, its arched roof and upper level wrapped with galvanized sheets. The lower level remained open to the elements.

In both end sections stacked hay reached to within three feet of the roof. The mid-section was left empty as a work area and a place to house farm machinery as well as farm implements like pitchforks and rakes. A ladder leaned against one of the two hay reeks. Bernard hadn't yet arrived. When Michael's eyes adjusted to the darkness he found a comfortable spot between a parked tractor and the reek. Leaning his back against the hay, he slumped crossed-legged on the chaff-covered floor to wait. It was 12:30 a.m.

At one o'clock, Bernard, who was usually as prompt as the rising and setting sun, hadn't arrived. Michael grew uneasy. He had come to rely on Bernard. Without him he wasn't sure he had the courage to make a break from his monastic home now turned into a prison. A half hour later, the crunch of approaching footsteps on gravel. Bernard ran up, out of breath and flustered. "I'm sorry for getting here so late, but I had a vet in to see to a sick animal and I couldn't get rid of him. He wanted to stay and chat once he determined the animal was out of danger. However, it's an ill wind that blows no good."

"I'm right glad to see you. I was beginning to think you weren't coming—or worse."

"As it happens, when the vet left, the lights of his car illuminated a figure advancing across the fields in the direction of the rear entrance. Although I only got a glimpse, it was long enough to determine that he wasn't a monk."

"So, your instincts were right. Someone is set to jump the gun."

"We can't afford to take chances," Bernard said. "Sleep on top of the hay; it's warm up there and also safe once I remove the ladder."

"Where are you going to sleep?"

"Don't worry about me. I'll find a spot down here out of sight. Should anyone come prowling around before morning … well, I'm a light sleeper."

Bernard gave him a fistful of pound notes and told him to be ready to move before the morning bell sounded at five o'clock. "The abbot won't miss you, in all likelihood, until after breakfast. Nevertheless, to be on the safe side it's best we get out of here as soon as the sun comes up."

Michael climbed the ladder and settled down in the soft hay. Before dropping off he felt Bernard remove the ladder. A sudden rain shower assaulted the galvanized roof. In spite of the din, sleep came quickly.

***

First light revealed a lone figure moving along the path among the headstones. Heavy boots ground the wet gravel. The early morning fog lingered, providing cover for which the interloper was grateful. As he passed out of the graveyard, large droplets from the overnight showers fell from the leaves and plopped on the rim of his felt hat. A solitary blackbird fluttered among the branches.

He skirted the yard to avoid meeting an early riser and moved along the fence to the orchard, where he waited among the apple trees. This afforded a good view of the hayshed. He picked an apple and bit into it, amazed by its sweetness. *These apples need picking, otherwise they'll rot.*

As the sun rose he held the apple between his teeth and removed the Luger from his raincoat pocket. He felt around some more for the silencer, and screwed it to the barrel. He took one more bite from the apple and threw the core among the beehives. Then he removed his hat and pulled a mask over his head and face. He remembered a line of Shakespeare from his school days: "If it were done when 'tis done, then 'twere well it were done quickly." "Amen!" he muttered and moved out of the orchard.

He had visited Brother Michael's cell first. Finding it empty, he was directed to the hayshed. The interior of the structure was still in shadow, but there was no mistaking the snoring atop the hay reek. As usual, the abbot was right. He stuck the gun under his belt and set the ladder against the wall of packed hay.

***

It may have been the rising chorus of birdsong or the squeaking of a loose step in the ladder. Bernard wasn't sure. Whatever the case, he awoke to see a figure climbing the repositioned ladder up the hay reek. He dove for the ladder and yanked it, his muscles bulging through his work shirt. The ladder swayed crazily toward the center of the shed, sending the climber flying like a trapeze artist across the open space into the wall of hay on the opposite side . As the intruder slid down the face of the haystack, he grabbed at it wildly, pulling out fistfuls that broke his fall and enabled him to land on his feet, dazed but unhurt. Bernard sprang. With a well-aimed blow to the chin, he sent the intruder sprawling to the floor on his back.

When Bernard closed in for a second go, the assailant drew up his knees and feet into a ball and released them against Bernard's shins, knocking him onto the tow bar of the tractor. Bernard lay there without

271

moving. Through blurred vision he watched his masked opponent pull a gun from his belt. Just as he fired, Michael's duffel landed on the gunman's head. The bullet ricocheted off one of the steel girders in a shower of sparks before embedding itself in the packed hay. Bernard staggered to his feet, but before he could engage the assailant a second time, he fled, taking a wild shot at Michael as he slid down the wall of hay.

Bernard grabbed a pitchfork and Michael followed suit. "Come on!" Bernard yelled." Michael ran to catch up. The interloper disappeared through the arch at the other end of the yard. "You follow him, but don't get too close," Bernard said. "I'll try to cut him off. To skirt the abbey he has to go through the graveyard. I'll be waiting there."

As Michael took up pursuit, Bernard turned into a field that ran parallel to the outer wall of the yard. Out of breath, but with enough adrenalin to pull a tractor, he reached the cemetery's western boundary wall and paused to listen. All was quiet except for the odd birdcall. Maybe I've misjudged it, Bernard thought, and he's taken refuge in one of the abbey buildings. The assailant obviously had allies within the monastic community. Bernard climbed over the moss-covered wall and hunkered down again to listen. Michael should have made an appearance, but he was nowhere in sight either.

Bernard took a few more steps through the long wet grass that grew between the graves and dropped to his haunches to reduce his profile. He grasped the hayfork lightly. He didn't trust the silence. Crouched within the long grass, he wondered if Michael was lying somewhere wounded, or worse.

Mustering his courage, he rose and started forward, swiveling his head from side to side to scrutinize the large crosses and statues that marked the final resting place of the dead. As if trying to restrain him, the wet grass clung to his Wellingtons. In his peripheral vision he thought he saw one of the statues step down from its pedestal. Were his eyes playing tricks on him?

He swiveled toward the motion. A masked shape leapt from a gravesite and came at him, flame erupting from the figure's right hand. As bullets ricocheted off the headstones, Bernard raised his arm over his shoulder. More from instinct than calculation, he heaved the pitchfork. Both prongs pierced the attacker's chest, pitching him backward into the gravesite atop the broken statue of the Virgin Mary that had toppled from its pedestal. Bernard stepped cautiously across the low granite wall of the grave and carefully removed the mask from the prone figure. The glassy, vacant eyes of Arthur Cusack glared back at him.

Michael emerged from the mist with the pitchfork dangling from his hand and stood motionless behind Bernard.

Bernard pulled his eyes away from Cusack. "Thanks for showing up."

"I'm sorry, Bernard, but I lost him almost immediately in the dim light and I spent the rest of the time wandering among the statues looking for him."

Bernard immediately regretted his brusque remark. "Listen, forgive my sharp comment, but the truth is I was beginning to think the worst."

They hurried from the graveyard. When they reached the moss-covered boundary wall they looked back at Cusack's body, raised above the ground on the prone statue of the Virgin. The pitchfork's thin handle stuck up amidst the granite crosses like a harpoon from a stricken whale. By the time they reached the cobblestone yard, smoke poured from the hayshed. The sparks caused by the bullets' ricocheting off the steel girders had slowly done their work. Three months' labor went up in smoke before their eyes. "We have to put this out!" Michael shouted.

"Are you out of your mind? We need to get away from here."

"But we can't walk off and leave it without doing something."

"Yes we can—and we shall, if you value your life." Braving the smoke and flames, Bernard leaped on the tractor and backed it from the shed. "Come on, hop on; there's no time to waste. Once they discover Cusack's body this place is going to be crawling with guards, not to mention the attention the fire is going to get."

As they drove through the back gate along the cart track, tongues of flame shot from the sides of the hayshed. Within minutes it was an inferno.

Chapter 53

Guard Ryan Goes AWOL

The phone rang. Guard Tom Ryan was sitting in the loo, in no frame of mind to engage the outside world, nor at a point in his business to easily break away. He had spent the entire weekend at his first cousin's wedding in the Travelers' Friend Hotel, arriving home late Monday afternoon. With only a few hours of fitful sleep, he lurched into work. When the sergeant smelled his breath and saw his bloodshot eyes, he reassigned him to the station instead of to a patrol car. "Can't let you out in public, Ryan, in worse condition than them you're supposed to be serving."

"Bollocks, if you had given me the day off like I requested, we wouldn't be having this discussion."

"If you show up to work again in this condition, I'll be forced to write you up. Hopefully it'll be a quiet night and you're still capable of answering the phone."

Ryan muttered to himself. "Pompous arsehole."

Within his pickled brain the phone resounded like a headache. He maneuvered out of the loo and grabbed it like an intruder choking a barking dog. He wasn't sure his mouth would work. When he heard Peter Coltrane on the other end, he exploded with a litany of obscenities. "You again? Do you ever fucking go to bed?"

"I thought you'd be at home after the wedding, and anyway, this can't wait."

"Don't tell me you woke the wife and kids?"

"Afraid so, I'm sorry."

Ryan bristled. "I'll get hell for this. What's got you so all fired up anyway?" Then it hit him what hell his friend was going through. His own inconvenience paled by comparison.

"Oh God, Pete, I'm sorry. I'm such a jerk."

"You are indeed. But don't worry about it. There's a major new development. Adler is alive and kicking and back in Ireland."

Ryan tried to focus, swaying over his cluttered desk. "Sweet suffering Jaysus, you're putting me on. It can't be … the Spitfires … how do you know this?"

"Look, he was smuggled in with the German spies from the submarine."

"But I checked those Krauts out. Wasn't a mention of him on the radio or in the newspapers."

"That's because he separated from the rest before they were apprehended."

"I'm rattled, I can hardly think."

"Well you better pull yourself together, man," Coltrane said, plenty of growl in his voice. "Report this to the brass. Then get down here as soon as possible. I need you." Then the line went dead. Ryan dropped the phone into its cradle with a clatter. Some unknown Kraut was responsible for beating up his friend Guard Daly and another, Adler, was responsible for the disappearance of his good friend's daughter. He blushed when he thought of his overreaction to Coltrane just now. As the girl's godfather, he felt a special responsibility beyond the tug of friendship. The wind whistling through the spaces in the window frames brushed his cheek. A terrible night. And Brigid Coltrane, an innocent fourteen-year-old, was out there lost in the darkness. It shocked him anew and sent adrenalin surging through his veins. His hands grew clammy. Screw the sergeant; he was heading to Cloonfin come the end of his shift. Damn the consequences. He had a score to settle with those murderous Krauts. Although deep down he wasn't convinced Adler was still alive. The Brits were quite adamant that the Spitfires did their job. Coltrane might have gotten hold of faulty information. Be that as it may, he would honor his friend's request.

***

Ryan arrived at Reagan's shop at about five o'clock the following afternoon. Mrs. Reagan ushered him down to the basement, where her husband, Coltrane, and Lost John awaited him. He cast his eyes around the room, knowing how he must have looked to them. Famished. "Well, Glory be to Jaysus, how cozy the three of you look, and I'm fucking wrecked."

Coltrane jumped to his feet and pumped Ryan's hand. "Welcome you auld scoundrel. It's good to see you."

The others crowded around him. After much backslapping and ribbing, they settled around the table. Reagan shouted up to his wife to bring down tea and sandwiches for the visitor.

Then Reagan addressed Ryan. "As you've heard by now, Adler is on the loose, and no one knows what he's up to."

"Can you confirm that? According to the brass, the Spitfire pilots said they nailed him, or at least the plane he was traveling in."

"That's the point. They killed the plane, but not Adler."

"But can you confirm it? That's what I'm asking," Ryan went on, his disbelief masking his disappointment.

Coltrane's face grew somber. "Heard it from the horse's mouth. A canon of the Church, in this case. He knew his life was on the line. I don't think he'd dare lie."

"You hope."

"Jesus, what is this, Ryan? Suddenly you've become a solicitor. I hope your skepticism didn't prevent you from reporting this on up the line," Coltrane chided.

"Don't worry. I may not have much regard for those clowns above me, but I did my duty in that regard."

Ryan returned from the Spanish Civil War just as disillusioned as Coltrane. He too fell victim to the bottle, so Coltrane harbored some sympathy for his antagonism to authority. However, this kind of foot dragging could put his daughter's life in jeopardy. "So what the hell was their reaction?" Coltrane asked.

Ryan threw up his hands like a schoolmaster irritated at a student's answer. "They proved what I've always suspected."

Reagan's lips twitched. "For Christ's sake, what?"

"They're a bunch of ignorant boneheads."

Coltrane dropped his head into his hands. "Ryan, don't make me regret bringing you in on this. What did they say?"

Ryan dropped his head. "They didn't fucking believe me, that's what, the pricks."

Coltrane looked at Reagan and then back at Ryan. "You're screwing with us."

"As a matter of fact, there was talk of investigating me, if you can believe that."

"Indeed I can, but not for this," Coltrane said, causing Reagan to smile.

"Did they think you were lying?" Reagan asked.

"I guess a Spitfire pilot has more clout than me, and they pretty much stuck with his story."

"Didn't they question the captured spies?"

"They did, but since the spies barely knew Adler and gave conflicting descriptions, they've shelved the investigation for now. They think it might be a diversionary tactic by the Germans to spread confusion and send us on a wild-goose chase, giving the ringleaders time to escape or regroup."

"Either that or our crowd wants to keep the general public in the dark to cover up their own incompetence and embarrassment," Reagan said.

Coltrane leaned back in his chair. "Either way, my guess is we can't rely on much help from that quarter."

Ryan wolfed down the tea and sandwiches, pausing to ask, "So what's the game plan?"

Coltrane's face hardened. "I'm for hunting him down right away. He might be after Brigid."

"You mean he came back from Germany to get revenge on a little girl?" Ryan said, raising his eyebrows.

"He's one frustrated Nazi right now. Since Operation Green seems to have imploded, he might try to hook up with Kincaid again. That would not be good for Brigid."

"So we all go after him, is that it?" Ryan asked.

"No, you and Reagan here handle that. Lost John and I continue our search for Brigid. We think we're getting close."

A worried look stretched across Lost John's weathered face. Coltrane noticed it, but didn't question him. He was afraid to.

Ryan finished his mug of tea and brushed the crumbs from his mouth with the back of his hand, then said, "Much as I hate to do this, I must put on my guard's cap and ask the following question: Since Adler must know the jig's up, why hasn't he gone into hiding or flown the coop?"

"He *is* in hiding; he's hiding in Galway," Reagan said.

Ryan turned to look at Reagan. "You're not too serious about hiding if you practically give your name to a prostitute and announce that within a few days the whole country will have heard of you."

"You could be if you're an arrogant, self-centered psychopath who can't accept that your last great chance at fame and glory has been snatched away."

"Unless … unless you believe you've got one more shot at making a name for yourself. One last chance to go out with a bang, so to speak," Ryan said.

"But why hide out in Galway since the place is going to be crawling with guards and military this week in preparation for—"

Ryan cut Coltrane off. "Holy shit, he's after Dev. Dev's giving a speech in Galway on Friday."

"That's it. The Taoiseach is addressing the nation about the attempted coup," Reagan said.

Ryan sucked in his breath. "That means we have less than two days to find Adler."

"Well, I'll leave that to you, lads. Lost John and I have our own challenge, so we must be away."

278

Coltrane rose and shook hands with Ryan and Reagan. As he and Lost John hurried out the door, he wondered how much sand remained in the hourglass. He waved. "Good luck, lads!"

"Good luck to all of us," Reagan said. "May we all have better news when we meet again."

Chapter 54

Some New Information

After a quick bite of breakfast, Reagan and Ryan hit the road for Galway in the semi-darkness. The sun squinted through the clouds over Loch Gorm. A solitary bird call rent the silence. Both men realized that, if wrong, this could be a wild-goose chase and result in major embarrassment for them and unnecessary turmoil for the Taoiseach and his security detail. For all they knew, Adler could be on his way back to Germany in the same submarine that delivered him to Killary a week before.

Ryan yawned. "So, Seamus, what's the game plan?"

"A good place to start would be to track down that prostitute. It's possible she forgot something—or didn't mention something—because she didn't think it was important."

"That's going to be a tall order."

"We have the address of the boarding house where she stays, so that should help."

"Where she works or where she lives?"

"Where she lives."

As soon as they reached a village with a phone, Reagan called Sergeant Cullen at Ryan's urging and told him about Adler, but not before he and Ryan had an argument about it. Reagan puckered his face. "You want me to inform the guards? Haven't you already tried that and they thought you were nuts?"

"I'm hoping that the local guards have more cop-on since Adler may be operating in their own backyard."

While Cullen didn't scoff at the information about Adler, he didn't react with alarm either. Instead he promised to pass it up the line. Reagan hung up the phone and filled Ryan in on the conversation.

"'Up the line.' That sounds awful like code for 'We'll put it in the get-to-it-later file.' It could sit on some detective's desk for a week or worse, never be seen by human eyes."

Reagan started the van and got underway again. "Now you know what we're dealing with."

"Well, at least the brass in Dublin and the locals are on the same page of stupidity." Ryan spat through the open window into the powdered dust gathered in waves along the side of the road. "That's comforting."

After stops at several checkpoints, they reached Galway about midday. The checkpoints indicated that the brass at last might be taking the Adler situation more seriously. They made their first call on the prostitute. She wasn't in. The landlady rolled her eyes when Reagan asked what time she might be back. "Faith, your guess is as good as mine." She cupped her hand against the side of her mouth. "She tends to keep irregular hours, if you know what I mean."

Fidgeting compulsively with the hem of her cardigan, she tossed her head and added, "Sure God help us, she's not holding down a regular job, you know."

Ryan nodded. "When she returns, have her call me at this number; I need to see her."

No sooner had he uttered the words than he knew he'd made a bollocks of the situation.

The landlady jerked as if she'd been stung by a wasp. "Well, I most certainly will not. I run a respectable establishment. You oughta be ashamed of yourself, and such a fine dacent-looking fella too, and you wearing a wedding ring. The Lord bless us and save us." She crossed herself and slammed the door in their faces.

"No, no!" Reagan protested. "You got it all wrong!"

It was no use. The door stayed closed. Ryan bent over with laughter. "Well, you did a fucking bang-up job on that."

"Could you have done any better?" Reagan asked, his face pinched in a scowl.

"Probably not, but at least I know enough not to ask her to act as the girl's pimp."

"That wasn't my intention, and you bloody well know it."

"Getting a rise outa ye, Seamus; don't be so serious."

"Well, we're on damn serious business," he replied, chastened and embarrassed by his screw-up.

They spent the rest of the afternoon scouring the neighborhood around Spanish Arch and the quays without any luck finding either Adler or the prostitute. They worked off the grainy *Irish Times* photo of Adler, but they only had a general description of the prostitute, Maraid: medium height, red hair, exotic-looking, a well-developed figure. They concentrated their efforts on the cheap boarding houses that looked as if they might support Maraid's line of work. An hour canvassing boarding houses and hotels yielded no more than blank looks and hostile stares. They would have to find the woman themselves. These people figured they were the law, which, given Ryan's presence, although he was AWOL, they were.

Down a side street, their luck turned. She almost collided with them while leaving a small thatched pub. "Maraid?" Reagan asked cautiously.

"Who wants to know?"

"I'm Seamus Reagan, and this is my friend Tom Ryan."

She looked them up and down, examining them carefully as a woman might examine a piece of clothing before buying. "Something tells me that you're not on the town this evening in pursuit of fun."

"Well, generally we never say no to fun, but you're right. Unfortunately that isn't what we're after this particular evening."

A look of recognition crossed Maraid's face. "Oh, I think I know who you blokes are. But I'm afraid I gave the lot to my contact on the phone last night." She tossed her long hair. "Unless you want to pay me again, which is fine by me."

"It's against my principles to pay for something twice, but if you join us in this wee pub, we'll stand you a few drinks for a replay."

"I suppose there's no harm in that, especially given how well I made out from that German creep."

"What do you fancy?" Ryan asked as they settled at a corner table.

"A brandy would hit the spot." She fished a pack of cigarettes from her handbag and lit up.

"I can tell you've never spent much time in the women's snug," Reagan laughed.

"Women's snug." She almost choked on the cigarette smoke. "Well, at least that's one giant piece of hypocrisy that ladies in my profession don't have to submit to, down here anyway, although there was a time not too long ago when snugs were all the rage in this area. That is, until the town fathers closed them down for being—I think the words they used were 'dens of iniquity.'" She laughed. "Apparently some of my more brazen co-workers weren't entirely using the snug for its intended purposes." She slapped her knee in merriment.

"Ah yes, another noble Victorian concept turned on its head," Reagan said.

"Victorian my arse; more like the long arm of the Catholic Church, if you ask me."

"Yer probably right," Reagan agreed, hoping to keep her in a positive frame of mind.

"By the way, did you know that creep last night pulled a pistol and tried to kill me?"

"Didn't know that."

"And on top of that he had the makings of a rifle in his duffel bag."

"The makings of a rifle? You're sure?"

She looked at him askance. "Well, it's not something I use in my line of work, but it looked more like a rifle than a bicycle pump, let's say, so yes, I'm sure."

Reagan raised his hands. "Sorry!"

"I went through his bag when he went to the john down the hall.

That's when I saw the gun."

"By the way, did this guy have an accent?" Ryan asked.

"Oh, begod, aye. Thick as a turnip. Kraut, I would say."

"Anything else?"

"As a matter of fact there was something rather peculiar for a guy like him, because he didn't look the type."

"What type would that be?" Ryan asked.

"A fisherman. He had two fishing reels, and oh, yeah, a telescope."

Reagan recalled that all the captured German spies were carrying detonators disguised as fishing reels.

"By any chance could you describe your customer for us?" Reagan asked.

"I can do better than that." She dug a pencil and piece of paper out of her handbag. "In my line of work paper and pencil can come in handy sometimes."

She started drawing. In about three minutes she sketched the profile of a man in his fifties with a receding hairline, prominent nose, and stubbled face.

Reagan pulled the *Irish Times* photo from his pocket and compared it to Maraid's sketch. "I'm impressed." Then he passed it to Ryan.

"There's no question this is him. It's sharper than the *Times* one."

He turned to Maraid. "You've captured him well. This could be a big break. Well done."

She acknowledged the compliment with a faraway look in her eyes. "Thanks. Once upon a time I had dreams of becoming an artist, but things turned out differently."

Reagan stood up and offered her his hand. "Remember, it's never too late to pursue a dream."

"I'd love to believe that, but it was kind of you to say it." Reagan and Ryan turned to leave.

Maraid touched her forehead with the tips of her fingers. "Begod, hold on. I forgot to mention this on the phone. He did say something about moving to posher digs up in Eyre Square. I laughed at him because I thought he was a blathering eejit. It was after that he nearly divulged his name and jabbered about how soon the whole of Ireland would know him."

What a break! "Good woman yourself, Maraid. You've been a big help, so thank you again. Let's go, Tom." When they reached the corner, Reagan looked back. Maraid was standing on the footpath gazing after them. He waved before he and Ryan turned up Shop Street and made a beeline for Eyre Square. As they drew close, the sounds of hammers and saws echoed off the buildings. Workmen scurried around putting the finishing touches on a platform for the Taoiseach. Following some cursory observations, they checked into the Clarence Hotel opposite the speakers' platform. Once situated they made the rounds of the square in hopes of spotting Adler. No luck. By the time they retired for the night, they were no closer to finding their elusive quarry.

The Taoiseach was due to arrive next day.

Chapter 55

Breaking and Entering

Coltrane and Lost John sped to Glenfar Abbey. A few minutes shy of 3:00 a.m. by Coltrane's pocket watch. Time was running out. Since Brother Michael's account corroborated that of the canon, it looked as if the abbot was indeed the one controlling Brigid's fate. Her survival might hinge on the abbot's emotional state, which according to Brother Michael appeared to be unstable. But since the coup had unraveled, had Brigid's captors lost the incentive to keep her alive? The thought terrified Coltrane. In the cruel calculus of the situation, it made sense not to leave any witnesses.

Upon arrival they met Brother Bernard near the abbey sacristy. "The place is locked up tighter than a drum at night by Brother Albert, who takes his duty as custodian of doors and windows very seriously," Bernard said. "However, the catch on the toilet window in the sacristy is broken, and because the window is small, nobody has gotten around to fixing it."

Coltrane narrowed his eyes. "Isn't that going to be a problem, Brother? None of us will fit through it either."

"Well, we better find someone who will, and fast, because by five o'clock the chapel will be full of monks at morning prayers."

Coltrane examined the window opening. "I think I know just the person. Wait here while I go roust him."

Fifteen minutes later he returned with a grumpy Tony Geraty slumped in the passenger seat. His beat-up Raleigh bike lay in a tangle on the floor of the van. Tony insisted on bringing the bike when he'd found out that Coltrane couldn't guarantee him a ride home.

"Like hell!" was his quick reply when Coltrane suggested that a young lad of his age shouldn't find it a bother to walk home.

"As I explained, Tony, all you have to do is get inside and open the sacristy door to the outside."

"Great, and after I do, will you promise not to wake me ever again out of a sound sleep at four in the morning? I'm getting tired of this. First the canon and now you."

"You got my word on it, kid, no more early morning roustings, but this could be the most important break-in of your entire life."

A startled look crossed Tony's face. "I'm not planning on making a career of breaking and entering."

Coltrane and Lost John lifted him up to the window. After a few minutes of futile twisting and turning, they lowered him headfirst by the ankles into the sacristy. Once inside, he quickly drew the bolt on the heavy oak door and let them in. "Now is that it?"

Coltrane wagged his finger before the boy's face. "Yes, but keep your mouth shut about this, you hear?"

"Do you think I'm a bloody eejit or something? I can hear myself saying to Eddy Flannery, 'Guess where I was at four o'clock this morning.'

'At home in bed, I hope?'

'No, breaking into Glenfar Abbey.'

'Ah, go on outa that, you're outa your mind.'

'Swear to God I'm not.' As proof, I'll show him the five-pound note you gave me for causing me such pain and bother and leading me into a life of crime." He extended his hand to Coltrane.

"By God, you're a right little knacker, but I'm sorry to disappoint you; I haven't a shilling to my name, let alone a fiver. Jaysus, Mary, and Joseph, you're a fucking extortionist."

"Well, somebody bloody well better have," the kid answered, gazing expectantly at Lost John and Brother Bernard.

"Don't be looking at me, you young tinker," Lost John said. "All I have is a plug of tobacco and a penknife."

"Christ, I can't believe we're standing here haggling with you, given the gravity of the situation. Get out of here before I give you a boot in the arse!" Coltrane barked.

"Hold on, hold on." Bernard withdrew a small leather pouch from inside his overalls. "For all the pain and bother." He filled Tony's hand with five one-pound notes. "There goes a chunk of my farm allowance, but come to think of it, I don't have a farm to worry about anymore, do I?"

"Thanks a lot!" Tony gave the notes a quick double snap as if to reassure himself that they were real before stuffing them into his pants pocket. He hopped on his bike and tore down the avenue, the familiar rat-tat-tat gradually fading into the morning cacophony of birdcalls and human commotion.

The interior sacristy door led to a concealed area behind the main altar. After pausing for a few moments to get their bearings, they followed Bernard's light down the nave of the darkened chapel and out into a hallway adjacent to the spiral staircase. The abbot's bedroom was located strategically at the top, giving him full view of the passing traffic when his door was open. At night, however, it was usually locked. They crept up the steps as the grandfather clock in the corner of the landing struck 4:30 a.m. Startled, Bernard dropped the flashlight. It bounced down the stairs, landing with a clatter on the tiled hallway. The transom above the abbot's door lit up, followed by the sound of footsteps.

In one fluid motion Bernard sprang toward the door. When the abbot rushed out, Bernard knocked him out with a well-placed blow. He dragged the abbot back into the room like a lion dragging its prey into the bush to conceal it.

Bernard noticed the startled looks on his visitors' faces. He shrugged sheepishly. "I worked on the docks in Liverpool in a former lifetime. Keep an eye on him while I retrieve the flashlight."

When he returned, Bernard took a length of surgical tape that he found in the abbot's well-stocked medicine chest, and placed it across the abbot's mouth. Since the abbot's room was isolated from the rest of the community there was little chance anyone else had heard the flashlight, but the community would miss the abbot at morning prayers and initiate a search.

From somewhere in the building a loud crash.

"Better stay here for a spell. If someone's prowling around it's not likely he'll visit the abbot's room," Bernard said. They stood in the darkened room, not speaking, the only sound their rapid breathing.

Bernard glanced nervously at his watch. "We have fifteen minutes to get him out the sacristy door before morning prayers."

"Then what are we waiting for? We'll fight our way out if we have to," Coltrane said. "Let's go!"

They manhandled the abbot's inert form down the spiral staircase and through the semi-darkened chapel to the inner sacristy door behind the altar. They turned the handle, but the door wouldn't budge. For a moment Coltrane thought they'd been discovered, since he had deliberately left the door open on the way in.

"This accounts for the crash we heard," Bernard whispered. "Drafts are common in an old building. Most likely it slammed shut from the wind."

The thin light of morning filtered through the rose-colored windows, giving form to the limestone statues set in niches along both walls and outlining the large wooden crucifix suspended above the altar. Bernard turned the key, but the door refused to budge. "The jambs must be swollen from the dampness. Stand back and let me shoulder it."

No use. He bounced off it like a tennis ball. Coltrane and Lost John each took turns, but to no avail. As the little group battled the door, the ghostly forms in the niches observed the contest impassively while the abbot lay oblivious on the flagstones.

Deep in the abbey recesses, a bell sounded. Five minutes until morning prayers.

Chapter 56

A Convenient Cover

Thursday

A short time after his altercation with the prostitute, Adler woke up on the floor in a pool of whiskey and urine with an oversized headache. He staggered to his feet and looked in the mirror, noticing the duck egg on his forehead where he connected with the chamber pot. He could never book into a respectable hotel in this condition.

He grabbed a towel and lurched down the hall to the bathroom. A sign on the door said, "No hot water." "*Scheisse!*" he said. He turned the tap on full blast, figuring that in his present condition it was better to freeze than stink. To lessen the shock of the cold water he attempted to lower himself gently into the tub, but lost his footing and plunged in face-first, splashing water all over the worn linoleum floor. "*Scheisse!*" he yelled again, nearly passing out from the cold. However, the shock sobered him up in a hurry. A few brutal minutes later he'd scrubbed off the filth with a half bar of Lifebuoy that lay almost caramelized in the soap dish.

So far his return to Ireland had carried him from one indignity to another, but this turn of events was the capper. To add insult to injury, several residents pounded on the walls, demanding to know what the hell was going on. The cold did put a brake on his rising temper. In the long run, he thought, it was more important to wash up and get the hell out of this kip as fast as his frozen joints would allow.

By the time he departed the boarding house the dustbin men were already cleaning the streets of the prior night's refuse. It was about seven o'clock when he walked stiffly up Shop Street, his teeth chattering. He clapped his hands and stamped his feet, but it didn't help much; the bath had chilled him to the bone. What he needed was a cup of hot tea or a shot of whiskey. Or both.

Halfway up the street, his luck turned. He stumbled on a little café that catered to early risers. After downing a few cups of strong Irish tea and a plate of rashers and black pudding, he felt himself again. Sensation returned to his feet. The warmth coursing through him raised his spirits.

He tuned into the conversations at neighboring tables.

Two men wearing what originally had been white overalls and now resembled artists' mixing palettes were engaged in an animated discussion. "He wants the bloody shop painted before Dev arrives on Friday, I'm telling you," the older man said to the younger.

"Well, he's out of his frigging mind if he thinks the two of us can get it done by then," his companion complained.

"We'll have to, or the miser won't pay us, because I promised him we'd finish it before the big day."

"But that was before Charlie went on a bender."

"I told him that and he said that was my effing problem."

"Then we're fucked, because with all the sprucing up that's going on, there's not a painter to be had for love or money."

"Tell me something I don't know," the older man replied gruffly, lighting up a cigarette and expelling a cloud of smoke with such ferocity that one might be forgiven for thinking it was either his last smoke, or his last breath.

Adler took a pack of cigarettes from his pocket. Pretending he was out of matches, he approached the painters and asked for a light. Without looking up, the older man extended the glowing cigarette and continued talking. "What about that kid of Miko Frawley's? Didn't I hear he did a spot of painting at one time?"

"Ah Jaysus, I wouldn't let that eejit near a henhouse. Besides, he left for England last week."

Adler passed the cigarette back. "Maybe I could be of some assistance." He'd seen a shop being painted in Eyre Square, and gambled that it might be the one in question.

The younger scrutinized him. "Got any experience?"

"What the hell difference does it make, he has two good hands, doesn't he?" the older one interrupted, giving Adler the once-over. "You're a foreigner, right?"

"That's correct."

"You're not a damn Kraut, I hope."

"Hardly. I'm a Dutch Jew."

"Humph," the older one continued, eyeing him up and down. "With the way things are going in this bloody country, you may be out of the frying pan into the fire, but be that as it may, you're hired if you want the job. By the way, I'd advise you to lose the suit and tie. You're going to be painting, not working in a bank."

"No problem." He nearly said *Danke*, but caught himself in the nick of time. "I'm obliged, and for the record, I was a painter in England for a while."

"Gallant! So you are not afraid of heights, then?"

"Not a bit."

"Nor the drink neither, by the looks of that goose egg on your forehead."

Adler checked himself from decking the guy on the spot. "A simple misunderstanding over a lady," he said.

"There's no such thing as a simple misunderstanding where women are concerned. That was your first mistake," the younger one volunteered with a leer.

Pricks like him will go down when the Führer takes over. Adler forced a laugh. "Well, you live and learn, don't you. By the way, where's the job?"

"O'Dowd's Drapery in the square. We start at nine o'clock."

"Righto! See you then." He moved to the checkout counter. After paying the bill he tipped his hat to the painters and left the restaurant. The narrow street was more crowded now with people hurrying to work. Added to that, commercial vehicles were parked chock-a-block on curbs and footpaths, off-loading bread, fruit, and vegetables to various business establishments. He walked with a lighter step and congratulated himself on guessing the right location of the job.

When he'd cased Eyre Square the previous afternoon, it occurred to him that the third-floor dormer window of O'Dowd's Drapery was a prime location from which to survey the speakers' platform. The problem was getting up there unseen and remaining hidden for several hours. In all probability the shop would be closed during the Taoiseach's speech, making access impossible. However, the painting job opened up several possibilities for clandestine entry and concealment. He would know more once inside the building.

Another reason drew him to the shop. As he reconnoitered the square he noticed several young guards making the rounds of all the hotels and boarding houses in the vicinity. He couldn't shake the sense that maybe it had something to do with him. He'd decided to put his suspicions to rest by discreetly checking on the nature of the guards' business. Today he wore his good suit, best shirt and tie, which raised the painter's eyebrows. Luckily he had hung these in the wardrobe in the flophouse, so they were unaffected by the chamber-pot fiasco.

When he reached the square he sat down on a wrought-iron bench and watched the men working on the platform. He lit a cigarette and pulled out the *Irish Press* which he acquired at a newsstand. While pretending to read, he scanned the area to get a grasp of the situation. He walked into a public toilet cubicle and attached a neatly trimmed moustache to his upper lip. No sense in taking chances; the guards may have shown his photograph to the hotel clerks or boarding-house owners. Since boarding houses, unlike hotels, were apt to keep the same person manning the door throughout the day, and therefore, more likely to know the purpose of the guards' visit, he decided to start his investigation with them.

He hit the boarding house directly across from the platform and rang the bell several times. Footsteps on a tiled floor. The door squeaked open. A woman in her sixties, with her hair tied in a bun, stood before him.

He tipped his hat. "Good day, Ma'am. I wish to rent a room for a few nights and I was wondering if you could accommodate me?"

She showed him into the sitting room while she consulted a ledger. "How many nights are you looking for?"

"That depends, Madam. I'm here for the races, and how long I stay depends on good fortune or lack thereof." He used his most polished British accent, figuring it would offer a more plausible cover.

Her unhappiness with that reply registered with the tightening of her jaw. Before he could explain, she said, "We require payment up front—in cash."

"That's no problem, but I do have one minor concern. Since I'm from the country, I live a quiet life and I'm looking for a place where I can get a peaceful night's sleep."

"My house has one of the best reputations in the city. I tolerate no carry-on."

"That's good to hear, but I have a further concern. I saw the guards come in here yesterday afternoon and was wondering if I should be—"

She cut him off. "No, no, goodness gracious, that had nothing to do with my establishment. The guards were checking on … here, let me show you." She took a photograph from a drawer and handed it to him. "They were telling me to be on the lookout for this man."

Adler's heart skipped a beat when he saw the grainy photo from the *Irish Times,* but regained his equilibrium when he realized its poor quality. With as much cool as he could muster, he inquired what the man had done.

"Oh, apparently he's mixed up in some trouble or other. I don't quite remember what it was all about. They told me that if he tried to rent a room, I should tell them right away, that's all." She looked at him without any hint of recognition, more concerned, it appeared, that her explanation calmed his fears.

"That makes me feel a lot better. If I see this chap, I certainly will report him to the guards."

"Aye. Will you be renting the room, then?"

"Yes, very definitely, but I'd prefer one overlooking the square, if possible." He swore silently, wondering if she caught his slip. He'd stated previously that he was looking for peace and quiet. But she went on, seeming not to notice.

"No problem. We have several with that view."

Adler decided to gamble, figuring he might be safer here than anywhere else. From the vehemence with which the landlady threw the picture back in the drawer and slammed it shut, he got the impression she wanted nothing more to do with the affair. He registered and gave her ten pounds to cover three nights' lodging. They made small talk, from which he discovered that the landlady, Mrs. Eberhard, was a widow and that he was the only guest. When he returned a half hour later with a suitcase that he had retrieved from a bus-station locker, she showed him to his room on the second floor.

A large chestnut tree blocked his view of the platform, but he wasn't too put out, having decided to avoid showing himself before a window unless it was a last resort. With his photo circulating, albeit a bad one, he couldn't chance switching to a hotel or another boarding house. The next registration clerk might be faster on the uptake. Even more reason to take the painting gig.

He looked at his watch. Fifteen minutes to change and get down to O'Dowd's. It was just a few hundred yards around the square. Then he thought of a possible hitch. What if Mrs. Eberhard walked by and recognized him while he was painting? It would be difficult to explain why somebody up from the country for a few days of leisure found it necessary to get a part-time job. He hoped that the boss had an extra pair of painting overalls, which would disguise him from casual passersby.

Chapter 57

The Gun Slot

When Adler arrived at the job site, the two painters were setting up. "By God, the knacker is here," the older one said. "Between me, you, and the wall, I wasn't expecting you to show."

He nodded toward a beat-up vehicle parked halfway up on the footpath. "You'll find a pair of overalls in the back of the van."

After Adler donned the overalls, the older man approached him. He inclined his head toward the younger painter. "Since you're okay with heights, not like this little sissy, I want you to start painting the outside sashes of the third-floor windows."

"You old bollocks; I don't see you jumping to do it either."

Great, Adler thought. House painters who are afraid of heights and don't get along.

Adler pointed to a ladder propped against the building."How sturdy is that? I don't mind climbing, but I don't want to fall and break my neck because of a rotten rung."

"You don't have to. Follow me."

The older painter led Adler into the shop and up the staircase to the second floor. "You can paint sitting on the sill from the inside. It's safer as long as you don't daydream and fall on your arse out the window."

Adler hardly heard the comments, so intent was he on scoping out the second-floor arrangement. The front half of the floor space was being used as an office. The back half looked like a staff area, containing a table with several chairs and, off in one corner, a potbellied stove with a kettle on it. A tall window with a locked iron gate pierced the back wall. *Wonder where that leads to?*

"Hey there! Are you comin' or what?"

He turned and saw the painter staring at him with a perplexed look from the narrow stairway that led to the third floor. "Remember what I said about daydreaming? In this job it could kill you."

"Oh, I'm sorry. That old stove distracted me. It looks like it's a hundred years, if it's a day."

"I don't give a fuck if it's a thousand years old. After you get the painting job done you can come back here and say the rosary in front of it, for all I care."

Adler followed him up the stairs. They hardly deserved that description, since they lacked a banister or any visible handholds. The third floor, a much smaller area than the second, included a skylight and a closet with its door ajar, stuffed with boxes of out-of-date footwear. In the middle of the room were several racks of men's suits that looked as if they hadn't been disturbed for twenty years. Two dormer windows overlooked the street, offering a panoramic view of the entire square.

With some difficulty the painter raised the windows and told him what he wanted done. Then he felt his way back down the steep stairway, muttering to himself. "How in the in the name of Jaysus did anyone get away with building such a death trap." He called back to Adler. "Watch your step." Adler followed, planting each foot with great care.

Once outside, Adler grabbed a paint can from where it was stacked on the sidewalk and headed back up. Under the ruse of bumming a light from a shop assistant on break, he sauntered into the staff room. "Nice setup you've got here."

"Yeah, sure it would be mighty if we could spend more time in it."

"So he keeps you on the go, hunh?"

"Like mice on a treadmill, he's an awful man for the money."

"Aren't they all? By the way, what's with the iron gate in front of the window?"

"Oh, that's the fire-escape exit. It leads out onto the roof of a shed."

"I sure as hell wouldn't want to be caught in a fire up here. Why is the damn thing locked?"

"That's for security purposes so no one can get in from the outside, but the key to the lock is here." The assistant pulled out a drawer underneath the table. "Everyone knows where to get it in case of an emergency."

"Oh, right, right." Adler nodded, trying to swallow the smile growing on his lips.

The shop assistant glanced toward the stairway. "Jaysus, the boss'll go for you bald-headed if he catches you dossing around up here, especially since you're a Brit."

"Not to worry, mate, I'm off. Well, 'twas good chatting with you and thanks for the light."

The left dormer window provided an excellent view of the platform and a perfect vantage point for a shot. However, it left him exposed to anyone scanning the upper stories with binoculars, which he assumed security would do. Upon discovering that the guards were distributing his photo, he realized that most likely other security measures were being put in place as well.

A voice rang out below. "Have you gone to sleep up there?"

He stuck his head out the window and yelled to the older painter down on the footpath. "Hold your horses! It takes a while to mix this stuff, you know."

Five minutes of shaking and stirring had him ready to begin. He eased out onto the third-floor windowsill and sat with his back to the street. Normally he wasn't afraid of heights, but this spooked him. It was an awkward setup. He decided to take it nice and easy until he got used to it. To keep his balance he pressed his calves against the interior wall and held on to the window frame with his left hand.

He had almost finished painting the window sashes when he noticed something that suggested possibilities. Two electrical cables snaked across the surface of the exterior wall before disappearing into the interior through a sloppily chiseled entry channel. When he finished the window, he eased back into the room and inspected the exit point of the cables on the interior wall. The plaster around the spot was flaky and soft. He poked around the edges with a putty knife until he saw daylight. The patching material wasn't very solid. He grabbed a long screwdriver, and in a short time he enlarged the hole enough to accommodate the barrel of a rifle.

He gazed through the hole, but he could only see the tops of the flags over the platform. That was a problem. He would need to angle the hole downward to get a direct bead on the platform itself. Not too difficult, he figured, since this part of the house had to be a hundred and fifty years old. Or more. Time had deteriorated the quality of the mortar, making it malleable, easy to penetrate. Before going down for lunch, he shifted a decade-old calendar from its spot on the opposite wall and placed it over the hole, securing it with a drawing pin that easily pierced the brittle mortar.

An hour after lunch, Adler started working on the three second-floor windows. Sitting on the sill facing the interior, he kept an eye on the activity in the staff room and waited until it was empty. On the pretext of going to the toilet, he slipped in and took the key to the iron security gate from the table drawer. After opening the lock he flipped the catch on the window behind the gate, returned the key to the drawer and hurried back to the front of the house.

By quitting time he had formulated a rough plan. All that remained was to find an access through the back garden. He planned to work on that later that evening.

Chapter 58

The Lodger

Adler washed up and descended to the dining room. The landlady served him a meal of lamb chops, mixed vegetables, and mashed potatoes. He had a ravenous appetite, exacerbated, he figured, by the stress of painting three stories up, but they had finished the job on schedule. He devoured the meal in no time and followed it up with apple tart and cream, which he washed down with a few cups of hot tea. Although he hated to admit it, he liked the national drink of his arch enemy.

When he finished he asked Mrs. Eberhard if he could take a stroll in her garden.

"As long as you don't tramp on my vegetables or mess with my roses, you're more than welcome."

Stupid old cow. Who does she think I am, some yahoo from the bog? For spite I'd like to piss on her roses, which indeed I may do before the night is out.

High privet hedges bordered the garden on both sides. Outside the back door several bushes of red and yellow roses swayed in the light breeze. A shingled path skirted a small turf shed and continued past some potato ridges, onion drills, and a bed of late-summer cabbage.

He followed the path to the bottom of the garden, where a blackthorn hedge interspersed with several young ash trees blocked his way forward. Beyond the hedge a well-worn path followed the contours of a little stream. After a brief search he found an opening between one of the trees and the bushes and squeezed through to the other side.

He walked along the path in the direction of O'Dowd's shop, hoping he would recognize it from the back. Some gardens had rear fences of privet hedges, others of barbed wire. As the path curved sharply, he knew he was approaching the general area where O'Dowd's was located. The shop stood diagonally across from Mrs. Eberhard's house, between a commercial bank and a florist.

Eventually he stopped before a garden with a barbed-wire fence that offered a clear view of a structure at the other end. He couldn't be sure, but the profile of the building from the back looked a lot like O'Dowd's. He enlarged the opening between the strands of wire by pressing the lower strand down with his boot while raising the top one with his hand, and squeezed through into a garden overgrown with weeds and dead stalks from an early potato crop. He wasn't likely to encounter anyone since O'Dowd's was closed for the day, and the owners didn't live on the premises.

He crept forward to the top of the garden. There was the shed with the galvanized roof. Clearly visible behind the second-storey window was the security gate, but no ladder. "Fuck! I'm screwed without that ladder. What kind of people have a fire-escape system without a ladder?"

Was this some cruel joke? Or an ugly insight into O'Dowd's head? It seemed O'Dowd was more concerned about people breaking in than facilitating their getting out in the event of a fire.

Adler was forced to acknowledge O'Dowd's shrewd, if callous, assessment of human nature. *Always look out for number one; then nothing is left to chance.* As an afterthought, Adler opened the shed door and found himself in the midst of discarded merchandise crates and boxes of all sizes. Some were made of wood and seemed sturdy enough to carry his weight. By stacking one on top of another, he figured he could pull himself up onto the roof.

Satisfied, he returned to the boarding house, stopping along the way to pick up a hammer and chisel from a hardware shop. When he got to his room he discovered that someone had entered it in his absence. A string of black thread, attached to a thumbtack, hung limply from the inside doorknob. He always rigged the door when he stayed in an unfamiliar place. His distrust of people also led him to remove anything incriminating before leaving his room, even for the briefest periods. Today was the exception. He violated his own rule because the landlady looked harmless and trusting. On entering the house from the garden, he heard an upstairs door close. When he encountered the landlady carrying a stack of laundered sheets and pillowcases down the stairs, he didn't think twice about it. He had told her not to bother making up his bed. As a reminder he hung the do-not-disturb sign on his door, so she couldn't have misunderstood.

He assumed that she searched through his belongings and saw the gun. Soon she would put two and two together. He slipped out of his room and crept down the staircase toward the sitting room. A shaft of light spilled onto the hallway floor through the partially opened door. He tiptoed toward it and peered inside.

Mrs. Eberhard stood before the open drawer of the sideboard examining the *Irish Times* photograph. His photograph. When she left the room he retreated into the shadows. She took her hat and coat from the hall rack and stepped toward the front door. His fingers closed around the ornamental handle of the gypsy knife.

One quick stroke did it. She buckled at the knees and slumped to the floor, emitting a gurgling sound as she drowned in her own blood.

Adler backtracked to the kitchen and washed the bloody knife in the sink before sheathing it in its leather scabbard. Draping a dishtowel around his neck, he returned to the hallway, hoisted the warm body over his shoulder like a sack of potatoes, and carried it out back. He would return later to clean up the mess in the hallway. *Where to conceal her?* His eyes fell on the little shed. Perfect. He buried her under a mound of stone turf, satisfied that it would be days, possibly weeks, before concerned relatives or guards found her. Nobody in that house would be lighting fires for a while.

Close to midnight Adler finished stacking the wooden crates

against the wall of O'Dowd's storage shed. By the time he let himself in through the gated window and took up his position on the third floor of the shop, he heard the pubs letting out for the night. He brought a small flashlight to illuminate his workspace, but when he reached the third storey he was surprised by the amount of ambient light entering the room from the street lamps. That would make it less cumbersome to move around, but it also increased the risk of being spotted from the outside.

Before setting to work on the hole, he poked around to find a hiding place for himself and his gear. The shop was closing tomorrow from eleven until after the Taoiseach's speech, which was scheduled to begin at one, so he needed to hide for several hours while the staff was on the premises. He pushed his way through several racks of discarded men's suits until he reached the back wall with the built-in closet. Spot on. After clearing out the shoes, which he stacked behind the clothes racks, he stowed his gear in the empty space.

Before setting to work on the hole he tied swatches of discarded cloth around the chisel head to muffle its sound. He fashioned a piece of scrap muslin into a pouch of sorts and placed it within the hole to trap the debris and prevent it from falling to the street. He gauged the angle of descent and patiently chipped away at the wall. It was sturdier than he thought. After an hour he was swearing profusely. In addition, the constant need to empty the hole of debris slowed him down considerably. To avoid electrocution he used the gypsy knife to gingerly excavate the channel on either side of the electrical wires. His face twisted in a crooked smile. *The gypsy was right after all. The knife turned out to be useful.*

By the time the slot was large enough, the sun peeked above the horizon. He wouldn't know for sure if the angle was correct until daylight, when he could sight the platform through his scope. He replaced the calendar over the slot, cleaned up the debris, and retreated behind the clothes racks. He assembled his rifle and stretched out on the floor for a short nap.

He awoke to thumping footsteps not two feet from his head. The door sprang open. "Look at the cut of this place, will ye?" O'Dowd yelled. "I want this shit outa here by tomorrow and down to McTierney at the secondhand stall. May as well get something for it. Is that clear? I've been at you lugs for the past month to get this place cleaned up and it never seems to get done."

"Yes, sir," a nervous assistant said. "I can start right now if you like."

Adler's heart raced. He gripped the handle of the gypsy knife in his inside pocket. Couldn't risk using his Glock.

"You will do nothing of the sort. Can't have you hauling this stuff through the shop with customers around."

"Right, sir."

"But come to think of it, you could get a start on it while we're closed for Dev's speech." He pointed to the hammer and chisel lying on the floor. "And what the hell is all this?"

"Oh, I bet the painters left them, sir. I'll get them outa here right away."

"Hunh! A tradesman who loses his tools. Well, he won't last too long."

O'Dowd tromped down the steep stairs, followed by the assistant. He rained curses on his miserly grandfather for building a contraption that would challenge a mountain goat.

Adler waited until the voices faded. He had a vision of his whole scheme going up in smoke. Worse, he knew no way out of the dilemma that now presented itself. If one assistant came up to clean the place, he could handle that, but what if there were more? When he crept from his hiding place he noticed the door to the room standing ajar. He closed it with utmost caution, fearing there might be someone in the staff room below.

He glanced at his watch: 8:15 a.m. He had slept longer than he planned. Gouging out that slot in the wall exhausted him. And it might all be for naught. Without thinking, he pounded his fists on the wall. *Damn! Damn! Damn!* When he calmed down, he eased open the door and listened. Silence. Lucky for him. His fist pounding could have given the game away. He must learn to control his temper. Closing the door, he retrieved the rifle and inserted it into the slot. He couldn't see the floor of the platform through his scope. The angle of the slope wasn't steep enough. "Fuck," he mouthed.

Then it occurred to him that the platform was about two feet off the ground and that the target was over six feet tall. Eight feet in all. He was certain he could angle the rifle that far. All he needed was a head shot.

Chapter 59

Up Against the Clock

Friday

Reagan looked at his watch. Four hours until the Taoiseach's speech. He panned the square through binoculars from a second-storey window of the Hotel Clarence. Worry clouded his eyes. "It's a perfect setup for a determined assassin. Dozens of ideal spots for an ambush, easy access to hotels and boarding houses, and relatively quick escape routes through backyards and gardens."

"Not to mention a security force that appears more hell-bent on keeping order than on the Taoiseach's safety," Ryan said.

Reagan removed the binoculars from his neck. "Oh, I wouldn't go that far. They're concerned with his safety all right, but they think good order will ensure that, which is laughable. Well, I suppose there's only so much we can do from up here, so let's head back down and burn some shoe leather."

Always a busy place, Eyre Square bustled with gawkers, musicians, and street vendors, as well as the usual traffic. The Taoiseach's speech was billed as an important address to the nation about the previous week's momentous events. Heavy press coverage was anticipated.

The visit would surely draw a huge crowd, because it wasn't often the Taoiseach left Dublin, owing to the tension in the country and the need to be close to the levers of power in case of a crisis. Unfortunately, large crowds were the friend of the assassin, providing anonymity, cover, confusion, and a nightmare for security. In an effort to get the lay of the land, Reagan and Ryan took stock of the preparations underway, trying to spot in advance any vulnerability in the security setup that an assassin could exploit.

No doubt Adler was doing the same, Reagan thought. The platform stood in the center of the square, itself a potential problem. A man using a high-powered rifle with a telescopic sight would have no difficulty picking off a speaker from a second- or third-storey window. There was no shortage of windows. The square perimeter was a mix of shops, hotels, banks, and insurance companies with the odd private residence interspersed among them. "That's a lot of glass," Reagan muttered.

Ryan exhaled loudly. "And a man hidden behind any piece of it would have an uninhibited view of the entire square."

"To be on the safe side, every room of every building overlooking the square should be searched and sealed off."

"But it would take a platoon of soldiers to do that."

"Right. A platoon we don't have, unfortunately."

Although daunted by the prospect of what lay ahead, they continued to visually catalog structures and objects in and around the square. Loudspeakers were positioned strategically, and green, white, and gold bunting decorated the speakers' platform. Irish flags of the same colors hung from poles and second-storey windows. The perimeter road was jammed with busses.

They walked around as inconspicuously as they could, trying to get inside Adler's head. They needed a lucky break to stop him. On the off chance that any of the guards might recognize him this far from Dublin, Ryan tipped his brown felt hat over his eyes. Turning to Reagan. "As I said, we'd need a platoon of soldiers to cover this place, not just the two of us."

Reagan slowed his pace and swiveled his head right and left. "Adler doesn't have a platoon either. He's one guy with a rifle. He may have a more limited number of vantage points than we think. Even fewer if he wants to make a successful getaway after it's done."

A puzzled look crossed Ryan's face. "That's hardly new information."

"The information isn't new, but the perspective is."

"How so?"

"Adler wants to escape, and that makes all the difference," Reagan said.

"Which means the choice of ambush site hinges on that consideration."

"Exactly. Now what we have to do is identify those sites that preclude him taking a shot for whatever reason. And from the remainder, eliminate those that don't provide an easy escape route."

"Sounds great, but what if Adler is suicidal?"

"We have to go with the odds. And the odds are he's going to select a spot that offers him the best chance of hightailing it out of there."

For the next hour they cased the square. They excluded some buildings because large trees or electrical poles stood in front of them, blocking a clear view of the platform. Others were oriented at such an angle that a gunman would have to practically sit with one leg hanging out over the windowsill to get a clear shot, thus exposing himself to security on the ground. Ryan made a note of these exclusions in a little notebook.

Reagan looked up at the clock over the Bank of Ireland. Three hours until the Taoiseach's speech. They had narrowed the field, but large gaps remained.

"I don't know about you," Ryan said, "but I can't take another step until I get some breakfast in me."

"It will have to be eat-and-run, because we're up against it."

They settled into a small pub down a side street and ordered the house special. Reagan spoke through mouthfuls of bacon and sausage. "Here's the rest of my plan."

"I'm listening, but barely. I didn't realize I was so hungry until I saw those sausages."

"As I was about to say ..."

"Go ahead," Ryan grunted.

"I'm afraid we'll have to gamble that Adler isn't going to try anything from the ground level. Since most of the ground floors of the perimeter buildings are either shops, banks, or hotel lobbies, all with lots of people around, we can eliminate them as possible ambush sites. No, to pull this off, he needs to remain hidden, which he couldn't do on the ground. So my guess is a second- or third-floor operation."

They finished eating. Reagan went up to the bar and placed a five-pound note on the counter in front of the barman. "Keep the change." Feeling a bit more chipper after a hearty breakfast, they hustled out the door.

"Okay, here's my idea. Since you're an officer of the law, I suspect you're good at questioning people and interpreting their reactions. So make the rounds of hotels and boarding houses and see if someone recognizes this." He withdrew Maraid's sketch of Adler from his pocket.

"And where will you be?"

"I'll hit the back gardens and see how many houses have fire escapes. Many of them might not, which eliminates them as ambush sites. In the meantime hang on to this." He handed Ryan a Glock pistol. "I assume you know how to use it."

Ryan rolled his eyes. "For God's sake, I carried one of these throughout my time in Spain."

"Gallant, so let's meet back at the hotel by twelve o'clock."

***

With the exception of one lodging house, where there was no response to the doorbell, Ryan received the same answer everywhere he went: no one remembered seeing Adler. Either the gunman changed his mind and wasn't staying in Eyre Square, or he was donning an effective disguise. He didn't fare any better when he stopped random people on the street and showed them the sketch. They shook their heads and continued about their business.

As the time slipped away, he racked his brains. Was he missing something? It was now five minutes to twelve by the bank clock. An hour to go. On his way back to the hotel to meet Reagan, he noticed a pub he hadn't surveyed. It was worth a try. The pub filled rapidly with patrons and soon there was standing room only. He had a time of it attracting the barman's attention to get a pint. Finally, with a glass of the black stuff in his hand, he circulated the sketch. No luck. All he got were puzzled frowns.

Then a man in white overalls slapped the sketch on the bar counter in front of him. He raised a glass of Guinness unsteadily to his lips. "Are you the f-f-fella looking for this b-b-bloke?"

"I'm your man. Did you see him?"

"Never saw that man in my life, but I did see t-t-his fella yesterday." He took out a flat carpenter's pencil and touched up Maraid's sketch with a moustache. "Him I saw. No q-question about it."

Chapter 60

Caught off Guard

The speeches began. Local politicians droned on so long that Adler nearly fell asleep from boredom and exhaustion. He felt the double strain of keeping one eye on the platform in front of him and the another on the stairway behind him. He left the door open, figuring it increased his odds of not being surprised. As one speaker succeeded another, Adler practiced getting the range and lining up their heads in his crosshairs. He was so focused on this routine and so distracted by the blaring loudspeakers that he failed to hear footsteps behind him.

"Who the hell are you?"

Adler whipped around. He faced O'Dowd's young assistant, his mouth agape. Before the assistant could sound the alarm, Adler struck him on the head with the barrel of his rifle, knocking him out the door and tumbling down the stairs. Unable to arrest his own forward motion without a handrail, he pitched headlong down the steps after the assistant. He wasn't sure how long he lay on top of the young man, but the roar of the crowd edged him back to reality. He staggered to his feet. Apart from another bump on his head and a little wooziness, he could manage.

He was lucky; his fall was broken by the victim, who, as far as he could tell in his dazed state, was dead. Fearing that another staff member might discover his colleague, Adler stashed him in the second-floor toilet near the gated window. Then he picked up his rifle and limped up the stairs. The noise from the square grew to a crescendo. The Lord Mayor was introduced. This was it.

Chapter 61

Time Running Out

Ryan's pulse quickened. "Quick! Where did you see him?" he asked the half-tipsy house painter.

"He helped me paint O' ... O' ... Dowd's Drapery in the sq-square."

"God Almighty, I saw you lads myself yesterday. One of you was sitting on the third-storey windowsill."

The painter pointed to the sketch. "R-r-right you are. That was your man here."

After thanking the painter he threw a ten-shilling note to the barman and said, "Give yer man here as many pints as this will buy," then he dashed out the door.

Running down the street toward the shop, he glanced at the clock: 12:15 p.m. The music of a fife and drum band and the scratchy sounds of PA system tests filled the square.

He ran to a spot across from O'Dowd's and scanned the building with his binoculars. The shop was closed and the upper-storey windows without curtains. Then he noticed a smudge on the wall to the right of a third-storey dormer. Tightening the focus of the binoculars, he spotted the slit. Its purpose hit him with a wallop: the assassin had made himself invisible. No point in checking windows. Adler had outfoxed them. Ryan ran across the square, debating whether there was time to alert Reagan. There wasn't. The bank clock struck half past twelve as the guards and military units took their places around the platform.

He rattled the front and side entrances to O'Dowd's. Locked tight. No way in from the front. No time to find the owner. He sprinted a hundred yards up the street and let himself into a backyard through a wicker door set in a six-foot-high boundary wall. Racing to the bottom of the garden, he cleared the privet hedge and landed on the path alongside the stream. A young shop assistant staggered toward him, holding a bloody hand to a gash on the side of his head.

"There's a guy with a gun," he stammered. "He was—"

"Where, where?"

"He attacked me … nearly did me in. In O'Dowd's, sir, on the third floor."

"Are you okay?"

"I think so."

"Quick! Go to the Clarence Hotel. Find a bloke called Seamus Reagan. Tell him what happened."

The assistant staggered off.

Ryan called after him. "And find a doctor for yourself!" Then he checked his Glock and raced flat-out toward O'Dowd's garden. He hauled himself onto the roof of the shed by way of the stacked crates. The national anthem blared across the housetops.

"Ladies and gentlemen, the Taoiseach Eamon De Valera …" At best, without a longwinded introduction, he had less than a minute to take out Adler.

A metal fire-escape ladder ran up the wall to the third-storey roof, where the assistant told Ryan he'd find an unlocked skylight. He reached the skylight and peered into the room below. Only the rifle barrel inserted into the wall slit was visible. No chance for a clean shot. He had to get into that room. Fast!

Ryan yanked the handgrip on the skylight upward. The wooden frame, sealed tight by overlapping coats of paint, wouldn't budge. It looked like it hadn't been opened in years. The Taoiseach's voice came over the PA system.

Chapter 62

Apples, Bees, and Gunfire

The tread of many feet echoing off the limestone walls of the chapel sounded like the rumble of a train coming through a tunnel. Coltrane clenched his teeth as the jammed door stood fast. This was the only entrance to the sacristy from the church interior. Unless they were prepared to hoist the abbot on their shoulders and charge the column of monks advancing up the main aisle, they were trapped.

Bernard dropped to the floor. Lying on his back, he propped the soles of his sturdy boots against the door. He pulled his legs to his chest and released his feet with explosive force, sending the door crashing into the sacristy, minus its hinges, as the first monks filled the pews. With Coltrane's help, he hoisted the limp body of the abbot over his shoulder and rushed out of the sacristy, joining Lost John in the van with the engine running.

Lost John shifted into first and the van fishtailed down the avenue, spitting stones and gravel into the hedgerow. "They probably heard that door crash in the next county."

Through the dust cloud they saw the monks streaming from the sacristy, shouting and pointing in their direction. A few even gave chase before giving up in frustration. Coltrane directed Lost John to circle back and re-enter the abbey grounds by way of a cart track. "Better hide right under their noses, where they least expect it," he said, instructing him to drive to the cobble-stoned yard.

They entered beneath the arch, passing the charred skeleton of the hayshed. Not a soul in sight. "Let's put him in the barn with the red door over to the right," Bernard suggested, jumping out to open the door while Lost John backed the van inside. Then Bernard closed the barn door.

When the abbot showed signs of coming around, Coltrane removed the surgical tape from his mouth. He ushered his captive out of the van and sat him down on a bale of hay along the back wall. The abbot gave him a menacing glare. Becoming aware of his predicament, he let loose a torrent of threats and dire predictions of what would happen if he wasn't released right away. "When General Sloan hears about this, he will have you shot!" he yelled, his eyes bulging.

Coltrane tightened his lips. "Apparently, Reverend Abbot, you haven't heard the news. Your crony Sloan has been arrested, and the rest of his lieutenants are being rounded up as we speak."

The abbot tilted his head to one side, closed his eyes, and laughed quietly, as if he was enjoying his own personal joke. "I can't be fooled that easily. We are on the verge of a mighty triumph, and very soon, riff-raff like you and this apostate," he motioned toward Bernard, "will be swept away in a cleansing wave of righteous anger by the forces of the blessed. Your day is done, mark my words."

"Your grim forecasts are coming true all right, but—ironically—for you, not for us," Bernard said. "It all came crashing down in the last few days."

"What are you talking about? I can spot brazen lies when I hear them."

"Brother Bernard isn't trying to bluff you, Abbot," Coltrane said. "Your patron Sloan is in Mountjoy Jail, and the IRA are hot on Major Adler's tail."

"Oh, yes. And in all the excitement we nearly forgot your *compadre*, Canon Roach. He's out of commission as well after spilling his guts about you and your nasty operation," Lost John chimed in. "Peter and I handled that little assignment and the good canon found our approach quite persuasive."

The abbot's face took on a puzzled look. "*Compadre*? You misspeak. I couldn't care less what happened to that pompous, arrogant ass."

Coltrane crouched to the abbot's eye level and rhythmically slapped the head of the ball-peen hammer against the palm of his left hand. "It's over, Abbot." Fear flickered in the abbot's eyes. "However, we didn't come here to bring you up to date on national or local affairs. There's one loose end that concerns me above all others, and if you want to live through the day, you'll clear it up: Where is my daughter?"

The abbot laughed loudly, but it sounded forced. "Your child! She's at the bottom of Lough Gorm where you put her, you blackguard."

"Have it your way." Coltrane smacked the abbot on the soft tissue of his left knee. The abbot screamed, startling the blackbirds from the hazel bushes. "I'll ask you one more time."

Silence. The abbot had passed out.

"John. Strange though it be, he appears clueless about the collapse of the coup, so he would have no reason to harm Brigid or move her again, right? Or maybe I'm grasping at straws."

"How could that be, unless he was on a pub crawl over the past week and blacked out? Which is highly unlikely. It's been all over the news."

"Whatever the reason, John, he doesn't know."

Lost John stared at the ground. "Kincaid and his cronies would have known; that's the problem."

"They would, but without orders from the abbot I'm betting they wouldn't do anything."

"Pray God you're right."

Brother Bernard had gone for a bucket of water, and when he returned Coltrane turned to him. "Bernard, can you venture a guess as to why the abbot seems clueless that Operation Green has collapsed?"

Bernard thought for a moment. "According to Brother Michael the abbot is an abuser of prescription drugs."

Coltrane's face darkened. "That would explain it; he was out of it. It would also account for the glazed look in his eyes."

317

Bernard picked up the bucket from the floor. "Let's see if a dash of this helps him refocus." When the cold water hit the abbot's face, his body spasmed as if an electric charge went through it. His eyes shot open and he grimaced with pain. In the semi-darkness of the shed it was difficult to read his face. Coltrane turned his flashlight on.

Groaning, the abbot raised an arm to shield his eyes from the glare. Dressed only in a nightshirt and sandals, he rocked back and forth. He looked like a harmless old man, his sinister nature temporarily camouflaged. Grasping the hammer by its head, Coltrane yanked it from his waistband and went toward him.

The abbot raised his hands. "Please! No more. I will confess … everything."

"Well, where is she?"

"In the boathouse … at Kildallogue Girls' School," he gasped, his face twisting in pain.

"How many people are guarding her?"

"Kincaid's in charge. I know little of those details."

Coltrane stood up, looked down at the broken monk, and wondered how the world had come to such a place that a supposed man of God could sink so low. The abbot fixed his gaze on Coltrane. "What's to become of me?"

"You'll spend the rest of your life in prison, if you're lucky. If you're linked to the killings on the island, you could be hanged."

He turned his back on the abbot and walked toward the door. Then he stopped and spun around. "If you've harmed my child, there will be no court, no trial. I will strangle you with my bare hands."

The abbot's face turned ashen. A faraway look crept into his eyes. "Don't plan on giving you the satisfaction. I've made my peace with the Lord."

Lost John turned off the van lights then he and Coltrane joined Bernard outside the barn door. "Bernard, it's going to be up to you to keep him under wraps until we sort this out. Lost John and I are going after Brigid. Please God, this nightmare will soon be over."

Barely had the words left Coltrane's mouth when a powerful boom rocked the morning stillness. The van smashed through the barn door

318

in an explosion of splinters, petrol fumes, and smoke. The vehicle swung in their direction. "Son of a—I left the keys in the ignition!" Lost John yelled.

While he and Bernard scrambled for cover behind a parked tractor, Coltrane raced through the arch toward the orchard, the van in hot pursuit. Caught in the open, Coltrane had to think fast to avoid being crushed against the farmyard wall. He spun around, pulled his Glock, and fired point-blank into the windshield. The vehicle veered wildly and crashed through the picket fence surrounding the orchard. It wiped out the first four beehives before slamming against an apple tree, pitching the abbot headfirst through the shattered windshield onto the hood.

The bees descended on the car in a turbulent cloud. In minutes the abbot was covered in a writhing brown carpet. Bernard and Lost John ran to Coltrane, who looked dazed. Despite their best efforts to rescue the abbot, it was futile. The angry buzzing hoard drove them back. A red stain oozed from under the bee mass and dripped slowly off the hood, carrying swatches of squirming insects onto the fallen apples beneath the tree.

"I don't understand what got into him," Bernard whispered. "He must have known he couldn't get away."

"My hunch is he didn't want to get away, Bernard. He wanted to end it quickly," Coltrane said. "That's why he came after us, or more precisely, why he came after me. It was as if he was offering me a chance to get even, to levy the ultimate punishment against him. In a weird way, that might have been his final act of contrition."

Lost John puckered his face. "He said he wasn't going to give you the satisfaction. I'd take him at his word. Trying to crush you against the wall is evidence enough for me that getting you before you got him is what he meant by that."

"You've got a point, but I'd still like to give him the benefit of the doubt."

Lost John shook his head. "All I can say is that you're a better man than I."

As they drove out of the abbey grounds, the hypnotic chant of the monks rose and fell muffing the angry buzzing of the bees still audible on the wind.

Chapter 63

Through the Skylight

Guard Ryan stood up, took a few steps backward, and leaped onto the skylight, plunging to the floor, where he landed among the coat racks in a shower of glass and splintered timber.

Adler jumped up and sprayed the shattered skylight with gunfire. Buried behind the coat racks, Ryan lost sight of his quarry until a shadow passed in front of the window, blocking the light.

Ryan emptied his Glock into the shadow, pulverizing the dormer window. Another erratic volley from Adler shredded the clothes racks. But Ryan's bullets had found their mark. Adler staggered and teetered unsteadily before the shattered window. Then like a sail losing the wind, he sagged and pitched out the window, plummeting to the pavement below.

Ryan lay motionless, his heart pounding like a bass drum, among the shredded suits that looked like Swiss cheese.

He stumbled to the window. Pandemonium reigned on the street. Pedestrians, cars, and bicycles competed with one another to flee the danger zone. Adler lay on a bed of broken glass about ten feet from his rifle. His black felt hat rested on its crown beside his broken body like a street busker's cap waiting for coins from passersby. The few who ventured close recoiled in horror from the mangled corpse.

Ryan slumped to the floor at the base of the window. For the first time he noticed that both his hands were bleeding. He looked up at the smashed skylight. Shards of glass protruded like translucent teeth around the rim. He'd been lucky. Very lucky. He sat for a while longer, until the sound of breaking glass and heavy footsteps on the stairs interrupted his reverie.

Reagan charged into the room, gun drawn. "Jaysus, how bad is it?"

"Not as bad as it looks. Just superficial wounds."

Ryan held up his bloodied hands. Reagan turned his head, nauseated by the sight of blood.

Reagan supported Ryan down the rickety stairs to the second floor, where the wounded man washed his hands in the sink. Reagan, despite his phobia, managed to bandage them from material he found in the shop.

"Good show. The country will be proud of you."

Ryan didn't feel pride, just an immense sense of satisfaction. He had finished the work of the Spitfires. That was honor enough.

Chapter 64

Closing In

His hand white-fisted on the tiller, Coltrane guided *No Pasarán II* through the choppy waters of Lough Gorm toward the boathouse at Kildallogue Girls' School. The storm had piled clumps of driftwood and reeds in a jagged wave along the shore. His heart raced. Surely this was his last chance to find Brigid alive. If he drew a blank now, it would indeed be the end. What if the abbot had lied to him as a final act of revenge? There was nowhere else to turn, now that the Abbot was dead. The sense that the day might as easily end in tragedy as in joyous celebration weighed heavily upon him.

Lost John navigated in the bow, two loaded shotguns at his side. When they drew within a quarter mile of the boathouse, Coltrane cut the engine. They rowed the remaining distance in silence. The school, still in summer recess, was located about a half mile inland from the boathouse. Because the opening of school was imminent, had Kincaid, in the absence of orders from the abbot, taken it upon himself to move Brigid to a new location—or worse? Coltrane drove the latter thought out of his mind.

The shoreline was dotted with stands of willow trees whose branches spilled over the water's edge. He wasn't a superstitious man, but seeing the willows brought back the terror of the day he lost the oar, the day the nightmare began. He recalled their comforting concealment then, and he used them again to sneak up on the boathouse.

In a small bay fronting the house, a motor launch bobbed at anchor. A wooden jetty extended from the shore about thirty feet into the lake. Holes appeared at intervals along the length of the wooden causeway, evidence of the storm's fury. From the water's edge a cement boat ramp ran up the beach to a double door in the front of the building. To the right of the door were two windows, as well as windows on both side walls. The back of the house faced inland. They tied their boat to a willow tree and struck off into the pine wood, each carrying a shotgun. Fearing that Kincaid might have placed lookouts, they reconnoitered the general area around the house. All clear as far as they could tell. A cold breeze coming off the lake set the pine trees singing, which added to the rawness of the morning and the general atmosphere of dread. Having completed their surveillance, they huddled behind a limestone boulder to strategize.

"John, I'm going round back to see if there's a way in. You check out the side windows and meet me here when you're done."

"Got it."

Approaching the house, Coltrane noticed a carpet of withered pine needles on the roof that skittered off in tufts before each fresh gust of wind. Here and there slates had turned green. On the back wall he found a door with a broken pane of glass that led to a kitchen. He tried to open it. No luck. Several male voices came from the front room. He leaned his gun against the wall, then removed his jacket and rolled up a shirtsleeve. The hole in the glass was barely big enough to accommodate his arm. As he scratched around to find the lock, he felt a sharp sting. Blood oozed from his wrist.

He pawed around some more until his fingers closed around the bolt. He slid it back gently. As he gingerly withdrew his arm through the jagged shards of glass, a chair scraped against the floor.

Rather than risk severing an artery, he stayed put. He pulled a handgun from his belt and waited, figuring he would have to kill whoever came into the kitchen. So much for the element of surprise.

A toilet flushed. Again the scraping of the chair. He stuck the gun back under his belt and extracted his arm from the glass maw. Then grabbing his coat and shotgun he raced to the cover of the trees.

Once back at the limestone boulder he examined his wrist. The cut was minor, but it had left a bloodstain on the glass. That could be a problem. He hunkered down and waited for Lost John.

The snap of a twig announced his arrival. Leaning into Coltrane he whispered from the side of his mouth, "Two men gambling in the front room. Bottle of Powers on the table. They're pretty sloshed. I'm almost sure the big guy is Kincaid. The other looks like a German. Both armed and—"

"—For Christ's sake, John, I'm about to jump out of my skin. Is Brigid there?" "Not sure it's Brigid, but there's a girl all right, lying on a bed with her face to the wall. The light is kinda dim in there so I can't say for certain it's her."

Coltrane shivered uncontrollably. Was this the final act of their nightmare, or the opening scene of more pain and uncertainty?

"Should we rush them?" Lost John asked.

"Too risky. They might kill her at the first sign of trouble."

"May come down to how fanatical these guys are about fighting for a lost cause." But they may not know it's a lost cause," Coltrane said, since the abbot himself didn't know. "They're isolated out here, so they may never have gotten the word about the collapse of their so-called revolution."

Lost John shook his head. "Hate to disagree with you, old friend, but that's highly unlikely. My hunch is something else stayed Kincaid's hand."

"Did you notice a radio?"

"No. They might have one, but if so it wasn't on. Got the impression they were preparing to leave. There are two packed duffle bags sitting beside the front door."

"Better to confront them indoors where they're contained than deal with them in the open. We need to separate these guys. And we need to do it fast, because if they discover the bolt drawn on the back door and blood on the window, no telling how they might react. We need a diversion."

Lost John moved closer. "I'm listening."

"Go back, get the boat, and row it into the little inlet. Make plenty of noise to attract their attention. If they don't respond, call out and tell them you've run out of petrol. That should bring at least one of them out to see what's going on. While you've got their attention, I'll check the side window to see if the girl is Brigid. Then I'll try the back door again. The rest we'll have to play by ear."

Lost John's face grew tense. He patted Coltrane on the arm and disappeared into the hazel trees.

***

Coltrane waited behind the boulder. The minutes dragged by. Silence. Nothing but the swoosh of the wind through the branches and the odd bird call. He checked his watch. Every minute that elapsed could be crucial. His legs cramped. He shifted his position. He checked his watch again. It had been ten minutes since John left. He should have heard from him by now. His breathing grew shallow. What in the hell was keeping him? Had he run into some kind of trouble? Maybe they had ambushed him. But if they did, surely he'd have heard the ruckus. At last Lost John's distinctive whistling of *The Wild Colonial Boy*.

Coltrane blessed himself and, crouching low, ran to the side of the house. In his haste to get to the window he kicked over an empty watering can lying in his path. It clattered down an incline and banged against the containment wall of a flower bed. That noise would arouse their attention for sure. He sprinted for cover in the pine wood. No sooner had he reached the tree line than Stiglitz came rushing out. From where he crouched he could eliminate Stiglitz, but Kincaid was still inside with the girl. No telling what he might do if he heard a shot. Stiglitz walked along the side of the house and back again before turning his attention to the wood. Coltrane eased back the hammers of his shotgun. Stiglitz brought his rifle up chest-high. He moved toward the wood. Coltrane backed farther into the trees.

The best outcome here would be to avoid an altercation with the

German if possible. Stiglitz broached the tree line ... stopped ... looked around ... advanced farther in a zigzag fashion. *Damn, this guy is like a bloodhound.* Coltrane had adequate cover where he stood. Problem was back of him the trees thinned out. If he moved again, Stiglitz was bound to see him. No option if he kept coming but to kill him and hope that Kincaid wouldn't panic when he heard the shotgun blast. But Kincaid knew that Stiglitz carried a rifle, not a shotgun. Coltrane got ready. In the silence of the wood the approaching footsteps crunching pine needles and dried brambles sounded like a giant's tread. Coltrane readied himself to step out from behind the tree and fire. He dare not peek first to determine the German's position for fear of being seen and losing the advantage of surprise. He'd have to step out blindly, do a quick scan, and fire before Stiglitz had time to react. Calm descended on him. His breathing settled down. He had faced worse than this at the Ebro River. Then a shout from the house.

"Stiglitz! Where are you? Get your arse back in here. Time to go!" The sound of the German's footsteps faded as he returned to the boathouse.

Coltrane eased the hammers back to their resting position. "'Time to go!'" Kincaid had said. That sounded ominous.

Chapter 65

Defiant to the End

Lost John climbed out of the boat and walked nonchalantly up the jetty, carrying an empty petrol can. One of the double doors flew open and a young man stormed out. He held one hand behind him. Lost John recognized him as the German. He suspected he was concealing a weapon behind his back.

"Good day to you, Guv'nr."

Stiglitz narrowed his eyes. "What's your business?"

"I ran out of petrol and I'm wondering if you wouldn't spare a quart to get me back to my car. Don't fancy rowing all the way back to Doyle's Cove in this wind."

"Does this place look like a petrol station to you?"

"I'm willing to pay you; not looking for charity."

Stiglitz advanced on Lost John in a threatening manner. "Go on, get out of here."

"Now that's a downright unfriendly attitude. Especially for someone who works for the nuns. I'm going to lodge a complaint with Mother Superior."

"I said get to hell away from here," Stiglitz repeated, pulling a gun from behind his back. Anticipating the move, Lost John swung the five-gallon petrol can, catching the gunman's elbow, which sent the weapon flying into the lake. Stiglitz howled and grabbed his arm.

Lost John swung the petrol can again and smacked him alongside the head. "Take that, you snot-nosed Kraut." The German collapsed in a heap on the wooden jetty. Lost John scrambled for cover in the adjacent brush.

***

Coltrane edged toward the side window again. This time he paid attention to where he placed his feet. A quick peek inside. Kincaid stood with his back to him, peering out the front window toward the lake. He held a rifle. Coltrane had a clear view of the jetty through the same window. Stiglitz lay there motionless. Lost John was nowhere in sight. The young girl had disappeared. His heart sank. He raised his shotgun and pointed it at Kincaid.

The sound of an engine from the front of the house sent him scurrying back to the pine wood.

A small car, looked like an Austin, labored up the dirt track. It swayed and bounced as the wheels slipped in and out of ruts and furrows. The suspension creaked with every bounce. Could these be reinforcements? Coltrane wondered. But it wasn't the black Bentley, Kinkaid's customary mode of transportation. The car pulled up to the back door and stopped. Two nuns got out carrying wicker baskets. The wind caught their black scapulars and stood them high above their heads like sails. They put the baskets down while they fought with their clothing. Then one unlocked the door to the house and the other placed the baskets inside. They didn't tarry but returned to their car, and soon they were lurching back down the path. When they disappeared around a bend, Coltrane tried the door where he had cut his wrist. A lucky break. The nuns had left it unlocked. He edged around the food baskets and tiptoed through the kitchen, stopping at the door to the front room to listen.

A rifle shot. He kicked the door in and charged into the room. Kincaid stood silhouetted in the open double doorway pointing his rifle at Lost John, who staggered up the jetty holding a bloody hand to the side of his head. Coltrane hit Kincaid in the small of the back and sent him flying out onto the cement ramp.

Unusually nimble for a man of his size, Kincaid quickly regained his balance and fled, still grasping his rifle. Coltrane didn't pursue him. He called out Brigid's name. No response. He ransacked the room, overturning the bed. He pulled clothes out of a closet and scoured a storage space off the main living area. It was filled with bric-a-brac, rain gear, fishing rods, Wellingtons, two old outboard motors. Suspended on the walls were framed pictures of fishing-competition winners and island picnics of bygone days.

No place to hide someone in here. He called her name again. There was nowhere left to search unless she was hidden outside, but that was unlikely. *Oh my god, the nuns.* Could they have spirited her away unbeknownst to him ? But that was impossible. He watched them leave the baskets and drive away. He thought he heard a thump. An old watering can had slipped from a shelf in the storage area and deposited a mound of rust fragments on the floor. "What the—? Brigid?" Another thump as another object fell. Something or someone was behind that wall. He banged his fist along the whitewashed wall to test its density until he came to a spot that sounded hollow.

Closer examination revealed the outline of a door camouflaged by framed pictures and raingear hanging from pegs. Not seeing a handle or latch, he applied pressure to the spot until it yielded. A further push opened a narrow door that turned on a swivel. He peered inside the hideaway and saw a shadowy figure bound hand and foot with a dirty gag in its mouth. No mistaking those big eyes. It was Brigid. His throat caught. He lifted her up and carried her to a chair in the front room. She wore a calico dress that once was grey but had turned black with grime. Her red hair was now a dirty brown. With trembling fingers he pulled the gag from her mouth and undid the bindings around her hands and feet.

"Daddy!" she wept, falling into his arms. They sat on the floor together and cried. Sobs came in great heaves. His tears were gradually replaced by a surge of white-hot anger. He would get the monster that had put his child through this horror.

Lost John staggered in from outside, blood dripping from his head. Coltrane ran to him. "I'm all right. He only nicked me." John pointed to a plume of water far out on the lake. "There he is; follow the bastard. Go now."

Coltrane nodded toward Brigid. "Mind her till I return."

"Have no fear; she's sound with me." Lost John put his arm around Brigid's thin shoulders. "Are we glad to see you, *a grá*."

Coltrane jumped into *No Pasarán* and followed Kincaid. Despite Kincaid's head start, Coltrane felt that his superior knowledge of the lake gave him the edge in any hide-and-seek contest. When his quarry turned toward the Priests' Island, Coltrane smiled. He suspected Kincaid was attempting to seek refuge in a spot now somewhat familiar to him.

Coming around the point, he spotted Kincaid trying to navigate the passage between the Priests' Island and the Mora Headland. No luck. The bow of his boat reared like a frightened horse startled by a swarm of bees. An underwater obstacle had apparently done its work.

The abrupt stop pitched Kincaid headfirst into the choppy waters, where he scrambled to cling to the half-submerged vessel. Aided by the current and his brute strength, the black-coated figure lumbered out of the shallows and plunged into the interior of the Priests' Island.

Coltrane guided *No Pasarán* onto the sandy shore. Shotgun in hand, he jumped out of the boat into the shallow water and dashed into the trees after his quarry. Tracking Kincaid through the maze of hazel trees and blackberry bushes was made easier by the cries of startled wildlife and the sounds of breaking branches. Since Kincaid didn't know where he was going, his progress would be slow and circuitous, enabling Coltrane to rapidly reduce the distance between them. He wanted to cut Kincaid off before he reached the cutaway bog. If he entered that maze, the likelihood of his survival was slim, which was okay, but Coltrane wanted to bag him alive. As he gave chase, he checked his shotgun to make sure the safety was in place.

He moved at a fast pace for another ten minutes, until he reached a small stream overhung with branches from a great beech tree that cast a giant shadow at its base. On the other side of the stream, he bent down to examine a footprint in the wet soil. It was the impression of a large boot. Except it pointed back in the opposite direction. He looked around nervously. Had Kincaid doubled back?

On instinct he hit the dirt. A volley of automatic fire came from behind a boulder pile, chiseling fist-sized chunks of bark off an adjacent tree, spraying the stream and the surrounding terrain. Coltrane circled around the boulders, hoping to get a clear shot at his nemesis, but the sounds of renewed slashing through the hazel bushes signaled that Kincaid was on the move again, this time in the direction of the cutaway bog.

Chunks of bog splashed into the water. He quickened his pace. When he exited the trees he spotted Kincaid less than a hundred yards away, moving unsteadily along a narrow turf bridge toward one of the bog islands. He raised his shotgun and leveled it at Kincaid's back. "Give it up, Kincaid! There's no way out."

Kincaid turned around unsteadily on the turf bridge to face his pursuer, awkwardly switching his rifle from one hand to the other. During that maneuver the lining of his coat snagged on the briars that reached from the banks like predatory fingers. Unable to disentangle himself, he shed his wet coat. It fell into the water, where it remained anchored to the surface by the briar tentacles. "Go to hell, you Irish bastard! I told them we should have killed that little bitch of yours when we had the chance, but that crazy monk knew better. Always the fucking monk. And against my better judgment I waited, hoping the money would come … until it was too late. And then the storm. Wasn't for it I'd be long gone by now. Oh, what the hell!"

"That and the bottle of brandy you and the Nazi consumed last night."

"The bottle nearly got *you* killed mate, so spare me the lecture."

Coltrane raised his shotgun. "Kincaid! Throw your rifle down. There's no way out. Don't want to kill you, but I will if you drive me to it."

It looked for a brief moment as if Kincaid would comply. But then his mouth fell open in a grotesque smile, showing tobacco-stained teeth. Raising the rifle to his shoulder, he leveled it at Coltrane and fired. The kick from the gun caused him to stagger and his shot went wild. Coltrane's return volley reverberated among the treetops, startling a flock of mallards from the rushes. Kincaid pitched backward into the bog hole.

The green algae sloshed and heaved to reclaim its territory, slowly closing around Kincaid's body, until all that remained visible was the raised arm stiffly holding the rifle above the water like a monument to some long-forgotten war. Coltrane watched for a few moments as the water gurgled and roiled, sending air bubbles to the surface that floated briefly on the algae like little glass igloos before bursting with a pop.

Coltrane grasped his shotgun by the barrel tip and swung it around and around over his head like a shot put before lofting it far into the maze. He waited for the splash, then withdrew the warm whiskey bottle from his inside pocket. The sunlight illuminated the golden liquid within. "Ah, time to celebrate." He raised the bottle to his lips. "*No Pasarán.*" He had bested his enemy as he had in Spain. He paused, lowered the bottle, and observed the golden brew, his old friend, so alluring yet so deadly. Then he grabbed it by its slim neck and hurled it far across the cutaway bog, and listened.

Nothing, nothing at all.

Everything grew still, as if nature were observing a moment of silence to mark Kincaid's return to its embrace. The waterlogged coat pulled free of its thorny fetters and sank slowly into the depths. The insect hum took up again.

With a final glance across the still-gurgling bog hole, he turned on his heel and walked back into the woods the way he had come. The faint bleating of a goat echoed across the water.

Authors Note

I'd like to remind the reader that this is a work of historical fiction and as such does not conform in all respects to the historical record, assuming, of course, that we ever know with certainty what the actual historical record is. In the interest of the story I've taken a few liberties and moved some things around. For example, I've brought forward the date of the Blueshirt March on Dublin to accommodate the plot. I hope this tampering doesn't hinder the reader's enjoyment of the story.

Glossary

A Grá: *An Irish form of address. Literally means "My love"*

Amadán: *An Irish term for a "fool"*

Banshee: *A female spirit in Irish mythology said to herald the death of a family member*

Bedford van: *An English motor vehicle of the 1940s*

Blueshirts: *An Irish fascist group during WWII*

Bog: *A marshy area from which turf or peat is extracted*

Crane: *A piece of hardware suspended over an open hearth fire from which kettles, pots, and other cooking utensils are hung*

DeValera: *The last name of the Irish Taoiseach in office during WWII*

Ebro: *A river in Spain*

Fianna Eireann: *An Irish youth group in 1930s Ireland*

Garda Síochána: *The name of the Irish police force, more commonly referred to as the **Gardaí** or "the **Guards**"*

Gillie: *An Gaelic word for a fishing and hunting guide*

Girleen: *A little girl in Irish*

Gregorian Chant: *A form of song now practiced mainly by men and women of religious orders*

Hapert: *A colloquialism for "a halfpenny"*

Il Duce: *The Italian title of the dictator Mussolini*

Jameson: *A brand of Irish whiskey*

Knock Holy Water: *Water blessed by a priest from the Marian Shrine in Knock*

Lifebuoy: *A brand of English soap*

Mizen Head: *The southernmost tip of Ireland*

Rake a fire: *To cover a fire with ashes before retiring for the night*

Shebeen: *An illegal bar or pub*

Slane: *A spade-like tool used for cutting turf*

Taoiseach: *The title of the Irish Prime Minister*

About the Author

Irish-born writer, Seamus Beirne, lives in Irvine, California with his wife Ann and their dog Lucy. The stress of retirement is alleviated by their three grown children and two grandsons!! Seamus spent thirty-five years as a high school English teacher and administrator. Before that he worked as a priest in a Catholic high school and in neighboring parishes. His first novel, *Breakout from Sugar Island* was published in the fall of 2015.

Visit the author's website at: http://www.seamusbeirne.com/

Other titles from Fireship Press

Last Dance in Kabul
Ken Czech

The Ultimate Dance Between Love and War

When his superiors ignore his warnings of an impending Afghan insurrection in 1841, British army captain Reeve Waterton vows never to return to Kabul. But then he rescues strong-willed Sarah Kane from an ambush and his plans for civilian life and self-preservation unravel around him

"Reeve Waterton, a dashing rogue, is a true hero who stands among the most valiant officers of British fiction. Sarah Kane is an assertive woman assured of her own mind yet vulnerable in her heart. Together they spark the blaze that energizes *Last Dance in Kabul*."

—**Rex Griffin,** historical writer.

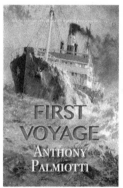

First Voyage
Anthony Palmiotti

It's 1938, America is still in a depression, jobs are hard to come by and the world is preparing for war…

The *Arrow* is an old tramp freighter with a diverse crew. Patrick Welch is a young seaman making his first trip on the *Arrow* and must weather storms and ports of call trying to win the respect of the tough captain and the friendship of the rough and ready crew.

Then, when the *Arrow* arrives in Hamburg, the Nazi movement is making life difficult for those who don't fit the mold of the new Germany. One of the crew wants to get his family out, but he has to rely on his crew mates. Will they rise to the challenge and bond together in order to outwit the pursuing Nazis?

"Wonderful read! This is the tale of a young merchant officer on his first ship on the eve of WWII. His adventures are compelling and enjoyable."

—**Capt. Dennis Schroeder**, Master Mariner

For the Finest in Nautical and Historical Fiction and Non-Fiction
www.FireshipPress.com

Interesting • Informative • Authoritative

All Fireship Press books are available through leading bookstores and wholesalers worldwide.

CPSIA information can be obtained
at www.ICGtesting.com
Printed in the USA
FSHW01n1522070918
52014FS